JACOB'S ROOM

Virginia Woolf is now recognized as a major twentieth-century author, a great novelist and essayist, and a key figure in literary history as a feminist and a modernist. Born in 1882, she was the daughter of the editor and critic Leslie Stephen, and suffered a traumatic adolescence after the deaths of her mother, in 1895, and her step-sister Stella, in 1897, leaving her subject to breakdowns for the rest of her life. Her father died in 1904 and two years later her favourite brother Thoby died suddenly of typhoid. With her sister, the painter Vanessa Bell, she was drawn into the company of writers and artists such as Lytton Strachey and Roger Fry, later known as the Bloomsbury Group. Among them she met Leonard Woolf, whom she married in 1912, and together they founded the Hogarth Press in 1917, which was to publish the work of T. S. Eliot, E. M. Forster and Katherine Mansfield as well as the earliest translations of Freud. Woolf lived an energetic life among friends and family, reviewing and writing, and dividing her time between London and the Sussex Downs. In 1941, fearing another attack of mental illness, she drowned herself.

Her first novel, *The Voyage Out*, appeared in 1915, and she then worked through the transitional *Night and Day* (1919) to the highly experimental and impressionistic *Jacob's Room* (1922). From then on her fiction became a series of brilliant and extraordinarily varied experiments, each one searching for a fresh way of presenting the relationship between individual lives and the forces of society and history. She was particularly concerned with women's experience, not only in her novels but also in her essays and her two books of feminist polemic, *A Room of One's Own* (1929) and *Three Guineas* (1938). Her major novels include *Mrs Dalloway* (1925), *To the Lighthouse* (1927), the historical fantasy *Orlando* (1928), written for Vita Sackville-West, the extraordinarily poetic vision of *The Waves* (1931), the family saga of *The Years* (1937), and *Between the Acts* (1941). All these are published by Penguin, as are her *Diaries*, Volumes I–V, and selections from her essays and short stories and *Flush* (1933), a reconstruction of the life of Elizabeth Barrett Browning's spaniel.

D0171681

Sue Roe is a novelist, poet and critic, and the author of *Writing and Gender: Virginia Woolf's Writing Practice* (Harvester Wheatsheaf & St Martin's Press, 1990). Her latest book (with Susan Sellers and Nicole Ward Jouve), on creative practice, is *The Semi-Transparent Envelope* (Marion Boyars, 1994).

Julia Briggs is General Editor for the works of Virginia Woolf in Penguin Twentieth-Century Classics.

JACOB'S ROOM

VIRGINIA WOOLF

EDITED WITH AN INTRODUCTION AND
NOTES BY SUE ROE

PENGUIN BOOKS

PENGUIN BOOKS

Published by the Penguin Group
Penguin Books Ltd, 27 Wrights Lane, London w8 5tz, England
Penguin Books USA Inc., 375 Hudson Street, New York, New York 10014, USA
Penguin Books Australia Ltd, Ringwood, Victoria, Australia
Penguin Books Canada Ltd, 10 Alcorn Avenue, Toronto, Ontario, Canada m4v 3b2
Penguin Books (NZ) Ltd, 182–190 Wairau Road, Auckland 10, New Zealand

Penguin Books Ltd, Registered Offices: Harmondsworth, Middlesex, England

Jacob's Room first published by The Hogarth Press 1922
This annotated edition published in Penguin Books 1992

10

Introduction and notes copyright © Sue Roe, 1992
All rights reserved

The moral right of the editor has been asserted

Set in 10/12 Monophoto Garamond
Made and Printed in England by Clays Ltd, St Ives plc

Except in the United States of America, this book is sold subject
to the condition that it shall not, by way of trade or otherwise, be lent,
re-sold, hired out, or otherwise circulated without the publisher's
prior consent in any form of binding or cover other than that in
which it is published and without a similar condition including this
condition being imposed on the subsequent purchaser.

CONTENTS

Bibliographical Note

The following is a list of abbreviated titles used in this edition.

MS: *Jacob's Room: The Holograph Notebooks* (New York Public Library, Astor, Lenox and Tilden Foundations).

JR: *Jacob's Room*, first British edn (Hogarth Press, 1922)

Letters: *The Letters of Virginia Woolf*, 6 vols., ed. Nigel Nicolson and Joanne Trautmann (Hogarth Press, 1975–80).

Diary: *The Diary of Virginia Woolf*, 5 vols., ed. Anne Olivier Bell (Hogarth Press, 1977; Penguin Books, 1979).

Essays: *The Essays of Virginia Woolf*, 3 vols. (to be 6 vols.), ed. Andrew McNeillie (Hogarth Press, 1986).

CE: *Collected Essays*, 4 vols., ed. Leonard Woolf (Chatto & Windus, 1966, 1967).

Moments of Being: *Moments of Being: Unpublished Autobiographical Writings of Virginia Woolf*, ed. Jeanne Schulkind (Chatto & Windus, 1976).

Passionate Apprentice: *A Passionate Apprentice: The Early Journals, 1897–1909*, ed. Mitchell A. Leaska (Hogarth Press, 1990).

Introduction

I

*For I figure that the approach will be entirely
different this time . . .*[1]

Written between 1920 and 1922, *Jacob's Room* is Virginia Woolf's third novel, and the work in which she retrospectively felt she had 'found out how to begin (at 40) to say something in my own voice'.[2] Set on the eve of the First World War, it evokes, to some extent, the halcyon days of pre-war innocence. Poised on the brink between being an Edwardian and a modernist novel, it is *about* thresholds, brinks and the layering in of character, in life and in the literary work. Subtle, delicate and tantalizingly suggestive, *Jacob's Room* is the novel in which Woolf examines for the first time the relationship between memory and desire. It is in this novel that she writes explicitly about sexuality; here that she ventures into what she called 'the dark places of psychology'.[3] As she gradually brings her central character into the limelight of Cambridge, London and the company of women, she shows him, simultaneously, in bas-relief, posing fundamental questions about the relationship between the human mind and the human form.

'If the old methods are obsolete,' Woolf would write of Henry James, in 1921, 'it is the business of a writer to discover new ones.'[4] She was ready to experiment with new forms in her own work, having served her apprenticeship as a novelist in her first two novels, *The Voyage Out* and *Night and Day*. In the former, she had tried to explore some of the more incommunicable regions of a young woman's mind, but the relatively conventional form of that novel had ultimately constrained her. She wrote *Night and Day* as a kind of corrective, she later noted, and as she was writing it, 'made [herself] copy from plaster casts, partly to tranquillise, partly to learn anatomy'.[5] Like her sister, Vanessa Bell, who had served her apprenticeship as a painter at the Slade 'copying from the Antique',[6] she reached the point at which she felt she knew enough about line-drawing, and was ready to begin drawing from life.

But what, for a novelist, was 'life'? In particular, how might 'life' be depicted in a novel? It was during this period that she considered this question in her famous essay, 'Modern Fiction'. There, she outlined her dissatisfaction with the novel form as she considered it to have been defined by her predecessors – she cites Bennett, Wells and Galsworthy – with their 'chapters that lead up and their chapters that lead down',[7] and their method of describing character by surrounding the hero or heroine with a wealth of material and geographical detail. By far the worst offender, she alleged, was Arnold Bennett: 'There is not so much as a draught between the frames of the windows, or a crack in the boards – and yet if life should refuse to live there?'[8] After reading Woolf's essay, *The Old Wives' Tale* becomes an irresistible Aunt Sally, seeming to epitomize all that is alienating about one kind of Edwardian style: 'The fact is, that while in the Five Towns they were also in the Square ... The Square ... contained five public-houses, a bank, a barber's, a confectioner's, three grocers', two chemists', an ironmonger's ...'[9] Eventually, and by an endlessly circuitous route, it contains Constance and Sophia Baines. Their place in the scheme of things, the narrator implies, is another unquestionable fact of life.

Virginia Woolf vehemently objected to this method, pleading that Bennett's characters lived 'abundantly, even unexpectedly, but ... what do they live for?'[10] In *Jacob's Room* she creates a character in such a way that she can begin to ask this enormous and unanswerable question, by moving him through the novel shadily and tantalizingly, like an obscure object of the reader's desire, and by consistently challenging our desire to locate and fix him in his room. 'Jacob's room', she tells us, in a discreet parody of the Edwardian mode,

> had a round table and two low chairs. There were yellow flags in a jar on the mantelpiece; a photograph of his mother; cards from societies ... books ... Lives of the Duke of Wellington, for example; Spinoza ... a *Manual of the Diseases of the Horse* ... Listless is the air in an empty room, just swelling the curtain; the flowers in the jar shift. One fibre in the wicker arm-chair creaks, though no one sits there. (p.31)

We can have access to Jacob's room if that is what we want, she is suggesting: she will take us inside, and we can note the contents, sample the atmosphere, but Jacob's room cannot necessarily tell us anything at all about Jacob.

It was clear to Woolf from the outset that she was about to write something 'entirely different this time': she wanted, she noted in her diary, 'no scaffolding; scarcely a brick to be seen; all crepuscular, but the heart, the passion, humour, everything as bright as fire in the mist'.[11] She had hit on the form already, she suspected, in three short stories which are little more than fragments, but which had all been well received. In each of these – 'Kew Gardens' (1917), 'The Mark on the Wall' (1919) and 'An Unwritten Novel' (1920) – she had stressed the effects of colour and light on the human being's vision of the natural world; the importance of the quality of the human voice; and the mystery of the human imagination. 'An Unwritten Novel', particularly, stresses the extent to which one human being must remain in ignorance of the vagaries of the mind of another. As she began writing *Jacob's Room* she noted, 'the theme is a blank to me; but I see immense possibilities in the form I hit upon by chance 2 weeks ago' – that is, in 'An Unwritten Novel'.[12] In that story, she explores the idea of the narrator/character as a fellow traveller in a railway carriage, piecing together in her imagination facts about the life of the woman sitting opposite. She is poor, lonely, isolated – but when the journey comes to an end and Minnie Marsh's son appears to meet her off the train, it is clear that the story, though entirely credible, has completely failed to correspond with the actual circumstances of the woman's life.

'An Unwritten Novel' may be seen as something of a preliminary sketch for the novel she did write – *Jacob's Room*. In chapter III Woolf wittily turns the tables on herself by having a 'Mrs. Norman' observe Jacob: she takes note of his socks '(loose)', his tie '(shabby)', but has the wit to realize that 'It is no use trying to sum people up. One must follow hints' (p.24). Mrs Norman is about to meet her own son; Jacob is in the process of leaving his mother. And although Virginia Woolf began with no fixed ideas about the nature of her theme (that of the relationship between mother and son) it had already established itself with some plangency in 'An Unwritten Novel' – '. . . the last look of them . . . brims me with wonder – floods me anew. Mysterious figures! Mother and son . . . Wherever

I go, mysterious figures, I see you ... mothers and sons; you, you, you.'[13] In *Jacob's Room* Woolf was to go on to develop this theme, and it is a crucial one: to some extent it determines the shape of Jacob's odyssey from boyhood to manhood, and casts one of the shadows over his brief life.

There are other discernible sources. The early 1920s were a sociable time for Woolf: she was living in London; she had a formidably active social life; and she entered with firm enthusiasm into the events of the art world, to which she had intimate access through her sister Vanessa and her circle. In April 1920 she went to see a show of negro carvings at the Chelsea Book Club and found them, she reported to Vanessa,

> dismal and impressive, but Heaven knows what real feeling I have ... after hearing Roger discourse. I dimly see that something in their style might be written, and also that if I had one on the mantelpiece I should be a different sort of character – less adorable, as far as I can make out, but somebody you wouldn't forget in a hurry.[14]

'Roger' was Roger Fry, who had taken the art world by storm by exhibiting, in 1910, the work of the French post-impressionists: Cézanne, Matisse and Picasso. In his introduction to a second exhibition, in 1912, he had stressed that these were painters who 'do not seek to imitate form, but seek to create form; not to imitate life, but to find an equivalent for life ... In fact they aim not at illusion but at reality.'[15]

Woolf was undeniably influenced by Fry's aesthetic theories. As she wrote *Jacob's Room* she read his *Vision and Design*,[16] which was published in 1920. Collected there is Fry's work on the negro carvings which had made such an impression on her, as well as his seminal piece, 'An Essay in Aesthetics', which outlines most clearly his theories about the difference between the world and the work, and his emphasis on the work of art as an aesthetic artifice, stripped of all moral and emotional implication. Fry believed the graphic arts to be the expression of the imaginative life rather than copies of nature; he makes the point in 'An Essay in Aesthetics' that artists may have a great deal to learn from the vision of children, who never 'as we say, "draw from nature", but express ... the mental images which make up their own imaginative lives'.[17]

Fry was one of the greatest admirers of Virginia Woolf's writing. He told her that she seemed to him to share with only the French novelists the relationship with her *matière* which he had identified first in the work of Gerald Brenan: 'he believes that everything must come out of the *matière* of his prose and not out of the ideas and emotions he describes.'[18] In his essay, 'Negro Sculpture', Fry closely echoes the style of Virginia Woolf in 'The Mark on the Wall', where she describes the disorientating rapidity which seems to characterize the modern world: 'And now, in the last sixty years, knowledge and perception have poured upon us so fast that the whole well-ordered system has been blown away, and we stand bare to the blast . . .'[19] As an example of what Fry was recognizing in modern art, the African sculptures seemed to him to epitomize the concentration on the power of plastic form, not merely to reproduce actual figures but to possess 'an inner life of their own'.[20]

Woolf would continue to be influenced by Fry's theories, and it is, perhaps, in *To the Lighthouse* that she was to bring them to bear most directly on her thinking about the capacity of the novel to encapsulate 'life'. *Jacob's Room* reflects a similar desire to make a shape which will enable the character of Jacob Flanders to show through, and it is notable that she employs the figure of the painter in the novel to mediate between the characters and the reader. It is Charles Steele, the unknown painter in the panama hat, who directs little Archer to the rock on which Jacob is playing, and this is how the reader first discovers him; and Nick Bramham, the painter who was originally Fanny Elmer's lover, will introduce Fanny to Jacob. But it is also important to note the extent to which Jacob is never quite captured by the vision of the artist within the text: Mrs Flanders (Steele's unwitting sitter) moves, causing all sorts of risks to the picture before we even encounter Jacob; it is the artist's model, Fanny Elmer, whom Jacob is interested in, rather than the artist, Nick Bramham; and when he finds himself in France with the painters Mallinson and Cruttendon, he steers the conversation as soon as he can (and with notably ill grace) from painting to literature – 'Shakespeare had more guts than all these damned frogs put together. "Hang there like fruit my soul . . ."' (p.110.) The notion of representation is challenged by Woolf throughout the composition of *Jacob's Room*, but the suggestion is that in *writing* the artist may need to substitute something other than (even something more complex than) 'significant form'. Writing to R. C. Trevelyan after the novel's publication she gives us, in its defence, something of a hint as to what she was actually after:

> Of course, the effort of breaking with strict representation is very unsettling, and many things were not controlled as they should have been . . . but the method was not so much at fault as my ignorance of how to use it psychologically.[21]

She drew the psychology of Jacob from life, though the novelist's relationship with his or her model or sitter can never be as clear-cut or as obviously discernible as that of the painter. The writer's model is always composed of a whole wealth of different influences, put together through a mixture of intimacy, imagination, reading, recollection and the myriad impressions which the mind receives (as Woolf noted in 'Modern Fiction') from all sides.[22] Fry's reference to the vision of a child is as likely as anything else in *Vision and Design* to have triggered a key idea in Woolf's mind, though the links she made as a result may well have remained unconscious and therefore undocumented. We, with her letters and diaries as well as the documentation relating to her reading matter, may speculate as to the influence, for example, of her small nephews on her creative perspectives at the time. Vanessa's little boys captivated her. She had had them to stay two years previously, while their sister Angelica was born, and had noted with admiration their facility of expression: 'How they get hold of all their language I don't know; it seems to me very superior – in fact their minds altogether seem much quicker and more intelligent than ours.' She speculated that she supposed 'the chief harm to human character comes from taking an interest in politics'[23] and was enchanted by their conscientiousness. Julian remarked that she and Leonard seemed very extravagant with their coal, and Quentin 'would only put a scraping of strawberry jam on his bread, because he said that it was very precious in war time' (this was 1918).

Who knows whether the immediate, intimate effect of the war on the life and sensibility of a small child profoundly affected Woolf? Certainly the children prompted in her all sorts of thoughts about the relationship between the world and the forms of human expression; equally importantly, they reminded her of her own child-hood. She revisited St Ives, the scene of her happy childhood summers, in 1921, and wrote to Vanessa, '... nothing but gorse between us and the sea ... the spray and the ships and the bees, peacock butterflies (tell Julian)'.[24] She took a keen interest in the children's education, urging Vanessa to teach Julian Greek, and wrote to her, on one occasion, to request the dispatch of one of his own books: they had tried a *Waverley* novel but found it a bit too difficult (he was ten at the time).[25] The extent to which she kept them in mind is exemplified by the fact that they entered into her dreams. Curiously, given the richness of her imaginative life, Woolf rarely records a dream, but in June 1921, she notes, 'all last night I dreamt of Julian. We were buying eclairs together.'[26] It is as if he really had given her access to something, enabling her to throw light on some new vision.

Perhaps most importantly of all, the boys reminded her of her own loved brother, Thoby Stephen, whose life had tragically been cut short at the age of twenty-six.[27] Watching Julian ('so like a brother with Angelica'[28]) she is put in mind of life in the day nursery at Hyde Park Gate and of her relationship with Thoby, on whose character she undoubtedly drew for Jacob Flanders. With Thoby she had enjoyed a vital connection: her letters to him are spirited, teasing, expectant. It was with him that she had learned to enjoy Shakespeare; it was he who had congratulated her on master-ing the *Antigone*; he was 'a charming great inarticulate creature, with torrents of things shut up in him'. Her bond with him was very strong, and his sudden death was unbearable. In the days following it, she had written to the family friend, Violet Dickinson, with imaginary descriptions of his recovery – she could at least keep him alive in writing.[29] She was to describe him, much later, in her 1939 autobiographical fragment, 'A Sketch of the Past'. She re-members him in a carriage of the underground (again, 'An Unwrit-ten Novel' comes to mind[30]) surveying the scene over the edge of his paper, 'motionless with a look ... of one equipped ... knowing his place, relishing his inheritance and his part in life'; he was, she reflects, 'melancholy; original ... I suppose he would have been more of a figure than a success'; and she recalls his 'strange awkward silence'.[31] They were intimate, trusting, 'naturally attracted to each other', and yet, she muses, she hardly knew him. How might it be possible to 'know' another person, even a loved, a cherished, familiar person? This is one of the key questions she poses in *Jacob's Room*.

II

There he stood pale, come out of the depths of darkness,
in the hot room, blinking at the light. (p.18)

Another dream may have influenced the creation of *Jacob's Room*. A dream related, this time, not by Virginia Woolf herself but by Walter Lamb (an old friend of the family who had once proposed to her). On 17 April 1920, she noted in her diary: 'I've begun Jacob's Room', then went on to describe going to the Bach Festival the night before.

> . . . as I settled into my seat, a voice said Virginia! It was Walter Lamb . . . 'I had such a vivid dream of Thoby the other night' he said. 'He came in after beagling, & said, something very important – I can't remember what. Very odd – for I don't think of him often.'[32]

The *stance* of this exchange is noteworthy: it sets the tone for the way the mind stores information about the important things by suddenly highlighting a figure in motion, in the act of speech, and as suddenly withdrawing the vision. This is very much a technique used by Woolf in *Jacob's Room*, particularly at the end of the novel, when Jacob is shown as he intrudes on the memories of the women who long for his presence. The desire for Jacob is evinced by the imaginary calling of his name, and triggered by a contiguous remark or incident: '"You are neglecting your friends," said Bowley [to Clara] . . . She started; acknowledged Mr. Lionel Parry's bow; wasted on him what had sprung for Jacob. ("Jacob! Jacob!" she thought.)' (p.147.)

Once lodged in the memory, he becomes almost a part of the women who have lost and who long for him. As Woolf composed her novel, she read Proust for the first time. She was captivated by the sensuousness of his language, in which she detected 'something sexual',[33] and fascinated by the way he moved his narrative backwards and forwards through time. The vividness of Jacob's image in the memory of another is one way in which she describes the force of his presence, and one critic has suggested that what Woolf is doing in this novel is creating the possibility for the reader to remember Jacob.[34]

Interesting though this idea is, and though the idea of memory plays a crucial part in the composition of *Jacob's Room*, I would suggest that that idea gives an impression of greater control on the part of the reader over the narrative than we in fact have, and that what Woolf is actually doing may come closer to the business of subjecting her character to a linear movement through time, in order for us to see what happens to him in the process. Jacob himself is in many ways conditioned by Edwardian social values, which he brings to bear on life as he progresses through it, but we, as readers, are being invited to be *critical* of this as a method of depicting the human consciousness in fiction. By the time Sandra Wentworth Williams gets her hook in his side, Jacob's attempts at good time-keeping and factual accuracy are more or less falling apart, and Woolf allows us to be poignantly amused at the grim spectacle of his efforts to hang on to these last vestiges of control and familiarity:

> He noted the slight irregularity in the line of the steps which 'the artistic sense of the Greeks preferred to mathematical accuracy,' he read in his guide-book . . . In short he was accurate and diligent; but profoundly morose. Moreover he was pestered by guides. This was on Monday . . . he was beginning to think a great deal about the problems of civilization, which were solved, of course, so very remarkably by the ancient Greeks, though their solution is no help to us. Then the hook gave a great tug in his side as he lay in bed on Wednesday night; and he turned over with a desperate sort of tumble, remembering Sandra Wentworth Williams with whom he was in love. Next day he climbed Pentelicus. (pp. 130–31)

Whereas Jacob must at all costs resist the chaotic nature of desire, the women know that there is nothing for it but to submit to it. In Jacob's absence, Fanny Elmer's idea of him was

> more statuesque, noble, and eyeless than ever. To reinforce her vision she had taken to visiting the British Museum, where, keeping her eyes downcast until she was alongside of the battered Ulysses,

she opened them and got a fresh shock of Jacob's presence, enough to last her half a day. But this was wearing thin. (pp.149–50)[35]

Fanny's strategy is (coincidentally) similar to that described by Proust in his preface to *By Way of Sainte-Beuve*.[36] He described how he halted beside a clump of trees, closed his eyes to make his mind a blank 'to recruit fresh energies for my pursuit of the past, and then suddenly reopened them, all in an attempt to see those same trees as if for the first time'. For Proust, however, this is an attempt to make a set of objects trigger a thread of association. Fanny Elmer, on the other hand, wishes, more simply, to behave *as if* she can re-create in the present a pleasurable experience in the past. It wears thin because nothing can compensate for Jacob's absence. She knows this, whereas Jacob is determined to resist the power of Sandra Wentworth Williams' disconcerting presence.

It is in the terms of the expectations, the disappointments and the shocks of childhood and adult desire that Woolf will continue to depict, within the formally experimental terms of the narrative's shape and structure, the developing psyche – and sexuality – of Jacob Flanders. She depicts him as a young man in relation to the women he both desires and resists, showing the extent to which he cannot help perceiving them as objects. In the earlier parts of the novel, she describes the developing shape of his personality in relation to the child's world of objects and of others. From the outset – with her depiction of him as a child on the beach – she experiments with the idea of perception and its bearing on narrative shape, so as to continue to use her method psychologically.

The very first time we encounter Jacob we watch him suffer as the narrative frame zooms out to encompass objects, and others, of which he had previously been oblivious. Straddling a rock on the beach, he is in his element: 'Rough with crinkled limpet shells and sparsely strewn with locks of dry seaweed, a small boy has to stretch his legs far apart, and indeed to feel rather heroic, before he gets to the top' (p.5). He observes a small crab on its journey across a pool of water; he is about to jump, when he is suddenly startled by something he had failed to notice before: the spectacle of the bodies of a man and woman, 'stretched motionless, with their heads on pocket-handkerchiefs, side by side . . .' (p.5.)

This is Jacob's first, startling insight into the limits of the world as he perceives it. Those limits extend beyond the boundaries of the current focus of attention, or object of desire. He does not understand the function of this couple, or how they got to be there, or what they are doing in his world. He panics, reels round, focuses on a black, rock-like figure which is how he perceives his Nanny, and pelts towards her, only to find that this black mass with the waves lapping round it is nothing but a rock. 'There he stood', and there we first encounter him: as a troubled child, in the act of discovering that his symbiotic connection with the world is imagined, rather than actual; confronted suddenly with the terrifying fact of his own isolation. When his mother appears to reassemble the illusion that he belongs, that he is integral to the world, that he can know who he is, she is all-encompassing. He needs her so much by this time that she is literally all he can see: '"There he is!" cried Mrs. Flanders, coming round the rock and covering the whole space of the beach in a few seconds' (pp. 5–6).

What is significant about Woolf's method at this stage of the book is that we experience all this as if we are Jacob. She trains our gaze on the rock, the crab, the pool, and suddenly on the sun-bathing couple so that we, too, are subject to Jacob's assumptions and to the shock of the external world, when it does intrude. We, too, see 'a large black woman . . . sitting on the sand' before we notice the waves lapping round her and realize she is not Nanny. So that when Mrs Flanders comes bustling in to make her presence felt, we know that the larger world she occupies may be observed, but not necessarily known: 'There were her spectacles, her sewing; and a letter with the Scarborough postmark.' But, having been admitted to the recesses of Jacob's mind, we are alert to Mrs Flanders' *non sequiturs*: '. . . She had not drawn the curtains either' (p.8). We may be comforted by the glimpse of her plotting, with Rebecca, 'the eternal conspiracy of hush and clean bottles' (p.8), but we are very far from knowing, in any detail, what that conspiracy actually consists of. This might apply, too, to our understanding of the role of Captain Barfoot in the story: who is he, and why does he carry the authority he does? Who is Rebecca?[37] Will she have a significant part to play in the story? And what about the sun-bathing couple on the sand? Will they put in a single appearance and then just disappear?

With, perhaps, some of these questions in mind, Virginia Woolf quietly takes us into the nursery, where Archer, Jacob and Johnny lie asleep. As our eyes adjust to the half-light, we may reflect that to describe such scenes as this Woolf may need to proceed more gently than the 'blast'[38] of post-impressionist theory, for example, would be capable of proceeding. In the boys' room, the narrative takes on a quality of *contre-jour* and, but for the presence of the sleeping children, this section might have anticipated the prose of the 'Time Passes' section of Woolf's later novel *To the Lighthouse*:

> The wind ... stirred the cloth on the chest of drawers, and let in a little light, so that the sharp edge of the chest of drawers was visible, running straight up, until a white shape bulged out; and a silver streak showed in the looking-glass ... (p.9)

The hush of the nursery at night is conveyed in a language which anticipates that of Woolf's later appreciation of the work of Walter Sickert (a painter with whom Fry was not in sympathy), whose paintings seem to suggest a special quality of complicity between painter and viewer, and between artist and sitter. In order to evoke the psychological dimensions of the human form, Sickert suggests a subtle, questioning relationship between subject and object. Woolf noted that, to convey a sense of innocence, for instance (or of pity, or squalor),

> Sickert merely takes his brush and paints a tender green light on the faded wallpaper. Light is beautiful falling through green leaves. He has no need of explanation; green is enough.[39]

Here, that little sliver of light glancing off the edge of the chest of drawers, the mass of the sheet (if that is what it is) are enough to suggest just a hint of restlessness as one of the boys (Archer, as it turns out, not Jacob) stirs: Jacob himself is 'profoundly unconscious'. If Woolf's reading of Proust has filtered in here, it may be that what she wants to suggest is Jacob's return to the realms of the unconscious where he may be most fully himself: back in his element, untroubled, for the duration of the night, by the sudden proximity of intruders or other challenges to his sense of orientation within the world. For Proust, the *néant* of sleep was the 'true home of the self',[40] the self-sufficient world unmediated by externality.

Woolf here paints a picture of the nursery 'bathed in time' – the state which the French *contre-jour* painter, Pierre Bonnard, had aimed to create in depicting the relationship between his figures and their settings.[41]

In a painting, such a scene, such a glimpse would be the whole story. In a novel, 'one thing should open out of another', as Virginia Woolf noted in her plans for *Jacob's Room*; one scene, one incident, one glimpse, should lead to another. In her depiction of the nursery she allows us a glimpse, perhaps, of the 'edge where painting breaks off and takes her way into the silent land': the novelist would need to depict the human form by opening up the silent land to the possibilities suggested by words. The appeal of a child's voice, searching the beach for a lost brother, rings out in this early section of the novel; as the narrative progresses, Woolf's characters will need to speak in order to identify themselves and to make contact with others.

What Virginia Woolf *didn't* want was to evolve a *theory* of unconscious desire, and the ways in which it might be expressed. She was not so much 'ignorant of how to use [her] method psychologically', as resistant to the idea that there might be such a thing as a formula. Her 1919 review of J. D. Beresford's novel, *An Imperfect Mother* ('Freudian Fiction'), warns against the danger of creating a novel in which 'all the characters have become cases'. Her complaint, she protested, was not that she objected to Beresford 'making use of any key that seems to him to fit the human mind', rather that his key 'is a patent key that opens every door'.[42] The key to her own achievement, in *Jacob's Room* as elsewhere, is in her refusal to believe that any theory of the 'shape' of the unconscious might be directly converted into, or transposed on to, the shape of a fictional narrative. When she came later to write *To the Lighthouse* she specifically resisted the idea that the lighthouse had any symbolic status: 'I can't manage Symbolism except in this vague, generalized way . . . directly I'm told what a thing means, it becomes hateful to me.'[43] As she offers us a glimpse into the nursery and we register a white shape, a silver streak reflected in the mirror, she is inviting us to ponder, perhaps, on the notion of origination, and to speculate on the shapes the mind of a child may make of the events of the preceding day; and to gain a sense of the essentially mysterious relation between subject and object: how far will the mass of white, the streak of silver, impinge upon the consciousness of Archer as he stirs? How many of the shapes of yesterday – the black rock, the crab, the strange faces – will Jacob remember in the morning? What will these things, processed and transformed and applied by the unconscious, come to mean?

As the novel progresses, we, as readers, will register, remember and forget the shapes, incidents, objects and subjects of the evolving narrative. There will be more to see; we will continue to be invited to make connections, observe repetitions, think about possible associations and reflect, too, on the *narrative's* ability to remember (we may observe, for instance, that Jacob's room at Cambridge is described twice, and that the description is unvarying). We, too, will continue to try to make sense of Jacob's world. In the language of the anonymous narrative and in the dialogue of the characters, Woolf will express not necessarily firm delineations, unvarying descriptions, 'facts', but at the very least we will be invited to observe, in the half-light, the desire to make sense, to remember, to gain and articulate a sense of being in the world, the desire to make contact with – even to possess – others, the desire to make cognitive and/or emotional discoveries, the desire to 'know'.

III

It's not catastrophes, murders, deaths, diseases, that age and kill us; it's the way people look and laugh, and run up the steps of omnibuses. (p.69)

In the Edwardian novel, love (except among the rebellious) is about romance, followed by constancy and continuity. Sons fall in love with ideal daughters; daughters, with ideal sons. Love which strays far from the family hearth is apt to end in disaster. Again, Bennett's *The Old Wives' Tale* is a good example of this: Sophia, tempted by her travelling salesman, is condemned to a life of independent loneliness; it is Constance, with her symbolic name, who will ensure the continuity of the spirit and moral standing of the family business.

The modernist novel, on the other hand, questions the relationship between the subject and the object of desire. If we cannot ever fully know ourselves, how could it ever be possible to possess another person? Desire is a striving for that which cannot be known; the object of desire constantly falls just outside the boundaries of the subject's reach. In the high modernist novel, *all* the characters are to some extent 'homeless', drifting, stranded, like the small Jacob on the beach, with the disorientating sense of human isolation, human separateness. But the implications of this for the modernist female subject are complex, since one aspect of female subjectivity may be to be able to identify oneself as an object of desire. If the male characters in a modernist novel are all, to some extent, drifting, perhaps there is a degree to which all the women characters are models; 'sitters' to a painter who is painting a picture of desire. In *Jacob's Room*, Virginia Woolf asks us to consider:

> the effect of sex – how between man and women it hangs wavy, tremulous, so that here's a valley, there's a peak, when in truth, perhaps, all's as flat as my hand. Even the exact words get the wrong accent on them. But something is always impelling one to hum vibrating . . . at the mouth of the cavern of mystery, endowing Jacob Flanders with all sorts of qualities he had not at all . . . Yet over him we hang vibrating. (p.61)

The passage is an example of the times when the narrative suddenly speaks for itself; the author of the text assumes complicity with us, and yet is somehow not there in person. On this issue, our position as readers is assured. Like the women in *Jacob's Room*, we are waiting. We hover, expectantly, in a state of anticipation. We do not know why, but we are waiting for Jacob.

At this stage in the novel, the women are in their bedrooms. Clara Durrant is asleep, 'on her dressing-table dishevelled roses and a pair of long white gloves' (p.65). When she wakes up, she will either attend or play hostess to yet another party: life, for her, is a question of 'little cards . . . with names engraved on them' (p.70), green-tufted puddings, dance cards and attendance on her mother.[44] When Jacob visited the Durrant household she took him out to the green-house where he held the ladder and she reached up to cut grapes from the vine. To Jacob, she looked 'semi-transparent, pale, wonderfully beautiful' (p.51), echoing the vocabulary in which Woolf, in 'Modern Fiction', described 'life itself'. Descending from the ladder, she placed two great leaves over her grapes 'where they lay curled warm in the basket', suggesting an imagery of maternity and of protection.

Jacob, of course, was captivated, as any good Edwardian son might well have been expected to be, by the sight of this vision reminiscent of, perhaps, Whistler's woman in white,[45] by this model daughter ('Ought she not to be grateful? Ought she not to be happy? Especially since her mother looked so well and enjoyed so much talking to Sir Edgar about Morocco ...' (p.146.) When he leaves her, she can do nothing but keep her place. She begins to record her feelings about him in her diary, but there is too much to say, and 'Mr. Letts allows little space in his shilling diaries. Clara was not one to encroach upon Wednesday. Humblest, most candid of women!' (p.59.)

Florinda's room is more reminiscent of a painting by Sickert or Gore.[46] Abandoned by Jacob after the Guy Fawkes party, so that he can stride home with his male friends and sound off about the Greeks, she succumbs to the nausea of suddenly being removed from the centre of his gaze. The bedroom seems 'fit for these catastrophes – cheap, mustard-coloured, half attic, half studio, curiously ornamented with silver paper stars, Welshwomen's hats, and rosaries pendent from the gas brackets' (p.65). She lives in lodging houses, studies at the Slade and has all the independence of illegitimacy: her name has been 'bestowed upon her by a painter who had wished it to signify that the flower of her maidenhood was still unplucked' (p.65). As an orphan, she has no home to which to return, no constraints against which to rebel, nothing to hark back to. As such, Jacob's comings and goings are baffling to her: having approached, she simply does not see why he has to retreat; her sickness is to do with the horror of being re-modelled by a man who, 'restless when she left him' (p.66), cannot take responsibility even for remembering who it was who left whom; who 'took her word for it that she was chaste'; who thinks her 'wild and frail and beautiful' (p.66), like the Greek women he has read about in the safety of his room.

Florinda is a tantalizing creature, full of appeal, despite her *demi-vierge* state, and her sexuality is strikingly suggestive. It is notable that sexuality is explicitly shown, in this novel, as nowhere else in Woolf's work. But what is also consistently revealed is the extent to which Jacob is forming a 'semi-transparent envelope' over the things he cannot allow himself to see. 'All night,' the narrative continues, men and women seethed up and down the well-known beats . . . Not a square in snow or fog lacked its amorous couple. All plays turned on the same subject. Bullets went through heads in hotel bedrooms almost nightly on that account . . . Yet we say it is a matter of no importance at all. (p.66)

So Jacob returns to his room with his friends, and 'this was life; and himself a man and Florinda chaste' (p.66).

He is disturbed by her, because she is sexually attractive, intelligent, and therefore dangerous. Having no parents, she cannot be cast as a daughter, which is convenient for Jacob because he cannot cast her in anything resembling a familiar mould. The narrator makes a fairly substantial contribution to this section of the book, as Woolf continues her discussion, apparently in the abstract, of the 'effects of sex':

What with Shakespeare and Adonais, Mozart and Bishop Berkeley – choose whom you like – the fact is concealed and the evenings for most of us pass reputably . . . But then concealment by itself distracts the mind from the print and the sound. If Florinda had had a mind, she might have read with clearer eyes than we can. (pp.66–67)

But unless we are very careful we will fall into the trap Jacob has fallen into at this point, and assume that it is all a matter of pre-established values to do with what is reputable and whose integrity is to be trusted. For what Florinda lacks is not a mind, but education: she may not understand Shelley but she understands Jacob all right. As they walk the streets, on a later occasion, passing 'here a girl for sale, or there an old woman with only matches to offer' (p.69), she observes his silence and comments, 'I don't like you when you look like that' (p.69). She sees evasion and intent, and it is not the suggestion of lust which unsettles her, but his disingenuousness. As fast as she picks up on the extent to which she can penetrate his facade, Jacob hurriedly resumes it:

In spite of defending indecency [he has written an essay on indecency in literature, at Cambridge], Jacob doubted whether he liked it in the raw. He had a violent reversion towards male society, cloistered rooms, and the works of the classics. (p.69)

And a reversion, too, towards the strategy which will eventually alienate him from the candid Florinda: 'Any excuse,' he reflects, 'serves a stupid woman.' And, of course, the more he brands her as stupid for seeing what he does not want her to see, the more successful he will be in silencing her.

Mrs Flanders, on the other hand, is never silent. When she cannot keep her son to herself by making her presence felt, she stakes her claim in writing. Her letter lies on the hall table; Florinda, coming in that night, takes it up with her and puts it on the table as she kisses Jacob: they leave it under the lamp, in the kind of clutter which might characterize the materialist Betty Flanders, 'between the biscuit-tin and the tobacco box'. Then they shut the bedroom door on it.

Desire is necessarily subversive because of its willingness to forget. As Jacob and Florinda make love, Mrs Flanders is temporarily forgotten, but the narrative cannot forget:

> if the pale blue envelope . . . had the feelings of a mother, the heart was torn by the little creak, the sudden stir. Behind the door was the obscene thing . . . Better, perhaps, burst in and face it than sit in the antechamber listening to the little creak, the sudden stir, for her heart was swollen, and pain threaded it. My son, my son – such would be her cry, uttered to hide her vision of him stretched with Florinda. (p.79)

Released from the obliteration of sex, this is, of course, the only narrative into which Jacob can regain consciousness: after all, it is *this* narrative, and no other, which is telling his story. As he emerges, 'amiable, authoritative, beautifully healthy, like a baby after an airing' (because sexuality also, of course, remembers our origins), he picks up his mother's letter and begins to read. The narrative is relentless. Now, it continues, 'Let us consider letters . . . Life would split asunder without them. "Come to tea, come to dinner, what's the truth of the story? have you heard the news?"' (p.79.) We are back in the world of trivia; Jacob is back in the world of the repressive grown-ups. Mrs Flanders wrote letters, he reflects, so did Mrs Jarvis, so did Florinda's landlady or guardian, Mother Stuart. Clara Durrant's letters, however, 'were those of a child. Florinda – the impediment between Florinda and her pen was something impassable . . . Her spelling was abominable. Her sentiments infantile . . .' (p.80.)

Mrs Flanders has triumphed by asserting the old, familial values. Jacob has only to read her words (any words – the narrative does not even need to tell us what she said) to revert back to his mode of recasting Florinda as an attractive, harmless child. But because she is equally sure of herself, equally protective of her own identity, Florinda reacts in the only way she can: 'Then he saw her turning up Greek Street upon another man's arm' (p.81).

In her first draft of *Jacob's Room*, Virginia Woolf included a woman character whom she deleted from the published text. The holograph drafts contain a section which was later revised and published as an essay (collected in *Atlanta's Garland* and entitled 'A Woman's College From Outside', it is reprinted in Appendix II of this edition).[47] Angela Williams, the character whom Woolf deleted from the text of the published novel, is a student being educated at Newnham 'for the purpose of earning her own living'. She has a card bearing her name on her door ('A. Williams')[48] and she lives in a corridor inhabited by similar girls, behind similar doors, bearing similar name cards. Clearly, what Woolf originally intended was to make a comparison between her life and Jacob's, and to introduce into the novel a 'modern' woman, in a room of her own, preparing to make her own way in the world.

Such a contrast would have been fascinating, but it would have gone against the grain of Virginia Woolf's whole method in this novel. The contrast she does make is between Jacob and the succession of desirous, powerless women he encounters in the course of his own journey towards adulthood and self-knowledge. The novel Woolf did publish is delicately constructed as a search to identify Jacob's interiority, his sexuality and the 'feelings of a man', of which we catch an early glimpse through the minor character Mr Dickens (p.19). (Virginia Woolf continually uses her walk-on characters, in *Jacob's Room*, in order to comment obliquely on what the central character may later think or feel.) As she continues her search to identify Jacob, Woolf gradually and subtly exposes to our gaze the interiority of the women, as Jacob moves from one woman to another in his modern, urban odyssey[49] from childhood to adulthood. As he progressively moves from virgin to adulteress in search of pleasure and knowledge, the narrative makes gradual disclosures about the nature of female desire.

Angela Williams, with her clearly stated identity ('A. Williams') and her firm location, would have interfered with the pattern Virginia Woolf makes, in *Jacob's Room*, out of the dynamics of male/female desire. In *Jacob's Room*, sexuality is central. But the question of sexual negotiation and the extent to which female desire becomes subject to male control, are issues which are carefully, delicately and subtly woven into the texture of her work of art. The women's desire is subject to Jacob's will; Jacob's desire is uncontrollable, confused and seems (and this is the irony which really engages Woolf) to compromise his integrity as a man. Each sexual contact or confrontation is therefore ambivalent, questionable and problematic. We deduce Woolf's statement about the dynamics of desire in this book by observing the women: how they sit, how they talk, how they dress, and, most revealingly of all, how they wait. The tone of Angela Williams' appeals would surely have been too plangent not to overbalance this delicate pattern. Angela has an insistent brightness – an earnest *claritas* – that distinguishes the passage concerning her from the published narrative's more muted tones.

The extent to which the Angela Williams material fails to fulfil Woolf's intention to show contrasting male and female rooms gives a fascinating insight into the importance of Woolf's method and of the subtle lights and shades of her narrative voice in this novel. It is interesting to note that the passage closely anticipates, in both style and sentiment, the essay portions Woolf would, much later, delete from her novel *The Years*, which also endeavours to discuss the question of women's independence. As is nearly always the case in passages which Woolf deleted, the material is over-insistent and over-written, as if the sentiments she wished to express were somehow top heavy. It is a prime example of the problem Woolf considered in 'Modern Fiction': that there are ideas which somehow fail to fit any form at the *artist's* disposal which would have been sufficient to contain them.

Firmly at the centre of this aspect of the history of the composition of *Jacob's Room*, however, resides the most fundamental aspect of Virginia Woolf's feminism. How might it be possible to reconcile the fragility, the delicacy of female desire – the plangent sensitivity exemplified by Angela Williams – with the issue of women's independence? Woolf was to continue the idea of contrasting male and female 'inside views' of college life in *A Room of One's Own*, where she draws graphic attention to the restrictions imposed on women in intellectual life at the time. She would take up the issue again in *Three Guineas*, where she explicitly poses the question of just what feminism would actually consist of, if in desiring social and sexual independence women were seeking something very much more subtle than simply rooms of their own in male institutions.

The framework of the world that men have made is subtly called into question throughout *Jacob's Room* (at Cambridge, in the City of London, in the British Museum and, at the end of the novel, in the Cabinet). To do this successfully Woolf needed to show Jacob's women tantalizingly and shadily almost-hidden in the interstices of such structures. Angela's articulate brightness would have interfered with the narrative's subtle method of shading-in. If Woolf had moved on to the question of women's education, the perspective of the book would have toppled. In making the *sexual* identity of her orphans, her artists' models and her adulteresses paramount, Woolf was doing something extremely daring, consistent with her overall attempt to revise the form of the novel. As it is, we have access to Virginia Woolf's creation of a uniquely feminist *demi-monde*. Catching glimpses, as Jacob does, of how Clara, Florinda, Fanny and Sandra feel – particularly about their actively felt sexuality – we are being offered an opportunity to revise our priorities in a style entirely in keeping with the novel's delicate mood.

Where Jacob, at Cambridge, is liberated from the external conditions of his mother's rule, while unconsciously moving homeward in all his attempts to establish relationships with women, Angela's dilemma would have been quite different. Angela (as the passage in Appendix II shows) is getting her education; her family supports the idea of her independence, but does she want it? At Newnham, her education and comradeship with other women are assured, but so is her celibacy. The rooms of the young women are flanked by the rooms of older women who, being successful, have remained at Newnham to continue the work of educating women: 'Elderly women slept ... surrounded ... supported, by the bodies of youth recumbent or grouped at the window ...' (p.191.) Sleepless, Angela Williams lay

in this good world, this new world, this world at the end of the
tunnel, until a desire to see it or forestall it drove her . . . to the
window, and there, looking out upon the garden . . . 'Oh,' she cried,
as if in pain. (p.192)

A point which Virginia Woolf would continue, throughout her
writing life, to attempt to convey is here expressed in embryo,
though it is more strikingly made, in my view, by Florinda. That
is that education for women might, in encompassing a 'good
world', a 'new world', succeed in assuring the sacrifice of something else: something fragile, delicate, something dangerously
destructible, a desire for 'life itself', which might differ radically in
quality from the kind of life towards which Jacob is striving.
The Angela Williams passage is significant in the sense that Woolf
herself would clearly like to believe that an access to independence,
to camaraderie and to the world of learning, will open the door
to a brave new world, but Angela, a 'wind-lashed sea in her heart'
as she roams around her room in a state of dizzy suspension, warns
us of the likely limits of this world. We cannot help feeling that,
in terms of her sexuality, she may simply have exchanged one
situation for another; one set of name cards for another. Woolf
clearly wanted to open up the world to her, but will the room of
her own turn out to be an entrée, or will it simply impose another
set of constraints?[50]

For a woman the process of origination has to be different. In a
sense, woman might become a metaphor for modernism in this
regard, because when a woman casts her mind back, what does she
think back *to*? In the holograph draft, there is a man with the
redoubtable name of Dick Midget, waiting back in Manchester for
Angela to name the day.[51] Clara Durrant will, it is hoped, procure
for her mother a husband who reminds Mrs Durrant of her youth
(' "I want to hear about your voyage," said. Mrs Durrant . . .
"Twenty years ago we did the same thing" ', p.50). For a woman
remembering, there would not be the same abrasive contrast between straddling rocks and returning to mother. The relationship
with the mother would be different: there would be different emotional debts to pay. So, too, the relationship with the father (though
fathers are notably absent from *Jacob's Room*). For a woman to
transcend tradition, for a woman to transgress, there would be a

price to pay; even the illegitimate Florinda suffers as Jacob attempts to reconstruct her in accordance with his myths. As she, herself, is the object of desire, how can she submit to the process of desiring without becoming completely unintelligible? The imagery of Angela Williams' desire ('immensely fertilizing, yet formless, chaotic, trailing and straying and tufting the rose-bushes with shreds of vapour', p.191) recalls and anticipates all that is evocative, vulnerable and irreducible to definition in Woolf's work.

Throughout Woolf's writing life she attempted to find a *shape* for sentiments such as these. Until she came to write *The Waves* she would go on taking up and relinquishing the attempt; elsewhere, she would relinquish to her minor characters (Minta in *To the Lighthouse*; Sara in *The Years*) the language of chaotic, uncontrolled desire. In the published text of *Jacob's Room* she came as close as she ever would to the possibility of articulating the desperation of desirous women, tormented by the emotional unreliability of men. By choosing orphans and artists' models as her characters, she was able to touch on the troubling connections between women as subjects and women as *desiring* objects. The narrative, though it teasingly weaves in and out of the legacy of Jacob's unconscious desire, continually, to return home, is suddenly blatant, uncompromising. At such moments, it calls to witness women as lovers: Florinda, with her integrity, or Fanny Elmer, the artist's model, who knows all about how to 'sit' to desire, and therefore makes no attempt to hide her longing.

> For he had grown to be a man . . . a fact that Florinda knew, as she knew everything, by instinct . . . Fanny Elmer felt it to desperation. For he would take his stick and his hat and would walk to the window . . . 'I am going,' he would say, 'to cadge a meal off Bonamy.'
> 'Anyhow, I can drown myself in the Thames,' Fanny cried, as she hurried past the Foundling Hospital. (p.122)

Men who organize women into position as the objects of desire and then 'forget' them, will be the death of women. He may well succeed in destroying Fanny Elmer, who has rearranged her life to accommodate him, but is – by the same token – certainly no Penelope:

She stitched or knitted.

'What's that?' asked Jacob.

'For the dance at the Slade.'

And she fetched her head-dress; her trousers; her shoes with red tassels. What should she wear?

'I shall be in Paris,' said Jacob.

And what is the point of fancy-dress dances? thought Fanny. You meet the same people; you wear the same clothes . . .

. . .

He would forget her. (p.107)

IV

'This is life. This is life,' said Fanny. (p.150)

Angela Williams' successor is Woolf's stroke of genius, and the pivotal character on whom the novel turns. Married to a Williams (though a Welsh, not a Mancunian Williams), she is a wonderful study in the power of suggestion, though her suggestions mean nothing at all, as her inane all-inclusiveness indicates. ('"Everything seems to mean so much," said Sandra', p.124.) More model than sitter, she chooses her novels because their jackets enhance her *ensemble*; constantly checking the limits of her world by regarding her image in the mirror, she succeeds in piercing to the root of Jacob Flanders because she panders to his myth. If Jacob has an inflated sense of his potential as a Greek hero, if his journey into adulthood is an unconscious odyssey homewards, Sandra is tailor-made as accomplice to his final fall, being of 'the English type which is so Greek, save that villagers have touched their hats to it . . .' (p.125.)[52]

The narrative, by the time Jacob succumbs to this fatal attraction and becomes himself an object (the helpless player in someone else's drama of the emotions), will have warned us that this passion of Jacob's for accuracy and precision will be the destruction of him. Since his quest is to be a figure in the external world, well, then, the external world is precisely what the narrative will supply. On his way to Greece, 'A motor car full of Italian officers ran along the flat road and kept up with the train, raising dust behind it. There were trees laced together with vines – as Virgil said' (p.118). Any reader with an eye on the external world of *Jacob's Room* – anyone with an eye for the allusive reportage which Woolf supplies as a kind of aside throughout the narrative – will have observed a closing of ranks, a gathering of forces; a succession of ominous warnings which have been sounding throughout the novel but which in this final section will bring the situation to a head.

From the outset, the imagery of *Jacob's Room* has hinted at the imminence of the First World War. Beginning with Jacob's name (which evokes, of course, the fields of Flanders), Woolf continues to lightly brush a succession of cryptic hints into the interstices of the narrative. In Cambridge, the stroke of the clock sounds 'as if generations of learned men heard the last hour go rolling through their ranks' (p.36); the smoke from the cottage chimney which Jacob and Timmy can see from their boat has 'the look of a mourning emblem, a flag floating its caress over a grave' (p.39). The ongoing discussions about history which Jacob has in Cambridge (encapsulated in his essay title) are contrasted with apparently throw-away references to walk-on characters such as Jimmy and Helen: the couple initially separated only by the conventions of the Edwardian tea-table, but now 'Jimmy feeds crows in Flanders and Helen visits hospitals' (p.83). So that by the time we hear, in Greece, the ships in the Piraeus firing their guns,[53] and the sound of the guns (like that of great carpets being beaten[54]) which Betty Flanders can hear from Scarborough, the narrator has already prepared us for the direction Jacob's brief life is to take.

Sandra, of course, is oblivious to all this.

> 'I am full of love for every one,' thought Mrs. Wentworth Williams, '– for the poor most of all – for the peasants coming back in the evenings with their burdens. And everything is soft and vague and very sad. It is sad, it is sad. But everything has meaning . . .' (p.124)

There is something dreadfully durable about Sandra. She is *almost* a comic character, echoing, perhaps, D. H. Lawrence's Hermione Roddice in *Women in Love* (which Woolf read as she was writing *Jacob's Room*), in that she cannot separate her sense of 'the modern' from an inflated and highly 'fashionable' sense of the significance of her own ego; to the extent that she controls Jacob by firmly keeping him at a convenient distance from her. Ironically, she resembles no-one more closely than Betty Flanders. 'Beautiful but dangerous' (p.125) is her disingenuous assessment of Jacob, and she sums up, in that stylish and derisive phrase, the sum total of her impact on him.

Woolf's genius in making Jacob fall for Sandra is that she thereby manages to substitute for her earlier idea (to use Angela Williams to compare male and female positions, male and female roles) the idea of having Jacob fall prey to the implications of his own assumptions, his own behaviour: Jacob becomes a kind of 'sitter' to Sandra and, thereby, the desirous, suffering object of desire. Schooled by his Cambridge training, he attempts to possess Sandra by improving his knowledge of Greece: he climbs the Pentelicus; he reaches the Acropolis; he reads; he observes the Erechtheum and is reminded of Sandra.[55] As he falls deeper and deeper prey to the controlling imagination of Sandra Wentworth Williams, he becomes increasingly subject to the sheer confusion – the mixed messages, the ambiguous signals, the impeded vision – of desire. Women madden him. He is interrupted in his attempt to draw a sketch of Sandra's nose by a group of French ladies 'opening and shutting their umbrellas' and exclaiming 'that one did not know what to expect – rain or fine weather?' (p.132.) Staring at a block of marble (probably, in fact, a famous statue) his vision is suddenly impeded by the figure of Madame Lucien Gravé,[56] who has 'her kodak pointed at his head' (p.132).

By now, the women have Jacob framed. Clara is reminded of him suddenly by a horse which gallops past without its rider;[57] Fanny makes her visits to the British Museum to look at the battered Ulysses; and Florinda is suddenly put in mind of him by an expression on the face of a waiter. Meanwhile, with the precision Jacob so admires in the Greeks,

> battleships ray out over the North Sea, keeping their stations accurately apart. At a given signal all the guns are trained on a target which ... flames into splinters. With equal nonchalance a dozen young men in the prime of life descend with composed faces into the depths of the sea; and there impassively ... suffocate uncomplainingly together. (p.136)

As they do so, Jacob encounters the Williamses in Hermes Street, and hatches his plans to take Sandra to the Acropolis. Returning to London, he manages to avoid all the waiting women who long for nothing so much as another opportunity to be in his presence. We never know where he goes after that, only that no sooner has he returned than he is nowhere to be found again, and that

> the red light was on the columns of the Parthenon, and the Greek women who were knitting their stockings and sometimes crying to a child to come ... were as jolly as sand-martins in the heat ... until the ships in the Piraeus fired their guns.

By the time 'Darkness drops like a knife over Greece' Jacob will have made his final leave-taking (p.154).

As the novel draws to its close, life goes on in London. Pickford's van swings down the street, omnibuses are locked together, engines throb, 'a harsh and unhappy voice cried something unintelligible' – the narrative remembering the sound of the child Archer on the beach calling his brother Jacob's name. With the ruthlessness of modernism, which refuses us happy endings, and in keeping with the ingenious narrative of *Jacob's Room*, which baldly exposes the patterns of habit in order to begin, just tentatively, to suggest that it is *these* patterns which we need to break, Betty Flanders bursts open the bedroom door. Bonamy, Jacob's trusted friend and confidant, the one with (in the ironic way of things) the Greek nose, turns to face her, for it is high time something was confronted.

The pair of old shoes she holds out to him is Woolf's final modernist gesture, for it is in these – not in any gesture of momentary heroism, nor in the embrace of some woman, nor indeed in any of the 'biographies of great men' – that Jacob has made his imprint, the unmistakable mark of his inimitable human form. It is in this gesture that Woolf reiterates the point which makes this a modern novel, and in artistic terms, a statement about the havoc wrought by the First World War. While 'the wires of the Admiralty shivered with some far-away communication', 'Prime Ministers and Viceroys spoke in the Reichstag', the 'Ambassador at Constantinople had audience with the Sultan' and 'the fleet was at Gibraltar' (p.151), the lives of thousands of young men were effectively being offered up for sacrifice. Or, to put it in personal terms, neither Clara, Florinda nor Fanny, neither Bonamy, Betty Flanders, Archer nor

INTRODUCTION

Johnny would ever see Jacob again. 'The policy of Sir Edward Grey' (p.146) was that England should remain at peace if at all possible. He, as Prime Minister, was as regretful as anyone when Britain went to war. On the eve of the war, he remarked that 'the lamps are going out all over Europe. We shall not see them lit again in our lifetime.' So what happened? The history books can tell us, but what they can never show us is the idiosyncratic, essentially tactile nature of an individual human being. They can give us the statistics, explain the political strategies but they can never show us who Jacob Flanders was, or what his potential consisted of, or why people loved him. The grand strategies of politicians and the large historical patterns could never show us such things: this is what Virginia Woolf means when she writes, 'It's not catastrophes, murders, deaths, diseases, that age and kill us; it's the way people look and laugh, and run up the steps of onmibuses' (p.69).

When she described the moving moment in which Betty Flanders holds out a pair of empty shoes, Woolf may have had in mind Van Gogh's painting, *A Pair of Shoes* [58] (was this, perhaps, the reproduction Jacob had on the wall of his college room? p.31): the epitome of what a painter may reveal to us about the relationship between what Lily Briscoe in *To the Lighthouse* calls 'subject and object and the nature of reality'.[59] In this moment (itself an exquisite encapsulation of both the spirit and the method of *Jacob's Room*), Woolf offers us a number of new possibilities: that of feeling a new sympathy with Betty Flanders; that of seeing a moment of interiority in her gesture; that of combining an emotional with an intellectual response to her text; and the possibility, also, of remembering Jacob after we put the book down. As we put this novel aside we might even perhaps imagine ourselves, just for a moment, in his shoes.

In the confrontation of Bonamy (the 'real' Greek; the homosexual)[60] with Jacob's mother, Woolf offers us one final opportunity to look backwards, forwards, inwards and outwards and perhaps also to reflect that here, in this final, unforgettable image, 'this is life', as Fanny would probably have said. It is in this novel that Virginia Woolf clearly determines the direction of all her future thinking, makes her final break with the conventional novel and brings us face to face with the intangible but not inexpressible vagaries of loss, longing, recollection and desire. If to sum up would be to misrepresent the whole nature, the whole point of *Jacob's Room*, I will leave it to someone else to supply the only statement remotely capable of paraphrasing this extraordinarily plangent, poised and subtle example of Virginia Woolf's achievement. 'Modernism begins,' Roland Barthes has suggested, 'with the search for a Literature which is no longer possible.'[61]

Sue Roe 1991

The Editor gratefully acknowledges the Henry W. and Albert A. Berg Collection (The New York Public Library, Astor, Lenox and Tilden Foundations) and Professor Quentin Bell, for permission to quote from unpublished sources. Also *Monks House Papers* (The Manuscripts Section, University of Sussex Library), for permission to quote from unpublished manuscripts. Particular thanks are due to Bet Inglis. Also to Bryan Berryman, John Boulter, Calum, John Davis, Beth Humphries, Angela Leighton, Ronald Milne, David Roe, Alison Sharpe, Joanne Shattock, John Spiers, Richard Stoneman, Jonathan Taylor, Jonathan Wilshere and, most warmly and especially, to Julia Briggs.

NOTES

1. On 26 January 1920, Virginia Woolf 'arrived at some idea of a new form for a new novel. Suppose,' she speculated, 'one thing should open out of another ...' She wanted, this time, to 'enclose everything, everything', yet worried that she was 'sufficiently mistress of my dialogue ... For I figure that the approach will be entirely different this time' (*Diary*, II, p. 13). She kept the idea in the back of her mind until 15 April, when she began the notebook which contains the early drafts of the novel. By this time she had hit on a new idea: 'Let us suppose that the Room will hold it together' (*MS*, p. 1).
2. *Diary*, II, 26 July 1922, p. 186.
3. In her essay 'Modern Fiction', Woolf stated that the modern novelist required the courage 'to say that what interests him is no longer "this" but "that" ... For the moderns "that", the point of interest, lies very likely in the dark places of psychology' (*CE*, II, p. 108).
4. 'Henry James' Ghost Stories' (*CE*, I, p. 288).
5. *Letters*, IV, p. 231.

6. That is, from plaster casts of Graeco-Roman statues.

7. 'Modern Fiction' (*CE*, II, p. 105).

8. ibid., p. 104.

9. Arnold Bennett, *The Old Wives' Tale* (Chapman and Hall, 1908; Penguin Books, 1983, p. 40).

10. 'Modern Fiction' (*CE*, II, p. 104).

11. *Diary*, II, 26 Jan. 1920, pp. 13–14.

12. Woolf was anxiously awaiting the public reaction to 'An Unwritten Novel' on 15 April 1920: it 'will certainly be abused', she worried. 'This slightly checks me from beginning *Jacob's Room*' (*Diary*, II, pp. 29–30). Nevertheless she began *JR* that same day. 'An Unwritten Novel' is collected (as are 'Kew Gardens' and 'The Mark on the Wall') in *A Haunted House and Other Stories* (Hogarth Press, 1944; Penguin Books, 1973).

13. 'An Unwritten Novel' (loc. cit., p. 27).

14. Letter to Vanessa Bell, 15 April 1920, *Letters*, II, p. 429.

15. Grafton Galleries, 1912; quoted in Gillian Naylor (ed.), *Bloomsbury: The Artists and Designers by Themselves* (Pyramid Books, 1990).

16. Roger Fry, *Vision and Design* (1920; Penguin Books, 1961). 'I'm in the middle of your book and fascinated,' Woolf wrote to Fry on 21 December 1920 (*Letters*, II, p. 450). She also praises the book in *Roger Fry: A Biography by Virginia Woolf* (1940; Penguin Books, 1979).

17. 'An Essay in Aesthetics' (*Vision and Design*, p. 26).

18. *Roger Fry*, p. 209.

19. 'Negro Sculpture' (*Vision and Design*, p. 86). Woolf wrote, 'What an accidental affair this living is after all our civilization . . . one must liken it to being blown through the Tube at fifty miles an hour . . . Shot out at the feet of God entirely naked!' ('The Mark on the Wall', loc. cit., pp. 44–5.)

20. 'Negro Sculpture' (loc. cit., p. 88).

21. Letter to R. C. Trevelyan, 23 Nov. 1922, *Letters*, II, p. 588.

22. 'Modern Fiction' (*CE*, II, pp. 103–10).

23. Letter to Vanessa Bell, 31 Dec. 1918, *Letters*, II, p. 311; Letter to Margaret Llewelyn Davies, 31 Dec. 1918, *Letters*, II, p. 313.

24. Letter to Vanessa Bell, 27 March 1921, *Letters*, II, p. 460; butterfly hunting (or 'bug-hunting') was a favourite pastime of the Stephen children during their long summer holidays at St Ives (see Quentin Bell, *Virginia Woolf*, vol. I, Hogarth Press, 1972, p. 33).

25. Letter to Duncan Grant, 29 Dec. 1918, *Letters*, II, p. 309. Woolf's father had read the *Waverley* novels to her when she was a child: see 'Impressions of Sir Leslie Stephen' (*Essays*, I, p. 128).

26. Letter to Vanessa Bell, June 1921, *Letters*, II, p. 475.

27. Thoby Stephen died on 20 November 1906, of typhoid fever.

28. Letter to Vanessa Bell, 11 April 1920, *Letters*, II, p. 429; this is oddly phrased, as Julian was Angelica's (half) brother. Perhaps Virginia Woolf can hardly believe it might be possible to re-create such a happy scene.

29. Virginia Woolf kept the news of Thoby's death from Violet Dickinson for a whole month: see *Letters*, I, pp. 248–66; Bell, op. cit., p. 110.

30. In 'An Unwritten Novel', the narrator surveys her fellow passenger, a middle-aged lady rather like Mrs Norman. In *JR* Woolf turns the tables: Mrs Norman has her eye on Jacob.

31. *Moments of Being*, pp. 139, 140, 127.

32. *Diary*, II, 17 April 1920, p. 31.

33. Letter to Roger Fry, 6 May 1922, *Letters*, II, p. 525.

34. John Mepham, 'Mourning and Modernism', in *Virginia Woolf: New Critical Essays* (Patricia Clements and Isobel Grundy (eds.), Vision Press, 1983).

35. The battered Ulysses also appears in a scene of unrequited love in chapter VI of *Night and Day* (cf. chapter IX, Note 28).

36. The material collected in *Contre Saint-Beuve* only came to light after Proust's death, in the 1950s, but evidence suggests that he wrote it in 1908–9. Marcel Proust, *By Way of Sainte-Beuve*, translated by Sylvia Townsend Warner (1958; Hogarth Press, 1984, p. 20).

37. Are she and Nanny one and the same person?

38. An emotive term. Wyndham Lewis launched his famous, controversial Vorticist journal of that name in 1914.

39. Walter Sickert (1860–1942) and Spencer Gore (1878–1914) were both founders of the Camden Town Group (founded in 1911), who experimented with the *contre-jour* effects of the play of light on form, and particularly with the play of artificial light on objects and the human figure in interiors. Woolf wrote a witty pamphlet, at Sickert's own request, about the 'stories' contained in his paintings (reprinted in *CE*, II, pp. 233–44).

40. Gabriel Josipovici develops this idea in 'Proust: A Voice in Search of Itself', in Josipovici, *The World and the Book* (Paladin, 1973, pp. 21–44).

41. Pierre Bonnard (1867–1947) was an important influence on the *contre-jour* painters. Gabriel Josipovici's novel about him, *Contre-Jour* (Paladin, 1988), quotes or paraphrases one of the main aims of his work: 'I want my people to be bathed in time as the Impressionists bathed them in light' (p. 20).

42. 'Freudian Fiction' (*A Woman's Essays*, Penguin Books, 1992, p. 23).

43. Letter to Roger Fry, 27 May 1927, *Letters*, III, p. 385.

44. This is very much the halcyon world of pre-war innocence, in which the upper classes existed in a round of parties. It is vividly evoked in Kirsty McLeod, *The Last Summer* (Collins, 1983).

45. James Abbott McNeill Whistler (1834–1903) was an American painter popular in the art world of Edwardian London, especially for his series of paintings of 'The White Girl'.

46. Frederick Spencer Gore (1878–1914), first President of the Camden Town Group, was a *contre-jour* painter mainly of interiors.

47. This material in its original form is chapter X of *Jacob's Room: The Holograph Notebook* (notebook I, pp. 85–91). In the holograph drafts the chapters are shorter, so that the material originally appeared in what has become (in the published text) chapter III. A revised version appears in Appendix II of this edition.

48. In the holograph draft, Angela is introduced to the reader as 'Angela Edwards', but the name on her door ('A. Williams') confirms that this is the same Angela (*Holograph Notebook*, I, p. 89). Virginia Woolf was never sure, in any case, about Edwards: 'was that her name?' (*Holograph Notebook*, I, p. 85.)

49. It is almost certainly for this reason that Virginia Woolf worried, at one point, that what she was doing might be 'being better done by Mr. Joyce' (*Diary*, II, 26 Sept. 1920, p. 69).

50. Virginia Woolf discusses this question most fully in the posthumously published drafts of the text she revised as *The Years*. The early drafts were called *The Pargiters: The Novel-Essay Portion of The Years* (edited with an introduction by Mitchell A. Leaska, Harcourt, Brace, Jovanovich, 1977). There, as in *A Room of One's Own* (1928), Virginia Woolf continues her discussion of women's independence and the question of women's education.

51. The women's talk, in the original draft, was of 'Bamborough Castle . . . "my father", "my mother"; Dick Midget. Then simply this – "I shall write & settle the day –"' (*Holograph Notebook*, I, p. 89–91.)

52. An 'English type' such as Sandra could have manufactured a Greek image, in this period, simply by following fashion. Poiret's 'frail and fragmentary' Greek fashions were all the rage in 1914 (McLeod, op. cit., p. 42).

53. It is worth noting that Virginia Woolf refers to this in her 1906 journal of her visit to Greece (published in *Passionate Apprentice*), so the firing of *these* guns may be nothing to do with the war: the suggestive imagery, however, is unmistakable; cf. chapter XII, Note 16.

54. Virginia Woolf first uses this image in a piece for *The Times*, 'Heard on the Downs' (*Essays*, II, p. 40). There the guns sound like 'the beating of

gigantic carpets by gigantic women': thus the imagery of war shifts from the imagery of the male to that of the female domain.

55. The Erechtheum is a temple at the Parthenon dedicated to (among others) the legendary half-divine King Erechtheus. One of its most striking and most controversial features is the caryatid, the pillars of which are sculpted in the form of a series of beautiful women, apparently supporting the architecture on their heads: an idiosyncrasy of Greek architecture which has long puzzled historians (see Rex Warner and Martin Hurlimann, *Eternal Greece*, Thames and Hudson, 1957). Sandra, with her mixture of the durable and the effete, similarly puzzles Jacob.

56. Virginia Woolf borrowed for this briefly and colourfully depicted character the name of her dressmaker, Madame Felix Gravé (see *Diary*, II, 4 Feb. 1920, p. 17).

57. In the *Phaedrus* (which Jacob has read, with difficulty) Plato compares the soul's journey through life to a chariot pulled by two horses: one horse represents reason, the other, base passions. Only the man who controls the chariot and lets his life be governed by reason can ever reach the truth: Sandra has triumphed; Jacob has lost his reason and succumbed to his base nature. It may be interesting to note here that in the original drafts of the novel (which only go as far as Jacob's encounter with Sandra) they have a more explicit affair. 'Well,' the narrator originally disclosed, 'it happened' (*Holograph Notebook*, III, p. 261). Sandra, moreover, was 'so daring'. So Clara *will* be forgotten.

58. *A Pair of Shoes*, 1886, by Vincent van Gogh (1853–90).

59. *To the Lighthouse* (Penguin Books, 1992, p. 28).

60. Bonamy, with his homosexuality and his capacity for loyal friendship, was probably modelled on Lytton Strachey. Certainly, Strachey recognized something of himself in the character: 'I am such a Bonamy', he remarked, on reading the novel for the first time (*Virginia Woolf and Lytton Strachey: Letters* (Harcourt, Brace, Jovanovich, 1956, p. 144, 9 Oct., 1922).

61. Roland Barthes, *Writing Degree Zero* (Farrar, Straus & Giroux, 1968, p. 38).

Further Reading

MATERIAL BY VIRGINIA WOOLF
Short stories

A Haunted House and Other Stories (Hogarth Press, 1944; Penguin Books, 1973); including 'An Unwritten Novel'.

Essays

A Room of One's Own (Hogarth Press, 1929; Penguin Books, 1992).

'Modern Fiction' (*CE*, II, pp. 103ff.).

'Mr Bennett and Mrs Brown' (*A Woman's Essays*, Penguin Books, 1992, pp. 69ff.).

'On Not Knowing Greek' (*A Woman's Essays*, pp. 93ff.).

'Walter Sickert' (*CE*, II, pp. 233ff.).

On Fry and Post-Impressionism

Roger Fry (Penguin Books, 1979).

Journals and Letters

The Diary of Virginia Woolf, II, ed. Anne Olivier Bell (Hogarth Press, 1978; Penguin Books, 1981).

Moments of Being: Unpublished Autobiographical Writings of Virginia Woolf, ed. Jeanne Schulkind (Chatto & Windus, 1976).

A Passionate Apprentice: The Early Journals, 1897–1909, ed. Mitchell A. Leaska (Hogarth Press, 1990).

The Letters of Virginia Woolf, II, ed. Nigel Nicolson and Joanne Trautmann (Hogarth Press, 1976).

MATERIAL ON VIRGINIA WOOLF
Biography

Quentin Bell, *Virginia Woolf: A Biography*, 2 vols. (Hogarth Press, 1972).

Criticism – on Jacob's Room

Rachel Bowlby, 'Jacob's Type', in *Virginia Woolf: Feminist Destinations* (Basil Blackwell, 1988).

Kate Flint, 'Revising *Jacob's Room*: Virginia Woolf, Women and Language', in the *Review of English Studies*, vol. XLII, 167, August 1991, pp. 361–79.

Winifred Holtby, 'Cinematograph', in *Virginia Woolf: A Critical Memoir* (Academy Press, 1978).

Judy Little, '*Jacob's Room* as Comedy: Woolf's Parodic Bildungs-roman', in Jane Marcus (ed.), *New Feminist Essays on Virginia Woolf* (Macmillan, 1981).

John Mepham, 'Mourning and Modernism', in Patricia Clements and Isobel Grundy (eds.), *Virginia Woolf: New Critical Essays* (Vision Press, 1983).

Beverley Ann Schlack, chapter two (on *Jacob's Room*) of *Continuing Presences: Virginia Woolf's Use of Literary Allusion* (Pennsylvania State University Press, 1979).

Criticism – on Woolf's methods of composition

C. Ruth Miller, *Virginia Woolf: The Frames of Art and Life* (Macmillan, 1988).

Sue Roe, *Writing and Gender: Virginia Woolf's Writing Practice* (Harvester/Wheatsheaf, 1990).

OTHER MATERIAL

Post-Impressionism

Roger Fry, *Vision and Design* (Penguin Books, 1961).

Simon Watney, *English Post-Impressionism* (Cassell, 1980).

Modernism

Roland Barthes, *Writing Degree Zero* (Farrar, Straus & Giroux, 1968).

Gabriel Josipovici, *The World and the Book* (Paladin, 1973).

A Note on the Text

Virginia Woolf began *Jacob's Room* on 15 April 1920, and completed the novel in July 1922. The first British edition was published on 27 October 1922 by the Hogarth Press. The Press's largest undertaking to date, it was printed for them by R. & R. Clark, of Edinburgh. It was set from a typescript which has not survived. The eight pages of typescript which do survive are unrevised, and are held in the Manuscripts Section of the University of Sussex Library.*

The Holograph Notebooks which contain Virginia Woolf's original drafts of the novel are held by the Berg Collection (New York Public Library, Astor, Lenox and Tilden Foundations). Notebooks I and II contain drafts of *Jacob's Room*; notebook III also contains the drafts of some stories and occasional pieces, including a few preliminary notes for *Mrs Dalloway*. The holograph drafts were clearly added to, re-ordered and revised before Virginia Woolf arrived at the published version. The most substantial change is the deletion of material relating to a character called, variously, Angela Edwards and Angela Williams (discussed in the Introduction to this edition), which was deleted from the novel and published separately, in a revised version, as an essay entitled 'A Woman's College From Outside' (reprinted in Appendix II of this edition).

Virginia Woolf herself made no further revisions to the text following the publication of the first British edition. In a letter to C. P. Sanger (30 October 1922), she declared, 'I think a close study of Jacob's Room, should you ever wish to approach the book again, will reveal many passages . . . where the mistakes are glaring. What about lilacs in April, fountains in Neville's Court, tulips in August etc. etc. etc. I am not going to pick them all out for your benefit.' As I indicate in the relevant notes, there are other 'glaring mistakes', particularly with regard to the geography of 'Scarborough' (the real Scarborough is not 700 miles from Cornwall, for

Monks House Papers, B. 12.

example). For obvious reasons, I have left all such 'mistakes' uncorrected.

The sales of the first British edition justified the immediate printing of a second edition. The first American edition followed in 1923 (from Harcourt, Brace, Jovanovich). A second American edition appeared in 1960, when *The Waves* and *Jacob's Room* were reset and bound in a single volume. In 1978, Harcourt, Brace, Jovanovich published a separate edition of both novels. The 1978 edition of *Jacob's Room* was offset from the pages of the 1960 combined edition, and, in 1977, the Hogarth Press published a Uniform edition.

Textual variants between (a) the first British edition and the first American edition, (b) the Uniform edition and the 1923 American edition, and (c) the Uniform edition and the 1978 American edition almost all represent errors of typography or punctuation, or errors arising out of editorial attempts to correct Virginia Woolf's text. Where editors' corrections have interfered with the sense (as in the change from 'ear-ring' to 'erring') I have reinstated the original printing. I have reinstated the version printed in the first British edition, in all but five instances. In these I have: added a comma and a diacritic; altered square to circular brackets; amended the curious word, 'squab' to 'squat'; and added the word 'the' to the line, 'It was the first time he had read his essay aloud.'

The corrections I have made to the text which have not before been listed as variants are listed in Appendix I. I have corrected the spelling of Van Gogh and of Boulevard Raspail. In a letter of 10 December 1922, to Jacques Raverat, Virginia Woolf admitted that 'Raspail was spelt wrong owing to Duncan [Grant] and Vanessa [Bell], whom I consulted. A letter more or less means nothing to them.' The toad which joins the company of insects on p. 25 I have not tampered with: 'Toads,' she told Raverat, 'are (essentially) insects, I maintain.'

JACOB'S ROOM

'So of course,' wrote Betty Flanders, pressing her heels rather deeper in the sand, 'there was nothing for it but to leave.'

Slowly welling from the point of her gold nib, pale blue ink dissolved the full stop; for there her pen stuck; her eyes fixed, and tears slowly filled them. The entire bay quivered; the lighthouse wobbled; and she had the illusion that the mast of Mr. Connor's little yacht was bending like a wax candle in the sun. She winked quickly. Accidents were awful things. She winked again. The mast was straight; the waves were regular; the lighthouse was upright; but the blot had spread.

'. . . nothing for it but to leave,' she read.

'Well, if Jacob doesn't want to play' (the shadow of Archer, her eldest son, fell across the notepaper and looked blue on the sand, and she felt chilly – it was the third of September already), 'if Jacob doesn't want to play' – what a horrid blot! It must be getting late.

'Where *is* that tiresome little boy?' she said. 'I don't see him. Run and find him. Tell him to come at once.' '. . . but mercifully,' she scribbled, ignoring the full stop, 'everything seems satisfactorily arranged, packed though we are like herrings in a barrel, and forced to stand the perambulator which the landlady quite naturally won't allow . . .'

Such were Betty Flanders's letters to Captain Barfoot – many-paged, tear-stained. Scarborough is seven hundred miles from Corn-wall:[1] Captain Barfoot is in Scarborough: Seabrook is dead. Tears made all the dahlias in her garden undulate in red waves and flashed the glass house in her eyes, and spangled the kitchen with bright knives, and made Mrs. Jarvis, the rector's wife, think at church, while the hymn-tune played and Mrs. Flanders bent low over her little boys' heads, that marriage is a fortress and widows stray solitary in the open fields, picking up stones, gleaning a few golden straws, lonely, unprotected, poor creatures. Mrs. Flanders had been a widow these two years.

*

'Ja–cob! Ja–cob!' Archer shouted.

'Scarborough,' Mrs. Flanders wrote on the envelope, and dashed a bold line beneath; it was her native town; the hub of the universe. But a stamp? She ferreted in her bag; then held it up mouth downwards; then fumbled in her lap, all so vigorously that Charles Steele in the Panama hat suspended his paint-brush.

Like the antennae of some irritable insect it positively trembled. Here was that woman moving – actually going to get up – confound her! He struck the canvas a hasty violet-black dab. For the landscape needed it. It was too pale – greys flowing into lavenders, and one star or a white gull suspended just so – too pale as usual. The critics would say it was too pale, for he was an unknown man exhibiting obscurely, a favourite with his landladies' children, wearing a cross on his watch chain, and much gratified if his landladies liked his pictures – which they often did.

'Ja–cob! Ja–cob!' Archer shouted.

Exasperated by the noise, yet loving children, Steele picked nervously at the dark little coils on his palette.

'I saw your brother – I saw your brother,' he said, nodding his head, as Archer lagged past him, trailing his spade, and scowling at the old gentleman in spectacles.

'Over there – by the rock,' Steele muttered, with his brush between his teeth, squeezing out raw sienna, and keeping his eyes fixed on Betty Flanders's back.

'Ja–cob! Ja–cob!' shouted Archer, lagging on after a second.

The voice had an extraordinary sadness. Pure from all body, pure from all passion, going out into the world, solitary, unanswered, breaking against rocks – so it sounded.

Steele frowned; but was pleased by the effect of the black – it was just *that* note which brought the rest together.[2] 'Ah, one may learn to paint at fifty! There's Titian . . .'[3] and so, having found the right tint, up he looked and saw to his horror a cloud over the bay.

Mrs. Flanders rose, slapped her coat this side and that to get the sand off, and picked up her black parasol.

*

The rock was one of those tremendously solid brown, or rather black, rocks which emerge from the sand like something primitive. Rough with crinkled limpet shells and sparsely strewn with locks of dry seaweed, a small boy has to stretch his legs far apart, and indeed to feel rather heroic, before he gets to the top.

But there, on the very top, is a hollow full of water, with a sandy bottom; with a blob of jelly stuck to the side, and some mussels. A fish darts across. The fringe of yellow-brown seaweed flutters, and out pushes an opal-shelled crab—

'Oh, a huge crab,' Jacob murmured— and begins his journey on weakly legs on the sandy bottom. Now! Jacob plunged his hand. The crab was cool and very light. But the water was thick with sand, and so, scrambling down, Jacob was about to jump, holding his bucket in front of him, when he saw, stretched entirely rigid, side by side, their faces very red, an enormous man and woman.

An enormous man and woman (it was early-closing day) were stretched motionless, with their heads on pocket-handkerchiefs, side by side, within a few feet of the sea, while two or three gulls gracefully skirted the incoming waves, and settled near their boots.

The large red faces lying on the bandanna handkerchiefs stared up at Jacob. Jacob stared down at them. Holding his bucket very carefully, Jacob then jumped deliberately and trotted away very nonchalantly at first, but faster and faster as the waves came creaming up to him and he had to swerve to avoid them, and the gulls rose in front of him and floated out and settled again a little farther on. A large black woman was sitting on the sand. He ran towards her.

'Nanny! Nanny!' he cried, sobbing the words out on the crest of each gasping breath.

The waves came round her. She was a rock. She was covered with the seaweed which pops when it is pressed. He was lost.

There he stood. His face composed itself. He was about to roar when, lying among the black sticks and straw under the cliff, he saw a whole skull – perhaps a cow's skull, a skull, perhaps, with the teeth in it.[4] Sobbing, but absent-mindedly, he ran farther and farther away until he held the skull in his arms.

'There he is!' cried Mrs. Flanders, coming round the rock and covering the whole space of the beach in a few seconds. 'What has he got hold of? Put it down, Jacob! Drop it this moment! Something horrid, I know. Why didn't you stay with us? Naughty little boy! Now put it down. Now come along both of you,' and she swept round, holding Archer by one hand and fumbling for Jacob's arm with the other. But he ducked down and picked up the sheep's jaw, which was loose.

Swinging her bag, clutching her parasol, holding Archer's hand, and telling the story of the gunpowder explosion in which poor Mr. Curnow had lost his eye, Mrs. Flanders hurried up the steep lane, aware all the time in the depths of her mind of some buried discomfort.

There on the sand not far from the lovers lay the old sheep's skull without its jaw. Clean, white, wind-swept, sand-rubbed, a more unpolluted piece of bone existed nowhere on the coast of Cornwall. The sea holly would grow through the eye-sockets; it would turn to powder, or some golfer, hitting his ball one fine day, would disperse a little dust. – No, but not in lodgings, thought Mrs. Flanders. It's a great experiment coming so far with young children. There's no man to help with the perambulator. And Jacob is such a handful; so obstinate already.

'Throw it away, dear, do,' she said, as they got into the road; but Jacob squirmed away from her; and the wind rising, she took out her bonnet-pin, looked at the sea, and stuck it in afresh. The wind was rising. The waves showed that uneasiness, like something alive, restive, expecting the whip, of waves before a storm. The fishing-boats were leaning to the water's brim. A pale yellow light shot across the purple sea; and shut. The lighthouse was lit. 'Come along,' said Betty Flanders. The sun blazed in their faces and gilded the great blackberries trembling out from the hedge which Archer tried to strip as they passed.

'Don't lag, boys. You've got nothing to change into,' said Betty, pulling them along, and looking with uneasy emotion at the earth displayed so luridly, with sudden sparks of light from greenhouses in gardens, with a sort of yellow and black mutability, against this blazing sunset, this astonishing agitation and vitality of nature, which stirred Betty Flanders and made her think of responsibility and danger. She gripped Archer's hand. On she plodded up the hill.

'What did I ask you to remember?' she said.

'I don't know,' said Archer.

'Well, I don't know either,' said Betty, humorously and simply, and who shall deny that this blankness of mind, when combined with profusion, mother wit, old wives' tales, haphazard ways, moments of astonishing daring, humour, and sentimentality – who shall deny that in these respects every woman is nicer than any man?

Well, Betty Flanders, to begin with.

She had her hand upon the garden gate.

'The meat!' she exclaimed, striking the latch down.

She had forgotten the meat.

There was Rebecca at the window.

The bareness of Mrs. Pearce's front room was fully displayed at ten o'clock at night when a powerful oil lamp stood on the middle of the table. The harsh light fell on the garden; cut straight across the lawn; lit up a child's bucket and a purple aster and reached the hedge. Mrs. Flanders had left her sewing on the table. There were her large reels of white cotton and her steel spectacles; her needle-case; her brown wool wound round an old postcard. There were the bulrushes and the *Strand* magazines;[5] and the linoleum sandy from the boys' boots. A daddy-long-legs shot from corner to corner and hit the lamp globe. The wind blew straight dashes of rain across the window, which flashed silver as they passed through the light. A single leaf[6] tapped hurriedly, persistently, upon the glass. There was a hurricane out at sea.

Archer could not sleep.

Mrs. Flanders stooped over him. 'Think of the fairies,' said Betty Flanders. 'Think of the lovely, lovely birds settling down on their nests. Now shut your eyes and see the old mother bird with a worm in her beak. Now turn and shut your eyes,' she murmured, 'and shut your eyes.'

The lodging-house seemed full of gurgling and rushing; the cistern overflowing; water bubbling and squeaking and running along the pipes and streaming down the windows.

'What's all that water rushing in?' murmured Archer.

'It's only the bath water running away,' said Mrs. Flanders.

Something snapped out of doors.

'I say, won't that steamer sink?' said Archer, opening his eyes.

'Of course it won't,' said Mrs. Flanders. 'The Captain's in bed long ago. Shut your eyes, and think of the fairies,[7] fast asleep, under the flowers.'

'I thought he'd never get off – such a hurricane,' she whispered to Rebecca, who was bending over a spirit-lamp in the small room next door. The wind rushed outside, but the small flame of the spirit-lamp burnt quietly, shaded from the cot by a book stood on edge.

'Did he take his bottle well?' Mrs. Flanders whispered, and Rebecca nodded and went to the cot and turned down the quilt, and Mrs. Flanders bent over and looked anxiously at the baby, asleep, but frowning. The window shook, and Rebecca stole like a cat and wedged it. The two women murmured over the spirit-lamp, plotting the eternal conspiracy of hush and clean bottles while the wind raged and gave a sudden wrench at the cheap fastenings.

Both looked round at the cot. Their lips were pursed. Mrs. Flanders crossed over to the cot.

'Asleep?' whispered Rebecca, looking at the cot.

Mrs. Flanders nodded.

'Good-night, Rebecca,' Mrs. Flanders murmured, and Rebecca called her ma'm, though they were conspirators plotting the eternal conspiracy of hush and clean bottles.

Mrs. Flanders had left the lamp burning in the front room. There were her spectacles, her sewing; and a letter with the Scarborough postmark. She had not drawn the curtains either.

The light blazed out across the patch of grass; fell on the child's green bucket with the gold line round it, and upon the aster which trembled violently beside it. For the wind was tearing across the coast, hurling itself at the hills, and leaping, in sudden gusts, on top of its own back. How it spread over the town in the hollow! How the lights seemed to wink and quiver in its fury, lights in the harbour, lights in bedroom windows high up! And rolling dark waves before it, it raced over the Atlantic, jerking the stars above the ships this way and that.

There was a click in the front sitting-room. Mr. Pearce had extinguished the lamp. The garden went out. It was but a dark patch. Every inch was rained upon. Every blade of grass was bent by rain. Eyelids would have been fastened down by the rain. Lying on one's back one would have seen nothing but muddle and confusion — clouds turning and turning, and something yellow-tinted and sulphurous in the darkness.

The little boys in the front bedroom had thrown off their blankets and lay under the sheets. It was hot; rather sticky and steamy. Archer[8] lay spread out, with one arm striking across the pillow. He was flushed; and when the heavy curtain blew out a little he turned and half-opened his eyes. The wind actually stirred the cloth on the chest of drawers, and let in a little light, so that the sharp edge of the chest of drawers was visible, running straight up, until a white shape bulged out; and a silver streak showed in the looking-glass.

In the other bed by the door Jacob lay asleep, fast asleep, profoundly unconscious. The sheep's jaw with the big yellow teeth in it lay at his feet. He had kicked it against the iron bed-rail.

Outside the rain poured down more directly and powerfully as the wind fell in the early hours of the morning. The aster was beaten to the earth. The child's bucket was half-full of rainwater; and the opal-shelled crab slowly circled round the bottom, trying with its weakly legs to climb the steep side; trying again and falling back, and trying again and again.

'Mrs. Flanders' – 'Poor Betty Flanders' – 'Dear Betty' – 'She's very attractive still' – 'Odd she don't marry again!' 'There's Captain Barfoot to be sure – calls every Wednesday as regular as clockwork, and never brings his wife.'

'But that's Ellen Barfoot's fault,' the ladies of Scarborough said. 'She don't put herself out for no one.'

'A man likes to have a son – that we know.'

'Some tumours have to be cut; but the sort my mother had you bear with for years and years, and never even have a cup of tea brought up to you in bed.'

(Mrs. Barfoot was an invalid.)

Elizabeth Flanders, of whom this and much more than this had been said and would be said, was, of course, a widow in her prime. She was half-way between forty and fifty. Years and sorrow between them; the death of Seabrook, her husband; three boys; poverty; a house on the outskirts of Scarborough; her brother, poor Morty's, downfall and possible demise – for where was he? what was he? Shading her eyes, she looked along the road for Captain Barfoot – yes, there he was, punctual as ever; the attentions of the Captain – all ripened Betty Flanders, enlarged her figure, tinged her face with jollity, and flooded her eyes for no reason that any one could see perhaps three times a day.

True, there's no harm in crying for one's husband, and the tombstone, though plain, was a solid piece of work, and on summer's days when the widow brought her boys to stand there one felt kindly towards her. Hats were raised higher than usual; wives tugged their husbands' arms. Seabrook lay six foot beneath, dead these many years; enclosed in three shells; the crevices sealed with lead,[1] so that, had earth and wood been glass, doubtless his very face lay visible beneath, the face of a young man whiskered, shapely, who had gone out duck-shooting and refused to change his boots.

'Merchant of this city,' the tombstone said; though why Betty Flanders had chosen so to call him when, as many still remembered, he had only sat behind an office window for three months, and before that had broken horses, ridden to hounds, farmed a few fields, and run a little wild – well, she had to call him something.[2] An example for the boys.

Had he, then, been nothing? An unanswerable question, since even if it weren't the habit of the undertaker to close the eyes, the light so soon goes out of them. At first, part of herself; now one of a company, he had merged in the grass, the sloping hillside, the thousand white stones,[3] some slanting, others upright, the decayed wreaths, the crosses of green tin, the narrow yellow paths, and the lilacs that drooped in April,[4] with a scent like that of an invalid's bedroom, over the churchyard wall. Seabrook was now all that; and when, with her skirt hitched up, feeding the chickens, she heard the bell for service or funeral, that was Seabrook's voice – the voice of the dead.[5]

The rooster had been known to fly on her shoulder and peck her neck, so that now she carried a stick or took one of the children with her when she went to feed the fowls.

'Wouldn't you like my knife, mother?' said Archer.

Sounding at the same moment as the bell, her son's voice mixed life and death inextricably, exhilaratingly.

'What a big knife for a small boy!' she said. She took it to please him. Then the rooster flew out of the hen-house, and, shouting to Archer to shut the door into the kitchen garden, Mrs. Flanders set her meal down, clucked for the hens, went bustling about the orchard, and was seen from over the way by Mrs. Cranch, who, beating her mat against the wall, held it for a moment suspended while she observed to Mrs. Page next door that Mrs. Flanders was in the orchard with the chickens.

Mrs. Page, Mrs. Cranch, and Mrs. Garfit could see Mrs. Flanders in the orchard because the orchard was a piece of Dods Hill[6] enclosed; and Dods Hill dominated the village. No words can exaggerate the importance of Dods Hill. It was the earth; the world against the sky; the horizon of how many glances can best be computed by those who have lived all their lives in the same village, only leaving it once to fight in the Crimea,[7] like old

George Garfit, leaning over his garden gate smoking his pipe. The progress of the sun was measured by it; the tint of the day laid against it to be judged.

'Now she's going up the hill with little John,' said Mrs. Cranch to Mrs. Garfit, shaking her mat for the last time, and bustling indoors.

Opening the orchard gate, Mrs. Flanders walked to the top of Dods Hill, holding John by the hand. Archer and Jacob ran in front or lagged behind; but they were in the Roman fortress when she came there, and shouting out what ships were to be seen in the bay. For there was a magnificent view – moors behind, sea in front, and the whole of Scarborough from one end to the other laid out flat[8] like a puzzle. Mrs. Flanders, who was growing stout, sat down in the fortress and looked about her.

The entire gamut of the view's changes should have been known to her; its winter aspect, spring, summer, and autumn; how storms came up from the sea; how the moors shuddered and brightened as the clouds went over; she should have noted the red spot where the villas were building; and the criss-cross of lines where the allotments were cut; and the diamond flash of little glass houses in the sun. Or, if details like these escaped her, she might have let her fancy play upon the gold tint of the sea at sunset, and thought how it lapped in coins of gold upon the shingle. Little pleasure boats shoved out into it; the black arm of the pier hoarded it up. The whole city was pink and gold; domed; mist-wreathed; resonate; strident. Banjoes strummed; the parade smelt of tar which stuck to the heels; goats suddenly cantered their carriages through crowds. It was observed how well the Corporation had laid out the flower-beds. Sometimes a straw hat was blown away. Tulips burned in the sun.[9] Numbers of sponge-bag trousers[10] were stretched in rows. Purple bonnets fringed soft, pink, querulous faces on pillows in bath chairs. Triangular hoardings were wheeled along by men in white coats. Captain George Boase had caught a monster shark. One side of the triangular hoarding said so in red, blue, and yellow letters; and each line ended with three differently coloured notes of exclamation.[11]

So that was a reason for going down into the Aquarium, where the sallow blinds, the stale smell of spirits of salt, the bamboo chairs, the tables with ash-trays, the revolving fish, the attendant knitting behind six or seven chocolate boxes (often she was quite alone with the fish for hours at a time) remained in the mind as part of the monster shark, he himself being only a flabby yellow receptacle, like an empty Gladstone bag in a tank. No one had ever been cheered by the Aquarium; but the faces of those emerging quickly lost their dim, chilled expression when they perceived that it was only by standing in a queue that one could be admitted to the pier. Once through the turnstiles, every one walked for a yard or two very briskly; some flagged at this stall; others at that. But it was the band that drew them all to it finally; even the fishermen on the lower pier taking up their pitch within its range.

The band played in the Moorish kiosk. Number nine went up on the board. It was a waltz tune. The pale girls, the old widow lady, the three Jews lodging in the same boarding-house, the dandy, the major, the horse-dealer, and the gentleman of independent means, all wore the same blurred, drugged expression, and through the chinks in the planks at their feet they could see the green summer waves, peacefully, amiably, swaying round the iron pillars of the pier.

But there was a time when none of this had any existence (thought the young man leaning against the railings). Fix your eyes upon the lady's skirt;[12] the grey one will do – above the pink silk stockings. It changes; drapes her ankles – the nineties; then it amplifies – the seventies; now it's burnished red and stretched above a crinoline – the sixties; a tiny black foot wearing a white cotton stocking peeps out. Still sitting there? Yes – she's still on the pier. The silk now is sprigged with roses, but somehow one no longer sees so clearly. There's no pier beneath us. The heavy chariot may swing along the turnpike road, but there's no pier for it to stop at, and how grey and turbulent the sea is in the seventeenth century! Let's to the museum. Cannon-balls; arrow-heads; Roman glass and a forceps green with verdigris. The Rev. Jaspar Floyd dug them up at his own expense[13] early in the forties in the Roman camp on Dods Hill – see the little ticket with the faded writing on it.

And now, what's the next thing to see in Scarborough?

*

Mrs. Flanders sat on the raised circle of the Roman camp, patching Jacob's breeches; only looking up as she sucked the end of her cotton, or when some insect dashed at her, boomed in her ear, and was gone.

John kept trotting up and slapping down in her lap grass or dead leaves which he called 'tea,' and she arranged them methodically but absent-mindedly, laying the flowery heads of the grasses together, thinking how Archer had been awake again last night; the church clock was ten or thirteen minutes fast; she wished she could buy Garfit's acre.

'That's an orchid leaf, Johnny. Look at the little brown spots. Come, my dear. We must go home. Ar–cher! Ja–cob!'

'Ar–cher–Ja–cob!' Johnny piped after her, pivoting round on his heel, and strewing the grass and leaves in his hands as if he were sowing seed. Archer and Jacob jumped up from behind the mound where they had been crouching with the intention of springing upon their mother unexpectedly, and they all began to walk slowly home.

'Who is that?' said Mrs. Flanders, shading her eyes.

'That old man in the road?' said Archer, looking below.

'He's not an old man,' said Mrs. Flanders. 'He's – no, he's not – I thought it was the Captain, but it's Mr. Floyd. Come along, boys.'

'Oh, bother Mr. Floyd!' said Jacob, switching off a thistle's head, for he knew already that Mr. Floyd was going to teach them Latin, as indeed he did for three years in his spare time, out of kindness, for there was no other gentleman in the neighbourhood whom Mrs. Flanders could have asked to do such a thing, and the elder boys were getting beyond her, and must be got ready for school, and it was more than most clergymen would have done, coming round after tea, or having them in his own room – as he could fit it in – for the parish was a very large one, and Mr. Floyd, like his father before him, visited cottages miles away on the moors, and, like old Mr. Floyd, was a great scholar, which made it so unlikely – she had never dreamt of such a thing. Ought she to have guessed? But let alone being a scholar he was eight years younger than she was. She knew his mother – old Mrs. Floyd. She had tea there. And it was that very evening when she came back from having tea with old Mrs. Floyd that she found the note in the hall and took it into the kitchen with her when she went to give Rebecca the fish, thinking it must be something about the boys.

'Mr. Floyd brought it himself, did he? — I think the cheese must be in the parcel in the hall — oh, in the hall—' for she was reading. No, it was not about the boys.

'Yes, enough for fish-cakes to-morrow certainly — Perhaps Captain Barfoot—' she had come to the word 'love.' She went into the garden and read, leaning against the walnut tree to steady herself. Up and down went her breast. Seabrook came so vividly before her. She shook her head and was looking through her tears at the little shifting leaves against the yellow sky when three geese, half-running, half-flying, scuttled across the lawn with Johnny behind them, brandishing a stick.

Mrs. Flanders flushed with anger.

'How many times have I told you?' she cried, and seized him and snatched his stick away from him.

'But they'd escaped!' he cried, struggling to get free.

'You're a very naughty boy. If I've told you once, I've told you a thousand times. I won't *have* you chasing the geese!' she said, and crumpling Mr. Floyd's letter in her hand, she held Johnny fast and herded the geese back into the orchard.

'How could I think of marriage!' she said to herself bitterly, as she fastened the gate with a piece of wire. She had always disliked red hair in men, she thought, thinking of Mr. Floyd's appearance, that night when the boys had gone to bed. And pushing her work-box away, she drew the blotting-paper towards her, and read Mr. Floyd's letter again, and her breast went up and down when she came to the word 'love', but not so fast this time, for she saw Johnny chasing the geese, and knew that it was impossible for her to marry any one — let alone Mr. Floyd, who was so much younger than she was, but what a nice man — and such a scholar too.

'Dear Mr. Floyd,' she wrote — 'Did I forget about the cheese?' she wondered, laying down her pen. No, she had told Rebecca that the cheese was in the hall. 'I am much surprised . . .' she wrote.

But the letter which Mr. Floyd found on the table when he got up early next morning did not begin 'I am much surprised', and it was such a motherly, respectful, inconsequent, regretful letter that he kept it for many years; long after his marriage with Miss Wimbush, of Andover; long after he had left the village. For he asked for a parish in Sheffield, which was given him; and, sending for Archer, Jacob, and John to say good-bye, he told them to choose whatever they liked in his study to remember him by. Archer chose a paper-knife, because he did not like to choose anything too good; Jacob chose the works of Byron in one volume; John, who was still too young to make a proper choice, chose Mr. Floyd's kitten, which his brothers thought an absurd choice, but Mr. Floyd upheld him when he said: 'It has fur like you.' Then Mr. Floyd spoke about the King's Navy (to which Archer was going); and about Rugby[14] (to which Jacob was going); and next day he received a silver salver and went – first to Sheffield, where he met Miss Wimbush, who was on a visit to her uncle, then to Hackney – then to Maresfield House, of which he became the principal, and finally, becoming editor of a well-known series of Ecclesiastical Biographies,[15] he retired to Hampstead with his wife and daughter, and is often to be seen feeding the ducks on Leg of Mutton Pond.[16] As for Mrs. Flanders's letter – when he looked for it the other day he could not find it, and did not like to ask his wife whether she had put it away. Meeting Jacob in Piccadilly lately, he recognized him after three seconds. But Jacob had grown such a fine young man that Mr. Floyd did not like to stop him in the street.

'Dear me,' said Mrs. Flanders, when she read in the *Scarborough and Harrogate Courier*[17] that the Rev. Andrew Floyd, etc., etc., had been made Principal of Maresfield House, 'that must be our Mr. Floyd.'

A slight gloom fell upon the table. Jacob was helping himself to jam; the postman was talking to Rebecca in the kitchen; there was a bee humming at the yellow flower which nodded at the open window. They were all alive, that is to say, while poor Mr. Floyd was becoming Principal of Maresfield House.

Mrs. Flanders got up and went over to the fender and stroked Topaz on the neck behind the ears.

'Poor Topaz,' she said (for Mr. Floyd's kitten was now a very old cat, a little mangy behind the ears, and one of these days would have to be killed).

'Poor old Topaz,' said Mrs. Flanders, as he stretched himself out in the sun, and she smiled, thinking how she had had him gelded, and how she did not like red hair in men. Smiling, she went into the kitchen.

Jacob drew rather a dirty pocket-handkerchief across his face. He went upstairs to his room.

The stag-beetle dies slowly (it was John who collected the beetles). Even on the second day its legs were supple. But the butterflies were dead. A whiff of rotten eggs had vanquished the pale clouded yellows which came pelting across the orchard and up Dods Hill and away on to the moor, now lost behind a furze bush, then off again helter-skelter in a broiling sun. A fritillary basked on a white stone in the Roman camp. From the valley came the sound of church bells. They were all eating roast beef in Scarborough; for it was Sunday when Jacob caught the pale clouded yellows in the clover field, eight miles from home.

Rebecca had caught the death's-head moth in the kitchen.

A strong smell of camphor came from the butterfly boxes.

Mixed with the smell of camphor was the unmistakable smell of seaweed. Tawny ribbons hung on the door. The sun beat straight upon them.

The upper wings of the moth which Jacob held were undoubtedly marked with kidney-shaped spots of a fulvous hue. But there was no crescent upon the underwing. The tree had fallen[18] the night he caught it. There had been a volley of pistol-shots suddenly in the depths of the wood. And his mother had taken him for a burglar when he came home late.[19] The only one of her sons who never obeyed her, she said.

Morris[20] called it 'an extremely local insect found in damp or marshy places.' But Morris is sometimes wrong. Sometimes Jacob, choosing a very fine pen, made a correction in the margin.

The tree had fallen, though it was a windless night, and the lantern, stood upon the ground, had lit up the still green leaves and the dead beech leaves. It was a dry place. A toad was there. And the red underwing had circled round the light and flashed and gone. The red underwing had never come back, though Jacob had waited. It was after twelve when he crossed the lawn and saw his mother in the bright room, playing patience, sitting up.

'How you frightened me!' she had cried. She thought something dreadful had happened. And he woke Rebecca, who had to be up so early.

There he stood pale, come out of the depths of darkness, in the hot room, blinking at the light.

No, it could not be a straw-bordered underwing.

The mowing-machine always wanted oiling. Barnet turned it under Jacob's window, and it creaked – creaked, and rattled across the lawn and creaked again.

Now it was clouding over.

Back came the sun, dazzlingly.

It fell like an eye upon the stirrups, and then suddenly and yet very gently rested upon the bed, upon the alarum clock, and upon the butterfly box stood open. The pale clouded yellows had pelted over the moor; they had zigzagged across the purple clover. The fritillaries flaunted along the hedgerows. The blues settled on little bones lying on the turf with the sun beating on them, and the painted ladies and the peacocks feasted upon bloody entrails dropped by a hawk. Miles away from home, in a hollow among teasles beneath a ruin, he had found the commas. He had seen a white admiral circling higher and higher round an oak tree, but he had never caught it. An old cottage woman living alone, high up, had told him of a purple butterfly which came every summer to her garden. The fox cubs played in the gorse in the early morning, she told him. And if you looked out at dawn you could always see two badgers. Sometimes they knocked each other over like two boys fighting,[21] she said.

'You won't go far this afternoon, Jacob,' said his mother, popping her head in at the door, 'for the Captain's coming to say good-bye.' It was the last day of the Easter holidays.

Wednesday was Captain Barfoot's day. He dressed himself very neatly in blue serge, took his rubber-shod stick – for he was lame and wanted two fingers on the left hand,[22] having served his country – and set out from the house with the flagstaff precisely at four o'clock in the afternoon.

At three Mr. Dickens, the bath-chair man, had called for Mrs. Barfoot.

'Move me,' she would say to Mr. Dickens, after sitting on the esplanade for fifteen minutes. And again,'That'll do, thank you, Mr. Dickens.' At the first command he would seek the sun; at the second he would stay the chair there in the bright strip.

An old inhabitant himself, he had much in common with Mrs. Barfoot – James Coppard's daughter. The drinking-fountain, where West Street joins Broad Street, is the gift of James Coppard, who was mayor at the time of Queen Victoria's jubilee, and Coppard is painted upon municipal watering-carts and over shop windows, and upon the zinc blinds of solicitors' consulting-room windows. But Ellen Barfoot never visited the Aquarium (though she had known Captain Boase who had caught the shark quite well), and when the men came by with the posters she eyed them superciliously, for she knew that she would never see the Pierrots, or the brothers Zeno,[23] or Daisy Budd and her troupe of performing seals. For Ellen Barfoot in her bath-chair on the esplanade was a prisoner – civilization's prisoner – all the bars of her cage falling across the esplanade on sunny days when the town hall, the drapery stores, the swimming-bath, and the memorial hall striped the ground with shadow.

An old inhabitant himself, Mr. Dickens would stand a little behind her, smoking his pipe. She would ask him questions – who people were – who now kept Mr. Jones's shop – then about the season – and had Mrs. Dickens tried, whatever it might be – the words issuing from her lips like crumbs of dry biscuit.

She closed her eyes. Mr. Dickens took a turn. The feelings of a man had not altogether deserted him, though as you saw him coming towards you, you noticed how one knobbed black boot swung tremulously in front of the other; how there was a shadow between his waistcoat and his trousers; how he leant forward unsteadily, like an old horse who finds himself suddenly out of the shafts drawing no cart. But as Mr. Dickens sucked in the smoke and puffed it out again, the feelings of a man were perceptible in his eyes. He was thinking how Captain Barfoot was now on his way to Mount Pleasant; Captain Barfoot, his master. For at home in the little sitting-room above the mews, with the canary in the window, and the girls at the sewing-machine, and Mrs. Dickens huddled up with the rheumatics – at home where he was made little of, the thought of being in the employ of Captain Barfoot supported him.

He liked to think that while he chatted with Mrs. Barfoot on the front, he helped the Captain on his way to Mrs. Flanders. He, a man, was in charge of Mrs. Barfoot, a woman.[24]

Turning, he saw that she was chatting with Mrs. Rogers. Turning again, he saw that Mrs. Rogers had moved on. So he came back to the bath-chair, and Mrs. Barfoot asked him the time, and he took out his great silver watch and told her the time very obligingly, as if he knew a great deal more about the time and everything than she did. But Mrs. Barfoot knew that Captain Barfoot was on his way to Mrs. Flanders.

Indeed he was well on his way there, having left the tram, and seeing Dods Hill to the south-east, green against a blue sky that was suffused with dust colour on the horizon. He was marching up the hill. In spite of his lameness there was something military in his approach. Mrs. Jarvis, as she came out of the Rectory gate, saw him coming, and her Newfoundland dog, Nero, slowly swept his tail from side to side.

'Oh, Captain Barfoot!' Mrs. Jarvis exclaimed.

'Good-day, Mrs. Jarvis,' said the Captain.

They walked on together, and when they reached Mrs. Flanders's gate Captain Barfoot took off his tweed cap, and said, bowing very courteously:

'Good-day to you, Mrs. Jarvis.'

And Mrs. Jarvis walked on alone.

She was going to walk on the moor. Had she again been pacing her lawn late at night? Had she again tapped on the study window and cried: 'Look at the moon, look at the moon, Herbert!'

And Herbert looked at the moon.

Mrs. Jarvis walked on the moor when she was unhappy, going as far as a certain saucer-shaped hollow, though she always meant to go to a more distant ridge; and there she sat down, and took out the little book hidden beneath her cloak and read a few lines of poetry, and looked about her. She was not very unhappy, and, seeing that she was forty-five, never perhaps would be very unhappy, desperately unhappy that is, and leave her husband, and ruin a good man's career, as she sometimes threatened.

Still there is no need to say what risks a clergyman's wife runs when she walks on the moor. Short, dark, with kindling eyes, a pheasant's feather in her hat, Mrs. Jarvis was just the sort of woman to lose her faith upon the moors – to confound her God with the universal that is – but she did not lose her faith, did not leave her husband, never read her poem through, and went on walking the moors, looking at the moon behind the elm trees, and feeling as she sat on the grass high above Scarborough ... Yes, yes, when the lark soars; when the sheep, moving a step or two onwards, crop the turf, and at the same time set their bells tinkling; when the breeze first blows, then dies down, leaving the cheek kissed; when the ships on the sea below seem to cross each other and pass on as if drawn by an invisible hand; when there are distant concussions in the air and phantom horsemen galloping, ceasing; when the horizon swims blue, green, emotional – then Mrs. Jarvis, heaving a sigh, thinks to herself, 'If only some one could give me ... if I could give some one ...' But she does not know what she wants to give, nor who could give it to her.[25]

'Mrs. Flanders stepped out only five minutes ago, Captain,' said Rebecca. Captain Barfoot sat him down in the arm-chair to wait. Resting his elbows on the arms, putting one hand over the other, sticking his lame leg straight out, and placing the stick with the rubber ferrule beside it, he sat perfectly still. There was something rigid about him. Did he think? Probably the same thoughts again and again. But were they 'nice' thoughts, interesting thoughts? He was a man with a temper; tenacious; faithful. Women would have felt, 'Here is law. Here is order. Therefore we must cherish this man. He is on the Bridge at night,' and, handing him his cup, or whatever it might be, would run on to visions of shipwreck and disaster, in which all the passengers come tumbling from their cabins, and there is the captain, buttoned in his pea-jacket, matched with the storm, vanquished by it but by none other. 'Yet I have a soul,' Mrs. Jarvis would bethink her, as Captain Barfoot suddenly blew his nose in a great red bandanna handkerchief, 'and it's the man's stupidity that's the cause of this, and the storm's my storm as well as his' ... so Mrs. Jarvis would bethink her when the Captain dropped in to see them and found Herbert out, and spent two or three hours, almost silent, sitting in the arm-chair. But Betty Flanders thought nothing of the kind.

* *

'Oh, Captain,' said Mrs. Flanders, bursting into the drawing-room, 'I had to run after Barker's man ... I hope Rebecca ... I hope Jacob ...'

She was very much out of breath, yet not at all upset, and as she put down the hearth-brush which she had bought of the oil-man, she said it was hot, flung the window further open, straightened a cover, picked up a book, as if she were very confident, very fond of the Captain, and a great many years younger than he was. Indeed, in her blue apron she did not look more than thirty-five. He was well over fifty.

She moved her hands about the table; the Captain moved his head from side to side, and made little sounds, as Betty went on chattering, completely at his ease – after twenty years.

'Well,' he said at length, 'I've heard from Mr. Polegate.'

He had heard from Mr. Polegate that he could advise nothing better than to send a boy to one of the universities.

'Mr. Floyd was at Cambridge ... no, at Oxford ... well, at one or the other,' said Mrs. Flanders.

She looked out of the window. Little windows, and the lilac and green of the garden were reflected in her eyes.

'Archer is doing very well,' she said. 'I have a very nice report from Captain Maxwell.'

'I will leave you the letter to show Jacob,' said the Captain, putting it clumsily back in its envelope.

'Jacob is after his butterflies as usual,' said Mrs. Flanders irritably, but was surprised by a sudden afterthought, 'Cricket begins this week, of course.'

'Edward Jenkinson has handed in his resignation,' said Captain Barfoot.

'Then you will stand for the Council?' Mrs. Flanders exclaimed, looking the Captain full in the face.

'Well, about that,' Captain Barfoot began, settling himself rather deeper in his chair.

Jacob Flanders, therefore, went up to Cambridge in October, 1906.[26]

III

'This is not a smoking-carriage,' Mrs. Norman protested, nervously but very feebly, as the door swung open and a powerfully built young man jumped in. He seemed not to hear her. The train did not stop before it reached Cambridge, and here she was shut up alone, in a railway carriage, with a young man.[1]

She touched the spring of her dressing-case, and ascertained that the scent-bottle and a novel from Mudie's[2] were both handy (the young man was standing up with his back to her, putting his bag in the rack). She would throw the scent-bottle with her right hand, she decided, and tug the communication cord with her left. She was fifty years of age, and had a son at college. Nevertheless, it is a fact that men are dangerous. She read half a column of her newspaper; then stealthily looked over the edge to decide the question of safety by the infallible test of appearance. . .[3] She would like to offer him her paper. But do young men read the *Morning Post*? She looked to see what he was reading – the *Daily Telegraph*.[4]

Taking note of socks (loose), of tie (shabby), she once more reached his face. She dwelt upon his mouth. The lips were shut. The eyes bent down, since he was reading. All was firm, yet youthful, indifferent, unconscious – as for knocking one down! No, no, no! She looked out of the window, smiling slightly now, and then came back again, for he didn't notice her. Grave, unconscious . . . now he looked up, past her . . . he seemed so out of place, somehow, alone with an elderly lady . . . then he fixed his eyes – which were blue – on the landscape. He had not realized her presence, she thought. Yet it was none of *her* fault that this was not a smoking-carriage – if that was what he meant.

Nobody sees any one as he is, let alone an elderly lady sitting opposite a strange young man in a railway carriage. They see a whole – they see all sorts of things – they see themselves . . . Mrs. Norman now read three pages of one of Mr. Norris's novels.[5] Should she say to the young man (and after all he was just the same age as her own boy): 'If you want to smoke, don't mind me'? No: he seemed absolutely indifferent to her presence ... she did not wish to interrupt.

But since, even at her age, she noted his indifference, presumably he was in some way or other – to her at least – nice, handsome, interesting, distinguished, well built, like her own boy? One must do the best one can with her report. Anyhow, this was Jacob Flanders, aged nineteen. It is no use trying to sum people up. One must follow hints, not exactly what is said, nor yet entirely what is done – for instance, when the train drew into the station, Mr. Flanders burst open the door, and put the lady's dressing-case out for her, saying, or rather mumbling: 'Let me' very shyly; indeed he was rather clumsy about it.

'Who ...' said the lady, meeting her son; but as there was a great crowd on the platform and Jacob had already gone, she did not finish her sentence. As this was Cambridge, as she was staying there for the week-end, as she saw nothing but young men all day long, in streets and round tables, this sight of her fellow-traveller was completely lost in her mind, as the crooked pin dropped by a child into the wishing-well twirls in the water and disappears for ever.

They say the sky is the same everywhere.[6] Travellers, the ship-wrecked, exiles, and the dying draw comfort from the thought, and no doubt if you are of a mystical tendency, consolation, and even explanation, shower down from the unbroken surface. But above Cambridge – anyhow above the roof of King's College Chapel[7] – there is a difference. Out at sea a great city will cast a brightness into the night. Is it fanciful to suppose the sky, washed into the crevices of King's College Chapel, lighter, thinner, more sparkling than the sky elsewhere? Does Cambridge burn not only into the night, but into the day?

Look, as they pass into service, how airily the gowns blow out, as though nothing dense and corporeal were within. What sculpted faces, what certainty, authority controlled by piety, although great boots march under the gowns. In what orderly procession they advance. Thick wax candles stand upright; young men rise in white gowns; while the subservient eagle bears up for inspection the great white book.[8]

An inclined plane of light comes accurately through each window, purple and yellow even in its most diffused dust, while, where it breaks upon stone, that stone is softly chalked red, yellow, and purple. Neither snow nor greenery, winter nor summer, has power over the old stained glass. As the sides of a lantern protect the flame so that it burns steady even in the wildest night – burns steady and gravely illumines the tree-trunks – so inside the Chapel all was orderly. Gravely sounded the voices; wisely the organ replied, as if buttressing human faith with the assent of the elements. The white-robed figures crossed from side to side; now mounted steps, now descended, all very orderly.

. . . If you stand a lantern under a tree every insect in the forest creeps up to it – a curious assembly, since though they scramble and swing and knock their heads against the glass, they seem to have no purpose – something senseless inspires them. One gets tired of watching them, as they amble round the lantern and blindly tap as if for admittance, one large toad being the most besotted[9] of any and shouldering his way through the rest. Ah, but what's that? A terrifying volley of pistol-shots rings out – cracks sharply; ripples spread – silence laps smooth over sound. A tree – a tree has fallen, a sort of death in the forest. After that, the wind in the trees sounds melancholy.

But this service in King's College Chapel – why allow women to take part in it? Surely, if the mind wanders (and Jacob looked extraordinarily vacant, his head thrown back, his hymn-book open at the wrong place), if the mind wanders it is because several hat shops and cupboards upon cupboards of coloured dresses are displayed upon rush-bottomed chairs. Though heads and bodies may be devout enough, one has a sense of individuals – some like blue, others brown; some feathers, others pansies and forget-me-nots. No one would think of bringing a dog into church.[10] For though a dog is all very well on a gravel path, and shows no disrespect to flowers, the way he wanders down an aisle, looking, lifting a paw, and approaching a pillar with a purpose that makes the blood run cold with horror (should you be one of a congregation – alone, shyness is out of the question), a dog destroys the service completely. So do these women – though separately devout, distinguished, and vouched for by the theology, mathematics, Latin, and Greek of their husbands.[11] Heaven knows why it is. For one thing, thought Jacob, they're as ugly as sin.

Now there was a scraping and murmuring. He caught Timmy Durrant's eye; looked very sternly at him; and then, very solemnly, winked.

'Waverley,'[12] the villa on the road to Girton was called, not that Mr. Plumer admired Scott or would have chosen any name at all, but names are useful when you have to entertain undergraduates, and as they sat waiting for the fourth undergraduate, on Sunday at lunchtime, there was talk of names upon gates.

'How tiresome,' Mrs. Plumer interrupted impulsively. 'Does anybody know Mr. Flanders?'

Mr. Durrant knew him; and therefore blushed slightly, and said, awkwardly, something about being sure – looking at Mr. Plumer and hitching the right leg of his trouser as he spoke. Mr. Plumer got up and stood in front of the fireplace. Mrs. Plumer laughed like a straightforward friendly fellow. In short, anything more horrible than the scene, the setting, the prospect, even the May garden being afflicted with chill sterility and a cloud choosing that moment to cross the sun, cannot be imagined. There was the garden, of course. Every one at the same moment looked at it. Owing to the cloud, the leaves ruffled grey, and the sparrows – there were two sparrows.

'I think,' said Mrs. Plumer, taking advantage of the momentary respite, while the young men stared at the garden, to look at her husband, and he, not accepting full responsibility for the act, nevertheless touched the bell.

There can be no excuse for this outrage upon one hour of human life, save the reflection which occurred to Mr. Plumer as he carved the mutton, that if no don ever gave a luncheon party, if Sunday after Sunday passed, if men went down,[13] became lawyers, doctors, members of Parliament, business men – if no don ever gave a luncheon party—

'Now, does lamb make the mint sauce, or mint sauce make the

lamb?' he asked the young man next him, to break a silence which had already lasted five minutes and a half.

'I don't know, sir,' said the young man, blushing very vividly.

At this moment in came Mr. Flanders. He had mistaken the time.

Now, though they had finished their meat, Mrs. Plumer took a second helping of cabbage. Jacob determined, of course, that he would eat his meat in the time it took her to finish her cabbage, looking once or twice to measure his speed – only he was infernally hungry. Seeing this, Mrs. Plumer said that she was sure Mr. Flanders would not mind – and the tart was brought in. Nodding in a peculiar way, she directed the maid to give Mr. Flanders a second helping of mutton. She glanced at the mutton. Not much of the leg would be left for luncheon.

It was none of her fault – since how could she control her father begetting her forty years ago in the suburbs of Manchester?[14] and once begotten, how could she do other than grow up cheese-paring, ambitious, with an instinctively accurate notion of the rungs of the ladder and an ant-like assiduity in pushing George Plumer ahead of her to the top of the ladder? What was at the top of the ladder? A sense that all the rungs were beneath one apparently; since by the time that George Plumer became Professor of Physics, or whatever it might be, Mrs. Plumer could only be in a condition to cling tight to her eminence, peer down at the ground, and goad her two plain daughters to climb the rungs of the ladder.

'I was down at the races yesterday,' she said, 'with my two little girls.'

It was none of *their* fault either. In they came to the drawing-room, in white frocks and blue sashes. They handed the cigarettes. Rhoda had inherited her father's cold grey eyes. Cold grey eyes George Plumer had, but in them was an abstract light. He could talk about Persia and the Trade winds, the Reform Bill[15] and the cycle of the harvests. Books were on his shelves by Wells and Shaw;[16] on the table serious sixpenny weeklies written by pale men[17] in muddy boots – the weekly creak and screech of brains rinsed in cold water and wrung dry – melancholy papers.

'I don't feel that I know the truth about anything till I've read them both!' said Mrs. Plumer brightly, tapping the table of contents with her bare red hand, upon which the ring looked so incongruous.

'Oh God, oh God, oh God!' exclaimed Jacob, as the four undergraduates left the house. 'Oh, my God!'

'Bloody beastly!' he said, scanning the street for lilac or bicycle – anything to restore his sense of freedom.

'Bloody beastly,' he said to Timmy Durrant, summing up his discomfort at the world shown him at lunch-time, a world capable of existing – there was no doubt about that – but so unnecessary, such a thing to believe in – Shaw and Wells and the serious sixpenny weeklies! What were they after, scrubbing and demolishing, these elderly people? Had they never read Homer, Shakespeare, the Elizabethans? He saw it clearly outlined against the feelings he drew from youth and natural inclination. The poor devils had rigged up this meagre object. Yet something of pity was in him. Those wretched little girls—

The extent to which he was disturbed proves that he was already agog. Insolent he was and inexperienced, but sure enough the cities which the elderly of the race have built upon the skyline showed like brick suburbs, barracks, and places of discipline against a red and yellow flame. He was impressionable; but the word is contradicted by the composure with which he hollowed his hand to screen a match. He was a young man of substance.

Anyhow, whether undergraduate or shop boy, man or woman, it must come as a shock about the age of twenty – the world of the elderly – thrown up in such black outline upon what we are; upon the reality; the moors and Byron;[18] the sea and the lighthouse; the sheep's jaw with the yellow teeth in it; upon the obstinate irrepressible conviction which makes youth so intolerably disagreeable – 'I am what I am, and intend to be it,' for which there will be no form in the world unless Jacob makes one for himself. The Plumers will try to prevent him from making it. Wells and Shaw and the serious sixpenny weeklies will sit on its head. Every time he lunches out on Sunday – at dinner parties and tea parties – there will be this same shock – horror – discomfort – then pleasure, for he draws into him at every step as he walks by the river such steady certainty, such reassurance from all sides, the trees bowing, the grey spires soft in the blue, voices blowing and seeming suspended in the air, the springy air of May, the elastic air with its particles – chestnut bloom, pollen, whatever it is that gives the May air its potency, blurring the trees, gumming the buds, daubing the green. And the river too runs past, not at flood, nor swiftly, but cloying the oar that dips in it and drops white drops from the blade, swimming green and deep over the bowed rushes, as if lavishly caressing them.

Where they moored their boat the trees showered down, so that their topmost leaves trailed in the ripples and the green wedge that lay in the water being made of leaves shifted in leaf-breadths as the real leaves shifted. Now there was a shiver of wind – instantly an edge of sky; and as Durrant ate cherries he dropped the stunted yellow cherries through the green wedge of leaves, their stalks twinkling as they wriggled in and out, and sometimes one half-bitten cherry would go down red into the green. The meadow was on a level with Jacob's eyes as he lay back; gilt with buttercups, but the grass did not run like the thin green water of the graveyard grass about to overflow the tombstones, but stood juicy and thick. Looking up, backwards, he saw the legs of children deep in the grass, and the legs of cows. Munch, munch, he heard; then a short step through the grass; then again munch, munch, munch, as they tore the grass short at the roots. In front of him two white butterflies circled higher and higher round the elm tree.

'Jacob's off,' thought Durrant, looking up from his novel. He kept reading a few pages and then looking up in a curiously methodical manner, and each time he looked up he took a few cherries out of the bag and ate them abstractedly. Other boats passed them, crossing the backwater from side to side to avoid each other, for many were now moored, and there were now white dresses and a flaw in the column of air between two trees, round which curled a thread of blue – Lady Miller's picnic party. Still more boats kept coming, and Durrant, without getting up, shoved their boat closer to the bank.

'Oh-h-h-h,' groaned Jacob, as the boat rocked, and the trees rocked, and the white dresses and the white flannel trousers drew out long and wavering up the bank.

'Oh-h-h-h!' He sat up, and felt as if a piece of elastic had snapped in his face.

*

'They're friends of my mother's,' said Durrant. 'So old Bow took no end of trouble about the boat.'

And this boat had gone from Falmouth to St. Ives Bay, all round the coast. A larger boat, a ten-ton yacht, about the twentieth of June, properly fitted out, Durrant said . . .

'There's the cash difficulty,' said Jacob.

'My people'll see to that,' said Durrant (the son of a banker, deceased).

'I intend to preserve my economic independence,' said Jacob stiffly. (He was getting excited.)

'My mother said something about going to Harrogate,' he said with a little annoyance, feeling the pocket where he kept his letters.

'Was that true about your uncle becoming a Mohammedan?' asked Timmy Durrant.

Jacob had told the story of his Uncle Morty in Durrant's room the night before.

'I expect he's feeding the sharks, if the truth were known,' said Jacob. 'I say, Durrant, there's none left!' he exclaimed, crumpling the bag which had held the cherries, and throwing it into the river. He saw Lady Miller's picnic party on the island as he threw the bag into the river.

A sort of awkwardness, grumpiness, gloom came into his eyes.

'Shall we move on . . . this beastly crowd . . .' he said.

So up they went, past the island.

The feathery white moon never let the sky grow dark; all night the chestnut blossoms were white in the green; dim was the cow-parsley in the meadows.

The waiters at Trinity[19] must have been shuffling china plates like cards, from the clatter that could be heard in the Great Court. Jacob's rooms, however, were in Neville's Court;[20] at the top; so that reaching his door one went in a little out of breath; but he wasn't there. Dining in Hall, presumably. It will be quite dark in Neville's Court long before midnight, only the pillars opposite will always be white, and the pavement. A curious effect the gate has, like lace upon pale green. Even in the window you hear the plates; a hum of talk, too, from the diners; the Hall lit up, and the swing-doors opening and shutting with a soft thud. Some are late.

Jacob's room had a round table and two low chairs. There were yellow flags in a jar on the mantelpiece; a photograph of his mother; cards from societies with little raised crescents, coats of arms, and initials; notes and pipes; on the table lay paper ruled with a red margin – an essay, no doubt – 'Does History consist of the Biographies of Great Men?'[21] There were books enough; very few French books; but then any one who's worth anything reads just what he likes,[22] as the mood takes him, with extravagant enthusiasm. Lives of the Duke of Wellington, for example; Spinoza; the works of Dickens; the *Faëry Queen*; a Greek dictionary with the petals of poppies pressed to silk between the pages; all the Elizabethans.[23] His slippers were incredibly shabby, like boats burnt to the water's rim. Then there were photographs from the Greeks, and a mezzotint from Sir Joshua[24] – all very English. The works of Jane Austen, too, in deference, perhaps, to some one else's standard.[25] Carlyle was a prize.[26] There were books upon the Italian painters of the Renaissance,[27] a *Manual of the Diseases of the Horse*,[28] and all the usual text-books. Listless is the air in an empty room, just swelling the curtain; the flowers in the jar shift. One fibre in the wicker arm-chair creaks, though no one sits there.

Coming down the steps a little sideways (Jacob sat on the window-seat talking to Durrant; he smoked, and Durrant looked at the map), the old man, with his hands locked behind him, his gown floating black, lurched, unsteadily, near the wall; then, upstairs he went into his room. Then another, who raised his hand and praised the columns, the gate, the sky; another, tripping and smug. Each went up a staircase; three lights were lit in the dark windows.

If any light burns above Cambridge, it must be from three such rooms; Greek burns here; science there; philosophy on the ground floor. Poor old Huxtable can't walk straight; – Sopwith, too, has praised the sky any night these twenty years; and Cowan[29] still chuckles at the same stories. It is not simple, or pure, or wholly splendid, the lamp of learning, since if you see them there under its light (whether Rossetti's on the wall, or Van Gogh reproduced,[30] whether there are lilacs in the bowl or rusty pipes), how priestly they look! How like a suburb where you go to see a view and eat a special cake! 'We are the sole purveyors of this cake.' Back you go to London; for the treat is over.

Old Professor Huxtable, performing with the method of a clock his change of dress, let himself down into his chair; filled his pipe; chose his paper; crossed his feet; and extracted his glasses. The whole flesh of his face then fell into folds as if props were removed. Yet strip a whole seat of an underground railway carriage of its heads and old Huxtable's head will hold them all. Now, as his eye goes down the print, what a procession tramps through the corridors of his brain, orderly, quick-stepping, and reinforced, as the march goes on, by fresh runnels, till the whole hall, dome, whatever one calls it, is populous with ideas. Such a muster takes place in no other brain. Yet sometimes there he'll sit for hours together, gripping the arm of the chair, like a man holding fast because stranded, and then, just because his corn twinges, or it may be the gout, what execrations, and, dear me, to hear him talk of money, taking out his leather purse and grudging even the smallest silver coin, secretive and suspicious as an old peasant woman with all her lies. Strange paralysis and constriction – marvellous illumination. Serene over it all rides the great full brow, and sometimes asleep or in the quiet spaces of the night you might fancy that on a pillow of stone he lay triumphant.

Sopwith, meanwhile, advancing with a curious trip from the fireplace, cut the chocolate cake into segments. Until midnight or later there would be undergraduates in his room, sometimes as many as twelve, sometimes three or four; but nobody got up when they went or when they came; Sopwith went on talking. Talking, talking, talking – as if everything could be talked – the soul itself slipped through the lips in thin silver disks which dissolve in young men's minds like silver, like moonlight. Oh, far away they'd remember it, and deep in dullness gaze back on it, and come to refresh themselves again.

'Well, I never. That's old Chucky. My dear boy, how's the world treating you?' And in came poor little Chucky, the unsuccessful provincial,[31] Stenhouse his real name, but of course Sopwith brought back by using the other everything, everything, 'all I could never be' – yes, though next day, buying his newspaper and catching the early train, it all seemed to him childish, absurd; the chocolate cake, the young men; Sopwith summing things up; no, not all; he would send his son there. He would save every penny to send his son there. Sopwith went on talking; twining stiff fibres of awkward speech – things young men blurted out – plaiting them round his own smooth garland, making the bright side show, the vivid greens, the sharp thorns, manliness. He loved it. Indeed to Sopwith a man could say anything, until perhaps he'd grown old, or gone under, gone deep, when the silver disks would tinkle hollow, and the inscription read a little too simple, and the old stamp look too pure, and the impress always the same – a Greek boy's head. But he would respect still. A woman, divining the priest, would, involuntarily, despise.

Cowan, Erasmus Cowan, sipped his port alone, or with one rosy little man, whose memory held precisely the same span of time; sipped his port, and told his stories, and without book before him intoned Latin, Virgil, and Catullus, as if language were wine upon his lips. Only – sometimes it will come over one – what if the poet strode in? '*This* my image?'[32] he might ask, pointing to the chubby man, whose brain is, after all, Virgil's representative among us, though the body gluttonize, and as for arms, bees, or even the plough,[33] Cowan takes his trips abroad with a French novel in his pocket, a rug about his knees, and is thankful to be home again in his place, in his line, holding up in his snug little mirror the image of Virgil, all rayed round with good stories of the dons of Trinity and red beams of port. But language is wine upon his lips. Nowhere else would Virgil hear the like. And though, as she goes sauntering along the Backs, old Miss Umphelby sings him melodiously enough, accurately too, she is always brought up by this question as she reaches Clare Bridge: 'But if I met him, what should I wear?' – and then, taking her way up the avenue towards Newnham, she lets her fancy play upon other details of men's meeting with women which have never got into print. Her lectures, therefore, are not half so well attended as those of Cowan, and the thing she might have said in elucidation of the text for ever left out.[34] In short, face a teacher with the image of the taught and the mirror breaks. But Cowan sipped his port, his exaltation over, no longer the representative of Virgil. No, the builder, assessor, surveyor, rather; ruling lines between names, hanging lists above doors. Such is the fabric through which the light must shine, if shine it can – the light of all these languages, Chinese and Russian, Persian and Arabic, of symbols and figures, of history, of things that are known and things that are about to be known.[35] So that if at night, far out at sea over the tumbling waves, one saw a haze on the waters, a city illuminated, a whiteness even in the sky, such as that now over the Hall of Trinity where they're still dining, or washing up plates, that would be the light burning there – the light of Cambridge.

'Let's go round to Simeon's room,' said Jacob, and they rolled up the map, having got the whole thing settled.

All the lights were coming out round the court, and falling on the cobbles, picking out dark patches of grass and single daisies. The young men were now back in their rooms. Heaven knows what they were doing. What was it that could *drop* like that? And leaning down over a foaming window-box, one stopped another hurrying past, and upstairs they went and down they went, until a sort of fulness settled on the court, the hive full of bees, the bees home thick with gold, drowsy, humming, suddenly vocal; the Moonlight Sonata[36] answered by a waltz.

The Moonlight Sonata tinkled away; the waltz crashed. Although young men still went in and out, they walked as if keeping engagements. Now and then there was a thud, as if some heavy piece of furniture had fallen, unexpectedly, of its own accord, not in the general stir of life after dinner. One supposed that young men raised their eyes from their books as the furniture fell. Were they reading? Certainly there was a sense of concentration in the air. Behind the grey walls sat so many young men, some undoubtedly reading, magazines, shilling shockers,[37] no doubt; legs, perhaps, over the arms of chairs; smoking; sprawling over tables, and writing while their heads went round in a circle as the pen moved – simple young men, these, who would – but there is no need to think of them grown old; others eating sweets; here they boxed; and, well, Mr. Hawkins must have been mad suddenly to throw up his window and bawl: 'Jo–seph! Jo–seph!' and then he ran as hard as ever he could across the court, while an elderly man, in a green apron, carrying an immense pile of tin covers, hesitated, balanced, and then went on. But this was a diversion. There were young men who read, lying in shallow arm-chairs, holding their books as if they had hold in their hands of something that would see them through; they being all in a torment, coming from midland towns, clergymen's sons. Others read Keats. And those long histories in many volumes – surely some one was now beginning at the beginning in order to understand the Holy Roman Empire, as one must. That was part of the concentration, though it would be dangerous on a hot spring night – dangerous, perhaps, to concentrate too much upon single books, actual chapters, when at any moment the door opened and Jacob appeared; or Richard Bonamy, reading Keats no longer, began making long pink spills from an old newspaper,[38] bending forward, and looking eager and contented no more, but almost fierce. Why? Only perhaps that Keats died young – one wants to write poetry too and to love – oh, the brutes! It's damnably difficult. But, after all, not so difficult if on the next staircase, in the large room, there are two, three, five young men all convinced of this – of brutality, that is, and the clear division between right and wrong. There was a sofa, chairs, a square table, and the window being open, one could see how they sat – legs issuing here, one there crumpled in a corner of the sofa; and, presumably, for you could not see him, somebody stood by the fender, talking. Anyhow, Jacob, who sat astride a chair and ate dates from a long box,[39] burst out laughing. The answer came from the sofa corner; for his pipe was held in the air, then replaced. Jacob wheeled round. He had something to say to *that*, though the sturdy red-haired boy at the table seemed to deny it, wagging his head slowly from side to side; and then, taking out his penknife, he dug the point of it again and again into a knot in the table, as if affirming that the voice from the fender spoke the truth – which Jacob could not deny. Possibly, when he had done arranging the date-stones, he might find something to say to it – indeed his lips opened – only then there broke out a roar of laughter.

The laughter died in the air. The sound of it could scarcely have reached any one standing by the Chapel, which stretched along the opposite side of the court. The laughter died out, and only gestures of arms, movements of bodies, could be seen shaping something in the room. Was it an argument? A bet on the boat races? Was it nothing of the sort? What was shaped by the arms and bodies moving in the twilight room?

A step or two beyond the window there was nothing at all, except the enclosing buildings – chimneys upright, roofs horizontal; too much brick and building for a May night, perhaps. And then before one's eyes would come the bare hills of Turkey – sharp lines, dry earth, coloured flowers, and colour on the shoulders of the women, standing naked-legged in the stream to beat linen on the stones. The stream made loops of water round their ankles. But none of that could show clearly through the swaddlings and blanketings of the Cambridge night. The stroke of the clock even was muffled; as if intoned by somebody reverent from a pulpit; as if generations of learned men heard the last hour go rolling through their ranks and issued it, already smooth and time-worn, with their blessing, for the use of the living.

Was it to receive this gift from the past that the young man came to the window and stood there, looking out across the court? It was Jacob. He stood smoking his pipe while the last stroke of the clock purred softly round him. Perhaps there had been an argument. He looked satisfied; indeed masterly; which expression changed slightly as he stood there, the sound of the clock conveying to him (it may be) a sense of old buildings and time; and himself the inheritor; and then to-morrow; and friends; at the thought of whom, in sheer confidence and pleasure, it seemed, he yawned and stretched himself.

Meanwhile behind him the shape they had made, whether by argument or not, the spiritual shape, hard yet ephemeral, as of glass compared with the dark stone of the Chapel, was dashed to splinters, young men rising from chairs and sofa corners, buzzing and barging about the room, one driving another against the bedroom door, which giving way, in they fell. Then Jacob was left there, in the shallow arm-chair, alone with Masham? Anderson? Simeon? Oh, it was Simeon. The others had all gone.

'. . . Julian the Apostate . . .'[40] Which of them said that and the other words murmured round it? But about midnight there sometimes rises, like a veiled figure suddenly woken, a heavy wind; and this now flapping through Trinity lifted unseen leaves and blurred everything. 'Julian the Apostate' – and then the wind. Up go the elm branches, out blow the sails, the old schooners rear and plunge, the grey waves in the hot Indian Ocean tumble sultrily, and then all falls flat again.

So, if the veiled lady stepped through the Courts of Trinity, she now drowsed once more, all her draperies about her, her head against a pillar.

'Somehow it seems to matter.'

The low voice was Simeon's.

The voice was even lower that answered him. The sharp tap of a pipe on the mantelpiece cancelled the words. And perhaps Jacob only said 'hum,' or said nothing at all. True, the words were inaudible. It was the intimacy, a sort of spiritual suppleness, when mind prints upon mind indelibly.

'Well, you seem to have studied the subject,' said Jacob, rising and standing over Simeon's chair. He balanced himself; he swayed a little. He appeared extraordinarily happy, as if his pleasure would brim and spill down the sides if Simeon spoke.

Simeon said nothing. Jacob remained standing. But intimacy – the room was full of it, still, deep, like a pool. Without need of movement or speech it rose softly and washed over everything, mollifying, kindling, and coating the mind with the lustre of pearl, so that if you talk of a light, of Cambridge burning, it's not languages only. It's Julian the Apostate.

But Jacob moved. He murmured good-night. He went out into the court. He buttoned his jacket across his chest. He went back to his rooms, and being the only man who walked at that moment back to his rooms, his footsteps rang out, his figure loomed large. Back from the Chapel, back from the Hall, back from the Library, came the sound of his footsteps, as if the old stone echoed with magisterial authority: 'The young man – the young man – the young man – back to his rooms.'[41]

IV

What's the use of trying to read Shakespeare, especially in one of those little thin paper editions whose pages get ruffled, or stuck together with sea-water? Although the plays of Shakespeare had frequently been praised, even quoted, and placed higher than the Greek,[1] never since they started had Jacob managed to read one through. Yet what an opportunity!

For the Scilly Isles had been sighted by Timmy Durrant lying like mountain-tops almost a-wash in precisely the right place. His calculations had worked perfectly, and really the sight of him sitting there, with his hand on the tiller, rosy gilled, with a sprout of beard, looking sternly at the stars, then at a compass, spelling out quite correctly his page of the eternal lesson-book, would have moved a woman. Jacob, of course, was not a woman. The sight of Timmy Durrant was no sight for him, nothing to set against the sky and worship; far from it. They had quarrelled. Why the right way to open a tin of beef, with Shakespeare on board, under conditions of such splendour, should have turned them to sulky schoolboys, none can tell. Tinned beef is cold eating, though; and salt water spoils biscuits; and the waves tumble and lollop much the same hour after hour – tumble and lollop all across the horizon. Now a spray of seaweed floats past – now a log of wood. Ships have been wrecked here. One or two go past, keeping their own side of the road. Timmy knew where they were bound, what their cargoes were, and, by looking through his glass, could tell the name of the line, and even guess what dividends it paid its shareholders. Yet that was no reason for Jacob to turn sulky.

The Scilly Isles had the look of mountain-tops almost a-wash . . . Unfortunately, Jacob broke the pin of the Primus stove.

The Scilly Isles might well be obliterated by a roller sweeping straight across.

But one must give young men the credit of admitting that, though breakfast eaten under these circumstances is grim, it is sincere enough. No need to make conversation. They got out their pipes.

Timmy wrote up some scientific observations; and – what was the question that broke the silence – the exact time or the day of the month? Anyhow it was spoken without the least awkwardness; in the most matter-of-fact way in the world; and then Jacob began to unbutton his clothes and sat naked, save for his shirt, intending, apparently, to bathe.

The Scilly Isles were turning bluish; and suddenly blue, purple, and green flushed the sea; left it grey; struck a stripe which vanished; but when Jacob had got his shirt over his head the whole floor of the waves was blue and white, rippling and crisp, though now and again a broad purple mark appeared, like a bruise; or there floated an entire emerald tinged with yellow. He plunged. He gulped in water, spat it out, struck with his right arm, struck with his left, was towed by a rope, gasped, splashed, and was hauled on board.

The seat in the boat was positively hot, and the sun warmed his back as he sat naked with a towel in his hand, looking at the Scilly Isles which – confound it! the sail flapped. Shakespeare was knocked overboard. There you could see him floating merrily away, with all his pages ruffling innumerably; and then he went under.

Strangely enough, you could smell violets, or if violets were impossible in July, they must grow something very pungent on the mainland then. The mainland, not so very far off – you could see clefts in the cliffs, white cottages, smoke going up – wore an extraordinary look of calm, of sunny peace, as if wisdom and piety had descended upon the dwellers there. Now a cry sounded, as of a man calling pilchards in a main street. It wore an extraordinary look of piety and peace, as if old men smoked by the door, and girls stood, hands on hips, at the well, and horses stood; as if the end of the world had come, and cabbage fields and stone walls, and coast-guard stations, and, above all, the white sand bays with the waves breaking unseen by any one, rose to heaven in a kind of ecstasy.

But imperceptibly the cottage smoke droops, has the look of a mourning emblem, a flag floating its caress over a grave. The gulls, making their broad flight and then riding at peace, seem to mark the grave.

No doubt if this were Italy, Greece, or even the shores of Spain, sadness would be routed by strangeness and excitement and the nudge of a classical education. But the Cornish hills have stark chimneys standing on them; and, somehow or other, loveliness is infernally sad. Yes, the chimneys and the coast-guard stations and the little bays with the waves breaking unseen by any one make one remember the overpowering sorrow. And what can this sorrow be?

It is brewed by the earth itself. It comes from the houses on the coast. We start transparent, and then the cloud thickens. All history backs our pane of glass. To escape is vain.

But whether this is the right interpretation of Jacob's gloom as he sat naked, in the sun, looking at the Land's End, it is impossible to say; for he never spoke a word. Timmy sometimes wondered (only for a second) whether his people bothered him . . . No matter. There are things that can't be said. Let's shake it off. Let's dry ourselves, and take up the first thing that comes handy . . . Timmy Durrant's notebook of scientific observations.

'Now . . .' said Jacob.

It is a tremendous argument.

Some people can follow every step of the way, and even take a little one, six inches long, by themselves at the end;[2] others remain observant of the external signs.

The eyes fix themselves upon the poker; the right hand takes the poker and lifts it; turns it slowly round, and then, very accurately, replaces it. The left hand, which lies on the knee, plays some stately but intermittent piece of march music. A deep breath is taken; but allowed to evaporate unused. The cat marches across the hearth-rug. No one observes her.

'That's about as near as I can get to it,' Durrant wound up.

The next minute is as quiet as the grave.

'It follows . . .' said Jacob.

Only half a sentence followed; but these half-sentences are like flags set on tops of buildings to the observer of external sights down below. What was the coast of Cornwall, with its violet scents, and mourning emblems, and tranquil piety, but a screen happening to hang straight behind as his mind marched up?

'It follows . . .' said Jacob.

'Yes,' said Timmy, after reflection. 'That is so.'

Now Jacob began plunging about, half to stretch himself, half in a kind of jollity, no doubt, for the strangest sound issued from his lips as he furled the sail, rubbed the plates – gruff, tuneless – a sort of paean, for having grasped the argument, for being master of the situation, sunburnt, unshaven, capable into the bargain of sailing round the world in a ten-ton yacht, which, very likely, he would do one of these days instead of settling down in a lawyer's office, and wearing spats.[3]

'Our friend Masham,' said Timmy Durrant, 'would rather not be seen in our company as we are now.' His buttons had come off.

'D'you know Masham's aunt?' said Jacob.

'Never knew he had one,' said Timmy.

'Masham has millions of aunts,' said Jacob.

'Masham is mentioned in Domesday Book,' said Timmy.

'So are his aunts,' said Jacob.

'His sister,' said Timmy, 'is a very pretty girl.'

'That's what'll happen to you, Timmy,' said Jacob.

'It'll happen to you first,' said Timmy.

'But this woman I was telling you about – Masham's aunt—'

'Oh, do get on,' said Timmy, for Jacob was laughing so much that he could not speak.

'Masham's aunt . . .'

Timmy laughed so much that he could not speak.

'Masham's aunt . . .'

'What is there about Masham that makes one laugh?' said Timmy.

'Hang it all – a man who swallows his tie-pin,' said Jacob.

'Lord Chancellor before he's fifty,' said Timmy.

'He's a gentleman,' said Jacob.

'The Duke of Wellington was a gentleman,' said Timmy.

'Keats wasn't.'

'Lord Salisbury was.'[4]

'And what about God?' said Jacob.

The Scilly Isles now appeared as if directly pointed at by a golden finger issuing from a cloud; and everybody knows how portentous that sight is, and how these broad rays, whether they light upon the Scilly Isles or upon the tombs of crusaders in cathedrals, always shake the very foundations of scepticism and lead to jokes about God.

> 'Abide with me:
> Fast falls the eventide;
> The shadows deepen;
> Lord, with me abide,'[5]

sang Timmy Durrant.

'At my place we used to have a hymn which began

> Great God, what do I see and hear?'[6]

said Jacob.

Gulls rode gently swaying in little companies of two or three quite near the boat; the cormorant, as if following his long strained neck in eternal pursuit, skimmed an inch above the water to the next rock; and the drone of the tide in the caves came across the water, low, monotonous, like the voice of some one talking to himself.

> 'Rock of Ages, cleft for me,
> Let me hide myself in thee,'[7]

sang Jacob.

Like the blunt tooth of some monster, a rock broke the surface; brown; overflown with perpetual waterfalls.

> 'Rock of Ages,'

Jacob sang, lying on his back, looking up into the sky at mid-day, from which every shred of cloud had been withdrawn, so that it was like something permanently displayed with the cover off.

By six o'clock a breeze blew in off an icefield; and by seven the water was more purple than blue; and by half-past seven there was a patch of rough gold-beater's skin round the Scilly Isles, and Durrant's face, as he sat steering, was of the colour of a red lacquer box polished for generations. By nine all the fire and confusion had gone out of the sky, leaving wedges of apple-green and plates of pale yellow; and by ten the lanterns on the boat were making twisted colours upon the waves, elongated or squat,[8] as the waves stretched or humped themselves. The beam from the lighthouse strode rapidly across the water. Infinite millions of miles away powdered stars twinkled; but the waves slapped the boat, and crashed, with regular and appalling solemnity, against the rocks.

Although it would be possible to knock at the cottage door and ask for a glass of milk, it is only thirst that would compel the intrusion. Yet perhaps Mrs. Pascoe[9] would welcome it. The summer's day may be wearing heavy. Washing in her little scullery, she may hear the cheap clock on the mantelpiece tick, tick, tick . . . tick, tick, tick. She is alone in the house. Her husband is out helping Farmer Hosken; her daughter married and gone to America. Her elder son is married too, but she does not agree with his wife. The Wesleyan minister came along and took the younger boy. She is alone in the house. A steamer, probably bound for Cardiff, now crosses the horizon, while near at hand one bell of a foxglove swings to and fro with a bumble-bee for clapper.

These white Cornish cottages[10] are built on the edge of the cliff; the garden grows gorse more readily than cabbages; and for hedge, some primeval man has piled granite boulders. In one of these, to hold, an historian conjectures, the victim's blood, a basin has been hollowed, but in our time it serves more tamely to seat those tourists who wish for an uninterrupted view of the Gurnard's Head.[11] Not that any one objects to a blue print dress and a white apron in a cottage garden.

'Look – she has to draw her water from a well in the garden.'

'Very lonely it must be in winter, with the wind sweeping over those hills, and the waves dashing on the rocks.'

Even on a summer's day you hear them murmuring.

Having drawn her water, Mrs. Pascoe went in. The tourists regretted that they had brought no glasses, so that they might have read the name of the tramp steamer.[12] Indeed, it was such a fine day that there was no saying what a pair of field-glasses might not have fetched into view. Two fishing luggers, presumably from St. Ives Bay, were now sailing in an opposite direction from the steamer, and the floor of the sea became alternately clear and opaque. As for the bee, having sucked its fill of honey, it visited the teasle and thence made a straight line to Mrs. Pascoe's patch, once more directing the tourists' gaze to the old woman's print dress and white apron, for she had come to the door of the cottage and was standing there.

There she stood, shading her eyes and looking out to sea.

For the millionth time, perhaps, she looked at the sea. A peacock butterfly now spread himself upon the teasle, fresh and newly emerged, as the blue and chocolate down on his wings testified. Mrs. Pascoe went indoors, fetched a cream pan, came out, and stood scouring it. Her face was assuredly not soft, sensual, or lecherous, but hard, wise, wholesome rather, signifying in a room full of sophisticated people the flesh and blood of life. She would tell a lie, though, as soon as the truth. Behind her on the wall hung a large dried skate. Shut up in the parlour she prized mats, china mugs, and photographs,[13] though the mouldy little room was saved from the salt breeze only by the depth of a brick, and between lace curtains you saw the gannet drop like a stone, and on stormy days the gulls came shuddering through the air, and the steamers' lights were now high, now deep. Melancholy were the sounds on a winter's night.

The picture papers were delivered punctually on Sunday, and she pored long over Lady Cynthia's wedding at the Abbey.[14] She, too, would have liked to ride in a carriage with springs. The soft, swift syllables of educated speech often shamed her few rude ones. And then all night to hear the grinding of the Atlantic upon the rocks instead of hansom cabs and footmen whistling for motor-cars ... So she may have dreamed, scouring her cream pan. But the talkative, nimble-witted people have taken themselves to towns. Like a miser, she has hoarded her feelings within her own breast. Not a penny piece has she changed all these years, and, watching her enviously, it seems as if all within must be pure gold.

The wise old woman, having fixed her eyes upon the sea, once more withdrew. The tourists decided that it was time to move on to the Gurnard's Head.

Three seconds later Mrs. Durrant rapped upon the door.

'Mrs. Pascoe?' she said.

Rather haughtily, she watched the tourists cross the field path. She came of a Highland race, famous for its chieftains.

Mrs. Pascoe appeared.

'I envy you that bush, Mrs. Pascoe,' said Mrs. Durrant, pointing the parasol with which she had rapped on the door at the fine clump of St. John's wort that grew beside it. Mrs. Pascoe looked at the bush deprecatingly.

'I expect my son in a day or two,' said Mrs. Durrant. 'Sailing from Falmouth with a friend in a little boat . . . Any news of Lizzie yet, Mrs. Pascoe?'

Her long-tailed ponies stood twitching their ears on the road twenty yards away. The boy, Curnow, flicked flies off them occasionally. He saw his mistress go into the cottage; come out again; and pass, talking energetically to judge by the movements of her hands, round the vegetable plot in front of the cottage. Mrs. Pascoe was his aunt. Both women surveyed a bush. Mrs. Durrant stooped and picked a sprig from it. Next she pointed (her movements were peremptory; she held herself very upright) at the potatoes. They had the blight. All potatoes that year had the blight. Mrs. Durrant showed Mrs. Pascoe how bad the blight was on her potatoes. Mrs. Durrant talked energetically; Mrs. Pascoe listened submissively. The boy Curnow knew that Mrs. Durrant was saying that it is perfectly simple; you mix the powder in a gallon of water; 'I have done it with my own hands in my own garden,' Mrs. Durrant was saying.

'You won't have a potato left – you won't have a potato left,' Mrs. Durrant was saying in her emphatic voice as they reached the gate. The boy Curnow became as immobile as stone.

Mrs. Durrant took the reins in her hands and settled herself on the driver's seat.

'Take care of that leg, or I shall send the doctor to you,' she called back over her shoulder; touched the ponies; and the carriage started forward. The boy Curnow had only just time to swing himself up by the toe of his boot. The boy Curnow, sitting in the middle of the back seat, looked at his aunt.

Mrs. Pascoe stood at the gate looking after them; stood at the gate till the trap was round the corner; stood at the gate, looking now to the right, now to the left; then went back to her cottage.

Soon the ponies attacked the swelling moor road with striving forelegs. Mrs. Durrant let the reins fall slackly, and leant backwards. Her vivacity had left her. Her hawk nose was thin as a bleached bone through which you almost see the light. Her hands, lying on the reins in her lap, were firm even in repose. The upper lip was cut so short that it raised itself almost in a sneer from the front teeth. Her mind skimmed leagues where Mrs. Pascoe's mind adhered to its solitary patch. Her mind skimmed leagues as the ponies climbed the hill road. Forwards and backwards she cast her mind, as if the roofless cottages, mounds of slag, and cottage gardens overgrown with foxglove and bramble cast shade upon her mind. Arrived at the summit, she stopped the carriage. The pale hills were round her, each scattered with ancient stones; beneath was the sea, variable as a southern sea; she herself sat there looking from hill to sea, upright, aquiline, equally poised between gloom and laughter. Suddenly she flicked the ponies so that the boy Curnow had to swing himself up by the toe of his boot.

The rooks settled; the rooks rose. The trees which they touched so capriciously seemed insufficient to lodge their numbers. The tree-tops sang with the breeze in them; the branches creaked audibly and dropped now and then, though the season was midsummer, husks or twigs. Up went the rooks and down again, rising in lesser numbers each time as the sager birds made ready to settle, for the evening was already spent enough to make the air inside the wood almost dark. The moss was soft; the tree-trunks spectral. Beyond them lay a silvery meadow. The pampas grass raised its feathery spears from mounds of green at the end of the meadow. A breadth of water gleamed. Already the convolvulus moth was spinning over the flowers. Orange and purple, nasturtium and cherry pie, were washed into the twilight, but the tobacco plant and the passion flower, over which the great moth spun, were white as china. The rooks creaked their wings together on the tree-tops, and were settling down for sleep when, far off, a familiar sound shook and trembled – increased – fairly dinned in their ears – scared sleepy wings into the air again – the dinner bell at the house.

After six days of salt wind, rain, and sun, Jacob Flanders had put on a dinner jacket. The discreet black object had made its appearance now and then in the boat among tins, pickles, preserved meats, and as the voyage went on had become more and more irrelevant, hardly to be believed in. And now, the world being stable, lit by candle-light, the dinner jacket alone preserved him. He could not be sufficiently thankful. Even so his neck, wrists, and face were exposed without cover, and his whole person, whether exposed or not, tingled and glowed so as to make even black cloth an imperfect screen. He drew back the great red hand that lay on the table-cloth. Surreptitiously it closed upon slim glasses and curved silver forks. The bones of the cutlets were decorated with pink frills – and yesterday he had gnawn ham from the bone! Opposite him were hazy, semi-transparent shapes of yellow and blue.[15] Behind them, again, was the grey-green garden, and among the pear-shaped leaves of the escallonia fishing-boats seemed caught and suspended. A sailing ship slowly drew past the women's backs. Two or three figures crossed the terrace hastily in the dusk. The door opened and shut. Nothing settled or stayed unbroken. Like oars rowing now this side, now that, were the sentences that came now here, now there, from either side of the table.

'Oh, Clara, Clara!' exclaimed Mrs. Durrant, and Timothy Durrant adding, 'Clara, Clara,' Jacob named the shape in yellow gauze Timothy's sister, Clara. The girl sat smiling and flushed. With her brother's dark eyes, she was vaguer and softer than he was. When the laugh died down she said: 'But, mother, it was true. He said so, didn't he? Miss Eliot agreed with us . . .'

But Miss Eliot, tall, grey-headed, was making room beside her for the old man who had come in from the terrace. The dinner would never end, Jacob thought, and he did not wish it to end, though the ship had sailed from one corner of the window-frame to the other, and a light marked the end of the pier. He saw Mrs. Durrant gaze at the light. She turned to him.

'Did you take command, or Timothy?' she said. 'Forgive me if I call you Jacob. I've heard so much of you.' Then her eyes went back to the sea. Her eyes glazed as she looked at the view.

'A little village once,' she said, 'and now grown . . .' She rose, taking her napkin with her, and stood by the window.

'Did you quarrel with Timothy?' Clara asked shyly. 'I should have.'

Mrs. Durrant came back from the window.

'It gets later and later,' she said, sitting upright, and looking down the table. 'You ought to be ashamed – all of you. Mr. Clutterbuck,[16] you ought to be ashamed.' She raised her voice, for Mr. Clutterbuck was deaf.

'We *are* ashamed,' said a girl. But the old man with the beard went on eating plum tart. Mrs. Durrant laughed and leant back in her chair, as if indulging him.

'We put it to you, Mrs. Durrant,' said a young man with thick spectacles and a fiery moustache. 'I say the conditions were fulfilled. She owes me a sovereign.'

'Not *before* the fish – *with* it, Mrs. Durrant,' said Charlotte Wilding.

'That was the bet; with the fish,' said Clara seriously. 'Begonias, mother. To eat them with his fish.'

'Oh dear,' said Mrs. Durrant.

'Charlotte won't pay you,' said Timothy.

'How dare you . . .' said Charlotte.

'That privilege will be mine,' said the courtly Mr. Wortley, producing a silver case primed with sovereigns and slipping one coin on to the table. Then Mrs. Durrant got up and passed down the room, holding herself very straight, and the girls in yellow and blue and silver gauze followed her, and elderly Miss Eliot in her velvet; and a little rosy woman, hesitating at the door, clean, scrupulous, probably a governess. All passed out at the open door.

'When you are as old as I am, Charlotte,' said Mrs. Durrant, drawing the girl's arms within hers as they paced up and down the terrace.

'Why are you so sad?' Charlotte asked impulsively.

'Do I seem to you sad? I hope not,' said Mrs. Durrant.

'Well, just now. You're *not* old.'

'Old enough to be Timothy's mother.' They stopped.

Miss Eliot was looking through Mr. Clutterbuck's telescope at the edge of the terrace. The deaf old man stood beside her, fondling his beard, and reciting the names of the constellations: 'Andromeda, Bootes, Sidonia, Cassiopeia . . .'

'Andromeda,' murmured Miss Eliot, shifting the telescope slightly.

Mrs. Durrant and Charlotte looked along the barrel of the instrument pointed at the skies.

'There are *millions* of stars,' said Charlotte with conviction. Miss Eliot turned away from the telescope. The young men laughed suddenly in the dining-room.

'Let *me* look,' said Charlotte eagerly.

'The stars bore me,' said Mrs. Durrant, walking down the terrace with Julia Eliot. 'I read a book once about the stars ... What are they saying?' She stopped in front of the dining-room window. 'Timothy,' she noted.

'The silent young man,' said Miss Eliot.

'Yes, Jacob Flanders,' said Mrs. Durrant.

'Oh, Mother! I didn't recognize you!' exclaimed Clara Durrant, coming from the opposite direction with Elsbeth. 'How delicious,' she breathed, crushing a verbena leaf.

Mrs. Durrant turned and walked away by herself.

'Clara!' she called. Clara went to her.

'How unlike they are!' said Miss Eliot.

Mr. Wortley passed them, smoking a cigar.

'Every day I live I find myself agreeing ...' he said as he passed them.

'It's so interesting to guess ...'[17] murmured Julia Eliot.

'When first we came out we could see the flowers in that bed,' said Elsbeth.

'We see very little now,' said Miss Eliot.

'She must have been so beautiful, and everybody loved her, of course,' said Charlotte. 'I suppose. Mr. Wortley ...' she paused.

'Edward's death was a tragedy,' said Miss Eliot decidedly.

Here Mr. Erskine joined them.

'There's no such thing as silence,' he said positively. 'I can hear twenty different sounds on a night like this without counting your voices.'

'Make a bet of it?' said Charlotte.

'Done,' said Mr. Erskine. 'One, the sea; two, the wind; three, a dog; four ...'

The others passed on.

'Poor Timothy,' said Elsbeth.

'A very fine night,' shouted Miss Eliot into Mr. Clutterbuck's ear.

'Like to look at the stars?' said the old man, turning the telescope towards Elsbeth.

'Doesn't it make you melancholy – looking at the stars?' shouted Miss Eliot.

'Dear me no, dear me no,' Mr. Clutterbuck chuckled when he understood her. 'Why should it make me melancholy? Not for a moment – dear me no.'

'Thank you, Timothy, but I'm coming in,' said Miss Eliot. 'Elsbeth, here's a shawl.'

'I'm coming in,' Elsbeth murmured with her eye to the telescope. 'Cassiopeia,' she murmured. 'Where are you all?' she asked, taking her eye away from the telescope. 'How dark it is!'

Mrs. Durrant sat in the drawing-room by a lamp winding a ball of wool. Mr. Clutterbuck read the *Times*. In the distance stood a second lamp, and round it sat the young ladies, flashing scissors over silver-spangled stuff for private theatricals. Mr. Wortley read a book.

'Yes; he is perfectly right,' said Mrs. Durrant, drawing herself up and ceasing to wind her wool. And while Mr. Clutterbuck read the rest of Lord Lansdowne's speech she sat upright, without touching her ball.

'Ah, Mr. Flanders,' she said, speaking proudly, as if to Lord Lansdowne [18] himself. Then she sighed and began to wind her wool again.

'Sit *there*,' she said.

Jacob came out from the dark place by the window where he had hovered. The light poured over him, illuminating every cranny of his skin; but not a muscle of his face moved as he sat looking out into the garden.

'I want to hear about your voyage,' said Mrs. Durrant.

'Yes,' he said.

'Twenty years ago we did the same thing.'

'Yes,' he said. She looked at him sharply.

'He is extraordinarily awkward,' she thought, noticing how he fingered his socks. 'Yet so distinguished-looking.'

'In those days . . .' she resumed, and told him how they had sailed . . . 'my husband, who knew a good deal about sailing, for he kept a yacht before we married' . . . and then how rashly they had defied the fishermen, 'almost paid for it with our lives, but so proud of ourselves!' She flung the hand out that held the ball of wool.

'Shall I hold your wool?' Jacob asked stiffly.

'You do that for your mother,' said Mrs. Durrant, looking at him again keenly, as she transferred the skein. 'Yes, it goes much better.'

He smiled; but said nothing.

Elsbeth Siddons hovered behind them with something silver on her arm.

'We want,' she said . . . 'I've come . . .' she paused.

'Poor Jacob,' said Mrs. Durrant, quietly as if she had known him all his life. 'They're going to make you act in their play.'

'How I love you!' said Elsbeth, kneeling beside Mrs. Durrant's chair.

'Give me the wool,' said Mrs. Durrant.

'He's come – he's come!' cried Charlotte Wilding. 'I've won my bet!'

'There's another bunch higher up,' murmured Clara Durrant, mounting another step of the ladder. Jacob held the ladder[19] as she stretched out to reach the grapes high up on the vine.

'There!' she said, cutting through the stalk. She looked semi-transparent, pale, wonderfully beautiful up there among the vine leaves and the yellow and purple bunches, the lights swimming over her in coloured islands. Geraniums and begonias stood in pots along planks; tomatoes climbed the walls.

'The leaves really want thinning,' she considered, and one green one, spread like the palm of a hand, circled down past Jacob's head.

'I have more than I can eat already,' he said, looking up.

'It does seem absurd . . .' Clara began, 'going back to London . . .'

'Ridiculous,' said Jacob, firmly.

'Then . . .' said Clara, 'you must come next year, properly,' she said, snipping another vine leaf, rather at random.

'If . . . if . . .'

A child ran past the greenhouse shouting. Clara slowly descended the ladder with her basket of grapes.

'One bunch of white, and two of purple,' she said, and she placed two great leaves over them where they lay curled warm in the basket.

'I have enjoyed myself,' said Jacob, looking down the green-house.

'Yes, it's been delightful,' she said vaguely.

'Oh, Miss Durrant,' he said, taking the basket of grapes; but she walked past him towards the door of the greenhouse.

'You're too good – too good,' she thought, thinking of Jacob, thinking that he must not say that he loved her. No, no, no.

The children were whirling past the door, throwing things high into the air.

'Little demons!' she cried. 'What have they got?' she asked Jacob.

'Onions, I think,' said Jacob. He looked at them without moving.

'Next August, remember, Jacob,' said Mrs. Durrant, shaking hands with him on the terrace where the fuchsia hung, like a scarlet ear-ring,[20] behind her ear. Mr. Wortley came out of the window in yellow slippers, trailing the *Times* and holding out his hand very cordially.

'Good-bye,' said Jacob. 'Good-bye,' he repeated. 'Good-bye,' he said once more. Charlotte Wilding flung up her bedroom window and cried out: 'Good-bye, Mr. Jacob!'

'Mr. Flanders!' cried Mr. Clutterbuck, trying to extricate himself from his beehive chair. 'Jacob Flanders!'

'Too late, Joseph,' said Mrs. Durrant.

'Not to sit for me,' said Miss Eliot, planting her tripod upon the lawn.

V

'I rather think,' said Jacob, taking his pipe from his mouth, 'it's in Virgil,' and pushing back his chair, he went to the window.

The rashest drivers in the world are, certainly, the drivers of post-office vans. Swinging down Lamb's Conduit Street, the scarlet van rounded the corner by the pillar box in such a way as to graze the kerb and make the little girl who was standing on tiptoe to post a letter look up, half frightened, half curious. She paused with her hand in the mouth of the box; then dropped her letter and ran away. It is seldom only that we see a child on tiptoe with pity – more often a dim discomfort, a grain of sand in the shoe which it's scarcely worth while to remove – that's our feeling, and so – Jacob turned to the bookcase.

Long ago great people lived here, and coming back from Court past midnight stood, huddling their satin skirts, under the carved door-posts while the footman roused himself from his mattress on the floor, hurriedly fastened the lower buttons of his waistcoat, and let them in. The bitter eighteenth-century rain rushed down the kennel. Southampton Row, however, is chiefly remarkable now-adays for the fact that you will always find a man there trying to sell a tortoise to a tailor. 'Showing off the tweed, sir; what the gentry wants is something singular to catch the eye, sir – and clean in their habits, sir!' So they display their tortoises.

At Mudie's corner in Oxford Street[1] all the red and blue beads had run together on the string. The motor omnibuses were locked. Mr. Spalding going to the city looked at Mr. Charles Budgeon bound for Shepherd's Bush.[2] The proximity of the omnibuses gave the outside passengers an opportunity to stare into each other's faces. Yet few took advantage of it. Each had his own business to think of. Each had his past shut in him like the leaves of a book known to him by heart; and his friends could only read the title, James Spalding, or Charles Budgeon, and the passengers going the opposite way could read nothing at all – save 'a man with a red moustache,' 'a young man in grey smoking a pipe.' The October sunlight rested upon all these men and women sitting immobile; and little Johnnie Sturgeon took the chance to swing down the staircase, carrying his large mysterious parcel, and so dodging a zigzag course between the wheels he reached the pavement, started to whistle a tune and was soon out of sight – for ever. The omnibuses jerked on, and every single person felt relief at being a little nearer to his journey's end, though some cajoled themselves past the immediate engagement by promise of indulgence beyond – steak and kidney pudding, drink, or a game of dominoes in the smoky corner of a city restaurant. Oh yes, human life is very tolerable on the top of an omnibus in Holborn, when the policeman holds up his arm and the sun beats on your back, and if there is such a thing as a shell secreted by man to fit man himself[3] here we find it, on the banks of the Thames, where the great streets join and St. Paul's Cathedral,[4] like the volute on the top of the snail shell, finishes it off. Jacob, getting off his omnibus, loitered up the steps, consulted his watch, and finally made up his mind to go in ... Does it need an effort? Yes. These changes of mood wear us out.

Dim it is, haunted by ghosts of white marble, to whom the organ for ever chaunts.[5] If a boot creaks, it's awful; then the order; the discipline. The verger with his rod has life ironed out beneath him. Sweet and holy are the angelic choristers. And for ever round the marble shoulders, in and out of the folded fingers, go the thin high sounds of voice and organ. For ever requiem – repose. Tired with scrubbing the steps of the Prudential Society's office, which she did year in year out, Mrs. Lidgett took her seat beneath the great Duke's tomb,[6] folded her hands, and half closed her eyes. A magnificent place for an old woman to rest in, by the very side of the great Duke's bones, whose victories mean nothing to her, whose name she knows not, though she never fails to greet the little angels opposite, as she passes out, wishing the like on her own tomb, for the leathern curtain of the heart has flapped wide, and out steal on tiptoe thoughts of rest, sweet melodies ... Old Spicer, jute[7] merchant, thought nothing of the kind though. Strangely enough he'd never been in St. Paul's these fifty years, though his office windows looked on the churchyard. 'So that's all? Well, a gloomy old place ... Where's Nelson's tomb?[8] No time now – come again – a coin to leave in the box ... Rain or fine is it? Well, if it would only make up its mind!' Idly the children stray in – the verger dissuades them – and another and another ... man, woman, man, woman, boy ... casting their eyes up, pursing their lips, the same shadow brushing the same faces; the leathern curtain of the heart flaps wide.

Nothing could appear more certain from the steps of St. Paul's than that each person is miraculously provided with coat, skirt, and boots; an income; an object. Only Jacob, carrying in his hand Finlay's *Byzantine Empire*,[9] which he had bought in Ludgate Hill, looked a little different; for in his hand he carried a book, which book he would at nine-thirty precisely, by his own fireside, open and study, as no one else of all these multitudes would do. They have no houses. The streets belong to them; the shops; the churches; theirs the innumerable desks; the stretched office lights; the vans are theirs, and the railway slung high above the street. If you look closer you will see that three elderly men at a little distance from each other run spiders along the pavement as if the street were their parlour, and here, against the wall, a woman stares at nothing, boot-laces extended, which she does not ask you to buy. The posters are theirs too; and the news on them. A town destroyed; a race won. A homeless people, circling beneath the sky whose blue or white is held off by a ceiling cloth of steel filings and horse dung shredded to dust.

There, under the green shade, with his head bent over white paper, Mr. Sibley transferred figures to folios, and upon each desk you observe, like provender, a bunch of papers, the day's nutriment, slowly consumed by the industrious pen. Innumerable overcoats of the quality prescribed hung empty all day in the corridors, but as the clock struck six each was exactly filled, and the little figures, split apart into trousers or moulded into a single thickness, jerked rapidly with angular forward motion along the pavement; then dropped into darkness. Beneath the pavement, sunk in the earth, hollow drains lined with yellow light for ever conveyed them this way and that, and large letters upon enamel plates represented in the underworld the parks, squares, and circuses of the upper. 'Marble Arch – Shepherd's Bush' – to the majority the Arch and the Bush are eternally white letters upon a blue ground. Only at one point – it may be Acton, Holloway, Kensal Rise, Caledonian Road – does the name mean shops where you buy things, and houses, in one of which, down to the right, where the pollard trees grow out of the paving stones, there is a square curtained window, and a bedroom.

Long past sunset an old blind woman sat on a camp-stool with her back to the stone wall of the Union of London and Smith's Bank,[10] clasping a brown mongrel tight in her arms and singing out loud,[11] not for coppers, no, from the depths of her gay wild heart – her sinful, tanned heart – for the child who fetches her is the fruit of sin, and should have been in bed, curtained, asleep, instead of hearing in the lamplight her mother's wild song, where she sits against the bank, singing not for coppers, with her dog against her breast.

Home they went. The grey church spires received them; the hoary city, old, sinful, and majestic. One behind another, round or pointed, piercing the sky or massing themselves, like sailing ships, like granite cliffs, spires and offices, wharves and factories crowd the bank; eternally the pilgrims trudge; barges rest in mid stream heavy laden; as some believe, the city loves her prostitutes.[12]

But few, it seems, are admitted to that degree. Of all the carriages that leave the arch of the Opera House,[13] not one turns eastward, and when the little thief is caught in the empty market-place no one in black-and-white or rose-coloured evening dress blocks the way by pausing with a hand upon the carriage door to help or condemn – though Lady Charles, to do her justice, sighs sadly as she ascends her staircase, takes down Thomas à Kempis,[14] and does not sleep till her mind has lost itself tunnelling into the complexity of things. 'Why? Why? Why?' she sighs. On the whole it's best to walk back from the Opera House. Fatigue is the safest sleeping draught.

The autumn season was in full swing. Tristan was twitching his rug up under his armpits twice a week; Isolde[15] waved her scarf in miraculous sympathy with the conductor's baton. In all parts of the house were to be found pink faces and glittering breasts. When a Royal hand attached to an invisible body slipped out and withdrew the red and white bouquet reposing on the scarlet ledge, the Queen of England seemed a name worth dying for. Beauty, in its hothouse variety (which is none of the worst), flowered in box after box; and though nothing was said of profound importance, and though it is generally agreed that wit deserted beautiful lips about the time that Walpole died – at any rate when Victoria in her nightgown[16] descended to meet her ministers, the lips (through an opera glass) remained red, adorable. Bald distinguished men with gold-headed canes strolled down the crimson avenues between the stalls, and only broke from intercourse with the boxes when the lights went down, and the conductor, first bowing to the Queen, next to the bald-headed men, swept round on his feet and raised his wand.

Then two thousand hearts in the semi-darkness remembered, anticipated, travelled dark labyrinths; and Clara Durrant said farewell to Jacob Flanders, and tasted the sweetness of death in effigy; and Mrs. Durrant, sitting behind her in the dark of the box, sighed her sharp sigh; and Mr. Wortley, shifting his position behind the Italian Ambassador's wife, thought that Brangäne[17] was a trifle hoarse; and suspended in the gallery many feet above their heads, Edward Whittaker surreptitiously held a torch to his miniature score; and . . . and . . .

In short, the observer is choked with observations. Only to prevent us from being submerged by chaos, nature and society between them have arranged a system of classification which is simplicity itself; stalls, boxes, amphitheatre, gallery. The moulds are filled nightly. There is no need to distinguish details. But the difficulty remains – one has to choose. For though I have no wish to be Queen of England – or only for a moment – I would willingly sit beside her; I would hear the Prime Minister's gossip; the countess whisper, and share her memories of halls and gardens; the massive fronts of the respectable conceal after all their secret code; or why so impermeable? And then, doffing one's own headpiece, how strange to assume for a moment some one's – any one's – to be a man of valour who has ruled the Empire; to refer while Brangäne sings to the fragments of Sophocles, or see in a flash, as the shepherd pipes his tune, bridges and aqueducts. But no – we must choose. Never was there a harsher necessity! or one which entails greater pain, more certain disaster; for wherever I seat myself, I die in exile. Whittaker in his lodging-house; Lady Charles at the Manor.

*

A young man with a Wellington nose, who had occupied a seven-and-sixpenny seat, made his way down the stone stairs when the opera ended, as if he were still set a little apart from his fellows by the influence of the music.

At midnight Jacob Flanders heard a rap on his door.

'By Jove!' he exclaimed. 'You're the very man I want!' and without more ado they discovered the lines which he had been seeking all day; only they come not in Virgil, but in Lucretius.[18]

'Yes; that should make him sit up,' said Bonamy,[19] as Jacob stopped reading. Jacob was excited. It was the first time he had read his essay aloud.

'Damned swine!' he said, rather too extravagantly; but the praise had gone to his head. Professor Bulteel, of Leeds, had issued an edition of Wycherley[20] without stating that he had left out, disembowelled, or indicated only by asterisks, several indecent words and some indecent phrases. An outrage, Jacob said; a breach of faith; sheer prudery; token of a lewd mind and a disgusting nature. Aristophanes and Shakespeare were cited. Modern life was repudiated. Great play was made with the professorial title, and Leeds as a seat of learning was laughed to scorn. And the extraordinary thing was that these young men were perfectly right – extraordinary, because, even as Jacob copied his pages, he knew that no one would ever print them; and sure enough back they came from the *Fortnightly*, the *Contemporary*, the *Nineteenth Century*[21] – when Jacob threw them into the black wooden box where he kept his mother's letters, his old flannel trousers, and a note or two with the Cornish postmark. The lid shut upon the truth.

This black wooden box, upon which his name was still legible in white paint, stood between the long windows of the sitting-room. The street ran beneath. No doubt the bedroom was behind. The furniture – three wicker chairs and a gate-legged table – came from Cambridge. These houses (Mrs. Garfit's daughter, Mrs. Whitehorn, was the landlady of this one) were built, say, a hundred and fifty years ago. The rooms are shapely, the ceilings high; over the door-way a rose, or a ram's skull, is carved in the wood. The eighteenth century has its distinction. Even the panels, painted in raspberry-coloured paint, have their distinction . . .

'Distinction' – Mrs. Durrant said that Jacob Flanders was 'distinguished-looking.' 'Extremely awkward,' she said, 'but so distinguished-looking.' Seeing him for the first time that no doubt is the word for him. Lying back in his chair, taking his pipe from his lips, and saying to Bonamy: 'About this opera now' (for they had done with indecency). 'This fellow Wagner' . . . distinction was one of the words to use naturally, though, from looking at him, one would have found it difficult to say which seat in the opera house was his, stalls, gallery, or dress circle. A writer? He lacked self-consciousness. A painter? There was something in the shape of his hands (he was descended on his mother's side from a family of the greatest antiquity and deepest obscurity) which indicated taste. Then his mouth – but surely, of all futile occupations this of cataloguing features is the worst. One word is sufficient. But if one cannot find it?

'I like Jacob Flanders,' wrote Clara Durrant in her diary. 'He is so unworldly. He gives himself no airs, and one can say what one likes to him, though he's frightening because . . .' But Mr. Letts[22] allows little space in his shilling diaries. Clara was not one[23] to encroach upon Wednesday. Humblest, most candid of women! 'No, no, no,' she sighed, standing at the greenhouse door, 'don't break – don't spoil' – what? Something infinitely wonderful.

But then, this is only a young woman's language, one, too, who loves, or refrains from loving. She wished the moment to continue for ever precisely as it was that July morning. And moments don't. Now, for instance, Jacob was telling a story about some walking tour he'd taken, and the inn was called 'The Foaming Pot,' which, considering the landlady's name . . . They shouted with laughter. The joke was indecent.

Then Julia Eliot said 'the silent young man,' and as she dined with Prime Ministers, no doubt she meant: 'If he is going to get on in the world, he will have to find his tongue.'

Timothy Durrant never made any comment at all.

The housemaid found herself very liberally rewarded.

Mr. Sopwith's opinion was as sentimental as Clara's, though far more skilfully expressed.

Betty Flanders was romantic about Archer and tender about John; she was unreasonably irritated by Jacob's clumsiness in the house.

Captain Barfoot liked him best of the boys; but as for saying why . . .

It seems then that men and women are equally at fault. It seems that a profound, impartial, and absolutely just opinion of our fellow-creatures is utterly unknown. Either we are men, or we are women. Either we are cold, or we are sentimental. Either we are young, or growing old. In any case life is but a procession of shadows, and God knows why it is that we embrace them so eagerly, and see them depart with such anguish, being shadows. And why, if this and much more than this is true, why are we yet surprised in the window corner by a sudden vision that the young man in the chair is of all things in the world the most real, the most solid, the best known to us – why indeed? For the moment after we know nothing about him.

Such is the manner of our seeing. Such the conditions of our love.

('I'm twenty-two. It's nearly the end of October. Life is thoroughly pleasant, although unfortunately there are a great number of fools about. One must apply oneself to something or other – God knows what. Everything is really very jolly – except getting up in the morning and wearing a tail coat.')

'I say, Bonamy, what about Beethoven?'

('Bonamy is an amazing fellow. He knows practically everything – not more about English literature than I do – but then he's read all those Frenchmen.')

'I rather suspect you're talking rot, Bonamy. In spite of what you say, poor old Tennyson . . .'

('The truth is one ought to have been taught French. Now, I suppose, old Barfoot is talking to my mother. That's an odd affair to be sure. But I can't see Bonamy down there. Damn London!') for the market carts were lumbering down the street.

'What about a walk on Saturday?'

('What's happening on Saturday?')

Then, taking out his pocket-book, he assured himself that the night of the Durrants' party came next week.

But though all this may very well be true – so Jacob thought and spoke – so he crossed his legs – filled his pipe – sipped his whisky, and once looked at his pocket-book, rumpling his hair as he did so, there remains over something which can never be conveyed to a second person save by Jacob himself. Moreover, part of this is not Jacob but Richard Bonamy – the room; the market carts; the hour; the very moment of history. Then consider the effect of sex – how between man and woman it hangs wavy, tremulous, so that here's a valley, there's a peak, when in truth, perhaps, all's as flat as my hand. Even the exact words get the wrong accent on them. But something is always impelling one to hum vibrating, like the hawk moth, at the mouth of the cavern of mystery, endowing Jacob Flanders with all sorts of qualities he had not at all – for though, certainly, he sat talking to Bonamy, half of what he said was too dull to repeat; much unintelligible (about unknown people and Parliament); what remains is mostly a matter of guess work. Yet over him we hang vibrating.

'Yes,' said Captain Barfoot, knocking out his pipe on Betty Flanders's hob, and buttoning his coat. 'It doubles the work, but I don't mind that.'

He was now town councillor. They looked at the night, which was the same as the London night, only a good deal more transparent. Church bells down in the town were striking eleven o'clock. The wind was off the sea. And all the bedroom windows were dark – the Pages were asleep; the Garfits were asleep; the Cranches were asleep – whereas in London at this hour they were burning Guy Fawkes on Parliament Hill.[24]

VI

The flames had fairly caught.

'There's St. Paul's!' some one cried.

As the wood caught the city of London was lit up for a second; on other sides of the fire there were trees. Of the faces which came out fresh and vivid as though painted in yellow and red, the most prominent was a girl's face. By a trick of the firelight she seemed to have no body. The oval of the face and hair hung beside the fire with a dark vacuum for background. As if dazed by the glare, her green-blue eyes stared at the flames. Every muscle of her face was taut. There was something tragic in her thus staring – her age between twenty and twenty-five.

A hand descending from the chequered darkness thrust on her head the conical white hat of a pierrot. Shaking her head, she still stared. A whiskered face appeared above her. They dropped two legs of a table upon the fire and a scattering of twigs and leaves. All this blazed up and showed faces far back, round, pale, smooth, bearded, some with billycock hats[1] on; all intent; showed too St. Paul's floating on the uneven white mist, and two or three narrow, paper-white, extinguisher-shaped spires.

The flames were struggling through the wood and roaring up when, goodness knows where from, pails flung water in beautiful hollow shapes, as of polished tortoiseshell; flung again and again; until the hiss was like a swarm of bees; and all the faces went out.

'Oh Jacob,' said the girl, as they pounded up the hill in the dark, 'I'm so frightfully unhappy!'

Shouts of laughter came from the others – high, low; some before, others after.

The hotel dining-room was brightly lit. A stag's head in plaster was at one end of the table; at the other some Roman bust blackened and reddened to represent Guy Fawkes, whose night it was. The diners were linked together by lengths of paper roses, so that when it came to singing 'Auld Lang Syne' [2] with their hands crossed a pink and yellow line rose and fell the entire length of the table. There was an enormous tapping of green wine-glasses. A young man stood up, and Florinda, taking one of the purplish globes that lay on the table, flung it straight at his head. It crushed to powder.[3]

'I'm so frightfully unhappy!' she said, turning to Jacob, who sat beside her.

The table ran, as if on invisible legs, to the side of the room, and a barrel-organ[4] decorated with a red cloth and two pots of paper flowers reeled out waltz music.

Jacob could not dance. He stood against the wall smoking a pipe.

'We think,' said two of the dancers, breaking off from the rest, and bowing profoundly before him, 'that you are the most beautiful man we have ever seen.'

So they wreathed his head with paper flowers.[5] Then somebody brought out a white and gilt chair and made him sit on it. As they passed, people hung glass grapes on his shoulders, until he looked like the figure-head of a wrecked ship. Then Florinda got upon his knee and hid her face in his waistcoat. With one hand he held her; with the other, his pipe.

'Now let us talk,' said Jacob, as he walked down Haverstock Hill between four and five o'clock in the morning of November the sixth arm-in-arm with Timmy Durrant, 'about something sensible.'

The Greeks[6] – yes, that was what they talked about – how when all's said and done, when one's rinsed one's mouth with every literature in the world, including Chinese and Russian (but these Slavs aren't civilized), it's the flavour of Greek that remains. Durrant quoted Aeschylus – Jacob Sophocles. It is true that no Greek could have understood or professor refrained from pointing out – Never mind; what is Greek for if not to be shouted on Haverstock Hill in the dawn? Moreover, Durrant never listened to Sophocles, nor Jacob to Aeschylus. They were boastful, triumphant; it seemed to both that they had read every book in the world; known every sin, passion, and joy. Civilizations stood round them like flowers ready for picking. Ages lapped at their feet like waves fit for sailing. And surveying all this, looming through the fog, the lamplight, the shades of London, the two young men decided in favour of Greece.

'Probably,' said Jacob, 'we are the only people in the world who know what the Greeks meant.'

They drank coffee at a stall where the urns were burnished and little lamps burnt along the counter.

Taking Jacob for a military gentleman, the stall-keeper told him about his boy at Gibraltar, and Jacob cursed the British army and praised the Duke of Wellington.[7] So on again they went down the hill talking about the Greeks.

A strange thing — when you come to think of it — this love of Greek, flourishing in such obscurity, distorted, discouraged, yet leaping out, all of a sudden, especially on leaving crowded rooms, or after a surfeit of print, or when the moon floats among the waves of the hills, or in hollow, sallow, fruitless London days, like a specific; a clean blade; always a miracle. Jacob knew no more Greek than served him to stumble through a play. Of ancient history he knew nothing. However, as he tramped into London it seemed to him that they were making the flagstones ring on the road to the Acropolis, and that if Socrates saw them coming he would bestir himself and say 'my fine fellows,' for the whole sentiment of Athens was entirely after his heart; free, venturesome, high-spirited . . . She had called him Jacob without asking his leave. She had sat upon his knee. Thus did all good women in the days of the Greeks.

At this moment there shook out into the air a wavering, quavering, doleful lamentation which seemed to lack strength to unfold itself, and yet flagged on; at the sound of which doors in back streets burst sullenly open; workmen stumped forth.

Florinda was sick.

Mrs. Durrant, sleepless as usual, scored a mark by the side of certain lines in the *Inferno*.[8]

*

Clara slept buried in her pillows; on her dressing-table dishevelled roses and a pair of long white gloves.

Still wearing the conical white hat of a pierrot, Florinda was sick.

The bedroom seemed fit for these catastrophes – cheap, mustard-coloured, half attic, half studio, curiously ornamented with silver paper stars, Welshwomen's hats, and rosaries pendent from the gas brackets. As for Florinda's story, her name had been bestowed upon her by a painter who had wished it to signify that the flower of her maidenhood was still unplucked. Be that as it may, she was without a surname,[9] and for parents had only the photograph of a tombstone beneath which, she said, her father lay buried. Sometimes she would dwell upon the size of it, and rumour had it that Florinda's father had died from the growth of his bones which nothing could stop; just as her mother enjoyed the confidence of a Royal master, and now and again Florinda herself was a Princess, but chiefly when drunk. Thus deserted, pretty into the bargain, with tragic eyes and the lips of a child, she talked more about virginity than women mostly do; and had lost it only the night before, or cherished it beyond the heart in her breast, according to the man she talked to. But did she always talk to men? No, she had her confidante: Mother Stuart. Stuart, as the lady would point out, is the name of a Royal house; but what that signified, and what her business was, no one knew; only that Mrs. Stuart got postal orders every Monday morning, kept a parrot, believed in the transmigration of souls, and could read the future in tea leaves. Dirty lodging-house wallpaper she was behind the chastity of Florinda.

Now Florinda wept, and spent the day wandering the streets; stood at Chelsea watching the river swim past; trailed along the shopping streets; opened her bag and powdered her cheeks in omnibuses; read love letters, propping them against the milk pot in the A.B.C. shop;[10] detected glass in the sugar bowl; accused the waitress of wishing to poison her; declared that young men stared at her; and found herself towards evening slowly sauntering down Jacob's street, when it struck her that she liked that man Jacob better than dirty Jews, and sitting at his table (he was copying his essay upon the Ethics of Indecency[11]), drew off her gloves and told him how Mother Stuart had banged her on the head with the tea-cosy.

Jacob took her word for it that she was chaste. She prattled, sitting by the fireside, of famous painters. The tomb of her father was mentioned. Wild and frail and beautiful she looked, and thus the women of the Greeks were, Jacob thought; and this was life; and himself a man and Florinda chaste.

She left with one of Shelley's poems beneath her arm. Mrs. Stuart, she said, often talked of him.

Marvellous are the innocent. To believe that the girl herself transcends all lies (for Jacob was not such a fool as to believe implicitly), to wonder enviously at the unanchored life – his own seeming petted and even cloistered in comparison – to have at hand as sovereign specifics for all disorders of the soul Adonais[12] and the plays of Shakespeare; to figure out a comradeship all spirited on her side, protective on his, yet equal on both, for women, thought Jacob, are just the same as men – innocence such as this is marvellous enough, and perhaps not so foolish after all.

For when Florinda got home that night she first washed her head; then ate chocolate creams; then opened Shelley. True, she was horribly bored. What on earth was it *about*? She had to wager with herself that she would turn the page before she ate another. In fact she slept. But then her day had been a long one. Mother Stuart had thrown the tea-cosy; – there are formidable sights in the streets, and though Florinda was ignorant as an owl, and would never learn to read even her love letters correctly, still she had her feelings, liked some men better than others, and was entirely at the beck and call of life. Whether or not she was a virgin seems a matter of no importance whatever. Unless, indeed, it is the only thing of any importance at all.

Jacob was restless when she left him.

All night men and women seethed up and down the well-known beats. Late home-comers could see shadows against the blinds even in the most respectable suburbs. Not a square in snow or fog lacked its amorous couple. All plays turned on the same subject. Bullets went through heads in hotel bedrooms almost nightly on that account.[13] When the body escaped mutilation, seldom did the heart go to the grave unscarred. Little else was talked of in theatres and popular novels. Yet we say it is a matter of no importance at all.

What with Shakespeare and Adonais, Mozart and Bishop Berkeley

– choose whom you like – the fact is concealed and the evenings for most of us pass reputably, or with only the sort of tremor that a snake makes sliding through the grass.[14] But then concealment by itself distracts the mind from the print and the sound. If Florinda had had a mind, she might have read with clearer eyes than we can. She and her sort have solved the question by turning it to a trifle of washing the hands nightly before going to bed, the only difficulty being whether you prefer your water hot or cold, which being settled, the mind can go about its business unassailed.

But it did occur to Jacob, half-way through dinner, to wonder whether she had a mind.

They sat at a little table in the restaurant.

Florinda leant the points of her elbows on the table and held her chin in the cup of her hands. Her cloak had slipped behind her. Gold and white with bright beads on her she emerged, her face flowering from her body, innocent, scarcely tinted, the eyes gazing frankly about her, or slowly settling on Jacob and resting there. She talked:

'You know that big black box the Australian left in my room ever so long ago? . . . I do think furs make a woman look old . . . That's Bechstein[15] come in now . . . I was wondering what you looked like when you were a little boy, Jacob.' She nibbled her roll and looked at him.

'Jacob. You're like one of those statues . . . I think there are lovely things in the British Museum, don't you? Lots of lovely things . . .' she spoke dreamily. The room was filling; the heat increasing. Talk in a restaurant is dazed sleep-walkers' talk, so many things to look at – so much noise – other people talking. Can one overhear? Oh, but they mustn't overhear *us*.

'That's like Ellen Nagle – that girl . . .' and so on.

'I'm awfully happy since I've known you, Jacob. You're such a *good* man.'

The room got fuller and fuller; talk louder; knives more clattering.

'Well, you see what makes her say things like that is . . .'

She stopped. So did every one.

'To-morrow . . . Sunday . . . a beastly . . . you tell me . . . go then!'
Crash! And out she swept.[16]

It was at the table next them that the voice spun higher and
higher. Suddenly the woman dashed the plates to the floor. The
man was left there. Everybody stared. Then – 'Well, poor chap, we
mustn't sit staring. What a go! Did you hear what she said? By
God, he looks a fool! Didn't come up to scratch, I suppose. All the
mustard on the table-cloth. The waiters laughing.'

Jacob observed Florinda. In her face there seemed to him something horribly brainless – as she sat staring.

Out she swept, the black woman with the dancing feather in her
hat.

Yet she had to go somewhere. The night is not a tumultuous
black ocean in which you sink or sail as a star. As a matter of fact it
was a wet November night. The lamps of Soho made large greasy
spots of light upon the pavement. The by-streets were dark enough
to shelter man or woman leaning against the doorways. One
detached herself as Jacob and Florinda approached.

'She's dropped her glove,'[17] said Florinda.

Jacob, pressing forward, gave it her.

Effusively she thanked him; retraced her steps; dropped her glove
again. But why? For whom?

Meanwhile, where had the other woman got to? And the man?

The street lamps do not carry far enough to tell us. The voices,
angry, lustful, despairing, passionate, were scarcely more than the
voices of caged beasts at night. Only they are not caged, nor beasts.
Stop a man; ask him the way; he'll tell it you; but one's afraid to ask
him the way. What does one fear? – the human eye. At once the
pavement narrows, the chasm deepens. There! They've melted into
it – both man and woman. Further on, blatantly advertising its
meritorious solidity, a boarding-house exhibits behind uncurtained
windows its testimony to the soundness of London. There they sit,
plainly illuminated, dressed like ladies and gentlemen, in bamboo
chairs. The widows of business men prove laboriously that they are
related to judges. The wives of coal merchants instantly retort that
their fathers kept coachmen. A servant brings coffee, and the crochet

basket has to be moved. And so on again into the dark, passing a girl here for sale, or there an old woman with only matches to offer, passing the crowd from the Tube station, the women with veiled hair, passing at length no one but shut doors, carved door-posts, and a solitary policeman, Jacob, with Florinda on his arm, reached his room and, lighting the lamp, said nothing at all.

'I don't like you when you look like that,' said Florinda.

The problem is insoluble. The body is harnessed to a brain.[18] Beauty goes hand in hand with stupidity. There she sat staring at the fire as she had stared at the broken mustard-pot. In spite of defending indecency, Jacob doubted whether he liked it in the raw. He had a violent reversion towards male society, cloistered rooms, and the works of the classics; and was ready to turn with wrath upon whoever it was who had fashioned life thus.

Then Florinda laid her hand upon his knee.

After all, it was none of her fault. But the thought saddened him. It's not catastrophes, murders, deaths, diseases, that age and kill us; it's the way people look and laugh, and run up the steps of omnibuses.

Any excuse, though, serves a stupid woman. He told her his head ached.

But when she looked at him, dumbly, half-guessing, half-understanding, apologizing perhaps, anyhow saying as he had said, 'It's none of my fault,' straight and beautiful in body, her face like a shell within its cap, then he knew that cloisters and classics are no use whatever. The problem is insoluble.

VII

About this time a firm of merchants having dealings with the East put on the market little paper flowers which opened on touching water.[1] As it was the custom also to use finger-bowls at the end of dinner, the new discovery was found of excellent service. In these sheltered lakes the little coloured flowers swam and slid; surmounted smooth slippery waves, and sometimes foundered and lay like pebbles on the glass floor. Their fortunes were watched by eyes intent and lovely. It is surely a great discovery that leads to the union of hearts and foundation of homes. The paper flowers did no less.

It must not be thought, though, that they ousted the flowers of nature. Roses, lilies, carnations in particular, looked over the rims of vases and surveyed the bright lives and swift dooms of their artificial relations. Mr. Stuart Ormond made this very observation; and charming it was thought; and Kitty Craster married him on the strength of it six months later. But real flowers can never be dispensed with. If they could, human life would be a different affair altogether. For flowers fade; chrysanthemums are the worst; perfect over night; yellow and jaded next morning – not fit to be seen. On the whole, though the price is sinful, carnations pay best; – it's a question, however, whether it's wise to have them wired. Some shops advise it. Certainly it's the only way to keep them at a dance; but whether it is necessary at dinner parties, unless the rooms are very hot, remains in dispute. Old Mrs. Temple used to recommend an ivy leaf – just one – dropped into the bowl. She said it kept the water pure for days and days. But there is some reason to think that old Mrs. Temple was mistaken.

The little cards, however, with names engraved on them,[2] are a more serious problem than the flowers. More horses' legs have been worn out, more coachmen's lives consumed, more hours of sound afternoon time vainly lavished than served to win us the battle of Waterloo, and pay for it into the bargain. The little demons are the source of as many reprieves, calamities, and anxieties as the battle itself. Sometimes Mrs. Bonham has just gone out; at others she is at home. But, even if the cards should be superseded, which seems unlikely, there are unruly powers blowing life into storms, disordering sedulous mornings, and uprooting the stability of the afternoon – dressmakers, that is to say, and confectioners' shops. Six yards of silk will cover one body; but if you have to devise six hundred shapes for it, and twice as many colours? – in the middle of which there is the urgent question of the pudding with tufts of green cream and battlements of almond paste. It has not arrived.

The flamingo hours fluttered softly through the sky. But regularly they dipped their wings in pitch black; Notting Hill, for instance, or the purlieus of Clerkenwell.[3] No wonder that Italian remained a hidden art, and the piano always played the same sonata.[4] In order to buy one pair of elastic stockings for Mrs. Page, widow, aged sixty-three, in receipt of five shillings out-door relief,[5] and help from her only son employed in Messrs. Mackie's dye-works, suffering in winter with his chest, letters must be written, columns filled up in the same round, simple hand that wrote in Mr. Letts's diary how the weather was fine, the children demons, and Jacob Flanders unworldly. Clara Durrant procured the stockings, played the sonata, filled the vases, fetched the pudding, left the cards, and when the great invention of paper flowers to swim in finger-bowls was discovered, was one of those who most marvelled at their brief lives.

Nor were there wanting poets to celebrate the theme. Edwin Mallett, for example, wrote his verses ending:

And read their doom in Chloe's eyes,

which caused Clara to blush at the first reading, and to laugh at the second, saying that it was just like him to call her Chloe when her name was Clara. Ridiculous young man! But when, between ten and eleven on a rainy morning, Edwin Mallett laid his life at her feet she ran out of the room and hid herself in her bedroom, and Timothy below could not get on with his work all that morning on account of her sobs.

'Which is the result of enjoying yourself,' said Mrs. Durrant

severely, surveying the dance programme all scored with the same
initials, or rather they were different ones this time – R.B. instead of
E.M.; Richard Bonamy it was now, the young man with the Wellington nose.

'But I could never marry a man with a nose like that,' said Clara.

'Nonsense,' said Mrs. Durrant.

'But I am too severe,' she thought to herself. For Clara, losing
all vivacity, tore up her dance programme and threw it in the
fender.

Such were the very serious consequences of the invention of
paper flowers to swim in bowls.

'Please,' said Julia Eliot, taking up her position by the curtain
almost opposite the door, 'don't introduce me. I like to look on.
The amusing thing,' she went on, addressing Mr. Salvin, who,
owing to his lameness, was accommodated with a chair, 'the amusing
thing about a party is to watch the people – coming and going,
coming and going.'

'Last time we met,' said Mr. Salvin, 'was at the Farquhars. Poor
lady! She has much to put up with.'

'Doesn't she look charming?' exclaimed Miss Eliot, as Clara Durrant passed them.

'And which of them . . . ?' asked Mr. Salvin, dropping his voice
and speaking in quizzical tones.

'There are so many . . .' Miss Eliot replied. Three young men
stood at the doorway looking about for their hostess.

'You don't remember Elizabeth as I do,' said Mr. Salvin, 'dancing
Highland reels at Banchorie. Clara lacks her mother's spirit. Clara is
a little pale.'

'What different people one sees here!' said Miss Eliot.

'Happily we are not governed by the evening papers,' said Mr.
Salvin.

'I never read them,' said Miss Eliot. 'I know nothing about
politics,' she added.

'The piano is in tune,' said Clara, passing them, 'but we may have
to ask some one to move it for us.'

'Are they going to dance?' asked Mr. Salvin.

'Nobody shall disturb you,' said Mrs. Durrant peremptorily as she passed.

'Julia Eliot. It *is* Julia Eliot!' said old Lady Hibbert, holding out both her hands. 'And Mr. Salvin. What is going to happen to us, Mr. Salvin? With all my experience of English politics – My dear, I was thinking of your father last night – one of my oldest friends, Mr. Salvin. Never tell me that girls of ten are incapable of love! I had all Shakespeare by heart before I was in my teens, Mr. Salvin!'

'You don't say so,' said Mr. Salvin.

'But I do,' said Lady Hibbert.

'Oh, Mr. Salvin, I'm so sorry . . .'

'I will remove myself if you'll kindly lend me a hand,' said Mr. Salvin.

'You shall sit by my mother,' said Clara. 'Everybody seems to come in here . . . Mr. Calthorp, let me introduce you to Miss Edwards.'

'Are you going away for Christmas?' said Mr. Calthorp.

'If my brother gets his leave,' said Miss Edwards.

'What regiment is he in?' said Mr. Calthorp.

'The Twentieth Hussars,' said Miss Edwards.

'Perhaps he knows my brother?' said Mr. Calthorp.

'I am afraid I did not catch your name,' said Miss Edwards.

'Calthorp,' said Mr. Calthorp.

'But what proof was there that the marriage service was actually performed?' said Mr. Crosby.

'There is no reason to doubt that Charles James Fox . . .' Mr. Burley began; but here Mrs. Stretton told him that she knew his sister well; had stayed with her not six weeks ago; and thought the house charming, but bleak in winter.

'Going about as girls do nowadays—' said Mrs. Forster.

Mr. Bowley looked round him, and catching sight of Rose Shaw moved towards her, threw out his hands, and exclaimed: 'Well!'

'Nothing!' she replied. 'Nothing at all – though I left them alone the entire afternoon on purpose.'

'Dear me, dear me,' said Mr. Bowley. 'I will ask Jimmy to breakfast.'

'But who could resist her?' cried Rose Shaw. 'Dearest Clara – I know we mustn't try to stop you . . .'

'You and Mr. Bowley are talking dreadful gossip, I know,' said Clara.

'Life is wicked – life is detestable!' cried Rose Shaw.

'There's not much to be said for this sort of thing, is there?' said Timothy Durrant to Jacob.

'Women like it.'

'Like what?' said Charlotte Wilding, coming up to them.

'Where have you come from?' said Timothy. 'Dining somewhere, I suppose.'

'I don't see why not,' said Charlotte.

'People must go downstairs,' said Clara, passing. 'Take Charlotte, Timothy. How d'you do, Mr. Flanders.'

'How d'you do, Mr. Flanders,' said Julia Eliot, holding out her hand. 'What's been happening to you?'

> 'Who is Silvia? what is she?
> That all our swains commend her?'[6]

sang Elsbeth Siddons.

Every one stood where they were, or sat down if a chair was empty.

'Ah,' sighed Clara, who stood beside Jacob, half-way through.

> 'Then to Silvia let us sing,
>   That Silvia is excelling;
> She excels each mortal thing
>   Upon the dull earth dwelling.
> To her let us garlands bring,'

sang Elsbeth Siddons.

'Ah!' Clara exclaimed out loud, and clapped her gloved hands; and Jacob clapped his bare ones; and then she moved forward and directed people to come in from the doorway.

'You are living in London?' asked Miss Julia Eliot.

'Yes,' said Jacob.

'In rooms?'

'Yes.'

'There is Mr. Clutterbuck. You always see Mr. Clutterbuck here. He is not very happy at home, I'm afraid. They say that Mrs. Clutterbuck . . .' she dropped her voice. 'That's why he stays with the Durrants. Were you there when they acted Mr. Wortley's play? Oh, no, of course not – at the last moment, did you hear – you had to go to join your mother, I remember, at Harrogate – At the last moment, as I was saying, just as everything was ready, the clothes finished and everything – Now Elsbeth is going to sing again. Clara is playing her accompaniment or turning over for Mr. Carter, I think. No, Mr. Carter is playing by himself – This is *Bach*,' she whispered, as Mr. Carter played the first bars.

'Are you fond of music?' said Mrs. Durrant.

'Yes. I like hearing it,' said Jacob. 'I know nothing about it.'

'Very few people do that,' said Mrs. Durrant. 'I daresay you were never taught. Why is that, Sir Jasper? – Sir Jasper Bigham – Mr. Flanders. Why is nobody taught anything that they ought to know, Sir Jasper?' She left them standing against the wall.

Neither of the gentlemen said anything for three minutes, though Jacob shifted perhaps five inches to the left, and then as many to the right. Then Jacob grunted, and suddenly crossed the room.

'Will you come and have something to eat?' he said to Clara Durrant.

'Yes, an ice. Quickly. Now,' she said.

Downstairs they went.

But half-way down they met Mr. and Mrs. Gresham, Herbert Turner, Sylvia Rashleigh, and a friend, whom they had dared to bring, from America, 'knowing that Mrs. Durrant – wishing to show Mr. Pilcher – Mr. Pilcher from New York – This is Miss Durrant.'

'Whom I have heard so much of,' said Mr. Pilcher, bowing low.

So Clara left him.

VIII

About half-past nine Jacob left the house, his door slamming, other doors slamming, buying his paper, mounting his omnibus, or, weather permitting, walking his road as other people do. Head bent down, a desk, a telephone, books bound in green leather, electric light ... 'Fresh coals, sir?' ... 'Your tea, sir.' ... Talk about football, the Hotspurs, the Harlequins;[1] six-thirty *Star*[2] brought in by the office boy; the rooks of Gray's Inn[3] passing overhead; branches in the fog thin and brittle; and through the roar of traffic now and again a voice shouting: 'Verdict – verdict – winner – winner,' while letters accumulate in a basket, Jacob signs them, and each evening finds him, as he takes his coat down, with some muscle of the brain new stretched.

Then, sometimes a game of chess;[4] or pictures in Bond Street,[5] or a long way home to take the air with Bonamy on his arm, meditatively marching, head thrown back, the world a spectacle, the early moon above the steeples coming in for praise, the sea-gulls flying high, Nelson on his column[6] surveying the horizon, and the world our ship.

Meanwhile, poor Betty Flanders's letter, having caught the second post, lay on the hall table – poor Betty Flanders writing her son's name, Jacob Alan Flanders, Esq., as mothers do, and the ink pale, profuse, suggesting how mothers down at Scarborough[7] scribble over the fire with their feet on the fender, when tea's cleared away, and can never, never say, whatever it may be – probably this – Don't go with bad women, do be a good boy; wear your thick shirts; and come back, come back, come back to me.

But she said nothing of the kind. 'Do you remember old Miss Wargrave, who used to be so kind when you had the whooping-cough?' she wrote; 'she's dead at last, poor thing. They would like it if you wrote. Ellen came over and we spent a nice day shopping. Old Mouse gets very stiff, and we have to walk him up the smallest hill. Rebecca, at last, after I don't know how long, went into Mr.

Adamson's. Three teeth, he says, must come out. Such mild weather for the time of year, the little buds actually on the pear trees. And Mrs. Jarvis tells me—' Mrs. Flanders liked Mrs. Jarvis, always said of her that she was too good for such a quiet place, and, though she never listened to her discontent and told her at the end of it (looking up, sucking her thread, or taking off her spectacles) that a little peat wrapped round the iris roots keeps them from the frost, and Parrot's great white sale[8] is Tuesday next, 'do remember,' – Mrs. Flanders knew precisely how Mrs. Jarvis felt; and how interesting her letters were, about Mrs. Jarvis, could one read them year in, year out – the unpublished works of women, written by the fireside in pale profusion, dried by the flame, for the blotting-paper's worn to holes and the nib cleft and clotted. Then Captain Barfoot. Him she called 'the Captain,' spoke of frankly, yet never without reserve. The Captain was enquiring for her about Garfit's acre; advised chickens; could promise profit; or had the sciatica; or Mrs. Barfoot had been indoors for weeks; or the Captain says things look bad, politics that is, for as Jacob knew, the Captain would sometimes talk, as the evening waned, about Ireland or India;[9] and then Mrs. Flanders would fall musing about Morty, her brother, lost all these years – had the natives got him, was his ship sunk – would the Admiralty tell her? – the Captain knocking his pipe out, as Jacob knew, rising to go, stiffly stretching to pick up Mrs. Flanders's wool which had rolled beneath the chair. Talk of the chicken farm came back and back, the woman, even at fifty, impulsive at heart, sketching on the cloudy future flocks of Leghorns, Cochin Chinas, Orpingtons;[10] like Jacob in the blur of her outline; but powerful as he was; fresh and vigorous, running about the house, scolding Rebecca.

The letter lay upon the hall table; Florinda coming in that night took it up with her, put it on the table as she kissed Jacob, and Jacob seeing the hand, left it there under the lamp, between the biscuit-tin and the tobacco-box. They shut the bedroom door behind them.

The sitting-room neither knew nor cared. The door was shut; and to suppose that wood, when it creaks, transmits anything save that rats are busy and wood dry is childish. These old houses are only brick and wood, soaked in human sweat, grained with human dirt. But if the pale blue envelope lying by the biscuit-box had the feelings of a mother,[11] the heart was torn by the little creak, the sudden stir. Behind the door was the obscene thing, the alarming presence, and terror would come over her as at death, or the birth of a child. Better, perhaps, burst in and face it than sit in the antechamber listening to the little creak, the sudden stir, for her heart was swollen, and pain threaded it. My son, my son – such would be her cry, uttered to hide her vision of him stretched with Florinda, inexcusable, irrational, in a woman with three children living at Scarborough. And the fault lay with Florinda. Indeed, when the door opened and the couple came out, Mrs. Flanders would have flounced upon her – only it was Jacob who came first, in his dressing-gown, amiable, authoritative, beautifully healthy, like a baby after an airing, with an eye clear as running water. Florinda followed, lazily stretching; yawning a little; arranging her hair at the looking-glass – while Jacob read his mother's letter.

Let us consider letters – how they come at breakfast, and at night, with their yellow stamps and their green stamps, immortalized by the postmark – for to see one's own envelope on another's table is to realize how soon deeds sever and become alien. Then at last the power of the mind to quit the body is manifest, and perhaps we fear or hate or wish annihilated this phantom of ourselves, lying on the table. Still, there are letters that merely say how dinner's at seven; others ordering coal; making appointments. The hand in them is scarcely perceptible, let alone the voice or the scowl. Ah, but when the post knocks and the letter comes always the miracle seems repeated – speech attempted. Venerable are letters, infinitely brave, forlorn, and lost.

Life would split asunder without them. 'Come to tea, come to dinner, what's the truth of the story? have you heard the news? life in the capital is gay; the Russian dancers . . .'[12] These are our stays and props. These lace our days together and make of life a perfect globe.[13] And yet, and yet . . . when we go to dinner, when pressing finger-tips we hope to meet somewhere soon, a doubt insinuates itself; is this the way to spend our days? the rare, the limited, so soon dealt out to us – drinking tea? dining out? And the notes accumulate. And the telephones ring. And everywhere we go wires and tubes surround us to carry the voices that try to penetrate before the last card is dealt and the days are over. 'Try to penetrate,' for as we lift the cup, shake the hand, express the hope, something whispers, Is this all? Can I never know, share, be certain? Am I doomed all my days to write letters, send voices, which fall upon the tea-table, fade upon the passage, making appointments, while life dwindles, to come and dine? Yet letters are venerable; and the telephone valiant, for the journey is a lonely one, and if bound together by notes and telephones we went in company, perhaps – who knows? – we might talk by the way.

Well, people have tried. Byron wrote letters. So did Cowper.[14] For centuries the writing-desk has contained sheets fit precisely for the communications of friends. Masters of language, poets of long ages, have turned from the sheet that endures to the sheet that perishes, pushing aside the tea-tray, drawing close to the fire (for letters are written when the dark presses round a bright red cave), and addressed themselves to the task of reaching, touching, penetrating the individual heart. Were it possible! But words have been used too often; touched and turned, and left exposed to the dust of the street. The words we seek hang close to the tree. We come at dawn and find them sweet beneath the leaf.

Mrs. Flanders wrote letters; Mrs. Jarvis wrote them; Mrs. Durrant too; Mother Stuart actually scented her pages, thereby adding a flavour which the English language fails to provide; Jacob had written in his day long letters about art, morality, and politics to young men at college. Clara Durrant's letters were those of a child. Florinda – the impediment between Florinda and her pen was something impassable. Fancy a butterfly, gnat, or other winged insect, attached to a twig which, clogged with mud, it rolls across a page. Her spelling was abominable. Her sentiments infantile. And for some reason when she wrote she declared her belief in God. Then there were crosses – tear stains; and the hand itself rambling and redeemed only by the fact – which always did redeem Florinda – by the fact that she cared. Yes, whether it was for chocolate creams, hot baths, the shape of her face in the looking-glass, Florinda could no more pretend a feeling than swallow whisky. Incontinent was her rejection. Great men are truthful, and these little prostitutes, staring in the fire, taking out a powder-puff, decorating lips at an inch of looking-glass, have (so Jacob thought) an inviolable fidelity.

Then he saw her turning up Greek Street[15] upon another man's arm.

The light from the arc lamp drenched him from head to toe. He stood for a minute motionless beneath it. Shadows chequered the street. Other figures, single and together, poured out, wavered across, and obliterated Florinda and the man.

The light drenched Jacob from head to toe.[16] You could see the pattern on his trousers; the old thorns on his stick; his shoe laces; bare hands; and face.

It was as if a stone were ground to dust; as if white sparks flew from a livid whetstone, which was his spine; as if the switchback railway, having swooped to the depths, fell, fell, fell. This was in his face.

Whether we know what was in his mind is another question. Granted ten years' seniority and a difference of sex, fear of him comes first; this is swallowed up by a desire to help – overwhelming sense, reason, and the time of night; anger would follow close on that – with Florinda, with destiny; and then up would bubble an irresponsible optimism. 'Surely there's enough light in the street at this moment to drown all our cares in gold!' Ah, what's the use of saying it? Even while you speak and look over your shoulder towards Shaftesbury Avenue, destiny is chipping a dent in him. He has turned to go. As for following him back to his rooms, no – that we won't do.

Yet that, of course, is precisely what one does. He let himself in and shut the door, though it was only striking ten on one of the city clocks. No one can go to bed at ten. Nobody was thinking of going to bed. It was January and dismal, but Mrs. Wagg stood on her doorstep, as if expecting something to happen. A barrel-organ played like an obscene nightingale beneath wet leaves. Children ran across the road. Here and there one could see brown panelling inside the hall door . . . The march that the mind keeps beneath the windows of others is queer enough. Now distracted by brown panelling; now by a fern in a pot; here improvising a few phrases to dance with the barrel-organ; again snatching a detached gaiety from a drunken man; then altogether absorbed by words the poor shout across the street at each other (so outright, so lusty) – yet all the while having for centre, for magnet, a young man alone in his room.[17]

'Life is wicked – life is detestable,' cried Rose Shaw.

The strange thing about life is that though the nature of it must have been apparent to every one for hundreds of years, no one has left any adequate account of it. The streets of London have their map; but our passions are uncharted. What are you going to meet if you turn this corner?

'Holborn straight ahead of you,' says the policeman. Ah, but where are you going if instead of brushing past the old man with the white beard, the silver medal, and the cheap violin, you let him go on with his story, which ends in an invitation to step somewhere, to his room, presumably, off Queen's Square, and there he shows you a collection of birds' eggs and a letter from the Prince of Wales's secretary, and this (skipping the intermediate stages) brings you one winter's day to the Essex coast, where the little boat makes off to the ship, and the ship sails and you behold on the skyline the Azores; and the flamingoes rise; and there you sit on the verge of the marsh drinking rum-punch, an outcast from civilization, for you have committed a crime, are infected with yellow fever as likely as not, and – fill in the sketch as you like.

As frequent as street corners in Holborn are these chasms in the continuity of our ways.[18] Yet we keep straight on.

Rose Shaw, talking in rather an emotional manner to Mr. Bowley at Mrs. Durrant's evening party a few nights back, said that life was wicked because a man called Jimmy refused to marry a woman called (if memory serves) Helen Aitken.

Both were beautiful. Both were inanimate. The oval tea-table invariably separated them,[19] and the plate of biscuits was all he ever gave her. He bowed; she inclined her head. They danced. He danced divinely. They sat in the alcove; never a word was said. Her pillow was wet with tears. Kind Mr. Bowley and dear Rose Shaw marvelled and deplored. Bowley had rooms in the Albany.[20] Rose was re-born every evening precisely as the clock struck eight. All four were civilization's triumphs, and if you persist that a command of the English language is part of our inheritance, one can only reply that beauty is almost always dumb. Male beauty in association with female beauty breeds in the onlooker a sense of fear. Often have I seen them – Helen and Jimmy – and likened them to ships adrift, and feared for my own little craft. Or again, have you ever watched fine collie dogs couchant at twenty yards' distance? As she passed him his cup there was that quiver in her flanks. Bowley saw what was up – asked Jimmy to breakfast. Helen must have confided in Rose. For my own part, I find it exceedingly difficult to interpret songs without words. And now Jimmy feeds crows in Flanders and Helen visits hospitals.[21] Oh, life is damnable, life is wicked, as Rose Shaw said.

The lamps of London uphold the dark as upon the points of burning bayonets. The yellow canopy sinks and swells[22] over the great four-poster. Passengers in the mail-coaches running into London in the eighteenth century looked through leafless branches and saw it flaring beneath them. The light burns behind yellow blinds and pink blinds, and above fanlights, and down in basement windows. The street market in Soho is fierce with light. Raw meat, china mugs, and silk stockings blaze in it. Raw voices wrap themselves round the flaring gas-jets. Arms akimbo, they stand on the pavement bawling – Messrs. Kettle and Wilkinson; their wives sit in the shop, furs wrapped round their necks, arms folded, eyes contemptuous. Such faces as one sees. The little man fingering the meat must have squatted before the fire in innumerable lodging-houses, and heard and seen and known so much that it seems to utter itself even volubly from dark eyes, loose lips, as he fingers the meat silently, his face sad as a poet's, and never a song sung. Shawled women carry babies with purple eyelids; boys stand at street corners; girls look across the road – rude illustrations, pictures in a book whose pages we turn over and over as if we should at last find what we look for. Every face, every shop, bedroom window, public-house, and dark square is a picture feverishly turned – in search of what? It is the same with books. What do we seek through millions of pages? Still hopefully turning the pages – oh, here is Jacob's room.

He sat at the table reading the *Globe*. The pinkish sheet was spread flat before him. He propped his face in his hand, so that the skin of his cheek was wrinkled in deep folds. Terribly severe he looked, set, and defiant. (What people go through in half an hour! But nothing could save him. These events are features of our landscape. A foreigner coming to London could scarcely miss seeing St. Paul's.) He judged life. These pinkish and greenish newspapers are thin sheets of gelatine pressed nightly over the brain and heart of the world. They take the impression of the whole. Jacob cast his eye over it. A strike, a murder, football, bodies found; vociferation from all parts of England simultaneously. How miserable it is that the *Globe* newspaper offers nothing better to Jacob Flanders! When a child begins to read history one marvels, sorrowfully, to hear him spell out in his new voice the ancient words.

The Prime Minister's speech was reported in something over five columns. Feeling in his pocket, Jacob took out a pipe and proceeded to fill it. Five minutes, ten minutes, fifteen minutes passed. Jacob took the paper over to the fire. The Prime Minister proposed a measure for giving Home Rule to Ireland. Jacob knocked out his pipe. He was certainly thinking about Home Rule in Ireland – a very difficult matter. A very cold night.

The snow, which had been falling all night, lay at three o'clock in the afternoon over the fields and the hill. Clumps of withered grass stood out upon the hill-top; the furze bushes were black, and now and then a black shiver crossed the snow as the wind drove flurries of frozen particles before it. The sound was that of a broom sweeping – sweeping.

The stream crept along by the road unseen by any one. Sticks and leaves caught in the frozen grass. The sky was sullen grey and the trees of black iron. Uncompromising was the severity of the country. At four o'clock the snow was again falling. The day had gone out.

A window tinged yellow about two feet across alone combated the white fields and the black trees ... At six o'clock a man's figure carrying a lantern crossed the field ... A raft of twigs stayed upon a stone, suddenly detached itself, and floated towards the culvert ... A load of snow slipped and fell from a fir branch ... Later there was a mournful cry ... A motor-car[23] came along the road shoving the dark before it ... The dark shut down behind it ...

Spaces of complete immobility separated each of these movements. The land seemed to lie dead ... Then the old shepherd returned stiffly across the field. Stiffly and painfully the frozen earth was trodden under and gave beneath pressure like a treadmill. The worn voices of clocks repeated the fact of the hour all night long.[24]

Jacob, too, heard them, and raked out the fire. He rose. He stretched himself. He went to bed.

IX

The Countess of Rocksbier[1] sat at the head of the table alone with Jacob. Fed upon champagne and spices for at least two centuries (four, if you count the female line), the Countess Lucy looked well fed. A discriminating nose she had for scents, prolonged, as if in quest of them; her underlip protruded a narrow red shelf; her eyes were small, with sandy tufts for eyebrows, and her jowl was heavy. Behind her (the window looked on Grosvenor Square) stood Moll Pratt on the pavement, offering violets for sale; and Mrs. Hilda Thomas, lifting her skirts, preparing to cross the road. One was from Walworth; the other from Putney. Both wore black stockings, but Mrs. Thomas was coiled in furs. The comparison was much in Lady Rocksbier's favour.[2] Moll had more humour, but was violent; stupid too. Hilda Thomas was mealy-mouthed, all her silver frames aslant; egg-cups in the drawing-room; and the windows shrouded. Lady Rocksbier, whatever the deficiencies of her profile, had been a great rider to hounds. She used her knife with authority, tore her chicken bones, asking Jacob's pardon, with her own hands.

'Who is that driving by?' she asked Boxall, the butler.

'Lady Fittlemere's carriage, my lady,' which reminded her to send a card to ask after his lordship's health. A rude old lady, Jacob thought. The wine was excellent. She called herself 'an old woman' – 'so kind to lunch with an old woman' – which flattered him. She talked of Joseph Chamberlain,[3] whom she had known. She said that Jacob must come and meet – one of our celebrities. And the Lady Alice came in with three dogs on a leash, and Jackie, who ran to kiss his grandmother, while Boxall brought in a telegram, and Jacob was given a good cigar.

A few moments before a horse jumps it slows, sidles, gathers itself together, goes up like a monster wave, and pitches down on the further side. Hedges and sky swoop in a semicircle. Then as if your own body ran into the horse's body and it was your own forelegs grown with his that sprang, rushing through the air you go, the ground resilient, bodies a mass of muscles, yet you have command too, upright stillness, eyes accurately judging. Then the curves cease, changing to downright hammer strokes, which jar; and you draw up with a jolt; sitting back a little, sparkling, tingling, glazed with ice over pounding arteries, gasping: 'Ah! ho! Hah!' the steam going up from the horses as they jostle together at the cross-roads, where the signpost is, and the woman in the apron stands and stares at the doorway. The man raises himself from the cabbages to stare too.

So Jacob galloped over the fields of Essex, flopped in the mud, lost the hunt, and rode by himself eating sandwiches, looking over the hedges, noticing the colours as if new scraped, cursing his luck.

He had tea at the Inn; and there they all were, slapping, stamping, saying, 'After you,' clipped, curt, jocose, red as the wattles of turkeys, using free speech until Mrs. Horsefield and her friend Miss Dudding appeared at the doorway with their skirts hitched up, and hair looping down. Then Tom Dudding rapped at the window with his whip. A motor-car throbbed in the courtyard. Gentlemen, feeling for matches, moved out, and Jacob went into the bar with Brandy Jones to smoke with the rustics. There was old Jevons with one eye gone, and his clothes the colour of mud, his bag over his back, and his brains laid feet down in earth among the violet roots and the nettle roots; Mary Sanders with her box of wood; and Tom sent for beer, the half-witted son of the sexton – all this within thirty miles of London.

Mrs. Papworth, of Endell Street, Covent Garden, did for[4] Mr. Bonamy in New Square, Lincoln's Inn, and as she washed up the dinner things in the scullery she heard the young gentlemen talking in the room next door. Mr. Sanders was there again; Flanders she meant; and where an inquisitive old woman gets a name wrong, what chance is there that she will faithfully report an argument? As she held the plates under water and then dealt them on the pile beneath the hissing gas, she listened: heard Sanders speaking in a loud rather overbearing tone of voice: 'good' he said, and 'absolute' and 'justice' and 'punishment,' and 'the will of the majority.' Then her gentleman piped up; she backed him for argument against Sanders. Yet Sanders was a fine young fellow (here all the scraps went swirling round the sink, scoured after by her purple, almost nailless hands). 'Women' – she thought, and wondered what Sanders and her gentleman did in *that* line, one eyelid sinking perceptibly as she mused, for she was the mother of nine – three still-born and one deaf and dumb from birth. Putting the plates in the rack she heard once more Sanders at it again ('He don't give Bonamy a chance,' she thought). 'Objective something,' said Bonamy; and 'common ground' and something else – all very long words, she noted. 'Book learning does it,' she thought to herself, and, as she thrust her arms into her jacket, heard something – might be the little table by the fire – fall; and then stamp, stamp, stamp – as if they were having at each other – round the room, making the plates dance.

'To-morrow's breakfast, sir,' she said, opening the door; and there were Sanders and Bonamy like two bulls of Bashan[5] driving each other up and down, making such a racket, and all them chairs in the way. They never noticed her. She felt motherly towards them. 'Your breakfast, sir,' she said, as they came near. And Bonamy, all his hair touzled and his tie flying, broke off, and pushed Sanders into the arm-chair, and said Mr. Sanders had smashed the coffee-pot and he was teaching Mr. Sanders –

Sure enough, the coffee-pot lay broken on the hearthrug.

'Any day this week except Thursday,' wrote Miss Perry, and this was not the first invitation by any means. Were all Miss Perry's weeks blank with the exception of Thursday, and was her only desire to see her old friend's son? Time is issued to spinster ladies of wealth in long white ribbons. These they wind round and round, round and round, assisted by five female servants, a butler, a fine Mexican parrot, regular meals, Mudie's library, and friends dropping in. A little hurt she was already that Jacob had not called.

'Your mother,' she said, 'is one of my oldest friends.'

Miss Rosseter, who was sitting by the fire, holding the *Spectator* between her cheek and the blaze, refused to have a fire screen, but finally accepted one. The weather was then discussed, for in deference to Parkes, who was opening little tables, graver matters were postponed. Miss Rosseter drew Jacob's attention to the beauty of the cabinet.

'So wonderfully clever in picking things up,' she said. Miss Perry had found it in Yorkshire. The North of England was discussed. When Jacob spoke they both listened. Miss Perry was bethinking her of something suitable and manly to say when the door opened and Mr. Benson was announced. Now there were four people sitting in that room. Miss Perry aged 66; Miss Rosseter 42; Mr. Benson 38; and Jacob 25.[6]

'My old friend looks as well as ever,' said Mr. Benson, tapping the bars of the parrot's cage; Miss Rosseter simultaneously praised the tea; Jacob handed the wrong plates; and Miss Perry signified her desire to approach more closely. 'Your brothers,' she began vaguely.

'Archer and John,' Jacob supplied her. Then to her pleasure she recovered Rebecca's name; and how one day 'when you were all little boys, playing in the drawing-room—'

'But Miss Perry has the kettle-holder,' said Miss Rosseter, and indeed Miss Perry was clasping it to her breast. (Had she, then, loved Jacob's father?)

'So clever' – 'not so good as usual' – 'I thought it most unfair,' said Mr. Benson and Miss Rosseter, discussing the Saturday *Westminster*.[7] Did they not compete regularly for prizes? Had not Mr. Benson three times won a guinea, and Miss Rosseter once ten and sixpence? Of course Everard Benson had a weak heart, but still, to win prizes, remember parrots, toady Miss Perry, despise Miss Rosseter, give tea-parties in his rooms (which were in the style of Whistler,[8] with pretty books on tables), all this, so Jacob felt without knowing him, made him a contemptible ass. As for Miss Rosseter, she had nursed cancer, and now painted water-colours.

'Running away so soon?' said Miss Perry vaguely. 'At home every afternoon, if you've nothing better to do – except Thursdays.'

'I've never known you desert your old ladies once,' Miss Rosseter was saying, and Mr. Benson was stooping over the parrot's cage, and Miss Perry was moving towards the bell . . .

*

The fire burnt clear between two pillars of greenish marble, and on the mantelpiece there was a green clock guarded by Britannia leaning on her spear. As for pictures – a maiden in a large hat offered roses over the garden gate to a gentleman in eighteenth-century costume.[9] A mastiff lay extended against a battered door. The lower panes of the windows were of ground glass, and the curtains, accurately looped, were of plush and green too.

Laurette[10] and Jacob sat with their toes in the fender side by side, in two large chairs covered in green plush. Laurette's skirts were short, her legs long, thin, and transparently covered. Her fingers stroked her ankles.

'It's not exactly that I don't understand them,' she was saying thoughtfully. 'I must go and try again.'

'What time will you be there?' said Jacob.

She shrugged her shoulders.

'To-morrow?'

No, not to-morrow.

'This weather makes me long for the country,' she said, looking over her shoulder at the back view of tall houses through the window.

'I wish you'd been with me on Saturday,' said Jacob.

'I used to ride,' she said. She got up gracefully, calmly. Jacob got up. She smiled at him. As she shut the door he put so many shillings on the mantelpiece.

Altogether a most reasonable conversation; a most respectable room; an intelligent girl. Only Madame herself seeing Jacob out had about her that leer, that lewdness, that quake of the surface (visible in the eyes chiefly), which threatens to spill the whole bag of ordure, with difficulty held together, over the pavement. In short, something was wrong.

Not so very long ago the workmen had gilt the final 'y' in Lord Macaulay's name, and the names stretched in unbroken file round the dome of the British Museum.[11] At a considerable depth beneath, many hundreds of the living sat at the spokes of a cart-wheel copying from printed books into manuscript books; now and then rising to consult the catalogue; regaining their places stealthily, while from time to time a silent man replenished their compartments.

There was a little catastrophe. Miss Marchmont's pile overbalanced and fell into Jacob's compartment. Such things happened to Miss Marchmont. What was she seeking through millions of pages, in her old plush dress, and her wig of claret-coloured hair, with her gems and her chilblains? Sometimes one thing, sometimes another, to confirm her philosophy that colour is sound[12] – or, perhaps, it has something to do with music. She could never quite say, though it was not for lack of trying. And she could not ask you back to her room, for it was 'not very clean, I'm afraid,' so she must catch you in the passage, or take a chair in Hyde Park to explain her philosophy. The rhythm of the soul depends on it – ('how rude the little boys are!' she would say) and Mr. Asquith's Irish policy,[13] and Shakespeare comes in, 'and Queen Alexandra[14] most graciously once acknowledged a copy of my pamphlet,' she would say, waving the little boys magnificently away. But she needs funds to publish her book, for 'publishers are capitalists – publishers are cowards.' And so, digging her elbow into her pile of books it fell over.

Jacob remained quite unmoved.

But Fraser, the atheist, on the other side, detesting plush, more than once accosted with leaflets, shifted irritably. He abhorred vagueness – the Christian religion, for example, and old Dean Parker's pronouncements. Dean Parker wrote books and Fraser utterly destroyed them by force of logic and left his children unbaptized – his wife did it secretly in the washing basin – but Fraser ignored her, and went on supporting blasphemers, distributing leaflets, getting up his facts in the British Museum, always in the same check suit and fiery tie, but pale, spotted, irritable. Indeed, what a work – to destroy religion!

Jacob transcribed a whole passage from Marlowe.

Miss Julia Hedge, the feminist,[15] waited for her books. They did not come. She wetted her pen. She looked about her. Her eye was caught by the final letters in Lord Macaulay's name. And she read them all round the dome – the names of great men which remind us— 'Oh damn,' said Julia Hedge, 'why didn't they leave room for an Eliot or a Brontë?'

Unfortunate Julia! wetting her pen in bitterness, and leaving her shoe laces untied. When her books came she applied herself to her gigantic labours, but perceived through one of the nerves of her exasperated sensibility how composedly, unconcernedly, and with every consideration the male readers applied themselves to theirs. That young man for example. What had he got to do except copy out poetry? And she must study statistics. There are more women than men. Yes; but if you let women work as men work, they'll die off much quicker. They'll become extinct. That was her argument. Death and gall and bitter dust were on her pen-tip; and as the afternoon wore on, red had worked into her cheek-bones and a light was in her eyes.

But what brought Jacob Flanders to read Marlowe in the British Museum?

Youth, youth – something savage – something pedantic. For example there is Mr. Masefield, there is Mr. Bennett. Stuff them into the flame of Marlowe[16] and burn them to cinders. Let not a shred remain. Don't palter with the second rate. Detest your own age. Build a better one. And to set that on foot read incredibly dull essays upon Marlowe to your friends. For which purpose one must collate editions in the British Museum. One must do the thing oneself. Useless to trust to the Victorians, who disembowel,[17] or to the living, who are mere publicists. The flesh and blood of the future depends entirely upon six young men.[18] And as Jacob was one of them, no doubt he looked a little regal and pompous as he turned his page, and Julia Hedge disliked him naturally enough.

But then a pudding-faced man[19] pushed a note towards Jacob, and Jacob, leaning back in his chair, began an uneasy murmured conversation, and they went off together (Julia Hedge watched them), and laughed aloud (she thought) directly they were in the hall.

Nobody laughed in the reading-room. There were shiftings, murmurings, apologetic sneezes, and sudden unashamed devastating coughs. The lesson hour was almost over. Ushers were collecting exercises. Lazy children wanted to stretch. Good ones scribbled assiduously – ah, another day over and so little done! And now and then was to be heard from the whole collection of human beings a heavy sigh, after which the humiliating old man would cough shamelessly, and Miss Marchmont hinnied like a horse.

Jacob came back only in time to return his books.

The books were now replaced. A few letters of the alphabet were sprinkled round the dome. Closely stood together in a ring round the dome were Plato, Aristotle, Sophocles, and Shakespeare;[20] the literatures of Rome, Greece, China, India, Persia. One leaf of poetry was pressed flat against another leaf, one burnished letter laid smooth against another in a density of meaning, a conglomeration of loveliness.

'One does want one's tea,' said Miss Marchmont, reclaiming her shabby umbrella.

Miss Marchmont wanted her tea, but could never resist a last look at the Elgin Marbles.[21] She looked at them sideways, waving her hand and muttering a word or two of salutation which made Jacob and the other man turn round. She smiled at them amiably. It all came into her philosophy – that colour is sound, or perhaps it has something to do with music. And having done her service, she hobbled off to tea. It was closing time. The public collected in the hall to receive their umbrellas.

For the most part the students wait their turn very patiently. To stand and wait while some one examines white discs is soothing. The umbrella will certainly be found. But the fact leads you on all day through Macaulay, Hobbes, Gibbon;[22] through octavos, quartos, folios; sinks deeper and deeper through ivory pages and morocco bindings into this density of thought, this conglomeration of knowledge.

Jacob's walking-stick was like all the others; they had muddled the pigeon-holes perhaps.

There is in the British Museum an enormous mind.[23] Consider that Plato is there cheek by jowl with Aristotle; and Shakespeare with Marlowe. This great mind is hoarded beyond the power of any single mind to possess it. Nevertheless (as they take so long finding one's walking-stick) one can't help thinking how one might come with a notebook, sit at a desk, and read it all through. A learned man is the most venerable of all – a man like Huxtable of Trinity, who writes all his letters in Greek,[24] they say, and could have kept his end up with Bentley. And then there is science, pictures, architecture, – an enormous mind.

They pushed the walking-stick across the counter. Jacob stood beneath the porch of the British Museum. It was raining. Great Russell Street[25] was glazed and shining – here yellow, here, outside the chemist's, red and pale blue. People scuttled quickly close to the wall; carriages rattled rather helter-skelter down the streets. Well, but a little rain hurts nobody. Jacob walked off much as if he had been in the country; and late that night there he was sitting at his table with his pipe and his book.

The rain poured down. The British Museum stood in one solid immense mound, very pale, very sleek in the rain, not a quarter of a mile from him. The vast mind was sheeted with stone; and each compartment in the depths of it was safe and dry. The night-watchmen, flashing their lanterns over the backs of Plato and Shakespeare, saw that on the twenty-second of February neither flame, rat, nor burglar was going to violate these treasures – poor, highly respectable men, with wives and families at Kentish Town,[26] do their best for twenty years to protect Plato and Shakespeare, and then are buried at Highgate.[27]

Stone lies solid over the British Museum, as bone lies cool over the visions and heat of the brain. Only here the brain is Plato's brain and Shakespeare's; the brain has made pots and statues, great bulls and little jewels, and crossed the river of death this way and that incessantly, seeking some landing, now wrapping the body well for its long sleep; now laying a penny piece on the eyes; now turning the toes scrupulously to the East. Meanwhile, Plato continues his dialogue; in spite of the rain; in spite of the cab whistles; in spite of the woman in the mews behind Great Ormond Street who has come home drunk and cries all night long, 'Let me in! Let me in!'

In the street below Jacob's room voices were raised.

But he read on. For after all Plato continues imperturbably. And Hamlet utters his soliloquy. And there the Elgin Marbles lie, all night long, old Jones's lantern sometimes recalling Ulysses,[28] or a horse's head; or sometimes a flash of gold, or a mummy's sunk yellow cheek. Plato and Shakespeare continue; and Jacob, who was reading the *Phaedrus*, heard people vociferating round the lamp-post, and the woman battering at the door and crying, 'Let me in!' as if a coal had dropped from the fire, or a fly, falling from the ceiling, had lain on its back, too weak to turn over.

The *Phaedrus* is very difficult.[29] And so, when at length one reads straight ahead, falling into step, marching on, becoming (so it seems) momentarily part of this rolling, imperturbable energy, which has driven darkness before it since Plato walked the Acropolis, it is impossible to see to the fire.

The dialogue draws to its close. Plato's argument is done. Plato's argument is stowed away in Jacob's mind, and for five minutes Jacob's mind continues alone, onwards, into the darkness. Then, getting up, he parted the curtains, and saw, with astonishing clearness, how the Springetts opposite had gone to bed; how it rained; how the Jews and the foreign woman, at the end of the street, stood by the pillar-box, arguing.

Every time the door opened and fresh people came in, those already in the room shifted slightly; those who were standing looked over their shoulders; those who were sitting stopped in the middle of sentences. What with the light, the wine, the strumming of a guitar, something exciting happened each time the door opened. Who was coming in?

'That's Gibson.'

'The painter?'

'But go on with what you were saying.'

They were saying something that was far, far too intimate to be said outright. But the noise of the voices served like a clapper in little Mrs. Withers's mind, scaring into the air flocks of small birds, and then they'd settle, and then she'd feel afraid, put one hand to her hair, bind both round her knees, and look up at Oliver Skelton nervously, and say:

'Promise, *promise*, you'll tell no one.' . . . so considerate he was, so tender. It was her husband's character that she discussed. He was cold, she said.

Down upon them came the splendid Magdalen, brown, warm, voluminous, scarcely brushing the grass with her sandalled feet. Her hair flew; pins seemed scarcely to attach the flying silks. An actress of course, a line of light perpetually beneath her. It was only 'My dear' that she said, but her voice went jodelling between Alpine passes.[30] And down she tumbled on the floor, and sang, since there was nothing to be said, round ah's and oh's. Mangin, the poet, coming up to her, stood looking down at her, drawing at his pipe. The dancing began.

Grey-haired Mrs. Keymer asked Dick Graves to tell her who Mangin was, and said that she had seen too much of this sort of thing in Paris (Magdalen had got upon his knees; now his pipe was in her mouth) to be shocked. 'Who is that?' she said, staying her glasses when they came to Jacob, for indeed he looked quiet, not indifferent, but like some one on a beach, watching.[31]

'Oh, my dear, let me lean on you,' gasped Helen Askew, hopping on one foot, for the silver cord round her ankle had worked loose. Mrs. Keymer turned and looked at the picture on the wall.

'Look at Jacob,' said Helen (they were binding his eyes for some game).

And Dick Graves, being a little drunk, very faithful, and very simple-minded, told her that he thought Jacob the greatest man he had ever known. And down they sat cross-legged upon cushions and talked about Jacob, and Helen's voice trembled, for they both seemed heroes to her, and the friendship between them so much more beautiful than women's friendships.[32] Anthony Pollett now asked her to dance, and as she danced she looked at them, over her shoulder, standing at the table, drinking together.

The magnificent world – the live, sane, vigorous world . . . These words refer to the stretch of wood pavement between Hammersmith and Holborn[33] in January between two and three in the morning. That was the ground beneath Jacob's feet. It was healthy and magnificent because one room, above a mews, somewhere near the river, contained fifty excited, talkative, friendly people. And then to stride over the pavement (there was scarcely a cab or policeman in sight) is of itself exhilarating. The long loop of Piccadilly, diamond-stitched, shows to best advantage when it is empty. A young man has nothing to fear. On the contrary, though he may not have said anything brilliant, he feels pretty confident he can hold his own. He was pleased to have met Mangin; he admired the young woman on the floor; he liked them all; he liked that sort of thing. In short, all the drums and trumpets were sounding. The street scavengers were the only people about at the moment. It is scarcely necessary to say how well-disposed Jacob felt towards them; how it pleased him to let himself in with his latch-key at his own door; how he seemed to bring back with him into the empty room ten or eleven people whom he had not known when he set out; how he looked about for something to read, and found it, and never read it, and fell asleep.

Indeed, drums and trumpets is no phrase. Indeed, Piccadilly and Holborn, and the empty sitting-room and the sitting-room with fifty people in it are liable at any moment to blow music into the air. Women perhaps are more excitable than men. It is seldom that any one says anything about it, and to see the hordes crossing Waterloo Bridge to catch the non-stop to Surbiton one might think that reason impelled them. No, no. It is the drums and trumpets. Only, should you turn aside into one of those little bays on Waterloo Bridge to think the matter over, it will probably seem to you all a muddle – all a mystery.

They cross the Bridge incessantly. Sometimes in the midst of carts and omnibuses a lorry will appear with great forest trees chained to it. Then, perhaps, a mason's van with newly lettered tombstones recording how some one loved some one who is buried at Putney. Then the motor-car in front jerks forward, and the tombstones pass too quick for you to read more. All the time the stream of people never ceases passing from the Surrey side to the Strand; from the Strand to the Surrey side. It seems as if the poor had gone raiding the town, and now trapesed back to their own quarters, like beetles scurrying to their holes, for that old woman fairly hobbles towards Waterloo, grasping a shiny bag, as if she had been out into the light and now made off with some scraped chicken bones to her hovel underground.[34] On the other hand, though the wind is rough and blowing in their faces, those girls there, striding hand in hand, shouting out a song, seem to feel neither cold nor shame. They are hatless. They triumph.

The wind has blown up the waves. The river races beneath us, and the men standing on the barges have to lean all their weight on the tiller. A black tarpaulin is tied down over a swelling load of gold. Avalanches of coal glitter blackly. As usual, painters are slung on planks across the great riverside hotels, and the hotel windows have already points of light in them. On the other side the city is white as if with age; St. Paul's swells white above the fretted, pointed, or oblong buildings beside it. The cross alone shines rosy-gilt. But what century have we reached? Has this procession from the Surrey side to the Strand gone on for ever? That old man has been crossing the Bridge these six hundred years, with the rabble of little boys at his heels, for he is drunk, or blind with misery, and tied round with old clouts of clothing such as pilgrims might have worn. He shuffles on. No one stands still. It seems as if we marched to the sound of music; perhaps the wind and the river; perhaps these same drums and trumpets – the ecstasy and hubbub of the soul. Why, even the unhappy laugh, and the policeman, far from judging the drunk man, surveys him humorously, and the little boys scamper back again, and the clerk from Somerset House has nothing but tolerance for him, and the man who is reading half a page of *Lothair*[35] at the bookstall muses charitably, with his eyes off the print, and the girl hesitates at the crossing and turns on him the bright yet vague glance of the young.

Bright yet vague. She is perhaps twenty-two. She is shabby. She crosses the road and looks at the daffodils and the red tulips in the florist's window. She hesitates, and makes off in the direction of Temple Bar. She walks fast, and yet anything distracts her. Now she seems to see, and now to notice nothing.

X

Through the disused graveyard in the parish of St. Pancras,[1] Fanny
Elmer strayed between the white tombs which lean against the wall,
crossing the grass to read a name, hurrying on when the grave-
keeper approached, hurrying into the street, pausing now by a
window with blue china, now quickly making up for lost time,
abruptly entering a baker's shop, buying rolls, adding cakes, going
on again so that any one wishing to follow must fairly trot. She was
not drably shabby, though. She wore silk stockings, and silver-
buckled shoes, only the red feather in her hat drooped, and the
clasp of her bag was weak, for out fell a copy of Madame Tussaud's[2]
programme as she walked. She had the ankles of a stag. Her face
was hidden. Of course, in this dusk, rapid movements, quick
glances, and soaring hopes come naturally enough. She passed right
beneath Jacob's window.

The house was flat, dark, and silent. Jacob was at home engaged
upon a chess problem, the board being on a stool between his
knees. One hand was fingering the hair at the back of his head. He
slowly brought it forward and raised the white queen from her
square; then put her down again on the same spot. He filled his
pipe; ruminated; moved two pawns; advanced the white knight;
then ruminated with one finger upon the bishop. Now Fanny Elmer
passed beneath the window.

She was on her way to sit to Nick Bramham the painter.

She sat in a flowered Spanish shawl, holding in her hand a yellow
novel. [3]

'A little lower, a little looser, so – better, that's right,' Bramham
mumbled, who was drawing her, and smoking at the same time,
and was naturally speechless. His head might have been the work of
a sculptor, who had squared the forehead, stretched the mouth, and
left marks of his thumbs and streaks from his fingers in the clay.
But the eyes had never been shut. They were rather prominent, and

rather bloodshot, as if from staring and staring, and when he spoke they looked for a second disturbed, but went on staring. An unshaded electric light hung above her head.

As for the beauty of women, it is like the light on the sea, never constant to a single wave. They all have it; they all lose it. Now she is dull and thick as bacon; now transparent as a hanging glass. The fixed faces are the dull ones. Here comes Lady Venice displayed like a monument for admiration, but carved in alabaster, to be set on the mantelpiece and never dusted. A dapper brunette complete from head to foot serves only as an illustration to lie upon the drawing-room table. The women in the streets have the faces of playing cards;[4] the outlines accurately filled in with pink and yellow, and the line drawn tightly round them. Then, at a top-floor window, leaning out, looking down, you see beauty itself; or in the corner of an omnibus; or squatted in a ditch — beauty glowing, suddenly expressive, withdrawn the moment after. No one can count on it or seize it or have it wrapped in paper. Nothing is to be won from the shops, and Heaven knows it would be better to sit at home than haunt the plate-glass windows in the hope of lifting the shining green, the glowing ruby, out of them alive. Sea glass in a saucer loses its lustre no sooner than silks do. Thus if you talk of a beautiful woman you mean only something flying fast which for a second uses the eyes, lips, or cheeks of Fanny Elmer, for example, to glow through.

She was not beautiful, as she sat stiffly; her underlip too prominent; her nose too large; her eyes too near together. She was a thin girl, with brilliant cheeks and dark hair, sulky just now, or stiff with sitting. When Bramham snapped his stick of charcoal she started. Bramham was out of temper. He squatted before the gas fire warming his hands. Meanwhile she looked at his drawing. He grunted. Fanny threw on a dressing-gown and boiled a kettle.

'By God, it's bad,' said Bramham.

Fanny dropped on to the floor, clasped her hands round her knees, and looked at him, her beautiful eyes — yes, beauty, flying through the room, shone there for a second. Fanny's eyes seemed to question, to commiserate, to be, for a second, love itself. But she exaggerated. Bramham noticed nothing. And when the kettle boiled, up she scrambled, more like a colt or a puppy than a loving woman.

Now Jacob walked over to the window and stood with his hands in his pockets. Mr. Springett opposite came out, looked at his shop window, and went in again. The children drifted past, eyeing the pink sticks of sweetstuff. Pickford's van swung down the street. A small boy twirled from a rope. Jacob turned away. Two minutes later he opened the front door, and walked off in the direction of Holborn.

Fanny Elmer took down her cloak from the hook. Nick Bramham unpinned his drawing and rolled it under his arm. They turned out the lights and set off down the street, holding on their way through all the people, motor-cars, omnibuses, carts, until they reached Leicester Square, five minutes before Jacob reached it, for his way was slightly longer, and he had been stopped by a block in Holborn waiting to see the King drive by, so that Nick and Fanny were already leaning over the barrier in the promenade at the Empire[5] when Jacob pushed through the swing doors and took his place beside them.

'Hullo, never noticed you,' said Nick five minutes later.

'Bloody rot,' said Jacob.

'Miss Elmer,' said Nick.

Jacob took his pipe out of his mouth very awkwardly.

Very awkward he was. And when they sat upon a plush sofa and let the smoke go up between them and the stage, and heard far off the high-pitched voices and the jolly orchestra breaking in opportunely he was still awkward, only Fanny thought: 'What a beautiful voice!' She thought how little he said yet how firm it was. She thought how young men are dignified and aloof, and how unconscious they are, and how quietly one might sit beside Jacob and look at him. And how childlike he would be, come in tired of an evening, she thought, and how majestic; a little overbearing perhaps; 'But I wouldn't give way,' she thought. He got up and leant over the barrier. The smoke hung about him.

And for ever the beauty of young men seems to be set in smoke, however lustily they chase footballs, or drive cricket balls, dance, run, or stride along roads. Possibly they are soon to lose it. Possibly they look into the eyes of far-away heroes, and take their station among us half contemptuously, she thought (vibrating like a fiddle-string, to be played on and snapped). Anyhow, they love silence, and speak beautifully, each word falling like a disc new cut, not a hubble-bubble of small smooth coins such as girls use; and they move decidedly, as if they knew how long to stay and when to go – oh, but Mr. Flanders was only gone to get a programme.

'The dancers come right at the end,' he said, coming back to them.

And isn't it pleasant, Fanny went on thinking, how young men bring out lots of silver coins from their trouser-pockets, and look at them, instead of having just so many in a purse?

Then there she was herself, whirling across the stage in white flounces, and the music was the dance and fling of her own soul, and the whole machinery, rock and gear of the world was spun smoothly into those swift eddies and falls, she felt, as she stood rigid leaning over the barrier two feet from Jacob Flanders.

Her screwed-up black glove dropped to the floor.[6] When Jacob gave it her, she started angrily. For never was there a more irrational passion. And Jacob was afraid of her for a moment – so violent, so dangerous is it when young women stand rigid; grasp the barrier; fall in love.

It was the middle of February. The roofs of Hampstead Garden Suburb[7] lay in a tremulous haze. It was too hot to walk. A dog barked, barked, barked down in the hollow. The liquid shadows went over the plain.

The body after long illness is languid, passive, receptive of sweetness, but too weak to contain it. The tears well and fall as the dog barks in the hollow, the children skim after hoops, the country darkens and brightens. Beyond a veil it seems. Ah, but draw the veil thicker lest I faint with sweetness, Fanny Elmer sighed, as she sat on a bench in Judges Walk looking at Hampstead Garden Suburb. But the dog went on barking. The motor-cars hooted on the road. She heard a far-away rush and humming. Agitation was at her heart. Up she got and walked. The grass was freshly green; the sun hot. All round the pond children were stooping to launch little boats; or were drawn back screaming by their nurses.

At mid-day young women walk out into the air. All the men are busy in the town. They stand by the edge of the blue pond. The fresh wind scatters the children's voices all about. *My* children, thought Fanny Elmer. The women stand round the pond, beating off great prancing shaggy dogs. Gently the baby is rocked in the perambulator. The eyes of all the nurses, mothers, and wandering women are a little glazed,[8] absorbed. They gently nod instead of answering when the little boys tug at their skirts, begging them to move on.

And Fanny moved, hearing some cry – a workman's whistle perhaps – high in mid air. Now, among the trees, it was the thrush trilling out into the warm air a flutter of jubilation, but fear seemed to spur him, Fanny thought; as if he too were anxious with such joy at his heart – as if he were watched as he sang, and pressed by tumult to sing. There! Restless, he flew to the next tree. She heard his song more faintly. Beyond it was the humming of the wheels and the wind rushing.

She spent tenpence on lunch.

'Dear, miss, she's left her umberella,' grumbled the mottled woman in the glass box near the door at the Express Dairy Company's shop.[9]

'Perhaps I'll catch her,' answered Milly Edwards, the waitress with the pale plaits of hair; and she dashed through the door.

'No good,' she said, coming back a moment later with Fanny's cheap umbrella. She put her hand to her plaits.

'Oh, that door!' grumbled the cashier.

Her hands were cased in black mittens, and the finger-tips that drew in the paper slips were swollen as sausages.

'Pie and greens for one. Large coffee and crumpets. Eggs on toast. Two fruit cakes.'

Thus the sharp voices of the waitresses snapped. The lunchers heard their orders repeated with approval; saw the next table served with anticipation. Their own eggs on toast were at last delivered. Their eyes strayed no more.

Damp cubes of pastry fell into mouths opened like triangular bags.

Nelly Jenkinson, the typist, crumbled her cake indifferently enough. Every time the door opened she looked up. What did she expect to see?

The coal merchant read the *Telegraph*[10] without stopping, missed the saucer, and, feeling abstractedly, put the cup down on the table-cloth.

'Did you ever hear the like of that for impertinence?' Mrs. Parsons wound up, brushing the crumbs from her furs.

'Hot milk and scone for one. Pot of tea. Roll and butter,' cried the waitresses.

The door opened and shut.

Such is the life of the elderly.

It is curious, lying in a boat, to watch the waves. Here are three coming regularly one after another, all much of a size. Then, hurrying after them comes a fourth, very large and menacing; it lifts the boat; on it goes; somehow merges without accomplishing anything; flattens itself out with the rest.

What can be more violent than the fling of boughs in a gale, the tree yielding itself all up the trunk, to the very tip of the branch, streaming and shuddering the way the wind blows, yet never flying in dishevelment away?

The corn squirms and abases itself as if preparing to tug itself free from the roots, and yet is tied down.

Why, from the very windows, even in the dusk, you see a swelling run through the street, an aspiration, as with arms outstretched, eyes desiring, mouths agape. And then we peaceably subside. For if the exaltation lasted we should be blown like foam into the air. The stars would shine through us. We should go down the gale in salt drops – as sometimes happens. For the impetuous spirits will have none of this cradling. Never any swaying or aimlessly lolling for them. Never any making believe, or lying cosily, or genially supposing that one is much like another, fire warm, wine pleasant, extravagance a sin.

'People are so nice, once you know them.'

'I couldn't think ill of her. One must remember—' But Nick perhaps, or Fanny Elmer, believing implicitly in the truth of the moment, fling off, sting the cheek, are gone like sharp hail.

'Oh,' said Fanny, bursting into the studio three-quarters of an hour late because she had been hanging about the neighbourhood of the Foundling Hospital [11] merely for the chance of seeing Jacob walk down the street, take out his latch-key, and open the door, 'I'm afraid I'm late'; upon which Nick said nothing and Fanny grew defiant.

'I'll never come again!' she cried at length.

'Don't, then,' Nick replied, and off she ran without so much as good-night.

How exquisite it was – that dress in Evelina's shop off Shaftesbury Avenue! It was four o'clock on a fine day early in April, and was Fanny one to spend four o'clock on a fine day indoors? Other girls in that very street sat over ledgers, or drew long threads wearily between silk and gauze; or, festooned with ribbons in Swan and Edgars,[12] rapidly added up pence and farthings on the back of the bill and twisted the yard and three-quarters in tissue paper and asked 'Your pleasure?' of the next comer.

In Evelina's shop off Shaftesbury Avenue the parts of a woman were shown separate.[13] In the left hand was her skirt. Twining round a pole in the middle was a feather boa. Ranged like the heads of malefactors on Temple Bar were hats – emerald and white, lightly wreathed or drooping beneath deep-dyed feathers. And on the carpet were her feet – pointed gold, or patent leather slashed with scarlet.

Feasted upon by the eyes of women, the clothes by four o'clock were flyblown like sugar cakes in a baker's window. Fanny eyed them too.

But coming along Gerrard Street was a tall man in a shabby coat. A shadow fell across Evelina's window – Jacob's shadow, though it was not Jacob. And Fanny turned and walked along Gerrard Street and wished that she had read books. Nick never read books, never talked of Ireland, or the House of Lords; and as for his finger-nails! She would learn Latin and read Virgil. She had been a great reader. She had read Scott; she had read Dumas.[14] At the Slade no one read. But no one knew Fanny at the Slade, or guessed how empty it seemed to her; the passion for ear-rings, for dances, for Tonks and Steer[15] – when it was only the French who could paint, Jacob said. For the moderns were futile; painting the least respectable of the arts; and why read anything but Marlowe and Shakespeare, Jacob said, and Fielding if you must read novels?

'Fielding,' said Fanny, when the man in Charing Cross Road asked her what book she wanted.

She bought *Tom Jones*.[16]

At ten o'clock in the morning, in a room which she shared with a school teacher, Fanny Elmer read *Tom Jones* – that mystic book. For this dull stuff (Fanny thought) about people with odd names is what Jacob likes. Good people like it. Dowdy women who don't mind how they cross their legs read *Tom Jones* – a mystic book; for there is something, Fanny thought, about books which if I had been educated I could have liked – much better than ear-rings and flowers, she sighed, thinking of the corridors at the Slade and the fancy-dress dance next week. She had nothing to wear.

They are real, thought Fanny Elmer, setting her feet on the mantelpiece. Some people are. Nick perhaps, only he was so stupid. And women never – except Miss Sargent,[17] but she went off at lunch-time and gave herself airs. There they sat quietly of a night, reading, she thought. Not going to music-halls; not looking in at shop windows; not wearing each other's clothes, like Robertson who had worn her shawl, and she had worn his waistcoat, which Jacob could only do very awkwardly; for he liked *Tom Jones*.

There it lay on her lap, in double columns, price three and sixpence; the mystic book in which Henry Fielding ever so many years ago rebuked Fanny Elmer for feasting on scarlet, in perfect prose, Jacob said. For he never read modern novels. He liked *Tom Jones*.

'I do like *Tom Jones*,' said Fanny at five-thirty that same day early in April when Jacob took out his pipe in the arm-chair opposite.

Alas, women lie! But not Clara Durrant. A flawless mind; a candid nature; a virgin chained to a rock (somewhere off Lowndes

Square) eternally pouring out tea for old men in white waistcoats, blue-eyed, looking you straight in the face, playing Bach. Of all women, Jacob honoured her most. But to sit at a table with bread and butter, with dowagers in velvet, and never say more to Clara Durrant than Benson said to the parrot when old Miss Perry poured out tea, was an insufferable outrage upon the liberties and decencies of human nature – or words to that effect. For Jacob said nothing. Only he glared at the fire. Fanny laid down *Tom Jones*.

She stitched or knitted.

'What's that?' asked Jacob.

'For the dance at the Slade.'

And she fetched her head-dress; her trousers; her shoes with red tassels. What should she wear?

'I shall be in Paris,' said Jacob.

And what is the point of fancy-dress dances? thought Fanny. You meet the same people; you wear the same clothes; Mangin gets drunk; Florinda sits on his knee. She flirts outrageously – with Nick Bramham just now.

'In Paris?' said Fanny.

'On my way to Greece,' he replied.

For, he said, there is nothing so detestable as London in May.

He would forget her.

A sparrow flew past the window trailing a straw – a straw from a stack stood by a barn in a farmyard. The old brown spaniel snuffs at the base for a rat. Already the upper branches of the elm trees are blotted with nests. The chestnuts have flirted their fans. And the butterflies are flaunting across the rides in the Forest. Perhaps the Purple Emperor is feasting, as Morris says, upon a mass of putrid carrion at the base of an oak tree.

Fanny thought it all came from *Tom Jones*. He could go alone with a book in his pocket and watch the badgers. He would take a train at eight-thirty and walk all night. He saw fire-flies, and brought back glow-worms in pill-boxes. He would hunt with the New Forest Staghounds. It all came from *Tom Jones*; and he would go to Greece with a book in his pocket and forget her.

She fetched her hand-glass. There was her face. And suppose one wreathed Jacob in a turban? There was his face. She lit the lamp. But as the daylight came through the window only half was lit up by the lamp. And though he looked terrible and magnificent and would chuck the Forest, he said, and come to the Slade, and be a Turkish knight or a Roman emperor (and he let her blacken his lips and clenched his teeth and scowled in the glass), still — there lay *Tom Jones*.

XI

'Archer,' said Mrs. Flanders with that tenderness which mothers so often display towards their eldest sons, 'will be at Gibraltar to-morrow.'

The post for which she was waiting (strolling up Dods Hill while the random church bells swung a hymn tune about her head, the clock striking four straight through the circling notes; the grass purpling under a storm-cloud; and the two dozen houses of the village cowering, infinitely humble, in company under a leaf of shadow), the post, with all its variety of messages, envelopes addressed in bold hands, in slanting hands, stamped now with English stamps, again with Colonial stamps, or sometimes hastily dabbed with a yellow bar,[1] the post was about to scatter a myriad messages over the world. Whether we gain or not by this habit of profuse communication it is not for us to say. But that letter-writing is practised mendaciously nowadays, particularly by young men travelling in foreign parts, seems likely enough.

For example, take this scene.

Here was Jacob Flanders gone abroad and staying to break his journey in Paris. (Old Miss Birkbeck, his mother's cousin, had died last June and left him a hundred pounds.)

'You needn't repeat the whole damned thing over again, Crut-tendon,' said Mallinson, the little bald painter who was sitting at a marble table, splashed with coffee and ringed with wine, talking very fast, and undoubtedly more than a little drunk.

'Well, Flanders, finished writing to your lady?' said Cruttendon, as Jacob came and took his seat beside them, holding in his hand an envelope addressed to Mrs. Flanders, near Scarborough, England.

'Do you uphold Velazquez?'[2] said Cruttendon.

'By God, he does,' said Mallinson.

'He always gets like this,' said Cruttendon irritably.

Jacob looked at Mallinson with excessive composure.

'I'll tell you the three greatest things that were ever written in the whole of literature,' Cruttendon burst out. '"Hang there like fruit my soul,"' he began . . .

'Don't listen to a man who don't like Velazquez,' said Mallinson.

'Adolphe, don't give Mr. Mallinson any more wine,' said Cruttendon.

'Fair play, fair play,' said Jacob judicially. 'Let a man get drunk if he likes. That's Shakespeare, Cruttendon. I'm with you there. Shakespeare had more guts than all these damned frogs put together. "Hang there like fruit my soul,"[3] he began quoting, in a musical rhetorical voice, flourishing his wine-glass. 'The devil damn you black, you cream-faced loon!'[4] he exclaimed as the wine washed over the rim.

'"Hang there like fruit my soul,"' Cruttendon and Jacob both began again at the same moment, and burst out laughing.

'Curse these flies,' said Mallinson, flicking at his bald head. 'What do they take me for?'

'Something sweet-smelling,' said Cruttendon.

'Shut up, Cruttendon,' said Jacob. 'The fellow has no manners,' he explained to Mallinson very politely. 'Wants to cut people off their drink. Look here. I want grilled bone. What's the French for grilled bone? Grilled bone, Adolphe. Now you juggins, don't you understand?'

'And I'll tell you, Flanders, the second most beautiful thing in the whole of literature,' said Cruttendon, bringing his feet down on to the floor, and leaning right across the table, so that his face almost touched Jacob's face.

'"Hey diddle diddle, the cat and the fiddle,"[5] Mallinson interrupted, strumming his fingers on the table. 'The most ex-qui-sitely beautiful thing in the whole of literature . . . Cruttendon is a very good fellow,' he remarked confidentially. 'But he's a bit of a fool.' And he jerked his head forward.

Well, not a word of this was ever told to Mrs. Flanders; nor what happened when they paid the bill and left the restaurant, and walked along the Boulevard Raspail.

* *

Then here is another scrap of conversation; the time about eleven in the morning; the scene a studio; and the day Sunday.

'I tell you, Flanders,' said Cruttendon, 'I'd as soon have one of Mallinson's little pictures as a Chardin. And when I say that . . .' he squeezed the tail of an emaciated tube . . . 'Chardin was a great swell . . . He sells 'em to pay his dinner now. But wait till the dealers get hold of him. A great swell – oh, a very great swell.'

'It's an awfully pleasant life,' said Jacob, 'messing away up here. Still, it's a stupid art, Cruttendon.' He wandered off across the room. 'There's this man, Pierre Louÿs⁶ now.' He took up a book.

'Now my good sir, are you going to settle down?' said Cruttendon.

'That's a solid piece of work,' said Jacob, standing a canvas on a chair.

'Oh, that I did ages ago,' said Cruttendon, looking over his shoulder.

'You're a pretty competent painter in my opinion,' said Jacob after a time.

'Now if you'd like to see what I'm after at the present moment,' said Cruttendon, putting a canvas before Jacob. 'There. That's it. That's more like it. That's . . .' he squirmed his thumb in a circle round a lamp globe painted white.

'A pretty solid piece of work,' said Jacob, straddling his legs in front of it. 'But what I wish you'd explain . . .'

Miss Jinny Carslake, pale, freckled, morbid, came into the room.

'Oh Jinny, here's a friend. Flanders. An Englishman. Wealthy. Highly connected. Go on, Flanders . . .'

Jacob said nothing.

'It's *that* – that's not right,' said Jinny Carslake.

'No,' said Cruttendon decidedly. 'Can't be done.'

He took the canvas off the chair and stood it on the floor with its back to them.

'Sit down, ladies and gentlemen. Miss Carslake comes from your part of the world, Flanders. From Devonshire. Oh, I thought you said Devonshire. Very well. She's a daughter of the church too. The black sheep of the family. Her mother writes her such letters. I say

– have you one about you? It's generally Sundays they come. Sort
of church-bell effect, you know.'

'Have you met all the painter men?' said Jinny. 'Was Mallinson
drunk? If you go to his studio he'll give you one of his pictures. I
say, Teddy . . .'

'Half a jiff,'[7] said Cruttendon. 'What's the season of the year?' He
looked out of the window.

'We take a day off on Sundays, Flanders.'

'Will he . . . ' said Jinny, looking at Jacob. 'You . . .'

'Yes, he'll come with us,' said Cruttendon.

And then, here is Versailles.[8]

Jinny stood on the stone rim and leant over the pond, clasped by
Cruttendon's arms or she would have fallen in. 'There! There!' she
cried. 'Right up to the top!' Some sluggish, sloping-shouldered fish
had floated up from the depths to nip her crumbs. 'You look,' she
said, jumping down. And then the dazzling white water, rough and
throttled, shot up into the air. The fountain spread itself. Through
it came the sound of military music far away. All the water was puck-
ered with drops. A blue air-ball[9] gently bumped the surface. How
all the nurses and children and old men and young crowded to the
edge, leant over and waved their sticks! The little girl ran stretching
her arms towards her air-ball, but it sank beneath the fountain.

Edward Cruttendon, Jinny Carslake, and Jacob Flanders walked in
a row along the yellow gravel path; got on to the grass; so passed
under the trees; and came out at the summer-house where Marie
Antoinette used to drink chocolate. In went Edward and Jinny, but
Jacob waited outside, sitting on the handle of his walking-stick.
Out they came again.

'Well?' said Cruttendon, smiling at Jacob.

Jinny waited; Edward waited; and both looked at Jacob.

'Well?' said Jacob, smiling and pressing both hands on his stick.

'Come along,' he decided; and started off. The others followed
him, smiling.

* *

And then they went to the little café in the by-street where people sit drinking coffee, watching the soldiers, meditatively knocking ashes into trays.

'But he's quite different,' said Jinny, folding her hands over the top of her glass. 'I don't suppose you know what Ted means when he says a thing like that,' she said, looking at Jacob. 'But I do. Sometimes I could kill myself. Sometimes he lies in bed all day long – just lies there . . . I don't want you right on the table'; she waved her hands. Swollen iridescent pigeons were waddling round their feet.

'Look at that woman's hat,' said Cruttendon. 'How do they come to think of it? . . . No, Flanders, I don't think I could live like you. When one walks down that street opposite the British Museum – what's it called? – that's what I mean. It's all like that. Those fat women – and the man standing in the middle of the road as if he were going to have a fit . . .'

'Everybody feeds them,' said Jinny, waving the pigeons away. 'They're stupid old things.'

'Well, I don't know,' said Jacob, smoking his cigarette. 'There's St. Paul's.'

'I mean going to an office,' said Cruttendon.

'Hang it all,' Jacob expostulated.

'But you don't count,' said Jinny, looking at Cruttendon. 'You're mad. I mean, you just think of painting.'

'Yes, I know. I can't help it. I say, will King George give way about the peers?'[10]

'He'll jolly well have to,' said Jacob.

'There!' said Jinny. 'He really knows.'

'You see, I would if I could,' said Cruttendon, 'but I simply can't.'

'I *think* I could,' said Jinny. 'Only, it's all the people one dislikes who do it. At home, I mean. They talk of nothing else. Even people like my mother.'

'Now if I came and lived here—' said Jacob. 'What's my share, Cruttendon? Oh, very well. Have it your own way. Those silly birds, directly one wants them – they've flown away.'

And finally under the arc lamps in the Gare des Invalides, with one

of those queer movements which are so slight yet so definite, which
may wound or pass unnoticed but generally inflict a good deal of
discomfort, Jinny and Cruttendon drew together; Jacob stood apart.
They had to separate. Something must be said. Nothing was said. A
man wheeled a trolley past Jacob's legs so near that he almost
grazed them. When Jacob recovered his balance the other two were
turning away, though Jinny looked over her shoulder, and Cruttendon, waving his hand, disappeared like the very great genius that
he was.

No – Mrs. Flanders was told none of this, though Jacob felt, it is
safe to say, that nothing in the world was of greater importance;
and as for Cruttendon and Jinny, he thought them the most remarkable people he had ever met – being of course unable to foresee
how it fell out in the course of time that Cruttendon took to
painting orchards; had therefore to live in Kent; and must, one
would think, see through apple blossom by this time, since his wife,
for whose sake he did it, eloped with a novelist; but no; Cruttendon
still paints orchards, savagely, in solitude. Then Jinny Carslake,
after her affair with Lefanu the American painter, frequented Indian
philosophers, and now you find her in pensions in Italy cherishing a
little jeweller's box containing ordinary pebbles picked off the road.
But if you look at them steadily, she says, multiplicity becomes
unity, which is somehow the secret of life, though it does not
prevent her from following the macaroni as it goes round the table,
and sometimes, on spring nights, she makes the strangest confidences to shy young Englishmen.

Jacob had nothing to hide from his mother. It was only that he
could make no sense himself of his extraordinary excitement, and as
for writing it down—

'Jacob's letters are so like him,' said Mrs. Jarvis, folding the
sheet.

'Indeed he seems to be having . . .' said Mrs. Flanders, and paused,
for she was cutting out a dress and had to straighten the pattern,
'. . . a very gay time.'

Mrs. Jarvis thought of Paris. At her back the window was open, for it was a mild night; a calm night; when the moon seemed muffled and the apple trees stood perfectly still.

'I never pity the dead,' said Mrs. Jarvis, shifting the cushion at her back, and clasping her hands behind her head. Betty Flanders did not hear, for her scissors made so much noise on the table.

'They are at rest,' said Mrs. Jarvis. 'And we spend our days doing foolish unnecessary things without knowing why.'

Mrs. Jarvis was not liked in the village.

'You never walk at this time of night?' she asked Mrs. Flanders.

'It is certainly wonderfully mild,' said Mrs. Flanders.

Yet it was years since she had opened the orchard gate and gone out on Dods Hill after dinner.

'It is perfectly dry,' said Mrs. Jarvis, as they shut the orchard door and stepped on to the turf.

'I shan't go far,' said Betty Flanders. 'Yes, Jacob will leave Paris on Wednesday.'

'Jacob was always my friend of the three,' said Mrs. Jarvis.

'Now, my dear, I am going no further,' said Mrs. Flanders. They had climbed the dark hill and reached the Roman camp.

The rampart rose at their feet – the smooth circle surrounding the camp or the grave. How many needles Betty Flanders had lost there! and her garnet brooch.[11]

'It is much clearer than this sometimes,' said Mrs. Jarvis, standing upon the ridge. There were no clouds, and yet there was a haze over the sea, and over the moors. The lights of Scarborough flashed, as if a woman wearing a diamond necklace turned her head this way and that.

'How quiet it is!' said Mrs. Jarvis.

Mrs. Flanders rubbed the turf with her toe, thinking of her garnet brooch.

Mrs. Jarvis found it difficult to think of herself to-night. It was so calm. There was no wind; nothing racing, flying, escaping. Black shadows stood still over the silver moors. The furze bushes stood perfectly still. Neither did Mrs. Jarvis think of God. There was a church behind them, of course. The church clock struck ten. Did the strokes reach the furze bush, or did the thorn tree hear them?

Mrs. Flanders was stooping down to pick up a pebble. Sometimes people do find things, Mrs. Jarvis thought, and yet in this hazy moonlight it was impossible to see anything, except bones, and little pieces of chalk.

'Jacob bought it with his own money, and then I brought Mr. Parker up to see the view, and it must have dropped—' Mrs. Flanders murmured.

Did the bones stir, or the rusty swords? Was Mrs. Flanders's twopenny-halfpenny brooch for ever part of the rich accumulation? and if all the ghosts flocked thick and rubbed shoulders with Mrs. Flanders in the circle, would she not have seemed perfectly in her place, a live English matron, growing stout?

The clock struck the quarter.

The frail waves of sound broke among the stiff gorse and the hawthorn twigs as the church clock divided time into quarters.

Motionless and broad-backed the moors received the statement 'It is fifteen minutes past the hour,' but made no answer, unless a bramble stirred.

Yet even in this light the legends on the tombstones could be read, brief voices saying, 'I am Bertha Ruck,' 'I am Tom Gage.'[12] And they say which day of the year they died, and the New Testament says something for them, very proud, very emphatic, or consoling.

The moors accept all that too.

The moonlight falls like a pale page upon the church wall, and illumines the kneeling family in the niche, and the tablet set up in 1780 to the Squire of the parish who relieved the poor, and believed in God – so the measured voice goes on down the marble scroll, as though it could impose itself upon time and the open air.

Now a fox steals out from behind the gorse bushes.

Often, even at night, the church seems full of people. The pews are worn and greasy, and the cassocks in place, and the hymn-books on the ledges. It is a ship with all its crew aboard. The timbers strain to hold the dead and the living, the ploughmen, the carpenters, the fox-hunting gentlemen and the farmers smelling of mud and brandy. Their tongues join together in syllabling the sharp-cut words, which for ever slice asunder time and the broad-backed moors. Plaint and belief and elegy, despair and triumph, but for the most part good sense and jolly indifference, go trampling out of the windows any time these five hundred years.

Still, as Mrs. Jarvis said, stepping out on to the moors, 'How quiet it is!' Quiet at mid-day, except when the hunt scatters across it; quiet in the afternoon, save for the drifting sheep; at night the moor is perfectly quiet.

A garnet brooch has dropped into its grass. A fox pads stealthily. A leaf turns on its edge. Mrs. Jarvis, who is fifty years of age, reposes in the camp in the hazy moonlight.

'. . . and,' said Mrs. Flanders, straightening her back, 'I never cared for Mr. Parker.'

'Neither did I,' said Mrs. Jarvis. They began to walk home.

But their voices floated for a little above the camp. The moonlight destroyed nothing. The moor accepted everything. Tom Gage cries aloud so long as his tombstone endures. The Roman skeletons are in safe keeping. Betty Flanders's darning needles are safe too and her garnet brooch. And sometimes at mid-day, in the sunshine, the moor seems to hoard these little treasures, like a nurse. But at midnight when no one speaks or gallops, and the thorn tree is perfectly still, it would be foolish to vex the moor with questions — what? and why?

The church clock, however, strikes twelve.

XII

The water fell off a ledge like lead – like a chain with thick white links. The train ran out into a steep green meadow, and Jacob saw striped tulips growing and heard a bird singing, in Italy.

A motor-car full of Italian officers ran along the flat road and kept up with the train, raising dust behind it. There were trees laced together with vines – as Virgil said.[1] Here was a station; and a tremendous leave-taking going on, with women in high yellow boots and odd pale boys in ringed socks. Virgil's bees had gone about the plains of Lombardy.[2] It was the custom of the ancients to train vines between elms. Then at Milan there were sharp-winged hawks, of a bright brown, cutting figures over the roofs.

These Italian carriages get damnably hot with the afternoon sun on them, and the chances are that before the engine has pulled to the top of the gorge the clanking chain will have broken. Up, up, up, it goes, like a train on a scenic railway. Every peak is covered with sharp trees, and amazing white villages are crowded on ledges. There is always a white tower on the very summit, flat red-frilled roofs, and a sheer drop beneath. It is not a country in which one walks after tea. For one thing there is no grass. A whole hillside will be ruled with olive trees. Already in April the earth is clotted into dry dust between them. And there are neither stiles nor footpaths, nor lanes chequered with the shadows of leaves nor eighteenth-century inns with bow-windows, where one eats ham and eggs. Oh no, Italy is all fierceness, bareness, exposure, and black priests shuffling along the roads. It is strange, too, how you never get away from villas.

Still, to be travelling on one's own with a hundred pounds to spend is a fine affair. And if his money gave out, as it probably would, he would go on foot. He could live on bread and wine – the wine in straw bottles – for after doing Greece he was going to knock off Rome. The Roman civilization was a very inferior affair, no doubt. But Bonamy talked a lot of rot, all the same. 'You ought to have been in Athens,' he would say to Bonamy when he got back. 'Standing on the Parthenon,' he would say, or 'The ruins of the Coliseum suggest some fairly sublime reflections,' which he would write out at length in letters. It might turn to an essay upon civilization. A comparison between the ancients and moderns, with some pretty sharp hits at Mr. Asquith – something in the style of Gibbon.[3]

A stout gentleman laboriously hauled himself in, dusty, baggy, slung with gold chains, and Jacob, regretting that he did not come of the Latin race, looked out of the window.

It is a strange reflection that by travelling two days and nights you are in the heart of Italy. Accidental villas among olive trees appear; and men-servants watering the cactuses. Black victorias[4] drive in between pompous pillars with plaster shields stuck to them. It is at once momentary and astonishingly intimate – to be displayed before the eyes of a foreigner. And there is a lonely hill-top where no one ever comes, and yet it is seen by me who was lately driving down Piccadilly on an omnibus. And what I should like would be to get out among the fields, sit down and hear the grasshoppers, and take up a handful of earth – Italian earth, as this is Italian dust upon my shoes.

Jacob heard them crying strange names at railway stations through the night. The train stopped and he heard frogs croaking close by, and he wrinkled back the blind cautiously and saw a vast strange marsh all white in the moonlight. The carriage was thick with cigar smoke, which floated round the globe with the green shade on it. The Italian gentleman lay snoring with his boots off and his waistcoat unbuttoned . . . And all this business of going to Greece seemed to Jacob an intolerable weariness – sitting in hotels by oneself and looking at monuments – he'd have done better to go to Cornwall[5] with Timmy Durrant . . . 'Oh–h,' Jacob protested, as the darkness began breaking in front of him and the light showed through, but the man was reaching across him to get something – the fat Italian man in his dicky, unshaven, crumpled, obese, was opening the door and going off to have a wash.

So Jacob sat up, and saw a lean Italian sportsman with a gun walking down the road in the early morning light, and the whole idea of the Parthenon came upon him in a clap.

'By Jove!' he thought, 'we must be nearly there!' and he stuck his head out of the window and got the air full in his face.

It is highly exasperating that twenty-five people of your acquaintance should be able to say straight off something very much to the point about being in Greece, while for yourself there is a stopper upon all emotions whatsoever. For after washing at the hotel at Patras, Jacob had followed the tram lines a mile or so out; and followed them a mile or so back; he had met several droves of turkeys; several strings of donkeys; had got lost in back streets; had read advertisements of corsets and of Maggi's consommé; children had trodden on his toes; the place smelt of bad cheese; and he was glad to find himself suddenly come out opposite his hotel. There was an old copy of the *Daily Mail*[6] lying among coffee-cups; which he read. But what could he do after dinner?

No doubt we should be, on the whole, much worse off than we are without our astonishing gift for illusion. At the age of twelve or so, having given up dolls and broken our steam engines, France, but much more probably Italy, and India almost for a certainty, draws the superfluous imagination. One's aunts have been to Rome; and every one has an uncle who was last heard of – poor man – in Rangoon. He will never come back any more. But it is the governesses who start the Greek myth. Look at that for a head (they say) – nose, you see, straight as a dart, curls, eyebrows – everything appropriate to manly beauty; while his legs and arms have lines on them which indicate a perfect degree of development – the Greeks caring for the body as much as for the face. And the Greeks could paint fruit so that birds pecked at it. First you read Xenophon; then Euripides. One day – that was an occasion, by God – what people have said appears to have sense in it; 'the Greek spirit'; the Greek this, that, and the other; though it is absurd, by the way, to say that any Greek comes near Shakespeare. The point is, however, that we have been brought up in an illusion.

Jacob, no doubt, thought something in this fashion, the *Daily Mail* crumpled in his hand; his legs extended; the very picture of boredom.

'But it's the way we're brought up,' he went on.

And it all seemed to him very distasteful. Something ought to be done about it. And from being moderately depressed he became like a man about to be executed. Clara Durrant had left him at a party to talk to an American called Pilchard.[7] And he had come all the way to Greece and left her. They wore evening-dresses, and talked nonsense – what damned nonsense – and he put out his hand for the *Globe Trotter*, an international magazine which is supplied free of charge to the proprietors of hotels.

In spite of its ramshackle condition modern Greece is highly advanced in the electric tramway system, so that while Jacob sat in the hotel sitting-room the trams clanked, chimed, rang, rang, rang imperiously to get the donkeys out of the way, and one old woman who refused to budge, beneath the windows. The whole of civilization was being condemned.

The waiter was quite indifferent to that too. Aristotle, a dirty man, carnivorously interested in the body of the only guest now occupying the only arm-chair, came into the room ostentatiously, put something down, put something straight, and saw that Jacob was still there.

'I shall want to be called early to-morrow,' said Jacob, over his shoulder. 'I am going to Olympia.'

This gloom, this surrender to the dark waters which lap us about, is a modern invention. Perhaps, as Cruttendon said, we do not believe enough. Our fathers at any rate had something to demolish. So have we for the matter of that, thought Jacob, crumpling the *Daily Mail* in his hand. He would go into Parliament and make fine speeches – but what use are fine speeches and Parliament, once you surrender an inch to the black waters? Indeed there has never been any explanation of the ebb and flow in our veins – of happiness and unhappiness. That respectability and evening parties where one has to dress, and wretched slums at the back of Gray's Inn – something solid, immovable, and grotesque – is at the back of it, Jacob thought probable. But then there was the British Empire which was beginning to puzzle him; nor was he altogether in favour of giving Home Rule to Ireland.[8] What did the *Daily Mail* say about that?

* *

For he had grown to be a man, and was about to be immersed in things – as indeed the chambermaid, emptying his basin upstairs, fingering keys, studs, pencils, and bottles of tabloids strewn on the dressing-table, was aware.

That he had grown to be a man was a fact that Florinda knew, as she knew everything, by instinct.

And Betty Flanders even now suspected it, as she read his letter, posted in Milan, 'Telling me,' she complained to Mrs. Jarvis, 'really nothing that I want to know'; but she brooded over it.

Fanny Elmer felt it to desperation. For he would take his stick and his hat and would walk to the window, and look perfectly absent-minded and very stern too, she thought.

'I am going,' he would say, 'to cadge a meal off Bonamy.'

'Anyhow, I can drown myself in the Thames,' Fanny cried, as she hurried past the Foundling Hospital.

'But the *Daily Mail* isn't to be trusted,' Jacob said to himself, looking about for something else to read. And he sighed again, being indeed so profoundly gloomy that gloom must have been lodged in him to cloud him at any moment, which was odd in a man who enjoyed things so, was not much given to analysis, but was horribly romantic, of course, Bonamy thought, in his rooms in Lincoln's Inn.

'He will fall in love,' thought Bonamy. 'Some Greek woman with a straight nose.'

It was to Bonamy that Jacob wrote from Patras – to Bonamy who couldn't love a woman and never read a foolish book.

There are very few good books after all, for we can't count profuse histories, travels in mule carts to discover the sources of the Nile, or the volubility of fiction.

I like books whose virtue is all drawn together in a page or two. I like sentences that don't budge[9] though armies cross them. I like words to be hard – such were Bonamy's views, and they won him the hostility of those whose taste is all for the fresh growths of the morning, who throw up the window, and find the poppies spread in the sun, and can't forbear a shout of jubilation at the astonishing fertility of English literature. That was not Bonamy's way at all.

That his taste in literature affected his friendships, and made him silent, secretive, fastidious, and only quite at his ease with one or two young men of his own way of thinking, was the charge against him.

But then Jacob Flanders was not at all of his own way of thinking – far from it, Bonamy sighed, laying the thin sheets of notepaper on the table and falling into thought about Jacob's character, not for the first time.

The trouble was this romantic vein in him. 'But mixed with the stupidity which leads him into these absurd predicaments,' thought Bonamy, 'there is something – something' – he sighed, for he was fonder of Jacob than of any one in the world.

Jacob went to the window and stood with his hands in his pockets. There he saw three Greeks in kilts; the masts of ships; idle or busy people of the lower classes strolling or stepping out briskly, or falling into groups and gesticulating with their hands. Their lack of concern for him was not the cause of his gloom; but some more profound conviction – it was not that he himself happened to be lonely, but that all people are.

Yet next day, as the train slowly rounded a hill on the way to Olympia, the Greek peasant women were out among the vines; the old Greek men were sitting at the stations, sipping sweet wine. And though Jacob remained gloomy he had never suspected how tremendously pleasant it is to be alone; out of England; on one's own; cut off from the whole thing. There are very sharp bare hills on the way to Olympia; and between them blue sea in triangular spaces. A little like the Cornish coast. Well now, to go walking by oneself all day – to get on to that track and follow it up between the bushes – or are they small trees? – to the top of that mountain from which one can see half the nations of antiquity—

'Yes,' said Jacob, for his carriage was empty, 'let's look at the map.'

Blame it or praise it, there is no denying the wild horse in us. To gallop intemperately; fall on the sand tired out; to feel the earth spin; to have – positively – a rush of friendship for stones and grasses, as if humanity were over, and as for men and women, let them go hang – there is no getting over the fact that this desire seizes us pretty often.

The evening air slightly moved the dirty curtains in the hotel window at Olympia.

'I am full of love for every one,' thought Mrs. Wentworth Williams, ' – for the poor most of all – for the peasants coming back in the evening with their burdens. And everything is soft and vague and very sad. It is sad, it is sad. But everything has meaning,' thought Sandra Wentworth Williams, raising her head a little and looking very beautiful, tragic, and exalted. 'One must love everything.'

She held in her hand a little book convenient for travelling – stories by Tchekov[10] – as she stood, veiled, in white, in the window of the hotel at Olympia. How beautiful the evening was! and her beauty was its beauty. The tragedy of Greece was the tragedy of all high souls. The inevitable compromise. She seemed to have grasped something. She would write it down. And moving to the table where her husband sat reading she leant her chin in her hands and thought of the peasants, of suffering, of her own beauty, of the inevitable compromise, and of how she would write it down. Nor did Evan Williams say anything brutal, banal, or foolish when he shut his book and put it away to make room for the plates of soup which were now being placed before them. Only his drooping bloodhound eyes and his heavy sallow cheeks expressed his melancholy tolerance, his conviction that though forced to live with circumspection and deliberation he could never possibly achieve any of those objects which, as he knew, are the only ones worth pursuing. His consideration was flawless; his silence unbroken.

'Everything seems to mean so much,' said Sandra. But with the sound of her own voice the spell was broken. She forgot the peasants. Only there remained with her a sense of her own beauty, and in front, luckily, there was a looking-glass.

'I am very beautiful,' she thought.

She shifted her hat slightly. Her husband saw her looking in the glass; and agreed that beauty is important; it is an inheritance; one cannot ignore it. But it is a barrier; it is in fact rather a bore.[11] So he drank his soup; and kept his eyes fixed upon the window.

'Quails,' said Mrs. Wentworth Williams languidly. 'And then goat, I suppose; and then . . .'

'Caramel custard presumably,' said her husband in the same cadence, with his toothpick out already.

She laid her spoon upon her plate, and her soup was taken away half finished. Never did she do anything without dignity; for hers was the English type which is so Greek, save that villagers have touched their hats to it, the vicarage reveres it; and upper-gardeners and under-gardeners respectfully straighten their backs as she comes down the broad terrace on Sunday morning, dallying at the stone urns with the Prime Minister to pick a rose – which, perhaps, she was trying to forget, as her eye wandered round the dining-room of the inn at Olympia, seeking the window where her book lay, where a few minutes ago she had discovered something – something very profound it had been, about love and sadness and the peasants.

But it was Evan who sighed; not in despair nor indeed in re-bellion. But, being the most ambitious of men and temperamentally the most sluggish, he had accomplished nothing; had the political history of England at his finger-ends, and living much in company with Chatham, Pitt, Burke, and Charles James Fox[12] could not help contrasting himself and his age with them and theirs. 'Yet there never was a time when great men are more needed,' he was in the habit of saying to himself, with a sigh. Here he was picking his teeth in an inn at Olympia. He had done. But Sandra's eyes wandered.

'Those pink melons are sure to be dangerous,' he said gloomily. And as he spoke the door opened and in came a young man in a grey check suit.

'Beautiful but dangerous,' said Sandra, immediately talking to her husband in the presence of a third person. ('Ah, an English boy on tour,' she thought to herself.)

And Evan knew all that too.

Yes, he knew all that; and he admired her. Very pleasant, he thought, to have affairs. But for himself, what with his height (Napoleon was five feet four, he remembered), his bulk, his inability to impose his own personality (and yet great men are needed more than ever now, he sighed), it was useless. He threw away his cigar, went up to Jacob and asked him, with a simple sort of sincerity which Jacob liked, whether he had come straight out from England.

'How very English!' Sandra laughed when the waiter told them next morning that the young gentleman had left at five to climb the mountain. 'I am sure he asked you for a bath?' at which the waiter shook his head, and said that he would ask the manager.

'You do not understand,' laughed Sandra. 'Never mind.'

Stretched on the top of the mountain, quite alone, Jacob enjoyed himself immensely. Probably he had never been so happy in the whole of his life.

But at dinner that night Mr. Williams asked him whether he would like to see the paper; then Mrs. Williams asked him (as they strolled on the terrace smoking – and how could he refuse that man's cigar?) whether he'd seen the theatre by moonlight; whether he knew Everard Sherborn; whether he read Greek and whether (Evan rose silently and went in) if he had to sacrifice one it would be the French literature or the Russian?

'And now,' wrote Jacob in his letter to Bonamy, 'I shall have to read her cursed book' – her Tchekov, he meant, for she had lent it him.

Though the opinion is unpopular it seems likely enough that bare places, fields too thick with stones to be ploughed, tossing sea-meadows half-way between England and America, suit us better than cities.

There is something absolute in us which despises qualification. It is this which is teased and twisted in society. People come together in a room. 'So delighted,' says somebody, 'to meet you,' and that is a lie. And then: 'I enjoy the spring more than the autumn now. One does, I think, as one gets older.' For women are always, always, always talking about what one feels, and if they say 'as one gets older,' they mean you to reply with something quite off the point.

Jacob sat himself down in the quarry where the Greeks had cut marble for the theatre. It is hot work walking up Greek hills at mid-day. The wild red cyclamen was out; he had seen the little tortoises hobbling from clump to clump; the air smelt strong and suddenly sweet, and the sun, striking on jagged splinters of marble, was very dazzling to the eyes. Composed, commanding, contemptuous, a little melancholy, and bored with an august kind of boredom, there he sat smoking his pipe.

Bonamy would have said that this was the sort of thing that made him uneasy – when Jacob got into the doldrums, looked like a Margate fisherman out of a job, or a British Admiral. You couldn't make him understand a thing when he was in a mood like that. One had better leave him alone. He was dull. He was apt to be grumpy.

He was up very early, looking at the statues with his Baedeker.

Sandra Wentworth Williams, ranging the world before breakfast in quest of adventure or a point of view, all in white, not so very tall perhaps, but uncommonly upright – Sandra Williams got Jacob's head exactly on a level with the head of the Hermes of Praxiteles.[13] The comparison was all in his favour. But before she could say a single word he had gone out of the Museum and left her.

Still, a lady of fashion travels with more than one dress, and if white suits the morning hour, perhaps sandy yellow with purple spots on it, a black hat, and a volume of Balzac, suit the evening. Thus she was arranged on the terrace when Jacob came in. Very beautiful she looked. With her hands folded she mused, seemed to listen to her husband, seemed to watch the peasants coming down with brushwood on their backs, seemed to notice how the hill changed from blue to black, seemed to discriminate between truth and falsehood, Jacob thought, and crossed his legs suddenly, observing the extreme shabbiness of his trousers.

'But he is very distinguished looking,' Sandra decided.

And Evan Williams, lying back in his chair with the paper on his knees, envied them. The best thing he could do would be to publish, with Macmillans, his monograph upon the foreign policy of Chatham. But confound this tumid, queasy feeling – this restlessness, swelling, and heat – it was jealousy! jealousy! jealousy! which he had sworn never to feel again.

'Come with us to Corinth, Flanders,' he said with more than his usual energy, stopping by Jacob's chair. He was relieved by Jacob's reply, or rather by the solid, direct, if shy manner in which he said that he would like very much to come with them to Corinth.

'Here is a fellow,' thought Evan Williams, 'who might do very well in politics.'

'I intend to come to Greece every year so long as I live,' Jacob wrote to Bonamy. 'It is the only chance I can see of protecting oneself from civilization.'

'Goodness knows what he means by that,' Bonamy sighed. For as he never said a clumsy thing himself, these dark sayings of Jacob's made him feel apprehensive, yet somehow impressed, his own turn being all for the definite, the concrete, and the rational.

Nothing could be much simpler than what Sandra said as she descended the Acro-Corinth,[14] keeping to the little path, while Jacob strode over rougher ground by her side. She had been left motherless at the age of four; and the Park was vast.

'One never seemed able to get out of it,' she laughed. Of course there was the library, and dear Mr. Jones, and notions about things. 'I used to stray into the kitchen and sit upon the butlers' knees,' she laughed, sadly though.

Jacob thought that if he had been there he would have saved her; for she had been exposed to great dangers, he felt, and, he thought to himself, 'People wouldn't understand a woman talking as she talks.'

She made little of the roughness of the hill; and wore breeches, he saw, under her short skirts.

'Women like Fanny Elmer don't,' he thought. 'What's-her-name Carslake didn't; yet they pretend . . .'

Mrs. Williams said things straight out. He was surprised by his own knowledge of the rules of behaviour; how much more can be said than one thought; how open one can be with a woman; and how little he had known himself before.

Evan joined them on the road; and as they drove along up hill and down hill (for Greece is in a state of effervescence, yet astonishingly clean-cut, a treeless land, where you see the ground between the blades, each hill cut and shaped and outlined as often as not against sparkling deep blue waters, islands white as sand floating on the horizon, occasional groves of palm trees standing in the valleys, which are scattered with black goats, spotted with little olive trees and sometimes have white hollows, rayed and criss-crossed, in their flanks), as they drove up hill and down he scowled in the corner of the carriage, with his paw so tightly closed that the skin was stretched between the knuckles and the little hairs stood upright. Sandra rode opposite, dominant, like a Victory[15] prepared to fling into the air.

'Heartless!' thought Evan (which was untrue).

'Brainless!' he suspected (and that was not true, either). 'Still . . .!' He envied her.

When bedtime came the difficulty was to write to Bonamy, Jacob found. Yet he had seen Salamis, and Marathon in the distance. Poor old Bonamy! No; there was something queer about it. He could not write to Bonamy.

'I shall go to Athens all the same,' he resolved, looking very set, with this hook dragging in his side.

The Williamses had already been to Athens.

Athens is still quite capable of striking a young man as the oddest combination, the most incongruous assortment. Now it is suburban; now immortal. Now cheap continental jewellery is laid upon plush trays. Now the stately woman stands naked, save for a wave of drapery above the knee. No form can he set on his sensations as he strolls, one blazing afternoon, along the Parisian boulevard and skips out of the way of the royal landau which, looking indescribably ramshackle, rattles along the pitted roadway, saluted by citizens of both sexes cheaply dressed in bowler hats and continental costumes; though a shepherd in kilt, cap, and gaiters very nearly drives his herd of goats between the royal wheels; and all the time the Acropolis surges into the air, raises itself above the town, like a large immobile wave with the yellow columns of the Parthenon firmly planted upon it.

The yellow columns of the Parthenon are to be seen at all hours of the day firmly planted upon the Acropolis; though at sunset, when the ships in the Piraeus fire their guns,[16] a bell rings, a man in uniform (the waistcoat unbuttoned) appears; and the women roll up the black stockings which they are knitting in the shadow of the columns, call to the children, and troop off down the hill back to their houses.

There they are again, the pillars, the pediment, the Temple of Victory and the Erechtheum,[17] set on a tawny rock cleft with shadows, directly you unlatch your shutters in the morning and, leaning out, hear the clatter, the clamour, the whip cracking in the street below. There they are.

The extreme definiteness with which they stand, now a brilliant white, again yellow, and in some lights red, imposes ideas of durability, of the emergence through the earth of some spiritual energy elsewhere dissipated in elegant trifles. But this durability exists quite independently of our admiration. Although the beauty is sufficiently humane to weaken us, to stir the deep deposit of mud – memories, abandonments, regrets, sentimental devotions – the Parthenon is separate from all that; and if you consider how it has stood out all night, for centuries, you begin to connect the blaze (at mid-day the glare is dazzling and the frieze almost invisible) with the idea that perhaps it is beauty alone that is immortal.

Added to this, compared with the blistered stucco, the new love songs rasped out to the strum of guitar and gramophone, and the mobile yet insignificant faces of the street, the Parthenon is really astonishing in its silent composure; which is so vigorous that, far from being decayed, the Parthenon appears, on the contrary, likely to outlast the entire world.

'And the Greeks, like sensible men, never bothered to finish the backs of their statues,' said Jacob, shading his eyes and observing that the side of the figure which is turned away from view is left in the rough.

He noted the slight irregularity in the line of the steps which 'the artistic sense of the Greeks preferred to mathematical accuracy,' he read in his guide-book.

He stood on the exact spot where the great statue of Athena used to stand,[18] and identified the more famous landmarks of the scene beneath.

In short he was accurate and diligent; but profoundly morose. Moreover he was pestered by guides. This was on Monday.

But on Wednesday he wrote a telegram to Bonamy, telling him to come at once. And then he crumpled it in his hand and threw it in the gutter.

'For one thing he wouldn't come,' he thought. 'And then I daresay this sort of thing wears off.' 'This sort of thing' being that uneasy, painful feeling, something like selfishness – one wishes almost that the thing would stop – it is getting more and more beyond what is possible – 'If it goes on much longer I shan't be able to cope with it – but if some one else were seeing it at the same time – Bonamy is stuffed in his room in Lincoln's Inn – oh, I say, damn it all, I say,' – the sight of Hymettus, Pentelicus, Lycabettus[19] on one side, and the sea on the other, as one stands in the Parthenon at sunset, the sky pink feathered, the plain all colours, the marble tawny in one's eyes, is thus oppressive. Luckily Jacob had little sense of personal association; he seldom thought of Plato or Socrates in the flesh; on the other hand his feeling for architecture was very strong; he preferred statues to pictures; and he was beginning to think a great deal about the problems of civilization, which were solved, of course, so very remarkably by the ancient Greeks, though their solution is no help to us. Then the hook gave a great tug in his side as he lay in bed on Wednesday night; and he turned over with a desperate sort of tumble, remembering Sandra Wentworth Williams with whom he was in love.

Next day he climbed Pentelicus.

The day after he went up to the Acropolis. The hour was early; the place almost deserted; and possibly there was thunder in the air. But the sun struck full upon the Acropolis.

Jacob's intention was to sit down and read, and, finding a drum of marble conveniently placed, from which Marathon could be seen, and yet it was in the shade, while the Erechtheum blazed white in front of him, there he sat. And after reading a page he put his thumb in his book. Why not rule countries in the way they should be ruled? And he read again.

No doubt his position there overlooking Marathon somehow raised his spirits. Or it may have been that a slow capacious brain has these moments of flowering. Or he had, insensibly, while he was abroad, got into the way of thinking about politics.

And then looking up and seeing the sharp outline, his meditations were given an extraordinary edge; Greece was over; the Parthenon in ruins; yet there he was.

(Ladies with green and white umbrellas passed through the court-yard – French ladies on their way to join their husbands in Constantinople.)

Jacob read on again. And laying the book on the ground he began, as if inspired by what he had read, to write a note upon the importance of history – upon democracy – one of those scribbles upon which the work of a lifetime may be based; or again, it falls out of a book twenty years later, and one can't remember a word of it. It is a little painful. It had better be burnt.

Jacob wrote; began to draw a straight nose; when all the French ladies opening and shutting their umbrellas just beneath him exclaimed, looking at the sky, that one did not know what to expect – rain or fine weather?

Jacob got up and strolled across to the Erechtheum. There are still several women standing there holding the roof on their heads. Jacob straightened himself slightly; for stability and balance affect the body first. These statues annulled things so! He stared at them, then turned, and there was Madame Lucien Gravé perched on a block of marble with her kodak[20] pointed at his head. Of course she jumped down, in spite of her age, her figure, and her tight boots – having, now that her daughter was married, lapsed with a luxurious abandonment, grand enough in its way, into the fleshy grotesque; she jumped down, but not before Jacob had seen her.

'Damn these women – damn these women!' he thought. And he went to fetch his book which he had left lying on the ground in the Parthenon.

'How they spoil things,' he murmured, leaning against one of the pillars, pressing his book tight between his arm and his side. (As for the weather, no doubt the storm would break soon; Athens was under cloud.)

'It is those damned women,' said Jacob, without any trace of bitterness, but rather with sadness and disappointment that what might have been should never be.

(This violent disillusionment is generally to be expected in young men in the prime of life, sound of mind and limb, who will soon become fathers of families and directors of banks.)

Then, making sure that the Frenchwomen had gone, and looking cautiously round him, Jacob strolled over to the Erechtheum and looked rather furtively at the goddess on the left-hand side holding the roof on her head. She reminded him of Sandra Wentworth Williams. He looked at her, then looked away. He was extraordinarily moved, and with the battered Greek nose in his head, with Sandra in his head, with all sorts of things in his head, off he started to walk right up to the top of Mount Hymettus, alone, in the heat.

That very afternoon Bonamy went expressly to talk about Jacob to tea with Clara Durrant in the square behind Sloane Street where, on hot spring days, there are striped blinds over the front windows, single horses pawing the macadam outside the doors, and elderly gentlemen in yellow waistcoats ringing bells and stepping in very politely when the maid demurely replies that Mrs. Durrant is at home.

Bonamy sat with Clara in the sunny front room with the barrel-organ piping sweetly outside; the water-cart going slowly along spraying the pavement; the carriages jingling, and all the silver and chintz, brown and blue rugs and vases filled with green boughs, striped with trembling yellow bars.

The insipidity of what was said needs no illustration – Bonamy kept on gently returning quiet answers and accumulating amazement at an existence squeezed and emasculated within a white satin shoe (Mrs. Durrant meanwhile enunciating strident politics with Sir Somebody in the back room) until the virginity of Clara's soul appeared to him candid; the depths unknown; and he would have brought out Jacob's name had he not begun to feel positively certain that Clara loved him – and could do nothing whatever.

'Nothing whatever!' he exclaimed, as the door shut, and, for a man of his temperament, got a very queer feeling, as he walked through the park, of carriages irresistibly driven; of flower-beds uncompromisingly geometrical; of force rushing round geometrical patterns in the most senseless way in the world. 'Was Clara,' he thought, pausing to watch the boys bathing in the Serpentine, 'the silent woman? – would Jacob marry her?'

*

But in Athens in the sunshine, in Athens, where it is almost impossible to get afternoon tea, and elderly gentlemen who talk politics talk them all the other way round, in Athens sat Sandra Wentworth Williams, veiled, in white, her legs stretched in front of her, one elbow on the arm of the bamboo chair, blue clouds wavering and drifting from her cigarette.

The orange trees which flourish in the Square of the Constitution, the band, the dragging of feet, the sky, the houses, lemon and rose coloured – all this became so significant to Mrs. Wentworth Williams after her second cup of coffee that she began dramatizing the story of the noble and impulsive Englishwoman who had offered a seat in her carriage to the old American lady at Mycenae (Mrs. Duggan) – not altogether a false story, though it said nothing of Evan, standing first on one foot, then on the other, waiting for the women to stop chattering.

'I am putting the life of Father Damien into verse,'[21] Mrs. Duggan had said, for she had lost everything – everything in the world, husband and child and everything, but faith remained.

Sandra, floating from the particular to the universal, lay back in a trance.

The flight of time which hurries us so tragically along; the eternal drudge and drone, now bursting into fiery flame like those brief balls of yellow among green leaves (she was looking at orange trees); kisses on lips that are to die; the world turning, turning in mazes of heat and sound – though to be sure there is the quiet evening with its lovely pallor, 'For I am sensitive to every side of it,' Sandra thought, 'and Mrs. Duggan will write to me for ever, and I shall answer her letters.' Now the royal band marching by with the national flag stirred wider rings of emotion, and life became something that the courageous mount and ride out to sea on – the hair blown back (so she envisaged it, and the breeze stirred slightly among the orange trees) and she herself was emerging from silver spray – when she saw Jacob. He was standing in the Square with a book under his arm looking vacantly about him. That he was heavily built and might become stout in time was a fact.

But she suspected him of being a mere bumpkin.

'There is that young man,' she said, peevishly, throwing away her cigarette, 'that Mr. Flanders.'

'Where?' said Evan. 'I don't see him.'

'Oh, walking away – behind the trees now. No, you can't see him. But we are sure to run into him,' which, of course, they did.

But how far was he a mere bumpkin? How far was Jacob Flanders at the age of twenty-six a stupid fellow? It is no use trying to sum people up. One must follow hints, not exactly what is said, nor yet entirely what is done. Some, it is true, take ineffaceable impressions of character at once. Others dally, loiter, and get blown this way and that. Kind old ladies assure us that cats are often the best judges of character. A cat will always go to a good man, they say; but then, Mrs. Whitehorn, Jacob's landlady, loathed cats.

There is also the highly respectable opinion that character-mongering[22] is much overdone nowadays. After all, what does it matter – that Fanny Elmer was all sentiment and sensation, and Mrs. Durrant hard as iron? that Clara, owing (so the character-mongers said) largely to her mother's influence, never yet had the chance to do anything off her own bat, and only to very observant eyes displayed deeps of feeling which were positively alarming; and would certainly throw herself away upon some one unworthy of her one of these days unless, so the character-mongers said, she had a spark of her mother's spirit in her – was somehow heroic. But what a term to apply to Clara Durrant! Simple to a degree, others thought her. And that is the very reason, so they said, why she attracts Dick Bonamy – the young man with the Wellington nose.[23] Now *he's* a dark horse if you like. And there these gossips would suddenly pause. Obviously they meant to hint at his peculiar disposition – long rumoured among them.

'But sometimes it is precisely a woman like Clara that men of that temperament need . . .' Miss Julia Eliot would hint.

'Well,' Mr. Bowley would reply, 'it may be so.'

For however long these gossips sit, and however they stuff out their victims' characters till they are swollen and tender as the livers of geese exposed to a hot fire, they never come to a decision.

'That young man, Jacob Flanders,' they would say, 'so distinguished looking – and yet so awkward.' Then they would apply themselves to Jacob and vacillate eternally between the two extremes. He rode to hounds – after a fashion, for he hadn't a penny.

'Did you ever hear who his father was?' asked Julia Eliot.

'His mother, they say, is somehow connected with the Rocks-biers,' replied Mr. Bowley.

'He doesn't overwork himself anyhow.'

'His friends are very fond of him.'

'Dick Bonamy, you mean?'

'No, I didn't mean that. It's evidently the other way with Jacob. He is precisely the young man to fall headlong in love and repent it for the rest of his life.'

'Oh, Mr. Bowley,' said Mrs. Durrant, sweeping down upon them in her imperious manner, 'you remember Mrs. Adams? Well, that is her niece.' And Mr. Bowley, getting up, bowed politely and fetched strawberries.

So we are driven back to see what the other side means – the men in clubs and Cabinets – when they say that character-drawing is a frivolous fireside art, a matter of pins and needles, exquisite outlines enclosing vacancy, flourishes, and mere scrawls.

The battleships ray out[24] over the North Sea, keeping their stations accurately apart. At a given signal all the guns are trained on a target which (the master gunner counts the seconds, watch in hand – at the sixth he looks up) flames into splinters. With equal nonchal-ance a dozen young men in the prime of life descend with composed faces into the depths of the sea; and there impassively (though with perfect mastery of machinery) suffocate uncomplainingly together. Like blocks of tin soldiers the army covers the cornfield, moves up the hillside, stops, reels slightly this way and that, and falls flat, save that, through field-glasses, it can be seen that one or two pieces still agitate up and down like fragments of broken match-stick.

These actions, together with the incessant commerce of banks, laboratories, chancellories, and houses of business, are the strokes which oar the world forward, they say. And they are dealt by men as smoothly sculpted as the impassive policeman at Ludgate Circus. But you will observe that far from being padded to rotundity his face is stiff from force of will, and lean from the effort of keeping it so. When his right arm rises, all the force in his veins flows straight from shoulder to finger-tips; not an ounce is diverted into sudden impulses, sentimental regrets, wire-drawn distinctions. The buses punctually stop.

It is thus that we live, they say, driven by an unseizable force. They say that the novelists never catch it; that it goes hurtling through their nets and leaves them torn to ribbons. This, they say, is what we live by – this unseizable force.

'Where are the men?' said old General Gibbons, looking round the drawing-room, full as usual on Sunday afternoons of well-dressed people. 'Where are the guns?'

Mrs. Durrant looked too.

Clara, thinking that her mother wanted her, came in; then went out again.

They were talking about Germany at the Durrants, and Jacob (driven by this unseizable force) walked rapidly down Hermes Street and ran straight into the Williamses.

'Oh!' cried Sandra, with a cordiality which she suddenly felt. And Evan added, 'What luck!'

The dinner which they gave him in the hotel which looks on to the Square of the Constitution was excellent. Plated baskets contained fresh rolls. There was real butter. And the meat scarcely needed the disguise of innumerable little red and green vegetables glazed in sauce.

It was strange, though. There were the little tables set out at intervals on the scarlet floor with the Greek King's monogram wrought in yellow. Sandra dined in her hat, veiled as usual. Evan looked this way and that over his shoulder; imperturbable yet supple; and sometimes sighed. It was strange. For they were English people come together in Athens on a May evening. Jacob, helping himself to this and that, answered intelligently, yet with a ring in his voice.

The Williamses were going to Constantinople early next morning, they said.

'Before you are up,' said Sandra.

They would leave Jacob alone, then. Turning very slightly, Evan ordered something — a bottle of wine — from which he helped Jacob, with a kind of solicitude, with a kind of paternal solicitude, if that were possible. To be left alone — that was good for a young fellow. Never was there a time when the country had more need of men. He sighed.

'And you have been to the Acropolis?' asked Sandra.

'Yes,' said Jacob. And they moved off to the window together, while Evan spoke to the head waiter about calling them early.

'It is astonishing,' said Jacob, in a gruff voice.

Sandra opened her eyes very slightly. Possibly her nostrils expanded a little too.

'At half-past six then,' said Evan, coming towards them, looking as if he faced something in facing his wife and Jacob standing with their backs to the window.

Sandra smiled at him.

And, as he went to the window and had nothing to say she added, in broken half-sentences:

'Well, but how lovely — wouldn't it be? The Acropolis, Evan — or are you too tired?'

At that Evan looked at them, or, since Jacob was staring ahead of him, at his wife, surlily, sullenly, yet with a kind of distress — not that she would pity him. Nor would the implacable spirit of love, for anything he could do, cease its tortures.

They left him and he sat in the smoking-room, which looks out on to the Square of the Constitution.

'Evan is happier alone,' said Sandra. 'We have been separated from the newspapers. Well, it is better that people should have what they want . . . You have seen all these wonderful things since we met . . . What impression . . . I think that you are changed.'

'You want to go to the Acropolis,' said Jacob. 'Up here then.'

'One will remember it all one's life,' said Sandra.

'Yes,' said Jacob. 'I wish you could have come in the day-time.'

'This is more wonderful,' said Sandra, waving her hand.

Jacob looked vaguely.

'But you should see the Parthenon in the day-time,' he said. 'You couldn't come to-morrow — it would be too early?'

'You have sat there for hours and hours by yourself?'

'There were some awful women this morning,' said Jacob.

'Awful women?' Sandra echoed.

'Frenchwomen.'

'But something very wonderful has happened,' said Sandra. Ten minutes, fifteen minutes, half an hour – that was all the time before her.

'Yes,' he said.

'When one is your age – when one is young. What will you do? You will fall in love – oh yes! But don't be in too great a hurry. I am so much older.'

She was brushed off the pavement by parading men.

'Shall we go on?' Jacob asked.

'Let us go on,' she insisted.

For she could not stop until she had told him – or heard him say – or was it some action on his part that she required? Far away on the horizon she discerned it and could not rest.

'You'd never get English people to sit out like this,' he said.

'Never – no. When you get back to England you won't forget this – or come with us to Constantinople!' she cried suddenly.

'But then . . .'

Sandra sighed.

'You must go to Delphi, of course,' she said. 'But,' she asked herself, 'what do I want from him? Perhaps it is something that I have missed . . .'

'You will get there about six in the evening,' she said. 'You will see the eagles.'

Jacob looked set and even desperate by the light at the street corner; and yet composed. He was suffering perhaps. He was credulous. Yet there was something caustic about him. He had in him the seeds of extreme disillusionment, which would come to him from women in middle life. Perhaps if one strove hard enough to reach the top of the hill it need not come to him – this disillusionment from women in middle life.

'The hotel is awful,' she said. 'The last visitors had left their basins full of dirty water. There is always that,' she laughed.

'The people one meets *are* beastly,' Jacob said.

His excitement was clear enough.

'Write and tell me about it,' she said. 'And tell me what you feel and what you think. Tell me everything.'

The night was dark. The Acropolis was a jagged mound.

'I should like to, awfully,' he said.

'When we get back to London, we shall meet . . .'

'Yes.'

'I suppose they leave the gates open?' he asked.

'We could climb them!' she answered wildly.

Obscuring the moon and altogether darkening the Acropolis the clouds passed from east to west. The clouds solidified; the vapours thickened; the trailing veils stayed and accumulated.

It was dark now over Athens, except for gauzy red streaks where the streets ran; and the front of the Palace was cadaverous from electric light. At sea the piers stood out, marked by separate dots; the waves being invisible, and promontories and islands were dark humps with a few lights.

'I'd love to bring my brother, if I may,' Jacob murmured.

'And then when your mother comes to London—,' said Sandra.

The mainland of Greece was dark; and somewhere off Euboea[25] a cloud must have touched the waves and splattered them – the dolphins circling deeper and deeper into the sea. Violent was the wind now rushing down the Sea of Marmara between Greece and the plains of Troy.

In Greece and the uplands of Albania and Turkey, the wind scours the sand and the dust, and sows itself thick with dry particles. And then it pelts the smooth domes of the mosques, and makes the cypresses, standing stiff by the turbaned tombstones of Mohammedans, creak and bristle.

Sandra's veils were swirled about her.

'I will give you my copy,' said Jacob. 'Here. Will you keep it?'

(The book was the poems of Donne.[26])

Now the agitation of the air uncovered a racing star. Now it was dark. Now one after another lights were extinguished.[27] Now great towns – Paris – Constantinople – London – were black as strewn rocks. Waterways might be distinguished. In England the trees were heavy in leaf. Here perhaps in some southern wood an old man lit dry ferns and the birds were startled. The sheep coughed; one flower bent slightly towards another. The English sky is softer, milkier than the Eastern. Something gentle has passed into it from the grass-rounded hills, something damp. The salt gale blew in at Betty Flanders's bedroom window, and the widow lady, raising herself slightly on her elbow, sighed like one who realizes, but would fain ward off a little longer – oh, a little longer! – the oppression of eternity.

But to return to Jacob and Sandra.

They had vanished. There was the Acropolis; but had they reached it? The columns and the Temple remain; the emotion of the living breaks fresh on them year after year; and of that what remains?

As for reaching the Acropolis who shall say that we ever do it, or that when Jacob woke next morning he found anything hard and durable to keep for ever? (Still, he went with them to Constantinople.)

Sandra Wentworth Williams certainly woke to find a copy of Donne's poems upon her dressing-table. And the book would be stood on the shelf in the English country house where Sally Duggan's *Life of Father Damien* in verse would join it one of these days. There were ten or twelve little volumes already. Strolling in at dusk, Sandra would open the books and her eyes would brighten (but not at the print), and subsiding into the arm-chair she would suck back again the soul of the moment; or, for sometimes she was restless, would pull out book after book and swing across the whole space of her life like an acrobat from bar to bar. She had had her moments. Meanwhile, the great clock on the landing ticked and Sandra would hear time accumulating, and ask herself, 'What for? What for?'

'What for? What for?' Sandra would say, putting the book back, and strolling to the looking-glass and pressing her hair. And Miss Edwards would be startled at dinner, as she opened her mouth to admit roast mutton, by Sandra's sudden solicitude: 'Are you happy, Miss Edwards?' – a thing Cissy Edwards hadn't thought of for years.

'What for? What for?' Jacob never asked himself any such question, to judge by the way he laced his boots; shaved himself; to judge by the depth of his sleep that night, with the wind fidgeting at the shutters, and half-a-dozen mosquitoes singing in his ears. He was young – a man. And then Sandra was right when she judged him to be credulous as yet. At forty it might be a different matter. Already he had marked the things he liked in Donne, and they were savage enough. However, you might place beside them passages of the purest poetry in Shakespeare.

But the wind was rolling the darkness through the streets of Athens, rolling it, one might suppose, with a sort of trampling energy of mood which forbids too close an analysis of the feelings of any single person, or inspection of features. All faces – Greek, Levantine, Turkish, English – would have looked much the same in that darkness. At length the columns and the Temples whiten, yellow, turn rose; and the Pyramids and St. Peter's arise, and at last sluggish St. Paul's looms up.

The Christians have the right to rouse most cities with their interpretation of the day's meaning. Then, less melodiously, dissenters of different sects issue a cantankerous emendation. The steamers, resounding like gigantic tuning-forks, state the old old fact – how there is a sea coldly, greenly, swaying outside. But nowadays it is the thin voice of duty, piping in a white thread from the top of a funnel, that collects the largest multitudes, and night is nothing but a long-drawn sigh between hammer-strokes, a deep breath – you can hear it from an open window even in the heart of London.

But who, save the nerve-worn and sleepless, or thinkers standing with hands to the eyes on some crag above the multitude, see things thus in skeleton outline, bare of flesh? In Surbiton[28] the skeleton is wrapped in flesh.

'The kettle never boils so well on a sunny morning,' says Mrs. Grandage, glancing at the clock on the mantelpiece. Then the grey Persian cat stretches itself on the window-seat, and buffets a moth with soft round paws. And before breakfast is half over (they were late to-day) a baby is deposited in her lap, and she must guard the sugar basin while Tom Grandage reads the golfing article in the *Times*, sips his coffee, wipes his moustaches, and is off to the office, where he is the greatest authority upon the foreign exchanges and marked for promotion.

The skeleton is well wrapped in flesh. Even this dark night when the wind rolls the darkness through Lombard Street and Fetter

Lane[29] and Bedford Square it stirs (since it is summer-time and the height of the season) plane trees spangled with electric light, and curtains still preserving the room from the dawn. People still murmur over the last word said on the staircase, or strain, all through their dreams, for the voice of the alarum clock. So when the wind roams through a forest innumerable twigs stir; hives are brushed; insects sway on grass blades; the spider runs rapidly up a crease in the bark; and the whole air is tremulous with breathing; elastic with filaments.

Only here – in Lombard Street and Fetter Lane and Bedford Square – each insect carries a globe of the world in his head, and the webs of the forest are schemes evolved for the smooth conduct of business; and honey is treasure of one sort and another; and the stir in the air is the indescribable agitation of life.

But colour returns; runs up the stalks of the grass; blows out into tulips and crocuses; solidly stripes the tree trunks; and fills the gauze of the air and the grasses and pools.

The Bank of England emerges; and the Monument with its bristling head of golden hair; the dray horses crossing London Bridge show grey and strawberry and iron-coloured. There is a whir of wings as the suburban trains rush into the terminus. And the light mounts over the faces of all the tall blind houses, slides through a chink and paints the lustrous bellying crimson curtains; the green wine-glasses; the coffee-cups; and the chairs standing askew.

Sunlight strikes in upon shaving-glasses; and gleaming brass cans; upon all the jolly trappings of the day; the bright, inquisitive, armoured, resplendent, summer's day, which has long since vanquished chaos; which has dried the melancholy mediaeval mists; drained the swamp and stood glass and stone upon it; and equipped our brains and bodies with such an armoury of weapons that merely to see the flash and thrust of limbs engaged in the conduct of daily life is better than the old pageant of armies drawn out in battle array upon the plain.

'The height of the season,' said Bonamy.

The sun had already blistered the paint on the backs of the green chairs in Hyde Park; peeled the bark off the plane trees; and turned the earth to powder and to smooth yellow pebbles. Hyde Park was circled, incessantly, by turning wheels.

'The height of the season,' said Bonamy sarcastically.

He was sarcastic because of Clara Durrant; because Jacob had come back from Greece very brown and lean, with his pockets full of Greek notes, which he pulled out when the chair man came for pence; because Jacob was silent.

'He has not said a word to show that he is glad to see me,' thought Bonamy bitterly.

The motor-cars passed incessantly over the bridge of the Serpentine; the upper classes walked upright, or bent themselves gracefully over the palings; the lower classes lay with their knees cocked up, flat on their backs; the sheep grazed on pointed wooden legs; small children ran down the sloping grass, stretched their arms, and fell.

'Very urbane,' Jacob brought out.

'Urbane' on the lips of Jacob had mysteriously all the shapeliness of a character which Bonamy thought daily more sublime, devastating, terrific than ever, though he was still, and perhaps would be for ever, barbaric, obscure.

What superlatives! What adjectives! How acquit Bonamy of sentimentality of the grossest sort; of being tossed like a cork on the waves; of having no steady insight into character; of being unsupported by reason, and of drawing no comfort whatever from the works of the classics?

'The height of civilization,' said Jacob.

He was fond of using Latin words.

Magnanimity, virtue — such words when Jacob used them in talk with Bonamy meant that he took control of the situation; that Bonamy would play round him like an affectionate spaniel;

and that (as likely as not) they would end by rolling on the floor.

'And Greece?' said Bonamy. 'The Parthenon and all that?'

'There's none of this European mysticism,'[1] said Jacob.

'It's the atmosphere, I suppose,' said Bonamy. 'And you went to Constantinople?'

'Yes,' said Jacob.

Bonamy paused, moved a pebble; then darted in with the rapidity and certainty of a lizard's tongue.

'You are in love!' he exclaimed.

Jacob blushed.

The sharpest of knives never cut so deep.

As for responding, or taking the least account of it, Jacob stared straight ahead of him, fixed, monolithic – oh, very beautiful! – like a British Admiral, exclaimed Bonamy in a rage, rising from his seat and walking off; waiting for some sound; none came; too proud to look back; walking quicker and quicker until he found himself gazing into motor-cars and cursing women. Where was the pretty woman's face? Clara's – Fanny's – Florinda's? Who was the pretty little creature?

Not Clara Durrant.

The Aberdeen terrier must be exercised, and as Mr. Bowley was going that very moment – would like nothing better than a walk – they went together, Clara and kind little Bowley – Bowley who had rooms in the Albany, Bowley who wrote letters to the *Times* in a jocular vein about foreign hotels and the Aurora Borealis – Bowley who liked young people and walked down Piccadilly with his right arm resting on the boss of his back.

'Little demon!' cried Clara, and attached Troy[2] to his chain.

Bowley anticipated – hoped for – a confidence. Devoted to her mother, Clara sometimes felt her a little, well, her mother was so sure of herself that she could not understand other people being – being – 'as ludicrous as I am,' Clara jerked out (the dog tugging her forwards). And Bowley thought she looked like a huntress[3] and turned over in his mind which it should be – some pale virgin with a slip of the moon in her hair, which was a flight for Bowley.

The colour was in her cheeks. To have spoken outright about her mother – still, it was only to Mr. Bowley, who loved her, as everybody must; but to speak was unnatural to her, yet it was awful to feel, as she had done all day, that she *must* tell some one.

'Wait till we cross the road,' she said to the dog, bending down.

Happily she had recovered by that time.

'She thinks so much about England,' she said. 'She is so anxious—'

Bowley was defrauded as usual. Clara never confided in any one.

'Why don't the young people settle it, eh?' he wanted to ask. 'What's all this about England?' – a question poor Clara could not have answered, since, as Mrs. Durrant discussed with Sir Edgar the policy of Sir Edward Grey,[4] Clara only wondered why the cabinet looked dusty, and Jacob had never come. Oh, here was Mrs. Cowley Johnson . . .

And Clara would hand the pretty china tea-cups, and smile at the compliment – that no one in London made tea so well as she did.

'We get it at Brocklebank's,' she said, 'in Cursitor Street.'

Ought she not to be grateful? Ought she not to be happy? Especially since her mother looked so well and enjoyed so much talking to Sir Edgar about Morocco, Venezuela, or some such place.

'Jacob! Jacob!' thought Clara; and kind Mr. Bowley, who was ever so good with old ladies, looked; stopped; wondered whether Elizabeth wasn't too harsh with her daughter; wondered about Bonamy, Jacob – which young fellow was it? – and jumped up directly Clara said she must exercise Troy.

They had reached the site of the old Exhibition.[5] They looked at the tulips. Stiff and curled, the little rods of waxy smoothness rose from the earth, nourished yet contained, suffused with scarlet and coral pink. Each had its shadow; each grew trimly in the diamond-shaped wedge as the gardener had planned it.

'Barnes never gets them to grow like that,' Clara mused; she sighed.

'You are neglecting your friends,' said Bowley, as some one, going the other way, lifted his hat. She started; acknowledged Mr. Lionel Parry's bow; wasted on him what had sprung for Jacob.

('Jacob! Jacob!' she thought.)

'But you'll get run over if I let you go,' she said to the dog.

'England seems all right,' said Mr. Bowley.

The loop of the railing beneath the statue of Achilles[6] was full of parasols and waistcoats; chains and bangles; of ladies and gentlemen, lounging elegantly, lightly observant.

'"This statue was erected by the women of England . . . ?"' Clara read out with a foolish little laugh. 'Oh, Mr. Bowley! Oh!' Gallop – gallop – gallop – a horse galloped past without a rider.[7] The stirrups swung; the pebbles spurted.

'Oh, stop! Stop it, Mr. Bowley!' she cried, white, trembling, gripping his arm, utterly unconscious, the tears coming.

'Tut-tut!' said Mr. Bowley in his dressing-room an hour later. 'Tut-tut!' – a comment that was profound enough, though inarticulately expressed, since his valet was handing his shirt studs.

Julia Eliot, too, had seen the horse run away, and had risen from her seat to watch the end of the incident, which, since she came of a sporting family, seemed to her slightly ridiculous. Sure enough the little man came pounding behind with his breeches dusty; looked thoroughly annoyed; and was being helped to mount by a policeman when Julia Eliot, with a sardonic smile, turned towards the Marble Arch on her errand of mercy. It was only to visit a sick old lady who had known her mother and perhaps the Duke of Wellington; for Julia shared the love of her sex for the distressed; liked to visit death-beds;[8] threw slippers at weddings; received confidences by the dozen; knew more pedigrees than a scholar knows dates, and was one of the kindliest, most generous, least continent of women.

Yet five minutes after she had passed the statue of Achilles she had the rapt look of one brushing through crowds on a summer's afternoon, when the trees are rustling, the wheels churning yellow, and the tumult of the present seems like an elegy for past youth and past summers, and there rose in her mind a curious sadness, as if time and eternity showed through skirts and waistcoats, and she saw people passing tragically to destruction. Yet, Heaven knows, Julia was no fool. A sharper woman at a bargain did not exist. She was always punctual. The watch on her wrist gave her twelve minutes and a half in which to reach Bruton Street. Lady Congreve expected her at five.

The gilt clock at Verrey's was striking five.

Florinda looked at it with a dull expression, like an animal. She looked at the clock; looked at the door; looked at the long glass opposite; disposed her cloak; drew closer to the table, for she was pregnant – no doubt about it, Mother Stuart said, recommending remedies, consulting friends; sunk, caught by the heel, as she tripped so lightly over the surface.

Her tumbler of pinkish sweet stuff was set down by the waiter; and she sucked, through a straw, her eyes on the looking-glass, on the door, now soothed by the sweet taste. When Nick Bramham came in it was plain, even to the young Swiss waiter, that there was a bargain between them. Nick hitched his clothes together clumsily; ran his fingers through his hair; sat down, to an ordeal, nervously. She looked at him; and set off laughing; laughed – laughed – laughed. The young Swiss waiter, standing with crossed legs by the pillar, laughed too.

The door opened; in came the roar of Regent Street, the roar of the traffic, impersonal, unpitying; and sunshine grained with dirt. The Swiss waiter must see to the newcomers. Bramham lifted his glass.

'He's like Jacob,' said Florinda, looking at the newcomer.

'The way he stares.' She stopped laughing.

Jacob, leaning forward, drew a plan of the Parthenon in the dust in Hyde Park, a network of strokes at least, which may have been the Parthenon, or again a mathematical diagram. And why was the pebble so emphatically ground in at the corner? It was not to count his notes that he took out a wad of papers and read a long flowing letter which Sandra had written two days ago at Milton Dower House with his book before her and in her mind the memory of something said or attempted, some moment in the dark on the road to the Acropolis which (such was her creed) mattered for ever.

'He is,' she mused, 'like that man in Molière.'

She meant Alceste.[9] She meant that he was severe. She meant that she could deceive him.

'Or could I not?' she thought, putting the poems of Donne back in the bookcase. 'Jacob,' she went on, going to the window and looking over the spotted flower-beds across the grass where the piebald cows grazed under beech trees, 'Jacob would be shocked.'

The perambulator was going through the little gate in the railing. She kissed her hand; directed by the nurse, Jimmy waved his.

'*He's* a small boy,' she said, thinking of Jacob.

And yet – Alceste?

'What a nuisance you are!' Jacob grumbled, stretching out first one leg and then the other and feeling in each trouser-pocket for his chair ticket.

'I expect the sheep have eaten it,' he said. 'Why do you keep sheep?'

'Sorry to disturb you, sir,' said the ticket-collector, his hand deep in the enormous pouch of pence.

'Well, I hope they pay you for it,' said Jacob. 'There you are. No. You can stick to it. Go and get drunk.'

He had parted with half-a-crown, tolerantly, compassionately, with considerable contempt for his species.[10]

Even now poor Fanny Elmer was dealing, as she walked along the Strand, in her incompetent way with this very careless, indifferent, sublime manner he had of talking to railway guards or porters; or Mrs. Whitehorn, when she consulted him about her little boy who was beaten by the schoolmaster.

Sustained entirely upon picture post cards for the past two months, Fanny's idea of Jacob was more statuesque, noble, and eyeless than ever. To reinforce her vision she had taken to visiting the British Museum, where, keeping her eyes downcast until she was alongside of the battered Ulysses, she opened them and got a fresh shock of Jacob's presence, enough to last her half a day. But this was wearing thin. And she wrote now – poems, letters that were never posted, saw his face in advertisements on hoardings, and would cross the road to let the barrel-organ turn her musings to rhapsody. But at breakfast (she shared rooms with a teacher), when the butter was smeared about the plate, and the prongs of the forks were clotted with old egg yolk, she revised these visions violently; was, in truth, very cross; was losing her complexion, as Margery Jackson told her, bringing the whole thing down (as she laced her stout boots) to a level of mother-wit, vulgarity, and sentiment, for she had loved too; and been a fool.

'One's godmothers ought to have told one,' said Fanny, looking in at the window of Bacon, the mapseller, in the Strand[11] – told one that it is no use making a fuss; this is life, they should have said, as Fanny said it now, looking at the large yellow globe marked with steamship lines.

'This is life. This is life,' said Fanny.

'A very hard face,' thought Miss Barrett, on the other side of the glass, buying maps of the Syrian desert[12] and waiting impatiently to be served. 'Girls look old so soon nowadays.'

The equator swam behind tears.

'Piccadilly?' Fanny asked the conductor of the omnibus, and climbed to the top. After all, he would, he must, come back to her.

But Jacob might have been thinking of Rome; or architecture; of jurisprudence; as he sat under the plane tree in Hyde Park.

The omnibus stopped outside Charing Cross; and behind it were clogged omnibuses, vans, motor-cars, for a procession with banners was passing down Whitehall, and elderly people were stiffly descending from between the paws of the slippery lions,[13] where they had been testifying to their faith, singing lustily, raising their eyes from their music to look into the sky, and still their eyes were on the sky as they marched behind the gold letters of their creed.

The traffic stopped, and the sun, no longer sprayed out by the breeze, became almost too hot. But the procession passed; the banners glittered far away down Whitehall; the traffic was released; lurched on; spun to a smooth continuous uproar; swerving round the curve of Cockspur Street; and sweeping past Government offices and equestrian statues down Whitehall to the prickly spires, the tethered grey fleet of masonry, and the large white clock of Westminster.

Five strokes Big Ben intoned; Nelson received the salute. The wires of the Admiralty shivered with some far-away communication. A voice kept remarking that Prime Ministers and Viceroys spoke in the Reichstag;[14] entered Lahore; said that the Emperor travelled; in Milan they rioted; said there were rumours in Vienna; said that the Ambassador at Constantinople had audience with the Sultan; the fleet was at Gibraltar. The voice continued, imprinting on the faces of the clerks in Whitehall (Timothy Durrant was one of them) something of its own inexorable gravity, as they listened, deciphered, wrote down. Papers accumulated, inscribed with the utterances of Kaisers, the statistics of rice-fields, the growling of hundreds of workpeople, plotting sedition in back streets, or gathering in the Calcutta bazaars, or mustering their forces in the uplands of Albania, where the hills are sand-coloured, and bones lie unburied.

The voice spoke plainly in the square quiet room with heavy tables, where one elderly man made notes on the margin of typewritten sheets, his silver-topped umbrella leaning against the bookcase.

His head – bald, red-veined, hollow-looking – represented all the heads in the building.[15] His head, with the amiable pale eyes, carried the burden of knowledge across the street; laid it before his colleagues, who came equally burdened; and then the sixteen gentlemen, lifting their pens or turning perhaps rather wearily in their chairs, decreed that the course of history should shape itself this way or that way, being manfully determined, as their faces showed, to impose some coherency upon Rajahs and Kaisers and the muttering in bazaars, the secret gatherings, plainly visible in Whitehall, of kilted peasants in Albanian uplands; to control the course of events.

Pitt and Chatham, Burke and Gladstone[16] looked from side to side with fixed marble eyes and an air of immortal quiescence which perhaps the living may have envied, the air being full of whistling and concussions, as the procession with its banners passed down

Whitehall. Moreover, some were troubled with dyspepsia; one had at that very moment cracked the glass of his spectacles; another spoke in Glasgow to-morrow; altogether they looked too red, fat, pale or lean, to be dealing, as the marble heads had dealt, with the course of history.

Timmy Durrant in his little room in the Admiralty, going to consult a Blue book,[17] stopped for a moment by the window, and observed the placard tied round the lamp-post.

Miss Thomas, one of the typists, said to her friend that if the Cabinet was going to sit much longer she should miss her boy outside the Gaiety.[18]

Timmy Durrant, returning with his Blue book under his arm, noticed a little knot of people at the street corner; conglomerated as though one of them knew something; and the others, pressing round him, looked up, looked down, looked along the street. What was it that he knew?

Timothy, placing the Blue book before him, studied a paper sent round by the Treasury for information. Mr. Crawley, his fellow-clerk, impaled a letter on a skewer.

Jacob rose from his chair in Hyde Park, tore his ticket to pieces, and walked away.

'Such a sunset,' wrote Mrs. Flanders in her letter to Archer at Singapore. 'One couldn't make up one's mind to come indoors,' she wrote. 'It seemed wicked to waste even a moment.'

The long windows of Kensington Palace[19] flushed fiery rose as Jacob walked away; a flock of wild duck flew over the Serpentine; and the trees were stood against the sky, blackly, magnificently.

'Jacob,' wrote Mrs. Flanders, with the red light on her page, 'is hard at work after his delightful journey . . .'

'The Kaiser,' the far-away voice remarked in Whitehall, 'received me in audience.'

'Now I know that face — ' said the Reverend Andrew Floyd, coming out of Carter's shop in Piccadilly, 'but who the dickens — ?' and he watched Jacob, turned round to look at him, but could not be sure—

'Oh, Jacob Flanders!' he remembered in a flash.

But he was so tall; so unconscious; such a fine young fellow.

'I gave him Byron's works,' Andrew Floyd mused, and started forward, as Jacob crossed the road; but hesitated, and let the moment pass, and lost the opportunity.

Another procession, without banners, was blocking Long Acre.[20] Carriages, with dowagers in amethyst and gentlemen spotted with carnations, intercepted cabs and motor-cars turned in the opposite direction, in which jaded men in white waistcoats lolled, on their way home to shrubberies and billiard-rooms in Putney and Wimbledon.

Two barrel-organs played by the kerb, and horses coming out of Aldridge's[21] with white labels on their buttocks straddled across the road and were smartly jerked back.

Mrs. Durrant, sitting with Mr. Wortley in a motor-car, was impatient lest they should miss the overture.

But Mr. Wortley, always urbane, always in time for the overture, buttoned his gloves, and admired Miss Clara.

'A shame to spend such a night in the theatre!' said Mrs. Durrant, seeing all the windows of the coachmakers in Long Acre ablaze.

'Think of your moors!' said Mr. Wortley to Clara.

'Ah! but Clara likes this better,' Mrs. Durrant laughed.

'I don't know – really,' said Clara, looking at the blazing windows. She started.

She saw Jacob.

'Who?' asked Mrs. Durrant sharply, leaning forward.

But she saw no one.

Under the arch of the Opera House large faces and lean ones, the powdered and the hairy, all alike were red in the sunset; and, quickened by the great hanging lamps with their repressed primrose lights, by the tramp, and the scarlet, and the pompous ceremony, some ladies looked for a moment into steaming bedrooms near by, where women with loose hair leaned out of windows, where girls – where children – (the long mirrors held the ladies suspended) but one must follow; one must not block the way.

Clara's moors were fine enough. The Phoenicians[22] slept under their piled grey rocks; the chimneys of the old mines pointed starkly; early moths blurred the heather-bells; cartwheels could be heard grinding on the road far beneath; and the suck and sighing of the waves [23] sounded gently, persistently, for ever.

Shading her eyes with her hand Mrs. Pascoe stood in her cabbage-garden looking out to sea. Two steamers and a sailing-ship crossed each other; passed each other; and in the bay the gulls kept alighting on a log, rising high, returning again to the log, while some rode in upon the waves and stood on the rim of the water until the moon blanched all to whiteness.

Mrs. Pascoe had gone indoors long ago.

But the red light was on the columns of the Parthenon, and the Greek women who were knitting their stockings and sometimes crying to a child to come and have the insects picked from its head were as jolly as sand-martins in the heat, quarrelling, scolding, suckling their babies, until the ships in the Piraeus fired their guns. [24]

The sound spread itself flat, and then went tunnelling its way with fitful explosions among the channels of the islands.

Darkness drops like a knife over Greece.

'The guns?' said Betty Flanders, half asleep, getting out of bed and going to the window, which was decorated with a fringe of dark leaves.

'Not at this distance,' she thought. 'It is the sea.'

Again, far away, she heard the dull sound, as if nocturnal women were beating great carpets. There was Morty lost, and Seabrook dead; her sons fighting for their country. But were the chickens safe? Was that some one moving downstairs? Rebecca with the toothache? No. The nocturnal women were beating great carpets. Her hens shifted slightly on their perches.

XIV

'He left everything just as it was,' Bonamy marvelled. 'Nothing arranged. All his letters strewn about for any one to read. What did he expect? Did he think he would come back?' he mused, standing in the middle of Jacob's room.

The eighteenth century has its distinction. These houses were built, say, a hundred and fifty years ago. The rooms are shapely, the ceilings high; over the doorways a rose or a ram's skull is carved in the wood. Even the panels, painted in raspberry-coloured paint, have their distinction.

Bonamy took up a bill for a hunting-crop.

'That seems to be paid,' he said.

There were Sandra's letters.

Mrs. Durrant was taking a party to Greenwich.[1]

Lady Rocksbier hoped for the pleasure . . .

Listless is the air in an empty room, just swelling the curtain; the flowers in the jar shift. One fibre in the wicker arm-chair creaks, though no one sits there.

Bonamy crossed to the window. Pickford's van swung down the street. The omnibuses were locked together at Mudie's corner.[2] Engines throbbed, and carters, jamming the brakes down, pulled their horses sharp up. A harsh and unhappy voice cried something unintelligible. And then suddenly all the leaves seemed to raise themselves.

'Jacob! Jacob!'[3] cried Bonamy, standing by the window. The leaves sank down again.

'Such confusion everywhere!' exclaimed Betty Flanders, bursting open the bedroom door.

Bonamy turned away from the window.

'What am I to do with these, Mr. Bonamy?'

She held out a pair of Jacob's old shoes.

THE END

Notes

1. *Scarborough is seven hundred miles from Cornwall*: Virginia Woolf's first hint to the reader of the fictitious status of *JR*. In fact, Scarborough is 442 miles from St Ives, but Betty Flanders may have a poor grasp of facts (like Mrs Ramsay in *To the Lighthouse* (1927) and Clarissa Dalloway in *Mrs Dalloway* (1925)), or she may feel farther from home than she actually is. In reading about Scarborough we should bear in mind that Woolf is, to some extent, parodying the conventions of the Edwardian novel, with its emphasis on minutiae. We should also, perhaps, heed the warning she gives in her essay, 'Literary Geography': 'A writer's country is a territory within his own brain; and we run the risk of disillusionment if we try to turn such phantom cities into tangible brick and mortar' (*Essays*, I, p. 35).

2. *it was just* that *note which brought the rest together*: Woolf read Roger Fry's important essay 'An Essay in Aesthetics', as she was writing *JR*. Fry argues there that 'One chief aspect of order in a work of art is unity ... In a picture this unity is due to a balancing of the attractions of the eye about the central line of the picture' (Roger Fry, *Vision and Design*, 1920; Penguin Books, 1961, p. 34). The first page of the *MS* of *JR* bears Virginia Woolf's note: 'Let us suppose that the Room will hold it together' (*MS*, p. 1).

3. *Titian*: Tiziano Vecellio (*c.* 1487–1576). Perhaps the most important painter of the sixteenth century, he painted many of the kings and princes of Europe. He was twenty-nine when he was appointed painter to the Venetian Republic, so Charles Steele's facts are as unreliable as Betty Flanders'.

4. *a skull, perhaps, with the teeth in it*: little boys tend to become attached to skulls in Virginia Woolf's novels. James Ramsay, in *To the Lighthouse*, refuses to sleep unless he can see his boar's skull, nailed to the bedroom wall (*To the Lighthouse*, Hogarth Press, 1927; Penguin Books, 1992, p. 124).

5. *the Strand magazines*: the *Strand* (founded in 1891) was the leading illustrated magazine of the day. It set a trend for large-format, generously illustrated magazines which included seralized fiction; Sherlock Holmes began life there.

6. *a single leaf*: while it would be a serious mistake to look for any consistent symbolism in Woolf's work, the single leaf is an important recurring image. In *A Room of One's Own* (1928) a single leaf detaches itself from a plane tree 'like a signal falling' when a man and woman meet.

7. *think of the fairies*: Mrs Ramsay offers James the same advice in *To the Lighthouse*, where she is sure they will love the skull from which he refuses to be parted (*To the Lighthouse*, Penguin Books, 1992, p. 124).

8. *Archer*: in the *MS*, Jacob is alone in the nursery. Archer did not originally appear in chapter I, except in Jacob's thoughts: 'Archer would know how old the bone was' (*MS*, p. 5). Jacob thus originally seemed a much lonelier child. The proximity of his brothers, in the published text, emphasizes his independence of mind, which withstands their (or indeed anybody's) interventions.

CHAPTER II

1. *enclosed in three shells; the crevices sealed with lead*: throughout the eighteenth and nineteenth centuries graves were vulnerable to the vandalism of grave-robbers, so the financially comfortable often had double or triple coffins. In 1818 the patent coffin (made of cast or wrought iron, with concealed spring catches) was devised by Edward Bridgeman. Sea-brook's sounds more like the old, triple-layered (wood–lead–wood) style of coffin.

2. *well, she had to call him something*: an example of the way Virginia Woolf undermines the conventions of the traditional Edwardian novel, in which a man's title – 'Merchant of this city', for example – would have summed him up. Woolf hated this kind of writing, of which she judged H. G. Wells to be a major offender (cf. p. xii); he was, she once wrote, 'taking upon his shoulders the work that ought to have been discharged by Government officials'. In *JR* by contrast, she aims to convey the 'varying . . . unknown and uncircumscribed spirit' of the human personality ('Modern Fiction', *CE*, II, pp. 105, 106).

3. *the thousand white stones*: another feature of nineteenth-century graveyards was that they were often severely overcrowded.

4. *lilacs that drooped in April*: they don't, as Woolf admitted in a letter to C. P. Sanger (*Letters*, II, pp. 577–8). This may be, she conceded, one of the novel's 'glaring mistakes'.

5. *the voice of the dead*: there are echoes of Romantic poetry running through the novel. Here, Woolf may have had in mind Tennyson's line from 'In

the Valley of the Cauteretz': 'The voice of the dead was a living voice to me.'

6. *Dods Hill*: a fictitious place; the real Scarborough is dominated by Castle Hill.

7. *the Crimea*: the Crimean War, 1854–6.

8. *the whole of Scarborough . . . laid out flat*: 'Scarborough', in this chapter, is a mixture of fact and fiction. There are the remains of a Roman signal station in the actual town of Scarborough, but the street plan of the town is far from flat, though it does lie partially between the moors and the sea. There was a pier between 1866 and 1905, but it was two miles from the Aquarium (so the queue would have been very long). There is a 'Moorish' bandstand (in Clarence Gardens), but 'Scarborough' is partly Woolf's invention; cf. chapter I, Note 1.

9. *Tulips burned in the sun*: another of the 'glaring mistakes' Woolf identified for C. P. Sanger; (cf. Note 4).

10. *sponge-bag trousers*: also feature in *Orlando* (1928), where they are one of the main signals that Orlando has entered the Edwardian age.

11. *triangular hoardings . . . exclamation*: the hoardings were used for advertising news. In the *MS*, 'A monster shark had been caught. One side of the triangular hoarding said so in red, blue and yellow letters, each sentence ending with three notes of exclamation' (*MS*, p. 15).

12. *Fix your eyes upon the lady's skirt*: the idea that the march of history might be marked by the changes in women's dress is one which also runs through *Orlando*. The suggestion is that this may be as reliable a way of documenting history as any; cf. the traditional male view (which *JR* questions) that history might 'consist of the biographies of great men' – an assertion of Thomas Carlyle's. See chapter III, Note 21.

13. *The Rev. Jaspar Floyd dug them up at his own expense*: the idea here may be that a more profound investigation of history might be made by the individual, but it would require a greater personal investment (amateur archaeologists, including clergymen in the nineteenth century, were among the first to investigate the remains of the Roman signal station at Scarborough).

14. *Rugby*: became one of the great English public schools under the direction of its famous headmaster, Dr Thomas Arnold (who was head of the school from 1828–42). It was immortalized in *Tom Brown's Schooldays* (written by Thomas Hughes, an 'Old Boy', and published in 1857).

15. *a well-known series of Ecclesiastical Biographies*: Mr Floyd is a traditionalist; cf. the essay Jacob will write at Cambridge, entitled 'Does History Consist of the Biographies of Great Men?' (p. 31).

16. *Leg of Mutton Pond*: at the western edge of Hampstead Heath.

17. *the Scarborough and Harrogate Courier*: another of Virginia Woolf's inspired inventions.

18. *The tree had fallen*: the tree-falling incident occurs several times in Virginia Woolf's essays, e.g. 'Reading' (*CE*, II, pp. 12–33).

19. *taken him for a burglar when he came home late*: Paul Rayley makes the same mistake in *To the Lighthouse*, when his wife comes home at three in the morning (*To the Lighthouse*, Penguin Books, 1992, p. 188).

20. *Morris*: Francis Orpen Morris (1810–93) was a famous Victorian naturalist, who wrote popular books on natural history. The Stephen children had a copy of one of his books for their 'bug-hunting activities'; cf. Introduction, Note 24.

21. *like two boys fighting*: cf. p. 88, where Sanders and Bonamy fight 'like two bulls of Bashan'.

22. *for he was lame and wanted two fingers on his left hand*: like Colonel Pargiter in *The Years* (1937), whose identity as a man is also an issue for speculation.

23. *the brothers Zeno*: this fictitious vaudeville act has a significant name. Zeno of Citium (336–264 BC) was a founder of Stoicism, the ancient Greek system of thought which has been called the religion of the public schools. The basis of it is that everything is material and that thought is an ethereal form of matter which has the power to control its grosser forms. Man's soul was believed to be part of the world-soul which made all human beings brothers (hence, the joke: the brothers Zeno). Jacob's stoical attitude towards the body and its 'gross' passions is a major issue for him, particularly in his relations with women; cf. p. 69.

24. *He, a man, was in charge of Mrs. Barfoot, a woman*: as though their respective gender-identities fixed the power relations between them. Woolf is being ironic: this is a basic patriarchal assumption which she questions throughout *JR*, and throughout her work as a whole. It is a major theme, particularly, of *A Room of One's Own*.

25. *give it to her*: 'give it her', in the first British edition.

26. *1906*: the year Thoby Stephen died (on 20 November) of typhoid fever.

CHAPTER III

1. *shut up alone, in a railway carriage, with a young man*: the railway carriage is one of Woolf's favourite locations. She exploits it to particular advantage in her short story, 'An Unwritten Novel', and in her famous essay about narrative technique, 'Mr Bennett and Mrs Brown', in which

'Mr Bennett' is Arnold Bennett and 'Mrs Brown' is a lady traveller ('Mr Bennett and Mrs Brown', *A Woman's Essays*, Penguin Books, 1992, pp. 69ff.).

2. *a novel from Mudie's*: Mudie's famous circulating library was founded in 1842, when Charles Edward Mudie began lending books from his stationer's shop in Bloomsbury. Between 1843 and 1848, the railways added 3,000 miles of track in England, one of the major factors in creating a vast new novel-reading public. In 1852, Mudie moved to larger premises at the corner of Oxford Street and Museum Street (the 'Mudie's Corner' referred to on p. 53).

3. *the infallible test of appearance*: this is, of course, ironic – it is one of the main assumptions Virginia Woolf undermines throughout *JR*.

4. *the Morning Post . . . the Daily Telegraph*: two of the principal London morning papers (of which there were nineteen in 1901, and twenty-eight by 1910; this was very much the era of the rise of the newspaper); cf. p. 104.

5. *one of Mr. Norris's novels*: W. E. (William Edward) Norris (1847–1925) was a popular novelist, whose books Virginia Woolf regularly reviewed on publication. His method, she noted, was to 'tell his simple story without any desire to discuss problems or suggest that everything is not precisely as it ought to be' ('Barham of Beltana', *Essays*, I, p. 36): the antithesis, of course, of her own method in *JR*.

6. *They say the sky is the same everywhere*: Virginia Woolf's sister Vanessa once asked, as a young child, if this was the case.

7. *the roof of King's College Chapel*: the vaulted roof (built by John Wastell between 1512 and 1515) is one of the Chapel's most noteworthy features. The distinctive light above the Chapel is such that the sky there seems to have a range of different 'moods'.

8. *the subservient eagle bears up for inspection the great white book*: another of Woolf's inventions – there is no lectern in the form of an eagle in King's College Chapel.

9. *every insect in the forest . . . one large toad being the most besotted*: 'Toads,' Virginia Woolf told Jacques Raverat in a letter, 'are (essentially) insects, I maintain' (*Letters*, II, pp. 591–2); cf. p. 143, where the City financiers behave like insects.

10. *No one would think of bringing a dog into church*: here, Woolf was surely thinking of Dr Johnson's assertion that 'a woman's preaching is like a dog's walking on his hind legs. It is not done well; but you are surprised to find it done at all.' The attitude of Cambridge towards women, Woolf is suggesting, is comparable. She develops this theme in *A Room of One's Own*.

NOTES

11. *vouched for by . . . their husbands*: again, the assumption Woolf is exposing is that women are unable to think for themselves.

12. *Waverley*: the Plumers have named their villa after the series of thirty-two novels by Sir Walter Scott (the first volume was published in 1814). Virginia Woolf was a great admirer of Scott, as was her father, Leslie Stephen, whose favourite volume, which he read aloud to his children, was *The Heart of Midlothian*, of which chapter IV bears the heading, 'The hour is come, but not the man': very much the situation here, as everyone waits for Jacob (cf. Introduction, Note 25).

13. *went down*: graduated from the university.

14. *the suburbs of Manchester*: for Woolf, a place of intellectual nullity (cf. chapter I of *Night and Day*). She visited Manchester in 1921, and found the dons and their wives 'provincial, smug, destitute of any character, hopelessly suburban, yet trying to live up to the metropolitan intellect (me, I mean) which they can't do' (Letter to Vanessa Bell, 17 March 1921, *Letters*, II, p. 458).

15. *the Reform Bill*: a measure designed, in 1832, to revise the British system of parliamentary representation and create a uniform basis for franchise (in place of such anomalies as the Rotten Boroughs and Pocket Boroughs, where patrons could secure the return of their own nominees). Effectively, it enfranchised the upper middle classes.

16. *Wells and Shaw*: H. G. (Herbert George) Wells (1866–1946), best known for his scientific-romance novels, and George Bernard Shaw (1856–1950), author of over fifty plays about mental and moral passions. Wells and Shaw were among those writers who for Woolf epitomized Edwardian 'materialism'. 'By the Edwardians,' she clearly stated, 'I mean Shaw, Wells, Galsworthy, the Webbs, Arnold Bennett' (Letter to Janet Case, 21 May 1922, *Letters*, II, p. 529).

17. *serious sixpenny weeklies written by pale men*: the intellectual weeklies, as opposed to the more popular journals. The *Spectator*, for example, cost 6d. at this date whereas the *Young Ladies Journal* cost 2d. and the *London Journal* 1d. The 'pale men' would undoubtedly be writing for the *Spectator* or the *Economist*, the 'higher journalism' aimed at the opinion-forming classes.

18. *Byron*: Lord George Gordon Byron (1788–1824), poet and notorious womanizer, pronounced 'mad, bad and dangerous to know' by his mistress, Lady Caroline Lamb. Author of *Don Juan* (1819) and of *Childe Harold's Pilgrimage* (1812–18), of which canto xxi is about Wellington and the Battle of Waterloo (cf. 'The Duke of Wellington', p. 41; and chapter IV, Note 4).

19. *Trinity*: Thoby Stephen went up to Trinity College, Cambridge, in 1899.

20. *Neville's Court*: the courtyard at Trinity College, flanked on one side by the Wren Library and on the others by fellows' and students' rooms. The Great Court adjoins Neville's Court.

21. *Does History Consist of the Biographies of Great Men?*: a question running throughout *JR*. Jacob's essay question invokes Thomas Carlyle (1795–1881) in *Heroes and Hero-Worship*, Lecture 1, 'The Hero as Divinity': 'The history of the world is but the biography of great men.' The assertion implies hero-worship of the kind that is consistently called into question throughout the novel (especially through the references to Wellington, see Note 18).

22. *any one who's worth anything reads just what he likes*: this was Leslie Stephen's firm belief, and Jacob's too, judging by the catholic tastes reflected in the bookshelves in his room.

23. *Lives of the Duke of Wellington . . . all the Elizabethans*: here the wide range of Jacob's tastes is detailed. Woolf wrote about most of these (in her essays), though her views are not necessarily always the same as Jacob's.

24. *Sir Joshua*: Reynolds, 1723–92, or 'Sir Sloshua' as his critics called him (his work was thought sloppy and sentimental by some). He was a famous portrait painter and founder-member and first president of the Royal Academy of Art.

25. *The works of Jane Austen, too, in deference, perhaps, to some one else's standard*: an example of the danger of confusing Virginia Woolf's standards with Jacob's. Woolf judged that the 'balance of her gifts was singularly perfect. Among her finished novels there are no failures' ('Jane Austen', *CE*, I, p. 151).

26. *Carlyle was a prize*: reflecting the University of Cambridge's, or perhaps Rugby's, standards; cf. pp. 16, 31; chapter III, Note 21.

27. *Italian painters of the Renaissance*: a group of painters – and a formation of style in the arts – generally thought to begin with Giotto (d. 1337) and to end some time in the sixteenth century between the deaths of Raphael (1520) and Tintoretto (1594). They claimed nothing less than a rebirth of letters and the arts after a sleep of 1,000 years. So Woolf is cryptically making the link – here as elsewhere in *JR* – between the artist and the making and remaking of history.

28. *a Manual of the Diseases of the Horse*: a serious component of any gentleman's library, since the motor car was still a very recent invention. By 1904, when compulsory registration was introduced, there were still only about 8,500 cars in the country.

29. *Huxtable . . . Sopwith . . . Cowan*: are all fictitious dons, but the narrator's refusal to put them on a pedestal is reminiscent of Woolf's

disappointment in G. E. Moore (1873–1958), philosopher, Fellow of Trinity College, and University Lecturer in Moral Sciences at Cambridge, whose book, *Principia Ethica* (1903), was deeply influential. She met him just after beginning *JR*, and noted 'A lack of mass, somewhere . . . I dont see altogether why he was the dominator & dictator of youth. Perhaps Cambridge is too much of a cave' (*Diary*, II, 23 June 1920, p. 49).

30. *Van Gogh reproduced*: Vincent Van Gogh (1853–90), painter of *A Pair of Shoes*; cf. p. xxxviii.

31. *Chucky, the unsuccessful provincial*: cf. Charles Tansley, the 'unsuccessful provincial', in *To the Lighthouse*. Woolf's portraits of 'provincials' are generally unsympathetic.

32. This *my image?*: the dialogue here between philosopher and poet may echo the dialogue of Yeats's poem, 'Ego Dominus Tuus', collected in *The Wild Swans at Coole* (1919), which Virginia Woolf read as she was writing *JR*:

> *Hic.* And I would find myself and not an image.
> *Ille.* That is our modern hope, and by its light
> We have lit upon the gentle, sensitive mind

33. *Virgil's . . . arms, bees, or even the plough*: *Georgics*, Book 2, cf. p. 118 and chapter XII, Note 2.

34. *the thing she might have said . . . for ever left out*: here, Virginia Woolf introduces the theme of the censorship of women's language, an issue she would go on to develop more fully in *A Room of One's Own*.

35. *things that are known and things that are about to be known*: possibly a Biblical echo: 'The thing that hath been, it is that which shall be; and that which is done is that which shall be done: and there is no new thing under the sun' (Eccles., 1:9); and a warning, perhaps, about the limitations of scholarship. The narrator of a novel, on the other hand, knows 'the things that are about to be known' – another reminder that the narrative continuum of *JR* has its own creative autonomy.

36. *the Moonlight Sonata*: the nickname (not Beethoven's, and fitting only the first movement) for Beethoven's piano sonata in C♯ minor, op. 27, no. 2 (1801). Rachel Vinrace plays Beethoven's sonatas, in *The Voyage Out* (1915).

37. *shilling shockers*: the early twentieth-century equivalent of 'penny dreadfuls'. *JR* cost 7/6 when published, as did many of Virginia Woolf's novels, whereas Jack London's novels ranged from 3/6 down to 6d. (the latter being a 'cheap' edition). This suggests that pulp fiction of a vaguely sensational nature had a lower price in expectation of larger markets.

38. *making long pink spills from an old newspaper*: the newspaper was probably the *Globe* which we see Jacob reading on p. 84; it was one of the principal London evening newspapers, and was printed on pink-tinted paper.

39. *ate dates from a long box*: as if to express his scorn for the traditional view of history and assert, instead, his casual, modern attitude.

40. *Julian the Apostate*: the Roman Emperor (332–63) who tried to destroy Christianity, persecuted Christians and promoted paganism; cf. Jacob's remark about 'European mysticism' on p. 145.

41. *The young man – the young man – the young man – back to his rooms*: Jacob's presence is here being evoked through the rhythm of his footsteps. A moment which adds particular poignancy when compared to the ending of the novel, with its focus on Jacob's uninhabited shoes.

CHAPTER IV

1. *Although the plays of Shakespeare had frequently been ... placed higher than the Greek*: Thoby Stephen placed Shakespeare higher than the Greeks, but he, unlike Jacob, had Shakespeare 'all in his grasp' (*Moments of Being*, pp. 138–9).

2. *and even take a little one ... by themselves at the end*: here, Virginia Woolf has another dig at the idea of rational man, and the imperviousness of the male sentence and the academic argument. She continues her attack in *A Room of One's Own* and, more lightheartedly, in *To the Lighthouse*, where the argument is portrayed in the form of an alphabet, and poor Mr Ramsay cannot even get as far as the letter 'R' (*To the Lighthouse*, Penguin Books, 1992, pp. 39–42).

3. *spats*: short cloth or leather anklets, worn on a pair of shoes, with buttons along the outer side: the footwear of the debonair.

4. *The Duke of Wellington ... Keats ... Lord Salisbury*: Arthur Wellesley, first Duke of Wellington (1769–1852), hero of the Battle of Waterloo (18 June 1815) and Prime Minister, 1828–30. Wellington was an archetypal military hero and Tory politician, known as the 'Iron Duke'. He is frequently invoked, throughout *JR*, as a figure who personifies the values of the British Empire; cf. pp. 54, 147. John Keats (1795–1821), poet and one of the principal figures in the Romantic movement. His tragically early death makes him a suitable figure for Jacob to invoke at this point, where the narrative subtly changes key. Lord Salisbury (Robert Gascoyne-Cecil, Marquess of Salisbury, 1830–1903) became Foreign Secretary in 1878, leader of the Conservative Party in 1881,

and subsequently headed three governments (1885–6, 1886–92, 1895–1902).

5. *Abide with me*: a popular Victorian hymn, by H. F. Lyte (1793–1847). The second verse begins, 'Swift to its close ebbs out life's little day': an ominous hint of what is to come.

6. *Great God, what do I see and hear?*: a hymn by anon. (1802); later revised by W. B. Collyer (1812), T. Cotterill (1819) and others.

7. *Rock of Ages*: by A. M. Toplady (1740–78), another popular hymn.

8. *squat*: 'squab' in the first edition.

9. *Mrs. Pascoe*: was a real person. She appears (though in name only) in Virginia Woolf's 1905 Cornwall journal. The *MS* is more explicit about her sexual experiences: in such a small cottage as hers 'there would be no escaping the body'. She would have known all kinds of things: 'copulation upstairs in the double bed', or even 'before the fire perhaps', but Woolf toned her down for publication, perhaps because she always found it difficult to write about the body – 'Its functions are detestable' (*MS*, pp. 99–101).

10. *These white Cornish cottages*: Leonard and Virginia Woolf owned, part-owned or rented three such cottages.

11. *the Gurnard's Head*: a rocky promontory on the north coast of Cornwall near Zennor, and accessible on foot from St Ives.

12. *tramp steamer*: a ship which takes goods irregularly to various parts.

13. *she prized mats, china mugs, and photographs*: one of Woolf's fantasies about 'the poor' was that 'they are very close to what they possess', because they have 'bought them off barrows in the street with money earned by their own hands' ('Walter Sickert', *CE*, II, pp. 238–9). The servant Crosby's possessions are similarly itemized, in an important section of Virginia Woolf's later novel, *The Years*.

14. *Lady Cynthia's wedding at the Abbey*: Lady Cynthia Charteris married the Prime Minister's younger son, Herbert Asquith, in Westminster Abbey in 1910.

15. *hazy, semi-transparent shapes of yellow and blue*: the women in their evening dresses, evoked in the imagery of 'life itself', as Woolf describes it in her essay 'Modern Fiction' (*CE*, II, pp. 103–10), and as seen by the nervous and perhaps slightly intoxicated Jacob.

16. *Mr. Clutterbuck*: Arthur Clutton-Brock (1868–1924) was art critic of *The Times*; Woolf may here be playing on his name; cf. p. 50.

17. *It's so interesting to guess*: Woolf here conveys the inconsequential remoteness of the conversation of the upper middle classes, very much as she did in her earlier story, 'Kew Gardens' (*A Haunted House and Other Stories*, Hogarth Press, 1944; Penguin Books, 1973).

18. *Lord Lansdowne*: Henry Petty Fitzmaurice (1845–1927), Unionist Foreign Secretary from 1900. From 1905–1915 he led the Conservative opposition in the Lords.

19. *Jacob held the ladder*: Woolf's gentle allusion here to Jacob's Biblical namesake is ironic, since it is Clara, not Jacob, who climbs the ladder.

20. *like a scarlet ear-ring*: the first American edition has 'erring', which is clearly a misprint. Virginia Woolf is here comparing the shape of the fuchsia with that of a woman's drop ear-ring.

CHAPTER V

1. *Mudie's corner in Oxford Street*: Mudie's circulating library moved to the corner of Oxford Street and Museum Street in 1852. See chapter III, Note 2.

2. *Mr. Spalding going to the city looked at Mr. Charles Budgeon bound for Shepherd's Bush*: the invention of the omnibus meant that the classes intermingled in public life as never before. Mr Spalding is on his way to London's business and financial centre, while Mr Charles Budgeon is bound for a lower-middle-class suburb.

3. *a shell secreted by man to fit man himself*: Woolf uses the same image in her later novel, *The Waves*.

4. *St. Paul's Cathedral*: Sir Christopher Wren's masterpiece stands at the top of Ludgate Hill. It boasts a dignified edifice in Renaissance style, dominated by the strikingly shaped dome.

5. *the organ for ever chaunts*: Woolf may have meant 'chants', but the word is 'chaunts' in the surviving pages of the typescript, and was retained in the first British edition.

6. *the great Duke's tomb*: another reference to the Duke of Wellington. His tomb is in the crypt of St Paul's Cathedral, below the centre of the dome.

7. *jute*: a plant fibre used for making canvas, sacking and twine. The jute industry dates from about 1806.

8. *Where's Nelson's tomb?*: it is in the crypt, with Wellington's (see Note 6).

9. *Finlay's Byzantine Empire*: George Finlay's *History of the Byzantine Empire, from 716 to 1057* (London, 1906). First published as *History of the Byzantine and Greek Empires, from 716 to 1453*, in 2 vols. (1854), but Jacob is obviously reading the Dent 1906, pocket-sized edition. Finlay, like Byron, was a supporter of Greece's declaration of independence; his obituary in the *Athenaeum* mentioned 'the loss caused to history and to English literature by the death of this last of the old generation of Philhellenes' (he died in Athens, in 1875).

10. *the Union of London and Smith's Bank*: in 1902, Smith's Bank merged with the Union Bank of London, a constituent company of the National Westminster Bank.

11. *clasping a brown mongrel tight in her arms and singing out loud*: in her diary for 8 June 1920, Virginia Woolf recorded the sight of 'an old beggar woman, blind, [who] sat against a stone wall in Kingsway holding a brown mongrel in her arms & sang aloud. There was a recklessness about her; much in the spirit of London. Defiant – almost gay, clasping her dog as if for warmth' (*Diary*, II, p. 47).

12. *as some believe, the city loves her prostitutes*: the surviving pages of the typescript contain this passage, but in the typescript the narrator claims a point of view: 'as I believe' rather than 'as some believe' (*Monks House Papers*, B. 12, p. 4).

13. *the arch of the Opera House*: the Covent Garden (Royal) Opera House, Bow Street, WC2, the most luxurious ever built in London, opened in 1732.

14. *Thomas à Kempis*: Thomas Hämmerlein or Hämmerken (1380–1471), the Augustinian monk and author of the *Imitation of the Life of Christ*.

15. *Tristan was twitching his rug . . . Isolde*: Richard Wagner's long opera, *Tristan und Isolde* (first performed in Munich in 1865), about love and passion. The 'rug' wittily refers to Tristan's long 'Liebestod'.

16. *Walpole . . . Victoria in her nightgown*: Horace Walpole died in 1797; Queen Victoria acceded to the throne in 1837, i.e. the opera is regarded as a rather Victorian institution.

17. *Brangäne*: Isolde's servant, in *Tristan und Isolde*.

18. *Virgil . . . Lucretius*: Publius Vergilius Maro Virgil (70–19 BC), Roman poet and author of the *Aeneid*, *Eclogues* and *Georgics*, whose poetry was generally held as rivalling that of the Greeks; Woolf alludes to the *Georgics* on pp. 33 and 118. Titus Lucretius Carus (*c.* 99–55 BC), Roman author of *De Rerum Natura*. The lines Jacob has been seeking may well be

> There is in all things a void, and to know this assists apprehension
> And leaves you not wandering in doubt . . . There is tangible space,
> A void and a room.
>
> (*De Rerum Natura*, I)

19. *Bonamy*: a character based, with his homosexuality and his capacity for loyal friendship, on Lytton Strachey, the great friend of Thoby Stephen, and later of Virginia Woolf. (On reading *JR* for the first time Strachey remarked, 'I am such a Bonamy'.)

20. *an edition of Wycherley*: the plays of William Wycherley (1641–1715) dealt with the themes of sexual morality and the marriage conventions, and were condemned by Macaulay as licentious and indecent. The Victorians were fond of bowdlerization, and the issue here of literary censorship extends to Virginia Woolf's theme in this novel of the censorship of sexuality. Jacob is outspoken (in his essay; with his male jokes about 'The Foaming Pot', p. 59; in giving Fanny a copy of *Tom Jones*, p. 106 and Sandra Wentworth Williams a copy of the poems of Donne), though the fact that 'the body is harnessed to a brain' is a problem for him in his relations with women (p. 69). Miss Umphelby always has to leave out of her work the thing she would really like to say: Woolf touches here on the issue of the censorship of sexuality in women's writing, a theme she would go on to develop in *A Room of One's Own*. The issue of intellectual snobbery also enters in, here: 'Leeds as a seat of learning was laughed to scorn.' Aristophanes and Shakespeare are cited because of their capacity for lewdness.

21. *the Fortnightly, the Contemporary, the Nineteenth Century*: all respectable literary periodicals, founded in the nineteenth century.

22. *Mr. Letts*: Virginia Woolf's jokey personification (cf. Professor Bulteel?) of the main printer of small, pocket-sized diaries. Again, the issue here is that Clara, as a woman (writer), is given no space to express her real thoughts and views.

23. *not one*: 'not the one', in the first British edition.

24. *Parliament Hill*: in North London, above Hampstead and Highgate – so-called because the Gunpowder Plotters were supposed to have planned to watch the destruction of the Houses of Parliament from there. The surviving pages of the typescript show that 'they were burning Guy Fawkes on Parliament Hill' was added later; in the typescript, the passage ends simply, 'whereas in London at this hour – '.

CHAPTER VI

1. *billycock hats*: introduced in the 1850s, they were otherwise named after the original hatter, William Bowler (they were called derbys in America; melons in France). At first worn for casual wear, they soon became acceptable as formal wear.

2. *Auld Lang Syne*: roughly, 'for old times' sake', in Scottish vernacular. From a poem by Robert Burns, set to music and usually sung, with arms clasped, by a group of friends breaking up at the end of an evening.

3. *taking one of the purplish globes . . . It crushed to powder*: an incident which may have been inspired by D. H. Lawrence's *Women in Love*, which Woolf read as she was writing *JR*, 'lured on by the portrait of Ottoline [Morrell, on whom Lawrence's character, Hermione Roddice, was based] . . . She has just smashed Lawrence's head open with a ball of lapis lazuli – but then balls are smashed on every other page' (Letter to Molly MacCarthy, 20 June 1921, *Letters*, II, p. 474).

4. *barrel-organ*: popular usage for a large automatic piano operated by a handle, played in the streets by itinerant musicians and popular at the time.

5. *they wreathed his head with paper flowers*: an idea Woolf may have taken from Shelley's *Hellas*, which she read as she was writing *JR*. There, the chorus of Greek women strew 'opiate flowers' on the pillow of the hero; cf. p. 64 where Jacob re-casts Florinda in his mind as one of the 'good women in the days of the Greeks'.

6. *The Greeks*: Jacob's passion for the Greeks is a strong theme running through the novel (later he will travel to Greece). Woolf's views here coincide with Jacob's: 'it is to the Greeks that we turn,' she wrote, 'when we are sick of the vagueness, of the confusion . . . of our own age' ('On Not Knowing Greek', *A Woman's Essays*, Penguin Books, 1992, p. 106). In *JR*, the civilization of Ancient Greece is regarded as a male domain. A point reiterated by the absurdity of Sandra Wentworth Williams' 'fashionable' preoccupation with the Greek style (see p. 124).

7. *Gibraltar . . . the British army . . . the Duke of Wellington*: there was a British peace-keeping truce at Gibraltar at this date. Jacob, though he despises the military, ironically praises the 'great Duke', who appears frequently throughout the novel; cf. pp. 41, 54, 147.

8. *the Inferno*: Dante's (Dante Alighieri, 1265–1321) great vision of Hell, from the *Divine Comedy*. Eleanor Pargiter, in Woolf's later novel *The Years*, also reads Dante.

9. *she was without a surname*: the idea of Florinda's illegitimacy may have been inspired by Defoe's *Moll Flanders*, which Woolf read with great enthusiasm as she was writing *JR*; she remarked that Moll reminded her of her sister Vanessa. The allusion adds a touch of female raciness to Jacob's name, even suggesting that what slender means of identification Florinda might have had has been subtly claimed by Jacob.

10. *the A.B.C. shop*: the Aerated Bread Company (bread and flour manufacturers) owned teashops all over London. The teashop was a vital component of female emancipation: until its emergence there had been nowhere a lady could eat or drink in public unaccompanied.

11. *his essay upon the Ethics of Indecency*: Woolf may have known about a paper Lytton Strachey wrote, *c.* 1908, entitled 'Art and Indecency' (in Paul Levy (ed.), *The Really Interesting Question and Other Papers*, Putnam, 1973). Jacob's essay of course continues the earlier discussion (on p. 58) about the bowdlerization of the Wycherley edition.

12. *Adonais*: Percy Bysshe Shelley's (1792–1822) elegy on the death of John Keats (1795–1821), written at Pisa and published in 1821.

13. *All plays turned on the same subject . . . on that account*: with the impact of Ibsen on Edwardian theatre, the subject of marital discord became a popular theme in drama. George Bernard Shaw pronounced himself an apostle of Ibsen's doctrine, and continued the good work. Ibsen's *Hedda Gabler* set the trend for 'bullets . . . through heads'.

14. *a snake . . . sliding through the grass*: Virgil's *Eclogue*, III, has 'Latet anguis in herba' ('A snake lurks in the grass'): a familiar way of referring to hidden sexual motives.

15. *Bechstein*: a generic name for one of the 'dirty Jews' referred to by Florinda on p. 65.

16. *Crash! And out she swept*: Virginia Woolf witnessed a similar scene in a London restaurant in March 1919: 'a prostitute who was dining at the next table suddenly threw her glass on the floor and upset the mustard and walked out, leaving her poor young man to look most uncomfortable' (Letter to Vanessa Bell, 23 March 1919, *Letters*, II, p. 341).

17. *She's dropped her glove*: the convention was that a prostitute would drop her glove to indicate availability. Woolf saw this happen, in Soho, while she was writing *JR* (*Diary*, II, 3 March 1920, p. 21). Jacob and Florinda seem to be innocently unfamiliar with the convention.

18. *The problem is insoluble. The body is harnessed to a brain*: Woolf may have had in mind the lines from Lucretius, *De Rerum Natura*, III – 'The intellect cannot spring up / Alone outside of the body, or live far from blood and sinews.' (The mind/body problem is also fundamental to most Western philosophy.) Woolf has referred to Lucretius earlier: cf. p. 58, where Jacob locates 'the lines which he had been seeking all day; only they come not in Virgil, but in Lucretius'.

CHAPTER VII

1. *little paper flowers which opened on touching water*: Japanese paper flowers, used to decorate fingerbowls at parties.

2. *little cards, with names engraved on them*: visiting cards were part of the whole system of paying calls, which was an important feature of Victorian and Edwardian upper-middle-class social life.

3. *Notting Hill . . . or the purlieus of Clerkenwell*: at the time, both would have been slum areas. The 'pitch black' is an indicator of the quality of life for 'the poor', which Woolf keeps in view throughout *JR*.

4. *Italian remained a hidden art, and the piano always played the same sonata*: Clara, like many nice girls of her class, is engaged in good work for the poor (like the Richmond Aunts in *The Voyage Out*), and therefore doesn't learn Italian or even a new piece on the piano – the typical situation of the upper-middle-class 'nice girl' at home.

5. *out-door relief*: organized poor relief, and the alternative to the work-house or hospital. Mrs Page would have got 5/- a week to live on, in the form of dole given out to the infirm or elderly (in the gift of Poor Law Guardians).

6. *Who is Silvia . . . commend her?*: a light, popular song, extolling the virtues of female chastity written in 1826, with English words by Shakespeare (from *The Two Gentlemen of Verona*) and music by Franz Schubert – 'Holy, fair, and wise is she . . . / . . . She excels each mortal thing'.

CHAPTER VIII

1. *the Hotspurs, the Harlequins*: by 1900, Tottenham Hotspur were one of the thirty-six firmly established association football clubs; the Har-lequins are a rugby team.

2. *Star*: a popular contemporary newspaper (edited, at the time, by T. P. O'Connor).

3. *Gray's Inn*: one of the four Inns of Court (of which the earliest records date from 1569) in London's West End. Jacob's office is located in the vicinity of Leonard Woolf's office at the *Nation*, which was in Great James Street (just north of Theobald's Road, near the junction with Gray's Inn Road).

4. *Then, sometimes a game of chess*: Woolf may here be echoing T. S. Eliot in *The Waste Land*, II, lines 137–8, who was in turn alluding to the game of chess in Middleton's *Women Beware Women*.

5. *pictures in Bond Street*: then as now, Bond Street was full of art galleries.

6. *Nelson on his column*: Nelson's Column stands on the south side of Trafalgar Square.

7. *down at Scarborough*: Virginia Woolf's (or Betty Flanders') geography has got the better of her again – the real Scarborough is 247 miles north of London.

8. *Parrot's great white sale*: the white sales were the large department stores' biannual stocktaking sales.

9. *Ireland or India*: the major political issue for both countries in the years leading up to the First World War was self-government. Gladstone's third Home Rule Bill was introduced in 1912; the Indian Councils Act (which marked a major step towards a self-governing India) came into force in 1909.

10. *Leghorns, Cochin Chinas, Orpingtons*: all different breeds of chicken.

11. *the feelings of a mother*: in the *MS*, Betty Flanders' feelings associated with her son's sexuality were even stronger and more closely associated with the violent imagery of (his?) birth. Woolf deleted from the *MS* the line, 'Behind the door knives cut human flesh from the bone, or death alights.' She retained 'Surgeons were there with their knives. Something was hinted that only austere [?] men or women in white capes might see; & having seen would never speak of' (*MS*, II, p. 5).

12. *the Russian dancers*: the first London appearance of Diaghileff's Russian ballet was at Covent Garden on 21 June 1909; they regularly appeared thereafter.

13. *make of life a perfect globe*: Virginia Woolf frequently uses this image of coherence in her work. Jacob also strives for a sense of coherence throughout the novel, which may be why he reads the *Globe*; cf. p. 84.

14. *Byron wrote letters. So did Cowper*: Byron has been referred to before; cf. pp. 16, 28, 80. Woolf reread his letters as she was writing *JR*, and she mentions Cowper's in the course of reviewing Swinburne's: 'There are people who would exchange all Byron's poems for half his letters . . . while Cowper's correspondence has the dog's ears, the sloping shoulders . . . of a loved companion' ('Swinburne Letters', *Essays*, II, p. 228).

15. *Greek Street*: a street in London's Soho.

16. *The light drenched Jacob from head to toe*: this passage shows a personality in crisis. Jacob is as vulnerable here as he was as a disoriented child on the beach. The power of the lamp to fix him in the moment may bear comparison with T. S. Eliot's 'Rhapsody on a Windy Night' (1917), although in her 1906 journal she imagines a rainy London street, 'with lamplight twisted on the pavement' (*Passionate Apprentice*, p. 345), so she is not necessarily being allusive here. Certainly, this is fine example of her modernist narrative technique: a far cry from the Edwardian 'stays and props', which seem to 'make of life a perfect globe' (p. 78).

17. *for centre, for magnet, a young man alone in his room*: cf. the note Woolf made on the first page of her *MS*: 'Let us suppose that the Room will hold it together' (*MS*, p. 1).

18. *As frequent as street corners in Holborn are these chasms in . . . our ways*: another (modernist) reminder that life is not 'a perfect globe': the directions we take are arbitrary; life is composed of contiguous, rather

than continuous, stories and a minor detour can culminate in quite a different story.

19. *The oval tea-table invariably separated them*: the tea-table dominated Victorian and Edwardian polite society. The Stephen family gathered round it daily at 4.30, at Hyde Park Gate, to entertain Sir Leslie Stephen's friends (or, as Adrian Stephen was later to call them, the 'Hyde Park Gaters'). Such occasions were the bane of Virginia Stephen's life (she parodies them in *Night and Day*), though she learned their conversational techniques which, she later recognized, influenced her ability to write witty essays and reviews.

20. *rooms in the Albany*: a mansion consisting of sixty-nine sets of bachelor chambers (residents have included Lord Byron, Aldous Huxley and Harold Nicolson) in Piccadilly, W1.

21. *And now Jimmy feeds crows in Flanders and Helen visits hospitals*: the series of proliferating narratives in this passage is an indicator of Florinda's power to move Jacob and to set him (and the narrative) moving in different directions, culminating in a story which, of course, sets the novel back in the political context of events leading up to the First World War (Jimmy's story, like Jacob's, will end on the fields of Flanders; Helen, like Clara Durrant, will visit the needy). The tragedy of missed opportunity is Virginia Woolf's message here.

22. *The yellow canopy sinks and swells*: Virginia Woolf's lyrical description of the London smog, which T. S. Eliot had rendered so strikingly animate in 'The Love Song of Alfred J. Prufrock' (1917). The obscuring of the double bed may also be seen to refer back to the sad fate of Jimmy and Helen.

23. *A motor-car*: Woolf's experiments with perspective in this sequence constitute another modernist departure from the narrative techniques of the Edwardian novel, and almost exactly echo her technique in her brief essay 'A Walk by Night' (1905, *Essays*, I, pp. 80–2). The motor car was an unusual sight before the war (though there were some around at the turn of the century).

24. *The worn voices of clocks ... all night long*: the fact of the hour is also repeated throughout the night in T. S. Eliot's 'Rhapsody on a Windy Night'; cf. Note 16.

CHAPTER IX

1. *The Countess of Rocksbier*: a made-up name, which Virginia Woolf had several stabs at inventing. In the *MS*, she lists possible alternatives: 'Rocksbier', 'Rookham', 'Rosckscave', 'Rockhold' and 'Rock' (*MS*, II, p. 32).

2. *Moll Pratt . . . Mrs. Hilda Thomas . . . Lady Rocksbier*: Virginia Woolf would have divided London, in her mind's eye, into three parts: the city, the suburbs and the slums, with their respective class associations. With these three figures she gives us an example of three kinds of Londoner: the flower seller from the slums, the respectable middle-class woman from the suburbs and the aristocrat.

3. *Joseph Chamberlain*: (1836–1914), was Gladstone's great opposer on the issue of Home Rule for Ireland. In 1886 he defected from the Liberal Party over this issue, a move which split the Party.

4. *did for*: cleaned his room.

5. *like two bulls of Bashan*: a Biblical reference; Bashan is the northernmost of the parts into which the region east of the Jordan was divided. The strong bulls of Bashan typify the fierce enemies that beset the righteous man (Ps. 22:12).

6. *Now there were four people . . . Jacob 25*: a witty parody of the Edwardian novelist's obsession with minutiae and classification, which approaches that of the journalist's or the 'Government Official's'; cf. p. xii.

7. *the Saturday Westminster*: a literary weekly which was sponsored as an offshoot of the Liberal penny evening paper, the *Westminster Gazette*, edited by J. A. Spender.

8. *Whistler*: James Abbott McNeill Whistler (1834–1903) was an American painter who appealed to British taste, particularly with his paintings on the theme of 'The White Girl'; cf. p. xxvi.

9. *a maiden in a large hat . . . a gentleman in eighteenth-century costume*: a typical scene of Edwardian over-the-fence courtship, and the subject of many popular nineteenth-century paintings.

10. *Laurette*: may have been inspired by Ralph Partridge (Leonard Woolf's assistant at the Hogarth Press) recounting his experiences with a prostitute. After the event, he said, they sat happily discussing the coal strike together. Woolf's point here is that Laurette *does* have a mind; cf. Jacob on Florinda, pp. 67–9.

11. *the names stretched in unbroken file round the dome of the British Museum*: Woolf here extends her evocative description of the British Museum Reading Room; cf. pp. 91, 93. The 'unbroken file' is suggestive of the continuity of the male canon and of the facility with which the world of male learning appears to proceed.

12. *her philosophy that colour is sound*: one of Roger Fry's post-impressionist theories was that art should be a kind of 'visual music'; others who experimented with this idea were the Russian composer, Scriabin, and the avant-garde poet, Apollinaire. Duncan Grant based his *Abstract*

Kinetic Scroll (1914) on this theory: Miss Marchmont is clearly a very progressive thinker.

13. *Mr. Asquith's Irish policy*: Herbert Henry Asquith (1852–1928) succeeded Campbell-Bannerman as Prime Minister in 1908, but it was not until 1912 that he was able to introduce a Home Rule Bill designed to give considerable self-government to the whole of Ireland. The Bill eventually passed the Commons in January 1913.

14. *Queen Alexandra*: (Danish) wife of Edward VII (who reigned from 1901–1910).

15. *Miss Julia Hedge, the feminist*: Julia encapsulates Virginia Woolf's strong views about the disadvantages which beset women scholars – a discussion she passionately continues in *A Room of One's Own*. It is symbolic of her plight that she 'waited for her books. They did not come.' If she wants to be independent she must study statistics, in order to qualify for a lucrative profession, as she would be unlikely ever to be admitted to Oxbridge as a university don. By contrast with the continuity – the 'unbroken file' – of male learning, there is no provision in the canon for the study of George Eliot, or Charlotte or Emily Brontë. The kind of education which consists of copying out poetry is closed to women and the struggles Julia must engage in, in order to achieve independence, jeopardize her femininity (she leaves her shoe laces untied, neglecting her appearance).

16. *Mr. Masefield ... Mr. Bennett ... Marlowe*: John Edward Masefield (1878–1967), prolific writer of some fifty volumes of verse, over twenty novels, eight plays and much miscellaneous work. (Enoch) Arnold Bennett (1867–1931), 'regional' English novelist, and one of the main butts of Woolf's attack on the Edwardian 'materialists'; cf. pp. xii, xiv. Christopher Marlowe (1564–93), playwright and author of *The Jew of Malta* (1633) and *Dr Faustus* (1604). All three are examples – spanning four centuries – of the range and breadth of the accepted male literary canon.

17. *the Victorians, who disembowel*: another reference to the issue of bowdlerization; cf. the earlier reference to the expurgated Wycherley edition (p. 58) which so enraged Jacob. The suggestion here is that modern scholarship must attend to the means and conditions of production, and not simply accept the literary canon at face value.

18. *The ... future depends entirely upon six young men*: perhaps a private reference to Thoby Stephen and his immediate circle: Clive Bell, Lytton Strachey, Saxon Sydney-Turner, Desmond MacCarthy and Maynard Keynes.

19. *a pudding-faced man*: Clive Bell (Virginia Woolf's brother-in-law) was 'pudding-faced'.

20. *Plato, Aristotle, Sophocles, and Shakespeare*: Plato (*c.* 428/7–348/7 BC), Greek philosopher. Aristotle (384–322 BC), Greek philosopher who studied under Plato. Sophocles (496–406 BC), first of the three great Attic tragedians. Shakespeare (allegedly 1564–1616), whose plays were influenced by all three. Another example of the range and continuity of the male canon.

21. *the Elgin Marbles*: so named after Lord Elgin, who 'reclaimed' a collection of Greek marbles and moved them from the Acropolis to the British Museum.

22. *Macaulay, Hobbes, Gibbon*: Thomas Babington Macaulay (1800–1859), author of the famous *History of England* (in 6 vols., 1849–55). Thomas Hobbes (1588–1679), philosopher of Nature and Man. Edward Gibbon (1737–94), author of *The History of the Decline and Fall of the Roman Empire* (vol. 1 published 1776), and cited by Virginia Woolf in *A Room of One's Own* as an exemplary stylist of the male sentence. Three further examples of the 'great men' of whose biographies history is traditionally held to consist.

23. *There is in the British Museum an enormous mind*: Virginia Woolf (with heavy 'male' emphasis) yet again reiterates her point that the male literary, historical and philosophical canons are wide-ranging, consistent and endlessly emphasized, in a range of comparisons such as that masters reside in the collective mind cheek by jowl with their prodigies; the 'great mind' of one century continues, along with that of another. (Still, there are no women thinkers mentioned.)

24. *writes all his letters in Greek*: like Thoby Stephen's friend Saxon Sydney-Turner (who wrote some of his letters in Greek).

25. *Great Russell Street*: in Bloomsbury, has been the location of the British Museum (originally Montagu House) since 1759. In 1852–7 the court-yard was converted into the Reading Room (its huge copper dome was designed by Sydney Smirke).

26. *Kentish Town*: in North London was originally a hamlet in a clearing in the great forest of Middlesex.

27. *Highgate*: in North London; the famous cemetery lies on both sides of Swains Lane.

28. *Ulysses*: the hero of Homer's epic poem of whom, at one level, Jacob Flanders may be seen to be a 'modern' version, which may be why Virginia Woolf began to worry, during the early stages of *JR*'s composition, that 'what I'm doing is probably being better done by Mr Joyce'. James Joyce's 1922 novel, *Ulysses*, also about a young man's 'modern'

odyssey, had much more explicit references to Homer's original than Woolf supplies in *JR*; cf. 'the battered Ulysses' (a statue in the British Museum), p. 150.

29. *The Phaedrus is very difficult*: perhaps because of its gist. It is Plato's dialogue (between Socrates and Phaedrus) on love. Erotic love is designated one of the four types of divine madness; Socrates also demonstrates that the soul is immortal, which would have been a problem for Jacob, who realizes that 'the body is harnessed to a brain', p. 69.

30. *the splendid Magdalen ... jodelling between Alpine passes*: Magdalen is a generic name, deriving from the New Testament, for the type of 'fallen woman'; 'jodelling between Alpine passes' is presumably a joke about falling.

31. *like some one on a beach, watching*: the narrator here casts the reader's mind back to the opening pages of *JR*, and invites us to remember Jacob as an independent, thoughtful and vulnerable child.

32. *the friendship between them so much more beautiful than women's friendships*: but that may be because, like the male intellect, male friendships have historical credence, whereas women's friendships are notably absent from traditional literary and historical accounts. This is another theme that Woolf expands on in *A Room of One's Own*, where she notes that 'almost without exception [women] are shown in their relation to men'.

33. *Hammersmith and Holborn ... Piccadilly ... Surbiton ... Putney*: Hammersmith is the most western of the London boroughs. Holborn is north of the Strand, near Lincoln's Inn and Gray's Inn (where Jacob seems to have his London rooms): quite a step, but the ground seems insubstantial beneath his feet (like a strip of temporary wood pavement) because Jacob is exhilarated by the party. Thence to the 'long loop of Piccadilly', 'diamond-stitched' with lights; and at the end of a long evening he lets himself in 'with his latch-key at his own door': another male privilege unlikely to be enjoyed by the feminist Julia Hedge (cf. p. 91), who probably does not have a room of her own (another theme Woolf discusses in the book of similar title). The 'hordes' are making their way home to the suburbs of Surbiton and Putney.

34. *her hovel underground*: another graphic description of the lives of the poor, in contrast to the privileges of Jacob's existence; cf. pp. 56, 83.

35. *Lothair*: the hugely popular novel by Benjamin Disraeli (1804–81), published in 1870.

CHAPTER X

1. *the disused graveyard in the parish of St. Pancras*: Woolf's choice of graveyard is significant. The most striking monument of the Greek revival in English architecture is W. H. Inwood's Church of St Pancras, with its porches modelled on the Erechtheum. The building was erected in 1822, soon after the arrival in London of the Elgin Marbles.

2. *Madame Tussaud's*: famous exhibition of waxworks.

3. *holding in her hand a yellow novel*: a cheap edition. This anticipates the debate on literature *v.* painting on p. 110. For an artist and his model, a book is merely a decorative object.

4. *The women in the streets have the faces of playing cards*: the increased use of cosmetics was a feature of the new pre-war fashions, which also liberated women from the constricting S-shape of Edwardian dresses, introducing simpler lines and brighter colours.

5. *the promenade at the Empire*: the promenade was one of the most popular features of the Empire music hall, in Leicester Square: it was there that prostitutes used to ply their trade.

6. *Her screwed-up black glove dropped to the floor*: she is issuing Jacob with a prostitute's invitation; cf. p. 68.

7. *Hampstead Garden Suburb*: purpose-built suburb in North London with wide, tree-lined roads; a variation on the 'Garden City' idea.

8. *The eyes of all the nurses, mothers, and wandering women are a little glazed*: 'a little glazed' by their preoccupation with the children. Woolf uses a similar image in her last novel, *Between the Acts* (1941), where nurses trundling perambulators up and down the terrace 'were talking – not shaping pellets of information . . . but rolling words . . . which . . . thinned to transparency'; cf. the 'fixed marble eyes' of the busts of dead politicians, p. 151.

9. *the Express Dairy Company's shop*: another cheap teashop; cf. the A.B.C. shop, on p. 65.

10. *the Telegraph*: cf. p. 104.

11. *the Foundling Hospital*: in Guilford Street, WC1 (near Gray's Inn, where Jacob has his rooms). Founded by Captain Thomas Coram in 1742, it housed the illegitimate first-born children of 'fallen' women.

12. *Swan and Edgars*: one of London's first large department stores, in Regent Street.

13. *In Evelina's shop . . . the parts of a woman were shown separate*: in the world of 'ladies' modes' a window display might offer radical new ways of presenting the female image, but it is still composed of scattered parts,

rather than the 'perfect globe' (p. 79) the male mind would prefer to see.

14. *Scott . . . Dumas*: Sir Walter Scott (1771–1832), author of the *Waverley* novels; cf. the reference to 'Waverley' on p. 26. Either 'Dumas père', Alexandre Dumas (1802–70), or 'Dumas fils', Alexandre Dumas (1824–95), both French playwrights; 'fils' was also a novelist.

15. *the Slade . . . Tonks and Steer*: the Slade School of Fine Art (University College, London WC1), which opened in 1871 (named after Felix Slade, who founded chairs in fine art at Oxford, Cambridge and London). Henry Tonks (1862–1937), English painter and Slade Professor of Fine Art, 1918–30. Philip Wilson Steer (1860–1942), English landscape painter.

16. *Tom Jones*: by Henry Fielding (1707–54), one of the first and most influential English novels, published in 1749: 'that mystic book' is ironic, it is a scurrilous work. Fanny is a character in Fielding's *Joseph Andrews* (1742). The eighteenth century might seem 'ever so many years ago' to Fanny, but to Jacob, the intellectual, it is the 'modern' period.

17. *Miss Sargent*: one of Virginia Woolf's private jokes. John Singer Sargent (1856–1925) was a fashionable portrait painter who taught at the Slade and had a following of devoted young women students.

CHAPTER XI

1. *or sometimes hastily dabbed with a yellow bar*: Post Office franking (seen through the eyes of Virginia Woolf, the artist).

2. *Velazquez*: Diego Rodriguez de Silva (1599–1660), painter of portraits and scenes.

3. *Hang there like fruit my soul*: the line – from *Cymbeline*, Act V, scene v, – which converted Virginia Woolf to Shakespeare. Encouraged by Thoby, she read the play 'just to see if there mightnt be more in the great William than I supposed . . . I am now let in to [the] company of worshippers' (*Letters*, I, pp. 45–6).

4. *The devil damn you black, you cream-faced loon!*: from *Macbeth*, Act V, scene iii.

5. *Hey diddle diddle, the cat and the fiddle*: one of the best-known English nursery rhymes (Mallinson is mocking Jacob's claims for literature).

6. *Pierre Louÿs*: pseudonym of Pierre Louis (1870–1925), French erotic poet and novelist, and a great exponent of the free life of Ancient Greece.

7. *Half a jiff*: (wait) just a moment.
8. *Versailles*: Marie Antoinette's famous residence, just outside Paris.
9. *air-ball*: balloon.
10. *will King George give way about the peers?*: this locates a discussion taking place during the constitutional crisis of 1911, when the Commons were trying to get finance measures through the House of Lords (who were blocking them). There was a proposal to create enough new Liberal peers to create a government majority (peerages being in the King's gift).
11. *and her garnet brooch*: Virginia Woolf lost her own Roman brooch while *JR* was in progress (*Diary*, II, 10 March 1921, p. 98).
12. *'I am Bertha Ruck,' 'I am Tom Gage'*: Woolf here innocently (as she thought) invented two names. When *JR* was published, however, the real Berta Ruck (the popular novelist, Mrs Oliver Onions) complained that Woolf had used her name in the novel, pronouncing her dead. The dispute was settled amicably, but then Woolf received a letter from an indignant Tom Gage, blaming her for the loss of his job as a lavatory attendant at Oxford Circus, as a consequence of her use of his name. The letter turned out to be a fake, written by Lytton Strachey and Dora Carrington. Woolf subsequently reported that he had accepted her conciliatory gift of an inscribed packet of Bromo (Letter to Dora Carrington, 25 Dec. 1922, *Letters*, II, p. 597).

CHAPTER XII

1. *There were trees laced together with vines – as Virgil said*: Virgil, *Georgics* Book 2, line 221: 'illa tibi laetas intexet vitibus ulmos' ('one kind of land will twine your vines with elms'). The grape vine cannot support itself, so needs to be held up, either by stakes or by trees planted for the purpose. Vine and tree thus become a stock image for marriage and widowhood (cf. p. 3), and the whole theme carried by Betty Flanders of continuity (motherhood) contrasted with loss (widowhood, and the First World War).
2. *Virgil's bees had gone about the plains of Lombardy*: cf. p. 33. Virgil came from Mantua (which may arguably be regarded as being in Lombardy).
3. *something in the style of Gibbon*: Edward Gibbon (1737–94) is regarded, in *A Room of One's Own*, as master of the style of the 'male sentence', which is pompous and self-perpetuating.
4. *Black victorias*: carriages (the ones in Greece reminded Virginia Woolf of hearses – *Passionate Apprentice*, p. 326).

5. *he'd have done better to go to Cornwall*: Virginia Woolf noted, in her 1906 journal of her visit to Greece, that Athens 'might have been a stretch of the Cornish coast'. Its narrow streets reminded her of St Ives (*Passionate Apprentice*, p. 321).

6. *Daily Mail*: English daily newspaper (founded in 1896), with a Conservative bias. cf. 'tabloids', p. 122 – a trademark for tablets.

7. *an American called Pilchard*: cf. p. 76; Jacob is being churlish – the American's name was Pilcher.

8. *Home Rule to Ireland*: cf. chapter VIII, Note 9 and chapter IX, Note 13.

9. *sentences that don't budge*: another reference to the 'male sentence'; cf. Note 3.

10. *Tchekov*: Anton Pavlovich Chekhov (1860–1904), Russian dramatist and short-story writer, immensely influential in England, who typically depicted a threatened upper class stifled by inactivity and ennui. Sandra models herself on such characters, oblivious that she is thereby setting herself up as a target of Chekhovian pastiche. Woolf refers to Chekhov in her essay, 'Modern Fiction'.

11. *beauty . . . is a barrier; it is in fact rather a bore*: Lily Briscoe comes to the same conclusion, in *To the Lighthouse*: 'Beauty had this penalty – it came too readily, came too completely. It stilled life – froze it' (*To the Lighthouse*, Penguin Books, 1992, p. 193).

12. *Chatham, Pitt, Burke, and Charles James Fox*: a list of eighteenth-century statesmen and politicians; cf. p. 151.

13. *the Hermes of Praxiteles*: from the Temple of Hera. The statue of the god, holding the infant Dionysius in his left arm, was discovered in 1877.

14. *the Acro-Corinth*: a high mountain on the isthmus of Corinth. The mountain is 2,000 feet high, with a temple of Venus at the summit; Corinth is built around the base.

15. *like a Victory*: the famous winged statue in Athens Museum.

16. *when the ships in the Piraeus fire their guns*: Virginia Woolf noted in her 1906 journal of her visit to Greece that perhaps the liveliest scene was 'that of the streets [of Athens] at evening, when the sun has just sunk & the boats in the Piraeus have fired their guns' (*Passionate Apprentice*, p. 325). Thus, not necessarily a sign of war, but later, of course, associated with it; cf. chapter XIII, Note 24.

17. *the Erechtheum*: built between 421 and 395 BC, its portico is supported by six caryatids – figures of 'fat maidens' – in place of columns, who thus appear to be supporting the roof on their heads; cf. p. xxxiv and Introduction, Note 55.

18. *the exact spot where the great statue of Athena used to stand*: the nave of the Parthenon forms a chapel which is illuminated through the great door-

way; the gold and ivory figure of Athena was made by Phidias. If you stand where the great statue used to stand, Woolf noted, 'It is like a panel, let in to the Parthenon to complete its beauty' (*Passionate Apprentice*, p.323).

19. *Hymettus, Pentelicus, Lycabettus*: Athens' three famous mountains.

20. *Madame Lucien Gravé ... with her kodak*: there was a real Madame Gravé, who was Virginia Woolf's dressmaker (*Diary*, II, 4 Feb. 1920, p. 17). The event which probably inspired this incident is described in Woolf's 1906 journal: 'A hoard of Teutons invaded us, & had the audacity to pose themselves in the midst of the Temple of Pluto; it was a photographers shop to them' (*Passionate Apprentice*, pp. 324–5).

21. *putting the life of Father Damien into verse*: a woman Virginia Woolf met on her 1906 Florentine holiday was doing just that.

22. *character-mongering*: 'The Character-Mongers and Comedians' is one of the sub-headings of Woolf's 1929 essay, 'Phases of Fiction' (*CE*, II, p. 71); she gives Charles Dickens as an example of a 'character-monger'.

23. *Wellington nose*: yet another reference to the Duke of Wellington, whose nickname was 'old nosey'.

24. *The battleships ray out*: this passage may be a flash-forward, or perhaps even a mock-up battle, staged by the military as part of their preparations. As such actions are staged, both in war and peacetime, by 'the incessant commerce of banks, laboratories, chancellories, and houses of business', Jacob, driven by an 'unseizable force', bumps into the Williamses in Hermes Street, and at the Durrants'. General Gibbons (who doubtless pontificates 'in the style of Gibbon', cf. p. 119) is worrying about the British lack of preparation for war with Germany: war, commerce, love and death are all thereby conflated at this point.

25. *Euboea*: also called Long Island, running to the north-west of Athens.

26. *the poems of Donne*: John Donne (1572–1631); Jacob almost certainly gives Sandra Donne's erotic love poems, though some of Donne's poetry is misogynist.

27. *one after another lights were extinguished*: anticipating Lord Grey's famous remark, on 3 August 1914: 'The lamps are going out all over Europe'; cf. p. xxxviii.

28. *Surbiton*: an urban district on the main railway line between London and Southampton and the South-West, whose inhabitants are ordinary working people, and so, like the working woman Mrs Pascoe (cf. p. 44), made of flesh and blood.

29. *Lombard Street and Fetter Lane*: two streets in the City of London's financial centre, where Tom Grandage will become anonymous: the financiers merge into the City like insects in the forest.

CHAPTER XIII

1. *European mysticism*: i.e., Christianity, and all it entails; cf. p. 145 – 'The Christians have the right to rouse most cities', and the Julian the Apostate discussion on p. 36. Jacob prefers the idea of the pagan rites of the Greeks.

2. *Troy*: Leslie Stephen once had a dog called Troy (though not an Aberdeen terrier). With the appearance of Clara's Troy, Woolf hints that Jacob is reaching the end of his odyssey.

3. *like a huntress*: Woolf here compares Clara with the goddess Diana. Her name means 'bright one', so that at this moment Clara may be compared with the deleted character, Angela Williams. In the *MS* Woolf stressed 'how bright she was, & how bright came back the reflection of herself from the square glass' (*MS*, p. 87).

4. *the policy of Sir Edward Grey*: Sir Edward Grey (1862–1933) became Foreign Secretary in December 1905, and advocated a consistent policy of peaceful negotiation. Nevertheless, in August 1914 he made it clear to Parliament that Britain had a duty to aid Belgium, so that it was effectively he who led the country into war.

5. *the site of the old Exhibition*: the Great Exhibition of 1851 was held in the Crystal Palace, which was specially erected in Hyde Park (between Rotten Row and the Carriage Road). After the Exhibition it was removed from Hyde Park and re-erected at Sydenham.

6. *the statue of Achilles*: the twenty-foot-high bronze statue, in Park Lane, was cast from captured French guns and erected by 'the women of England to Arthur Duke of Wellington and his brave companions in arms'.

7. *a horse galloped past without a rider*: a cryptic reference to the *Phaedrus*; cf. Introduction, Note 57 and chapter IX, Note 29.

8. *for Julia ... liked to visit death-beds*: as did Virginia Woolf's mother, Julia Stephen (on whom Mrs Ramsay in *To the Lighthouse* is modelled). (So, too, did Julia's mother, Maria Jackson, who was married to a doctor.) Julia Stephen even produced a small booklet entitled *Notes From Sickrooms*. 'Everyone who wanted help turned to her knowing that it would not be denied' (Quentin Bell, *Virginia Woolf*, I, Hogarth Press, 1972, p. 38).

9. *Alceste*: Molière's character, from *Le Misanthrope* (produced in 1666), who is exasperated by the corruption of society and in love with a worldly, older woman.

10. *contempt for his species*: Jacob is still, throughout this passage, modelling himself on Alceste.

11. *Bacon, the mapseller, in the Strand*: the mapsellers' business boomed at the end of the summer of 1914, as large-scale maps of Europe sold to an anxious public.

12. *the Syrian desert*: Syria remained part of the Turkish Empire until the end of the First World War, but had been territory coveted by the French for many years (it was created a French mandated territory in April 1920).

13. *the paws of the slippery lions*: the four bronze lions at the foot of Nelson's Column (20 feet long and 22 feet high). The procession is a pro-war demonstration (by implicit contrast with the anti-war demonstration located in Note 20).

14. *the Reichstag*: Parliament building in Berlin. This passage is an important one: it is five o'clock on the afternoon of 4 August 1914, war is about to break out, and Woolf here contrasts male activity with women's waiting. The wires of the Admiralty 'shivered with some far-away communication', echoing the *frissons* just experienced by Jacob's women. Prime Ministers and Viceroys are speaking in the Reichstag, presumably declaring war. The Austro-Hungarian Emperor (Franz-Josef) is travelling. The rumours in Vienna are presumably of war. The Ambassador at Constantinople is trying to persuade the Sultan of Turkey either to remain neutral or to join Britain and France against Turkey. The fleet is in Gibraltar (in readiness – but there is a British presence there anyway). The voice speaking is the Prime Minister, Asquith, announcing war to the other fifteen gentlemen of the Cabinet. The description of the Cabinet echoes Woolf's earlier description of the British Museum Reading Room, with its 'names stretched in unbroken file round the dome' (p. 90), where men copy out the works of other men under the illusion that they will thereby create an impression of coherence and continuity. Woolf is here describing what the men are planning (which involves blowing hundreds of thousands of other men to smithereens) while the women wait expectantly for Jacob, who (as a direct result of all this political activity) will never return. What *is* 'life'? Woolf implicitly asks, here as at the beginning of the novel. Florinda's pregnancy makes her 'like an animal' (p. 148), but do the strategies of men really make them appear contrastingly civilized?

15. *all the heads in the building*: cf. Note 14; and p. 31 where Jacob's essay will question the assumption that history consists 'of the Biographies of Great Men'.

16. *Pitt and Chatham, Burke and Gladstone*: the four great statesmen, William Pitt, first Earl of Chatham (1708–78); his second son (also William Pitt,

1759–1806); Edmund Burke (1729–97); and William Ewart Gladstone (1809–98). Their air of immortality is put to question: they look from side to side 'with fixed marble eyes', and can't do much for anyone now.

17. *Blue book*: a parliamentary paper ordered by one of the Houses of Parliament; a Royal Commission, for example.

18. *the Gaiety*: popular music hall in the Strand, at the west end of the Aldwych.

19. *Kensington Palace*: Jacobean house with state apartments, at the west end of Hyde Park.

20. *Another procession, without banners, was blocking Long Acre*: probably the anti-war Suffragette meeting in Kingsway Hall, addressed by Mrs Fawcett on behalf of the National Union of Women's Suffrage Societies – one kind of feminist interpretation of events.

21. *Aldridge's*: the 'Horse Bazaar' in Upper St Martin's Lane (WC2). A well-known mart for horses, until the motor-car took over as the main form of transport (the firm began to sell cars in 1907; the last horse sale was in 1926).

22. *the Phoenicians*: were supposed to have reached Cornwall, and there traded in tin.

23. *the suck and sighing of the waves*: an important image running throughout Virginia Woolf's work of natural, organic continuity capable of withstanding attempts to 'shape the course of history'. The image is crucial in *To the Lighthouse* and, of course, *The Waves*.

24. *Greek women ... until the ships in the Piraeus fired their guns*: a conflation of two events in Woolf's 1906 Greek journal. She noted that the people of Athens lounged in the Acropolis in the evenings just as we stroll in our parks: 'They sit about on classic marble, chatting & knitting.' But the liveliest scene was that of the streets at evening, 'when the sun has just sunk & the boats in the Piraeus have fired their guns' (*Passionate Apprentice*, pp. 325, 328); cf. chapter XII, Note 16.

CHAPTER XIV

1. *Greenwich*: the Palace, on the banks of the Thames, is set in 200 acres of parkland, through which the Greenwich meridian passes.

2. *locked together at Mudie's corner*: the location of the famous Circulating Library; cf. p. 53. The image is one of congestion: of movement, knowledge, and perhaps even the course of history.

3. *Jacob! Jacob!*: the appeal recalls the voice of Archer, searching for his

brother on the beach, in the opening pages of the novel. At the close of the novel, Virginia Woolf reminds us that it is Jacob's life-span, Jacob's history, with which we have been concerned all along.

Appendix I

The Concordance to *Jacob's Room* lists variants between the 1977 British edition and the first and second American editions. I have in most cases reinstated the printing of the first British edition (see the Note on the Text). I have made the following corrections to the text (not listed in the list of variants given in the Concordance). The first reading is from the 1922 Hogarth Press edition, the second reading is from this Penguin edition. Page and line numbers are for this edition.

12.30   Tulips burnt in the sun.   ]   Tulips burned in the sun.
21.17   nor who could give it her.   ]   nor who could give it to her.
31.36   Van Goch   ]   Van Gogh
40.30   quiet as the grave.   ]   as quiet as the grave.
56.19   Bank   ]   bank
57.16   Brangaena   ]   Brangäne
59.19   Clara was not the one   ]   Clara was not one
105.16   Fanny the one   ]   Fanny one
109.28   Velasquez   ]   Velazquez
110.4   Velasquez   ]   Velazquez
110.35   Boulevard Raspaille   ]   Boulevard Raspail
133.1   wind and limb   ]   mind and limb
136.34   smoothly sculpture   ]   smoothly sculpted

Appendix II

This passage is a revised version of a passage which appears in the *MS* (*MS*, I, pp. 85–91; originally chapter X, Woolf later reorganized her material into longer chapters). It would have begun on p. 30 at paragraph 2, of the present edition. The revised version originally appeared in *Atlanta's Garland* (Edinburgh University Press, 1926).

A WOMAN'S COLLEGE FROM OUTSIDE

The feathery-white moon never let the sky grow dark; all night the chestnut blossoms were white in the green, and dim was the cow-parsley in the meadows. Neither to Tartary nor to Arabia went the wind of the Cambridge courts, but lapsed dreamily in the midst of grey-blue clouds over the roofs of Newnham. There, in the garden, if she needed space to wander, she might find it among the trees; and as none but women's faces could meet her face, she might unveil it, blank, featureless, and gaze into rooms where at that hour, blank, featureless, eyelids white over eyes, ringless hands extended upon sheets, slept innumerable women. But here and there a light still burned.

A double light one might figure in Angela's room, seeing how bright Angela herself was, and how bright came back the reflection of herself from the square glass. The whole of her was perfectly delineated – perhaps the soul. For the glass held up an untrembling image – white and gold, red slippers, pale hair with blue stones in it, and never a ripple or shadow to break the smooth kiss of Angela and her reflection in the glass, as if she were glad to be Angela. Anyhow the moment was glad – the bright picture hung in the heart of night, the shrine hollowed in the nocturnal blackness. Strange indeed to have this visible proof of the rightness of things; this lily floating flawless upon Time's pool, fearless, as if this were sufficient – this reflection. Which meditation she betrayed by turning, and the mirror held nothing at all, or only the brass bedstead, and she, running here and there, patting and darting, became like a woman in a house, and changed again, pursing her lips over a black book and marking with her finger what surely could not be a firm grasp of the science of economics. Only Angela Williams was at Newnham for the purpose of earning her living, and could not forget even in moments of impassioned adoration the cheques of her father at Swansea: her mother washing in the scullery: pink frocks out to dry on the line; tokens that even the lily no longer floats flawless upon the pool, but has a name on a card like another.

A. Williams – one may read it in the moonlight; and next to it some Mary or Eleanor, Mildred, Sarah, Phoebe upon square cards on their doors. All names, nothing but names. The cool white light withered them and starched them until it seemed as if the only purpose of all these names was to rise martially in order should there be a call on them to extinguish a fire, suppress an insurrection, or pass an examination. Such is the power of names written upon cards pinned upon doors. Such too the resemblance, what with tiles, corridors, and bedroom doors, to dairy or nunnery, a place of seclusion or discipline, where the bowl of milk stands cool and pure and there's a great washing of linen.

At that very moment soft laughter came from behind a door. A prim-voiced clock struck the hour – one, two. Now if the clock were issuing his commands, they were disregarded. Fire, insurrection, examination, were all snowed under by laughter, or softly uprooted, the sound seeming to bubble up from the depths and gently waft away the hour, rules, discipline. The bed was strewn with cards. Sally was on the floor. Helena in the chair. Good Bertha clasping her hands by the fire-place. A. Williams came in yawning.

'Because it's utterly and intolerably damnable,' said Helena.

'Damnable,' echoed Bertha. Then yawned.

'We're not eunuchs.'

'I saw her slipping in by the back gate with that old hat on. They don't want us to know.'

'They?' said Angela. 'She.'

Then the laughter.

The cards were spread, falling with their red and yellow faces on the table, and hands were dabbled in the cards. Good Bertha, leaning with her head against the chair, sighed profoundly. For she would willingly have slept, but since night is free pasturage, a limitless field, since night is unmoulded richness, one must tunnel into its darkness. One must hang it with jewels. Night was shared in secret, day browsed on by the whole flock. The blinds were up. A mist was on the garden. Sitting on the floor by the window (while the others played), body, mind, both together, seemed blown through the air, to trail across the bushes. Ah, but she desired to stretch out in bed and to sleep! She believed that no one felt her desire for sleep; she believed humbly – sleepily – with sudden nods and lurchings, that other people were wide awake. When they laughed all together a bird chirped in its sleep out in the garden, as if the laughter –

Yes, as if the laughter (for she dozed now) floated out much like mist and attached itself by soft elastic shreds to plants and bushes, so that the garden was vaporous and clouded. And then, swept by the wind, the bushes would bow themselves and the white vapours blow off across the world.

From all the rooms where women slept this vapour issued, attaching itself to shrubs, like mist, and then blew freely out into the open. Elderly women slept, who would on waking immediately clasp the ivory rod of office. Now smooth and colourless, reposing deeply, they lay surrounded, lay supported, by the bodies of youth recumbent or grouped at the window; pouring forth into the garden this bubbling laughter, this irresponsible laughter: this laughter of mind and body floating away rules, hours, discipline: immensely fertilizing, yet formless, chaotic, trailing and straying and tufting the rose-bushes with shreds of vapour.

'Ah,' breathed Angela, standing at the window in her nightgown. Pain was in her voice. She leant her head out. The mist was cleft as if her voice parted it. She had been talking, while the others played, to Alice Avery, about Bamborough Castle; the colour of the sands at evening; upon which Alice said she would write and settle the day, in August, and stooping, kissed her, at least touched her head with her hand, and Angela, positively unable to sit still, like one possessed of a wind-lashed sea in her heart, roamed up and down the room (the witness of such a scene) throwing her arms out to relieve this excitement, this astonishment at the incredible stooping of the miraculous tree with the golden fruit at its summit – hadn't it dropped into her arms? She held it glowing to her breast, a thing not to be touched, thought of, or spoken about, but left to glow there. And then, slowly putting there her stockings, there her slippers, folding her petticoat neatly on top, Angela, her other name being Williams, realized – how could she express it? – that after the dark churning of myriad ages here was light at the end of the tunnel; life; the world. Beneath her it lay – all good; all lovable. Such was her discovery.

Indeed, how could one then feel surprise if, lying in bed, she could not close her eyes? – something irresistibly unclosed them – if in the shallow darkness chair and chest of drawers looked stately, and the looking-glass precious with its ashen hint of day? Sucking her thumb like a child (her age nineteen last November), she lay in this good world, this new world, this world at the end of the tunnel, until a desire to see it or forestall it drove her, tossing her blankets, to guide herself to the window, and there, looking out upon the garden, where the mist lay, all the windows open, one fiery-bluish, something murmuring in the distance, the world of course, and the morning coming, 'Oh,' she cried, as if in pain.